TRAVELS THROUGH
LOST WORLDS

TRAVELS THROUGH
LOST WORLDS

THE LIVING DEATH
IN AMUNDSEN'S TENT
DROME

JOHN MARTIN LEAHY

COACHWHIP PUBLICATIONS
Greenville, Ohio

Travels Through Lost Worlds: The Living Death, In Amundsen's Tent, Drome
© 2015 Coachwhip Publications

Front cover: Ice glacier caving © H. Budzynski

John Martin Leahy (1886-1967)

"The Living Death" published 1924-1925, serially in *Science & Invention*. No renewals.
"In Amundsen's Tent" published 1928, in *Weird Tales*. No renewals.
"Drome" published 1927, serially in Weird Tales. No renewal. Reprinted 1952 as *Drome* by Fantasy Publishing Co. No renewals.
Select illustrations for "The Living Death" by Frank R. Paul.
Illustrations for *Drome* by John Martin Leahy.
No claims made on public domain material.

CoachwhipBooks.com

ISBN 1-61646-315-5
ISBN-13 978-1-61646-315-1

CONTENTS

JOHN MARTIN LEAHY
(1886-1967)

Little is known about the life of science fiction (fantasy?) author
John Martin Leahy. Biographical details from the 1952 *Drome*
jacket cover give us:

> "John Martin Leahy was born in New Castle, Wash-
> ington. When he was a year old his family moved to
> a log-cabin in the great forest which at that time
> covered virtually the whole Puget Sound country. His
> first job was at the age of twelve years, carrying mail
> to a mine that was being opened up not far off in the
> forest primeval. Soon after he obtained his second
> job, water-boy for a railroad construction gang at a
> pay of seventy-five cents for a ten hour day.
> "Schools did not amount to much out in the
> woods, and one year in a town in which he lived in
> the Coos Bay country, there was no school at all. But
> Leahy wanted to be an illustrator and painter, and
> in his words, 'a struggle for knowledge began that
> was to be long, at times wellnigh hopeless and heart-
> breaking. I do not even like to think of those years.'"

A handful of serial novels and short stories from the 1920s are all
known of his literary output, but his obituary in the Seattle (WA)
Daily Times, March 29, 1967, makes no mention of his writing,
noting only that he had retired from the Northwest Cooperage Co.

7

(Artistically, the *Drome* cover notes, "His work and drawings have appeared in *Recreation, Sports Afield, Outdoor Life* and *The Westerner*.") Leahy appears to have lived in King County, Washington, most of his adult life, with no indication that he married. (A 1940 census record shows he was single, living with his widowed father at the time. At his death, Leahy was living with his sister, Mrs. Robert Barkley.)

We can infer from his writing, however, that Leahy was interested in science, widely read, and highly imaginative. His writing straddled genres from different periods: a cross between earlier "lost race" romances and technically scientific fiction that was just coming into its own. His earliest serial, "Draconda," was an off-world H. Rider Haggard imitation (not well liked by some science fiction critics) published in *Weird Tales*. He followed up with "The Living Death" (in *Science & Invention*) and "Drome" (in *Weird Tales*), which share similar plots though in very different environments. The former is set in Antarctica, while Drome is a land far underground, entered via a crevasse on Mt. Rainier.

In 1952, Leahy republished "Drome" as a book, adding material to connect it further to "The Living Death." (That is the version reprinted here.) He intended to republish "The Living Death" under the title *Zandara*, but that never appeared. Typically, science fiction commentators note the short story "In Amundsen's Tent" is a sequel to "The Living Death." What is intriguing, however, is that there are many less obvious connections between all three stories. Only when read together can they be appreciated as a whole.

Leahy did not create two disjunct worlds, but an underlying groundwork that could have been used and broadened in future stories. Sadly, Leahy appears to have given up writing after the end of the 1920s. (Perhaps the 1952 *Drome* reprint was intended to restart his career.) It's interesting to see that several of today's science fiction authors have taken on the Lost World theme: Warren Fahy (*Fragment, Pandemonium*), Greig Beck (*Beneath the Dark Ice*), and James Rollins (*Subterranean*), among others. Even today, readers enjoy the idea of hidden worlds and lost wonders still to explore on our planet.

THE LIVING DEATH

The LIVING DEATH

By JOHN MARTIN LEAHY

"'The true may sometimes not be probable.'
But science takes accounting of the truth, not
of the probability."—Victor Laporte.

1
THE DISCOVERY

What I had read was surprising, simply amazing. And yet why should I be surprised at my surprise and amazement? For *this* was not the first time. Yes, more than once, arriving at Darwin Frontenac's home, I had been surprised, and once or twice shocked with an accompanying shudder. For some of the studies and experiments of my friend—a strange friend, but one as true as strange—were as unearthly as ever entered the mind of man.

I thought of some of these things; but never the faintest thought came, as I sent my automobile spinning along the smooth road, that this was the most momentous day ever to be known in all my life.

However, as I drove along, I was not a little puzzled. For, after all, what was I to make of those amazing stories in the newspapers? The first word of his discovery had been given to print (under somewhat unusual circumstances, it seemed) only a few days before; yet already the world was buzzing with interest and comment, from Seattle to London and Paris and even on to Shanghai.

Some of that comment makes curious reading now; but how was the world to know? No wonder there were "Doubting Thomases." The thing was too bizarre, too gruesome.

Why, even I, who knew the man and his work as, I felt sure, no other man knew, doubted.

"Yes," I thought, "this must be another of those wild newspaper yarns! It can not be otherwise. When did a reporter ever get a scientific story straight? That there was some foundation for the story—or, rather, stories—I did not doubt for one moment.

I had been away five months, and (if it had been any one else) I could have sworn that he was not even interested in such a thing on my departure, let alone experimenting. And now this! Not the slightest mention of it had occurred in a single one of his letters.

The stories should be taken *cum grano salis.*

If I had only known the truth—above all, what was to follow!

TO THE HOUSE

At length I left the main road, taking one that led off to the right. A few moments, and the summit of the gentle acclivity was reached, whence an extensive view meets the eye. There, stretching from south to north, glittered Puget Sound. A short distance before, the red roof of Frontenac's house came into view.

The road gave a sudden turn and I, a sudden exclamation. A few curious persons would have seemed no surprise, but what I saw certainly was. There must have been twenty cars parked along the fence, and all of two hundred people gathered at the house. Here and yon little crowds were clustered about some wiseacre, and, as I rolled forward, I heard "bunk" and "faker" and sundry phrases and epithets no more complimentary than these.

And, there inside, puttering about the flowers and shrubs, was Blubs, the gardener and general handy man about the place. It was obvious, however, that the work engaging his hands was not taking his whole attention. Blubs, in reality, was on guard.

From the look he fixed on the car, I thought he was expecting some one. There was a sudden look of recognition, and the next instant he was moving toward the gate.

"Well, well," he said, as he swung the gate open, "if it isn't Mr. McQuestion back!"

"Not expecting me, eh, Blubs?"

"No," he answered. "I thought at first that it was—you see, I thought it was somebody else."

WELCOMED

My ring was answered by Frontenac himself. A look of surprise crossed his lean features and lighted up the somber gray of his eyes:

"Bond!" he exclaimed, and thrust out his hands and grasped me by the shoulders. "So it's you! When did you arrive?"

"You didn't know I'd returned?"

"Not until I opened the door and saw you here."

"I tried to get you on the phone. Sherrill answered, said you were expected back any moment, and he said that—"

"Oh, I see! And, when I did get back, Sherrill suddenly found so many matters on hand he forgot to tell me about it."

"Come in, Bond, come in!" he exclaimed with a sudden alteration of tone and manner. "You mustn't be surprised if things are a little upset about the place, though it would be rather difficult to say precisely why they should be so. Certainly I can't tell you. All this hullabaloo!"

He waved me into a chair and took another himself, crossing his legs and elbows resting on the arms of the chair, placed his chin on his long clasped fingers.

"Well, well, I'm certainly glad to see you again. Alaska seems to agree with you."

"And," I returned, "it seems you have been making a little Alaska of your own down here."

A smile touched his face.

"So you have been reading the papers?"

I nodded. "And tell me this, have the papers got this business straight?"

"Not straight, of course, Bond; they never do get scientific things straight. Why, your reporter is a wonder if he knows that Polaris isn't Archaeopteryx!"

"What I mean," I told him, "is this, have you really done what these accounts say?"

"I have," said Frontenac, "and a few things beside which they know nothing about."

"You mean to tell me— Great Heaven, you mean to say that you can?"

"Certainly I can! It was not my intention to have it made public so soon, however. This has—well, disarranged things a little. I'll have more sense next time. It was that old fuddlecap Professor

Archimedes Bukink that gave the story away—the old rattlebrained bagpipe. Oh, well, it's all my own fault. I ought to have had more sense than to let him know of it."

AN ARRIVAL

"But look here—" I began.

"There," interrupted Frontenac, "there he is at last."

He was looking out the window, towards the gate, which Blubs had just opened and through which an automobile was moving.

"Who?"

The look he gave made me wonder.

"Stanley Livingstone," he said.

"Stanley Livingstone!"

"Yes, Captain Stanley Livingstone. There in the back seat."

"That faker!" I exclaimed,

Frontenac held up a finger.

"Easy, Bond. Not so precipitate. Remember, even Newton and Columbus were fakers once."

"Shades of the great Münchausen!" I exclaimed. "Do you really believe in that man?"

"This is not the moment to say what I believe or do not believe. I have been waiting this visit with more interest than you can easily imagine. It has me guessing in more ways than one. Why is he coming—he of all men? What is this strange tale he has to tell me, and why has my discovery brought that man here?"

"You'll soon have the answer to that," I smiled. "But what is the Captain doing in Seattle?"

"Outfitting for another expedition."

"To the *North* Pole, this time?"

"No. To the Antarctic Continent again. I understand, however, that his health has caused some hitch in the plans."

"Well," I observed, "here he comes. I want to meet the man, but don't worry; I'll soon excuse myself and leave you two to your mysterious confab."

"By no means, Bond!"

He placed a hand on my arm, and the seriousness of his manner astonished me.

"I want you to remain—well, as a witness, say. Something tells me the story will prove no common one."

And the next moment he was moving toward the door to receive the arrival.

2
CAPTAIN STANLEY LIVINGSTONE

The meeting with Captain Stanley Livingstone left my thoughts in confusion.

This man I had set down as an unmitigated faker. Yet, as I saw his rugged, weather-beaten face, his clear blue eyes, doubts as to the correctness of my opinion arose. The impression produced upon me by the captain's personal appearance was very much in his favor.

This was not the face of a faker. And yet it was not pleasant to look upon. There was an unsightly puffiness about the features and a livid hue which stood out even through the tan. Captain Livingstone was a sick man. His troubled breathing, and the alacrity with which he sank into the chair pushed forward by Frontenac attested to his illness.

The captain lost little time in the small talk customary on such occasions.

"I have come to you, Mr. Frontenac," he said suddenly, "to tell you the strangest story one man ever told another. And, as I am a living and honorable man (though dishonorable, or worse, in the eyes of the world) every syllable of it is true."

He paused, and for an instant his eyes rested on me with a look the meaning of which could not be mistaken.

THE CAPTAIN SPEAKS

"I assure you, Captain Livingstone," Frontenac said in reply to the look, "that I am very sensible of the honor thus accorded me. Also,

18

I assure you that you may thoroughly rely on the discretion of my friend McQuestion here. Should there be anything in your story you wish held secret, you need have no fear of either of us betraying the trust."

The captain gave something like a bow.

"I believe it," he said after a momentary pause, "and so I will tell you my story; tell you of the strangest, the most astounding scientific discovery ever made. The world sneered and jibed at what I did tell. So why should I have taken the trouble to bring out proof—even if I had not the horrible stares of the curious and the vile publicity she would have been subjected to."

Darwin Frontenac leaned forward.

"She?" he queried.

And I caught at the eagerness in his voice.

"Yes," said Captain Livingstone. "In a—a museum!"

He gave a fierce gesture.

"Yes, that is what they would have done to her, that or something even worse—after all these thousands of years. I have been in something akin to despair ever since that awful day I found her. But now, Mr. Frontenac, your discovery changes everything. You are the one man in the world who can save her. And even you—no, will not think that."

"Save *her?*" queried Darwin Frontenac.

"Yes, sir: *save* her."

"From what?"

"From eternal sleep—or one of the foulest of deaths."

"All this, Captain Livingstone, is something of a riddle to me."

"Yes, yes; but I will make all plain." He was silent for a moment, then added: "As for me, gentlemen, I am finished—I am a doomed man."

His head sank forward, but the weakness was ephemeral: the next moment he raised his head and fixed his look once more on Frontenac.

"Aneurism of the aorta," he grunted.

That explained the puffiness and livid hue of his skin. Such a man, I knew, was not certain of his life from one minute to the next.

The explorer went on, "My days on this earth are numbered. Well, so be it. Glad have I lived, and I believe that I can, like Stevenson, gladly die. The only question is: what time remains to me? A day, a week, a month, six months? Who can tell?"

There was a pause. A moment, and a smile touched the captain's face.

"Well, what does it matter?" He made a gesture of resignation. "Life cannot be very rosy to a man who knows that any breath he draws may be his last. If I can only live to tell you my story! And I can await death with resignation when I have told you all if you will enter upon this undertaking."

"I must first," suggested Frontenac, "know what that undertaking is."

QUESTIONS

"A terrible one," Livingstone answered. "But, before entering upon my story, Mr. Frontenac, I am anxious to know if the version which we have of your discovery is correct."

Darwin Frontenac nodded.

"Yes; substantially it is correct—though the accounts are somewhat exaggerated."

"Then you really can bring an animal back to life?"

"Hardly that," Frontenac smiled. "It is not dead; the animal is merely in a state of suspended animation."

The captain looked puzzled.

"If an animal is frozen stiff, incased in a solid block of ice—is not dead, then what is it? Surely it is not living."

"No," said Darwin Frontenac.

"And it isn't dead?"

"Of course not."

"That," said the captain, "is just what poor Hampden said."

"The condition," I put in, "in which we find it in its block of ice must be one new to science."

"By no means, Bond," returned Frontenac. "If it were dead, life could not be restored. But life may be restored from suspended animation after many years—thousands of years."

"Thousands?" exclaimed the captain.

"Thousands, so I truly believe," Frontenac nodded.

"And if it were living?" I queried. "You say that it is neither alive nor dead."

"If it were living, we could kill it."

"Good Heaven, can't we do that?"

"No," said Frontenac, "in that state of suspended animation, remember. We kill it—if death results—not in its state of suspended animation, but in the *very act of restoring it to life*. What I am striving to express is this: What science calls suspended animation is neither life nor death."*

The captain and I looked at each other; the captain shook his head.

"That is what Hampden told me," he said. "I'm afraid, though, I do not grasp it.

"However," he added, "I can see there is a difference *if the animal is drugged* before it is frozen."

I thought a faint smile touched the corners of Frontenac's mouth, but he made no comment.

* "If, as seems certainly to be the case, the animal dies because in the very act of trying to restore it some inequality in the process is almost sure to determine a fatal issue, some vital center passing into the pectous state, the animal could not have been dead before restoration was attempted; for the dead cannot die again."—R. A. Proctor.

3
INCASED IN ICE

"That is what gives me hope," the captain added. "As I understand it, you produce with some drug, a state of hibernation, so to speak, and maintain this condition by freezing; and that any time you wish restore the animal to normal activity and life."

Frontenac nodded. "That is just what I do. Suspending the vital processes is the easiest part of the matter. Some of the chemical agents capable of producing the semblance of death have long been known—mandragora and belladonna, for instance, and others of the Solanaceae. Dioscorides employed plants of this order, though it is uncertain whether he speaks of belladonna, mandragora or datura stramonium. Belladonna is, perhaps, the *strychnos manicos* of the ancients. The effects of all these agents are similar, though the dose must be varied to secure the same results.

"To these may be added amyl nitrite and chloral hydrate. The latter is very effective in suspending the vital functions.

"However, the agent employed in my work is none of these, but a discovery of my own. There are undoubtedly hundreds of such agents in organic chemistry and I have chanced upon one of them."

The captain leaned forward; eagerness marked his expression; also, I thought, there was something akin to fear in his look.

"If one of the old drugs has been used, belladonna, let us say, would that mean that the chance of a complete recovery would in any way be diminished?"

"No," Frontenac told him, "provided always, of course, that the drug was not administered in a quantity to prove fatal *before the subject was frozen.* My agent possesses some marked advantages, that is all: I can not say it adds to the certainty of the recovery."

THE EXPERIMENT

The captain settled back in his chair with an audible sigh of relief.

"I thank God for that," he said. "For then there is hope."

Frontenac waited, hoping, no doubt, that the other would go on; but the captain seemed to have fallen into a profound reverie.

So Frontenac continued: "To the general public I am a faker. It makes me a little sad, though, to hear what some men who ought to know better think of my work. They seem to be utterly ignorant of what has been done along this very line. The marvels of hibernation (and estivation) should have shown them the virtue of true scientific caution.

"In a state of complete hibernation, animals—mammals, remember—live for months without drawing a single breath. That respiration is completely suspended was proved long ago by Spallanzani: he left a marmot for four hours in carbonic acid gas, repeating the experiment with a bat as the subject. To a *breathing* mammal, it is scarcely necessary to remark, this gas proves almost instantly fatal. Also, as a further proof of the complete suspension of respiration, the oxygen was found unaffected after a bat had remained in a pneumatometer for ten hours.

"As for my own experiments, I will mention but one: I kept a bat for two whole months in a vacuum as perfect as could be made, and it still lived. A little vapor of ammonia brought him out of his long snooze as though nothing whatever had happened.

"However, the blood of an animal in a condition of complete torpor continues to circulate, though slowly; and this marks the great difference between hibernation and artificial suspension of vitality."

"I knew," said the captain, "that some strange things could be done with cold-blooded creatures; but I never dreamed such marvels were possible with warm-blooded mammals."

"One can do the same things to a warm-blooded animal as to one of cold blood if he only knows how," said Frontenac. "The thing is more difficult, that is all. At any rate, such is my belief. It is not impossible.

"It has long been known that fish can be restored to perfect life though completely frozen. Why, then, all this excitement of the public because I have succeeded in resuscitating a frozen mammal?"

"I had heard," said the captain, "that fish frozen in solid ice could be thawed out and brought back to life; but I confess I had some doubts as to the accuracy of the story—even though Hampden said it was so. I placed it in the same category as those stories of petrified men."

Darwin Frontenac arose. "Would you care to see it done?"

"Would I?" exclaimed Livingstone.

"I'll fetch a fish from the freezer," Frontenac said, "and show you." He turned and left the room.

Livingstone gazed at me for some moments with a quizzical expression.

COMMERCIAL POSSIBILITIES

"No doubt, Mr. McQuestion, this is somewhat matter of fact to you; but to me it is very strange. And I assure you, sir, that I have seen some strange things in my day—as you will see when I tell my story."

"It is just as new and strange to me," I said. "And, you know, apart from its scientific interest and value, the discovery has great commercial possibilities."

"Oh," the captain nodded, "probably."

I wondered at the man's obtuseness.

"Great!" I ejaculated. "Why, the possibilities of this discovery are unlimited."

The captain looked at me questioningly. "Probably. But—that is—well, in what way, Mr. McQuestion?"

"In what way? Why, for instance, if you want to ship livestock from the Western ranches to the great packing-houses, simply *kill* the animals and pack them in the freezing cars like so many hams or slabs of bacon, like so much cordwood. Think of the saving in fodder—to say nothing of the freight!"

"And here's another application. During the long winter months, what a saving for the farmer! The stock which eats but gives no value will be killed, piled in the freezer, save a winter's feed. Simple, isn't it?"

"Oh, yes. Undoubtedly, as you say, Mr. McQuestion, there are—well—ahum, great possibilities in that direction. But there are greater, more interesting, more wonderful possibilities elsewhere."

At this moment came the sound of footfalls, and soon Frontenac entered—a pail, heavy with water, in one hand, a piece of ice in the other. The fish, a trout about seven inches in length, could be seen plainly encased in the ice, as though held in glass. The captain's hands trembled as he examined the little creature. He turned the ice this way and that and over and over.

"And, Mr. Frontenac," the captain exclaimed suddenly, his voice eager, his eyes wistful, "you can thaw him out, make him live once more?"

"Of course. That is what I am going to do now—though the fish is not dead, else it could not be done."

"And tell me," exclaimed the captain, his voice shaking a little, "could you restore a *human being* if frozen thus in solid ice?"

Frontenac scrutinized the captain closely for a moment, and asked, "A human being?"

"A human being—yes."

"I believe," Frontenac told him, "I could."

"I know you can!" the explorer cried.

"Captain Livingstone, what do you mean?"

There was a brief silence. "It means that—well, you see—" He raised a finger and pointed to the fish, resting again in Frontenac's hand. "I am as anxious to tell you what I found down there, Mr. Frontenac. But the fish. The story as soon as I see that trout swimming once more."

"That you will soon see, Captain. For I dare say you are not nearly so anxious to see this creature restored to life as I am to hear what you have to tell."

4

THE CAPTAIN BEGINS HIS STORY

In silence Darwin Frontenac proceeded with his thawing. The captain and I sat watching.

More than once my look lingered on the explorer's face, held there by that strange, indescribable expression which had come over his weather-beaten features.

And, while watching, I kept wondering about the story the man was to tell us. Strange was this scene before me, Frontenac in the act of restoring to life a fish that had been incased in solid ice for months. I found myself growing impatient. The captain's story, I thought, would be of things even stranger than this experiment of Frontenac's.

I kept turning over in my mind the few words he had uttered, endeavoring to find some idea which would cast a bit of light on the forthcoming story.

Her. What had he meant by her? Who was she? What was she, where was she? A woman in the Antarctic? His words could mean nothing else. No woman had ever set foot on the Antarctic Continent, according to all accounts. And Frontenac to head an expedition to this land of snow and ice (and, if one could believe our captain, palm-trees) to save her! From what? From one of the foulest of deaths, the captain had said, or from sleep eternal.

THE FISH SWIMS
My musing was interrupted by an exclamation from the captain— a boyish exclamation of surprise and joy. The fish, now wholly free

from its ice, was showing unmistakable signs of life. And the interval was not a very long one before he was swimming slowly around the pail as though nothing unusual had happened to him.

"Who would have believed it?" exclaimed Livingstone.

"I don't see what there is so very strange about it," Frontenac said. "In my mind, hibernation or estivation is more wonderful."

"Or," added the other, "the artificial suspension of vitality in warm-blooded creatures."

"Yes," nodded Frontenac; "or the artificial suspension of the vital functions—and their restoration."

"Of course," the captain added, "I realize that, in an ultimate sense, nothing can be any stranger than anything else. But it seems so to us, because, through our own ignorance or through the teachings of others, we come to believe things very possible are simply impossible. For instance, we are taught that life is a weak thing, whereas it seems no one knows how strong it really is."

"No one knows," said Frontenac, "or can know. And those who ought to know how wondrous and mysterious it is are the very ones we find so cocksure and dogmatic. For instance, these fellows declared life was utterly impossible in great depths of the sea. There was the frightful pressure; no living thing could stand it for an

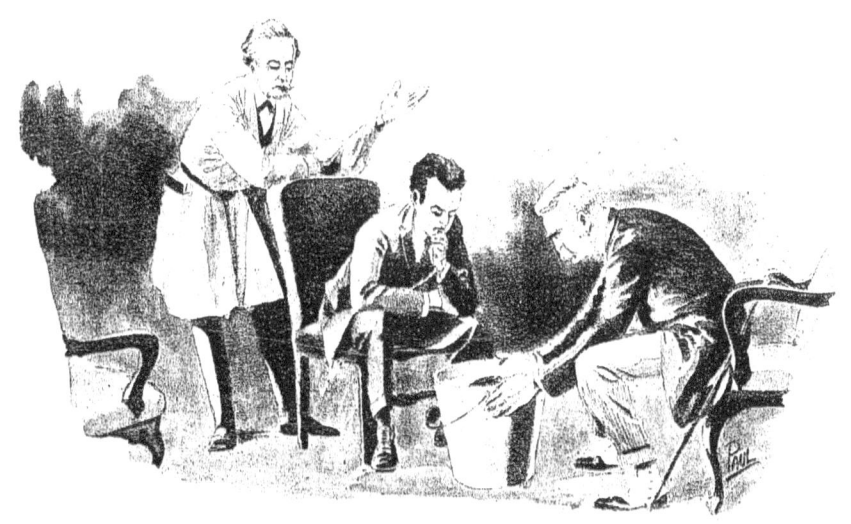

instant. And the total want of light; those depths are pitch black.
And then came deep-sea dredging, and, to the amazement of
the scientific know-it-alls, those deeps in which no creature could
exist even for a single instant were found to be teeming with a
myriad forms of life."

The captain nodded.

"Some of these scientific gentlemen are the very personification of cocksureness when, as a matter of fact, they haven't a single
toe to stand on. I remember, for instance, how the great scientist
Croll *proved* that there could be no elevated land in the Antarctic."

Frontenac nodded.

"Yes; I remember that, too. Had there been mountains, table-
lands and so on, the bergs would have shown tilted and broken
stratification, whereas the strata were always horizontal."

"Just so. And yet," said the captain, "when Roald Amundsen
and his four companions raised the flag of Norway over the South
Pole, they stood nearly two miles above the level of the sea."*

"A good lesson, that," nodded Darwin Frontenac, "in scientific
caution."

"Our scientists certainly need it," said Livingstone. "Perhaps
the bitterness I feel on this subject is not wholly warranted, but it
was a scientist who first covered me with ridicule and—well, worse."

"But ridicule and worse are what the discoverer should be *prepared* to meet. There is an old saying that Truth finds foes where
she makes none."

"But one doesn't expect to find foes in the very palace of Science herself."

"One should expect to find them there," Frontenac told him,
"for your scientist, with all his learning, is but a man, a man with
weaknesses and passions very like those of the butcher, the baker
and the candlestick-maker.

* "This is an awful place and terrible enough for us
to have labored to it without the reward of prior-
ity."—Captain Scott's Journal.

"The scientist, Captain Livingstone, is often myopic or blind when the intelligent layman sees things very clearly. Have you forgotten Agassiz and evolution? That Francis Bacon rejected the Copernican system, as did the great Tycho Brahe, and Leibnitz the law of gravitation? That Darwin's name was rejected by the French Academy of Sciences, that those omniscient academicians *suppressed* Peyssonel because his observations showed coral not to be a plant but an animal? And, coming down to our own day, that scientists, showing about as much courtesy as we find in a political campaign, have for years declared the lines cobwebbing Mars are optical illusions.

"At the risk of offending you, Captain Livingstone," Frontenac finished, "I will say—" But Frontenac did not say it.

"Well, sir?" demanded the captain. He had straightened up in his chair and fixed his look on the other—the gray eyes flashing as though shooting tiny points of steel.

"I think, Captain Livingstone," continued Frontenac, "you have suffered your sensitiveness to get the better of your judgment. However, you stand in distinguished company, for Newton himself was by no means free of this weakness.

"The public heard about the palm-trees, though!" added Frontenac.

The captain laughed a sardonic, bitter laugh. "But there my story ended. Of course, in any event, it is only a question of time before others see what I saw and the world learns what I told was the truth. But what good will vindication do me when I am dead?"

A silence fell. It was broken by Frontenac, who arose and said:

"You will excuse me for a moment, Captain, while I return this trout to the freezer. Then your story."

"Are you going to freeze him again?"

"Again," said Frontenac. "This will be the third time."

"However, Mr. Frontenac, I believe, after all, everything has been for the best. Yes, yes, for you are the only man in all the world that can save her."

"There it is again!" said Darwin Frontenac, sinking into his chair. "Save *her?*"

"Yes, Mr. Frontenac, save her! In other words, *awake* her!

"And now, gentlemen," he added, "listen to the strangest tale that ever a man had to tell."

5

"The frozen regions about the Poles," the captain began, "have always had a great interest for me, a fascination even. I read everything about Arctic and Antarctic exploration and discovery I could get my hands on, from Pytheas down. And, speaking of Pytheas,—whom we may regard as the first of Arctic explorers, though he reached only Thule and her utmost isles—that reminds me, gentlemen, that those explorers of ancient time, as well as some of our own day, had to meet doubt and derision on their return.

"According to the learned Strabo, Pytheas was a faker—a liar of the first magnitude, Strabo calls him. I believe that he called Eudorus something very similar, and other men too. And I remember that the great Herodotus voiced his disbelief in the circumnavigation of Africa by the Phoenicians engaged by Necho—because the Phoenicians reported that they had had the sun *on their right!*

"But I digress.

"Though so keenly interested, I never dreamed, in those days, that I should ever be an explorer myself—above all, that I should be branded by the modern Strabos as a liar of the first magnitude.

"I visited the Arctic—two cruises on a whaler. I was mate then. During the second cruise, we passed Amundsen in the *Gjoa* near Herschel Island. I did not take to whaling. On my return to San Francisco, I determined never to set foot on a whaler's deck again.

"Little did I dream that I would soon be a shipowner—above all, that within a few years, I would be rich. However, it was so. A rover all my life, I had often thought—dreamed, rather—of settling down and, as they say, taking things easy. I tried it then. But my restlessness was a torture. And, as they say in novels, the Unknown was calling.

"Though no longer as young as I had once been, I was by no means old. I could, I believed, stand fatigue and hardships as well as another. Youth, in these matters had been greatly exaggerated. There was nothing to hold me back. I had never married.

"As for means I had enough to fit out a dozen expeditions, and to spare. My thoughts went south. There, within the Antarctic circle, lay the last of the great unknown lands. Peary had reached the North Pole, and Amundsen the South. So I was too late to bid for achievement and fame in that direction. But there were other ways to turn. And the Antarctic was calling.

PREVIOUS EXPLORATIONS

"The flag of Norway flew over the Pole, 'tis true; the explorations of Shackleton and Scott, also, had immensely increased the world's knowledge of that mighty and terrible land. But, after all, what these three great men had won was only a ribbon of land. On either side of the long road they had marked, stretching clear around, lay vast unvisited regions in the Antarctic, snow-clad, with great plains, mighty mountain ranges; a region nearly three thousand miles across, lifeless, terrible; a world that (so men thought, and so I did then) had never been trod by any human foot."

"And you discovered that belief was all wrong?"

"I did. And, if it hadn't been for ill-luck and disaster, I would now be able to place in your hands photographic proof of that fact."

Darwin Frontenac leaned forward.

"Men down there? According to the belief of all Antarctic explorers before you, not a single living thing is to be found in the whole extent of that vast continent. It is described as an abode of silence and death. Not a fox—not so much as a single miserable snowshoe-rabbit—not even, after one leaves the sea, a single bird.

"And yet," Captain Livingstone said with something like a smile, "down there below the eighty-fourth parallel, Amundsen saw skua gulls. And I remember his amazement at seeing them. Amazement, too, must have been mutual, for the gulls came down to see the men. And, when they resumed their flight do you remember the direction that they took?"

"South!" Frontenac exclaimed.

"South!" Livingstone nodded. "I have an idea nothing Amundsen saw in all his journey surprised more than the sight of those birds. 'Were they,' he said, 'going over to the other side?'

"I think," the captain added after a little pause, "I know where those birds were going—and that strange one too that flew right over the heads of Shackleton's men. Then there was the skua seen by Scott at the eighty-seventh parallel."

A QUESTION

Again there was a silence, suddenly broken by Frontenac:

"Men! Captain Livingstone, are there men somewhere down there?"

I heard the captain's answer with surprise.

"I don't know," he said. "It is my belief, though, that there may be.

"Yes," continued the captain. "I believe there may be an unknown race somewhere in the heart of Antarctica. That, however, is a question exploration only can settle. But this I did discover: men once lived down there—*before the land had become covered with snow and ice.*"

The look of Frontenac now was strange and questioning.

"It puzzles me, Captain. Before the snow and ice? That takes us back thousands of years!"

"I know it. But I don't see why it should surprise or puzzle a scientist. When it comes to flying dragons, dinosaurs and such things, he thinks nothing of counting the time by millions of years. And even then the world was old! Why, therefore, be surprised when a discovery takes us back to a time when the Antarctic, now so frozen and forbidding, enjoyed a warm and genial climate?"

"It isn't," Frontenac told him. "It has long been known that the polar regions were formerly temperate. Nordenskjold's expedition to Palmer Land found fossils that told of a rich Jurassic flora there. The snow and ice of the polar regions are, in a geological sense, a very recent phenomenon. It seems certain there were no polar icecaps in Miocene times, perhaps not even in the Pliocene. In the Quaternary, though, the ice had come.

"No, Captain Livingstone, it is not the warm climate that worries me; it is man before the Ice Age."

"No doubt it is a startling statement," the explorer said. "But the evidence shows that man lived there before the Glacial Period."

"It seems to me," I observed, "that he would have had a hard time living there after the advent of the snow and ice."

"Mr. McQuestion," the captain answered a little dryly, "there are things in the Antarctic besides snow and glaciers. . . . Evidently, the flight of those gulls that so amazed Amundsen doesn't suggest anything to you."

"No. They must, as Amundsen himself suggested, have been going across."

"Clear across!" he answered. "I cannot see why they should fly two thousand miles or so if the region before them was covered with nothing but snow and ice."

Frontenac evidently thought that there might be something in the wild yarn about Antarctic palm-trees. Shades of Lemuel Gulliver!

OLD TIMES

"That, according to Croll," Frontenac was saying, "would take us back at least two hundred and forty thousand years!"

"In view of Croll's *proof* that Antarctica must be perfectly flat or merely a collections of low islands, I don't think," the captain smiled, "that we need pay much attention to his other ideas. Look at the theories and hypotheses scientists have spun in their endeavor to explain the cause of the Glacial Period! And yet, after all their reasoning, and guessing, they must admit it remains a mystery."

"The scientists have no evidence whatever that man appeared before the ice."

Darwin Frontenac nodded.

"Why," the explorer demanded, "should man have waited until the snow and ice and the glaciers had come?"

"I do not know," answered Frontenac. "I wish I did."

"I think I know," the captain told him.

"Where could he have been waiting?"

"I think I know that too. At any rate, here is my theory:

"Before the Great Cold, man could not have endured the terrific heat of the tropics or even the heat of what we call the temperate zones. The equatorial regions must have been to him what they are today to the right whale—a region of fire. But, when the Great Cold came, the survivors fled to the low latitudes, whence, in time, the human race was to spread over all the earth. In other words, gentlemen, I believe that the cradle of mankind is not to be looked for in Asia, but in that Antarctic land now so desolate and terrible.

"And here is another thing. It is now believed that the cold came on gradually, that the spread of the ice equatorward was so slow that men (had there been men on the earth at that time) would not have been aware of any change."

"That is the belief," Frontenac nodded.

THE CHANGE

"All the evidence teaches us the change was a slow one—not sudden, as it was at one time supposed."

"I know that the evidence is construed that way. The great Cuvier, you know, believed the change was a sudden one—instantaneous, in fact."

"Yes," Frontenac said, "I remember. And I remember, too, that he rejected the theory of epigenesis and clung to the absurd theory of preformation."

"Any man," returned the captain, "is liable to make a mistake."

"And I remember, also," added Frontenac, "that he said the penguins 'can only reach their nests by trailing on their bellies.' Yet the penguin has been known to journey eighty miles inland."

The captain seemed to fidget a little.

"The mistake, after all, Mr. Frontenac, is but a trifling one. As I remarked, any man—even the most learned of men—is liable to make a mistake."

"Of course," said Frontenac, and I could see a sly twinkle in his eye.

"Speaking of the rhinoceroses and elephants found preserved in the ice in Siberia, Cuvier says:

"'If they had not been frozen as soon as killed, putrefaction would have decomposed them: and, on the other hand, this eternal frost could not have previously prevailed in the place where they died; for they could not have lived in such a temperature. It was, therefore, at the same instant when these animals perished that the country they inhabited was rendered glacial. These events must have been sudden, instantaneous, and without any gradation.'"

"How," asked Frontenac, "could any such cold have fallen suddenly, instantaneously?"

"I don't know," replied Livingstone. "I believe I can prove that it came in an instant; however."

THE JOURNEY

"And so I return to my story. I organized my expedition, and at last the *Multnomah*—that is the name of my schooner—cleared Tatoosh and stood away on her course.

"After an uneventful passage—we entered the pack just east of Circle Island and in latitude 58° 15' S. You will see from this that I was indeed headed for the Unknown.

"There is another great Unknown, stretching from Ross Sea eastward to Palmer Land; but had I chosen a base there in moving Poleward, I would have been *converging* toward the route of Shackleton and Scott and that of Amundsen, whereas it was my intention to explore from a point as nearly opposite as possible. In other words, if I could reach the Pole itself, a trail would be blazed clear across the Antarctic Continent!

"Such, I confess, was my ambition. You will soon see what came of it.

"Finally, after twenty-two days in the ice, land was sighted in latitude 76—land (so we thought then) never seen by human eyes before.

"For six days we coasted along it, kept away from the land by the great barrier and held up half the time by floes. Then, on the seventh day, what appeared to be an entrance opened up to the south, and we stood for it.

"An entrance it proved to be, and pretty well jammed with ice driven down by the northeast breeze. Twice we were held up, and once I thought the *Multnomah* was in for a good squeeze. I never saw ice close so suddenly as it did. It was fifteen to twenty feet high in places. But there is no accounting for the movements of ice in those seas. Without any cause whatever, so far as we could see, a lead opened up, and we got through.

"And now I come to the first of our surprises.

"We had soon left the ice behind us. The *Multnomah* was moving through water as clear of ice as the Sound out there. I began to look about me with something like astonishment.

"The temperature of the water, we now found, had suddenly risen from 31° to 39° Fahrenheit. That of the air had not changed, it was still 28° below zero.

"On either side, rose high rounded hills, covered with snow, dark volcanic rocks showing through here and there. These hills were closing in before us, and I thought our way was barred. But such was not the case. The passage, now a narrow one, took a sharp turn to the right. And there, in the midst of it, appeared an island, rising up like a great ruined castle.

STRANGE THINGS

"The channel to the right was the larger, and we took it. It was, however, no more than three hundred feet in width. Soundings gave bottom at six fathoms.

"It now seemed that we *were* nearing the end—that the channel terminated half a mile beyond Castle, as I named the island.

"But wrong again! It was not the end but another turn, this time sharp to the left, or to the southward. Again we had deep water. No bottom with fifty fathoms out. The channel was gradually widening.

"The *Multnomah* stood steadily on, the chug of her engines echoing and re-echoing weirdly from the hills. There was not a particle of ice in the water; ice and snow, though, covered the hills, coming down to the water's edge. As I have mentioned, however, here and there dark volcanic rocks showed through.

"Again the *Multnomah* came to a turn, a gentle turn to the left, and in a few minutes we were gliding out into a large bay, expanding to some three miles and stretching away to the southward as far as we could see. A thin mist arose from the water and hung low over it as it moved before the wind—in appearance, very much like frost-smoke.

"High rounded hills rose on either side, and, to the southward, a jagged range of mountains was dimly visible, trending away in to the interior as far as the eye could reach. And further on, their bases touching, two great rounded peaks rose up.

"The one on the left I named Mount Theodore Roosevelt, that on the right Mount Woodrow Wilson.

"The *Multnomah* stood on, bays and inlets opening as we advanced. Still not a particle of ice was anywhere to be seen on that wonderful sheet of water—which I named Summer Haven. Evidently no glacier debouched into it. And this, as we afterwards found, was the case. The great glaciers of Mount Theodore Roosevelt and Mount Woodrow Wilson go westward to the sea—a range of hills rising between those mountains and Summer Haven.

"But how to explain this strange scene about us? Here, in this terrible ice-bound coast, in the midst of hills covered with snow and ice, was a sheet of water miles in extent and not a particle of ice to be found floating anywhere on its surface!

"Another thermometer reading was taken. Temperature at surface of water 44°—a rise of thirteen degrees. Temperature of air the same—minus 28°.

"I was, however, already suspecting the truth.

"And then we opened a view behind a bluff-like hill, and a few minutes afterwards a white column—a half mile from the shore, as we subsequently learned, and two miles distant—was seen to suddenly shoot into the air, the steam from it ascending to a height of two thousand feet or more!"

The captain looked at us inquiringly. "You know, I suppose, what that was, gentlemen?"

"Geyser," said Darwin Frontenac.

"Just so; the largest geyser in the world, as it proved. It erupts every seventy minutes, sends its columns of boiling water to a height of over four hundred feet and plays for twenty-five minutes. I called it Hero's Fountain.

"But Hero's Fountain is not the only one. In short, we had discovered another Yellowstone—though this Yellowstone of ours was by far the most wonderful.

"Fortune had smiled upon us—though, as you will see, discoveries more wonderful were to follow.

OTHER'S WORK

"But we had done very well, even if this were all. Wilkes had discovered that land of continental proportions exist in the Antarctic; Ross had discovered the sea that bears his name and, a discovery more interesting than that, the volcano Erebus; Nordenskjold had found fossils that proved this terrible land had once been clothed in luxuriant vegetation; Shackleton had found coal; Scott, copper in workable quantity; and now here was this discovery of ours.

"Here were all the secondary volcanic phenomena, as I believe the scientists call them—hot springs, fumaroles, solfataras, mud-volcanoes and geysers!

"The warmth of the water was now explained: they owed that warmth to volcanic fires somewhere below. The high temperature—it was found to be 51° near the end of the Haven—was, however, in no small measure due to the marrow and comparative shallowness of the entrance, to which I gave the name Multnomah Pass. Much of the heat was, of course, lost by radiation. Had the entrance been wide and deep a different story would be told. For the cold water, in large quantities, would have been continuously replacing the warm, while, as it was, the cold water from the sea could get in only very slowly as the warm flowed out through Multnomah Pass, and that narrow channel allowed small escape.

"A great change was now made in the expedition's plans. After landing the dogs and stores, the erection of the hut and so on, the *Multnomah*, according to these plans, was to make her way back through the pack and come again for us the next summer. But all that was changed. She would winter here in Summer Haven. There were no icebergs to go ploughing with the wind. The wildest gale could never send floe or berg in through Multnomah Pass."

"Was any vegetation found?" asked Frontenac, for the captain had paused.

"Moss, some pretty moss-flowers and a few shrubs, and that was all."

"Ah," I said to myself, "no palm-trees yet!"

"Of course," the discoverer went on, "I did not have any illusions. I felt sure that the bitterest cold of the bitter Antarctic could never freeze this haven over. But I well knew that everything else would be frozen. There could be no appreciable atmospheric warmth. The winds would carry all that away. Even in still weather, it would be the same thing. For there would be a steady indraught of cold air from the frozen waste.

6

THE SECOND DISCOVERY

"Now for the palm-trees!" I thought.

And I was right, though it did not come at once.

But he had made even more strange discoveries. Imagine a sleeper in a bed of crystal, his poor wondrous Sleeping Beauty; there in that dreamless, awful slumber, a slumber terrible as death, unbroken through centuries unnumbered, through ages even, ages unrecorded; a sleep never to be broken until that day of doom for all things earthly or until the foulest of deaths of which the captain had spoken overtook her unless, as in the fairy tale, there came a prince to awake her!

But I anticipate.

After a slight pause, Livingstone went on with his story:

"For a time we were very busy. There was much to be done, much to explore, depots to be laid down, before the long Antarctic night closed in on us.

"And how much different things were to be than we had planned—here in this wondrous spot! The erection of the hut was begun at once.

"Of course, in one way, our work, thanks to our discovery of Summer Haven, was considerably shortened: there was no need to land all the stores at once, as otherwise would have been the case.

"After our exploration of the region round-about, I turned to the southward. We passed the rising land between Summer Haven and Mounts Roosevelt and Wilson, passed between those mighty peaks and out upon the great glacier beyond. This glacier, which I

41

named Washington Glacier, was to be seen stretching for mile after mile to the southward.

"'There lies our way to the Pole—for a long distance at any rate,' I said.

"Little did I dream that this terrible highway of ice was to direct us to something far more wonderful than the Pole!

"I now turned back and ascended the side of Mount Woodrow Wilson to reconnoiter the country. Up we went until our aneroid told us we stood five thousand feet above sea level. From the mountain-top we could trace the glacier much further, and it ran on as wide as ever. The ranges of mountains that flanked it on either side continued for a hundred miles or more.

"Three days later, we set forth from Summer Haven. We made our way up the glacier for some seventy miles and laid down our first depot in latitude 78° 50'; the hut, near the southern extremity of Summer Haven, was in latitude 77° 45'. In getting those seventy-five miles of southing, our sled-meters logged eighty-four miles, so you see we had been going pretty straight all the time.

THE SECOND STOP

"Again we went southward, with supplies for our second depot. I determined to push on as far as possible. Ten miles or so beyond Depot One, however, we got into a crevassed and pressure-twisted region which slowed our progress. We got through with much trouble and labor, came to the end of the glacier, ascended to a broken plateau and at last reached latitude 80° 15'—one hundred and seventy miles from Summer Haven. With this we stopped and we had cause for satisfaction.

"You shall have details, if, when you have heard my story, you decided to go and see for yourself."

He smiled at us a little bitterly and with a strange sadness.

"Heaven knows, I should not blame you if you think it was all a dream.

"So we had laid down number two in latitude 80° 15'. Once more, though the season was getting late, we went south; this time

we pushed on to latitude 82° 10', where we put down the third depot. This ended our southern work for that year.

"The sun left us on the 25th of April, and we did not see it again
until August the 18th.

"There is no need to dwell on that long Antarctic night. Let us
hasten on to the southern journey in the spring.

"We got away on the first of November—myself and four men.
November 15 found us at depot three. Before us now lay the unknown—tumbled, shaggy mountains on every side, five hundred
miles between us and the Pole.

"To get through, we had to swing off to the left. After a terrible
time among glaciers, we made the passage of the mountains and
entered a great snowy plain. Here at times for miles the surface
was as smooth as a lawn, and then the dogs—there were four sleds
and sixty dogs—went on at a spanking rate. Then again we would
of a sudden find ourselves in the terrible sastrugi, and the going
was such as to make a bishop swear.

"At latitude 85° we laid down depot five and made our second
discovery. This discovery we owe to the geologizing fever of
Hampden. I should have explained that we had left the great plain
behind us and were once more in the midst of mountains. In the
spot where we had fixed upon for the depot, the mountains rose
up no more than a mile away on either hand, and the steep sides
were remarkably free from snow. The rocks lay in strata, showing
out black, gray, red, green and yellow, and I must say it made a
very striking picture.

ANOTHER DISCOVERY

"Hampden had gone off to one of them in search of geological data.
After some hours, I saw him returning, and at the sight of him I
stood up and stared. He was coming on as fast as his legs could
carry him, much excited. Indeed, this excitement was so remarkable that I caught it too and went out to meet him.

"'Wowee!' was his first word.

"'Why the wowee?' I wanted to know.

"Hampden blew like a whale for some moments; when he had recovered his breath sufficiently to speak, he said:

"'A discovery, Captain! The greatest discovery—yes,' he cried, 'the greatest discovery in all Antarctic history!'

"'Lead me to it!' I told him.

"'Come on!'

"We went. The others had heard and seen and were coming on after us. Even some of the dogs had caught the fever.

"'A gold mine?' I queried.

"'A gold mine!' echoed Hampden with a look of disgust. 'Something more wonderful than a gold mine, Captain!'

"And away he went again, and away I went with him. As we proceeded, I tried to get some light on this extraordinary discovery of his, but all I could get out of him was:

"'You'll soon see.'

"We reached the base of the mountain. There were the beautifully colored strata directly before us a talus, from which the wind had swept almost every trace of snow.

"Hampden headed straight for this mass of debris and started to climb. Without a word, I followed him.

"When he had reached a point about fifty feet above the level of the glacier, Hampden stopped. Hanging onto a piece of jutting stone to keep his balance, he pointed and said:

"'Look at that!'

"In a moment I was there and saw the object. I stared.

"'What did I tell you, Captain?' cried Hampden in triumph.

"What I saw was a fragment of a column; it was the capital, or, to be precise, part of one. It was beautifully sculptured. There were figures of harpies and palm-trees upon it."

Frontenac unwound his long legs, seemed to pop out of his chair and then made two or three turns before us.

"Captain Livingstone," he said, "was it of *those* palm-trees that you spoke to that witty fool Professor Kelp?"

"It was *not!*"

"Ah!" exclaimed Frontenac. "I am glad to hear you say that!"

The next moment he had sunk into his chair again and resumed his attitude of profound attention.

"Pray go on, Captain," he said.

"As for *those* palm-trees, Mr. Frontenac—well, sir," said the captain, "just wait till I come to the real ones!

"However, to return to Hampden's discovery.

"'Human beings, Captain!' exclaimed Hampden, a tone of awe in his voice.

A DISCUSSION

"His hand made a sweep as though to point out the forbidding aspect of this frozen, terrible land—the utter desolation and horror of this solitude that hemmed us in.

"'No,' he went on, 'we are not the first men here, Captain Livingstone. Who can say, though, how many centuries, how many ages even, have come and gone since human beings moved among these mountains?'

"'That carved stone,' and he pointed to the harpies and the palm-trees, 'proves that this Continent was inhabited by human beings before the coming of the great ice-sheets. What is a relic of the Neolithic or the Paleolithic age to this? It takes us back to a time when even the polar regions enjoyed a temperate climate—perhaps even a tropical one.'

"Soon the others had come up and were staring and expressing their astonishment.

"Suddenly Hampden thrust a hand toward the rocks towering above us.

"'It came from somewhere up there,' he said.

"'Of course,' I nodded, gazing up and wondering what we should find if we went up there.

"We went up. Ascent by the talus was too steep and difficult, so we went off to the left, made our way up a canyon and so out onto the shelf above. And there we found the spot from which our capital had fallen. Little of the ruin was left, however, only a scattered heap of stones and fragments of two columns.

"We stayed two days longer in the spot, searching about, but we found nothing more.

"On the third day we left depot five. Hampden looked over towards his mountain with longing and regret; if he could have followed his own desires, he would have remained there exploring all the rest of the spring and all summer!

"Hampden—poor fellow! My poor comrades! If I could have peered into the future! Had such power been vouchsafed me—well, all the wealth of Ormus and of Ind could never have moved me forward one single mile!"

7
AS THROUGH A CURTAIN

"You'll remember that this depot was in latitude 85°; it was in latitude 85° 7′, to be precise.

"On December the 5th we reached latitude 86° 10′. And here I figuratively scratched my head. We seemed to be in for a tough job. Great mountains barred our way to the south. Indeed, mountains rose up on every hand, some of the peaks majestic and beautiful beyond all words.

"There to the south, less than three hundred miles away, lay our goal. But those awful mountains rose up between. The chance of getting through in that direction seemed to me, and to the others, a desperate one. Things looked better off to the east, though anything but rosy. To try to get through in that direction meant that we should have to travel many miles without gaining a single mile of southing. And, besides, there was no telling what we might find after making our way to the other side.

"We had a council on the matter, and it was decided to steer off in that direction.

"The surface soon became extremely difficult. That day we made only six miles.

"The next day things were no better, but we managed to make ten miles. We were now at the very base of the range; on the morrow would begin the passage.

"On the afternoon of this same day, the 8th of December, we saw three enormous skua gulls. They circled and wheeled about us for a time, and one even alighted a short distance off; and then

47

they flew away toward the mountain peaks, went off in that same direction in which they had come to us.

"I must say the sight of those birds amazed every man of the party. What were they doing down here? Why had they flown back across the range? What could there be over there beyond those mountains to attract gulls?

"I thought of Amundsen's surprise at seeing two of these birds (on the opposite side of the Pole) in latitude 84°, and of the one seen by Scott in latitude 87°, and I confess that my surprise became greater than ever.

"But the gulls were not the only thing we found ourselves unable to account for: the dogs could be seen gazing away to the eastward, up at those mountains, as if some sudden and strange message, one not fully understood, as it were, had been borne to their acute senses. They would erect their ears, their eyes would shine brightly and eagerly. They thrust up their muzzles to sniff the air.

"'What the devil,' said Thompson, gazing up at the mountains and actually beginning to sniff the air himself.

"This was after we had made camp. The nearest dog arose at the sound of Thompson's voice, whined in a strange manner, then came over to Thompson, squatted at his feet and once more turned his eyes to the eastward and once more began his mysterious sniffing.

"'Something there,' said Thompson, waving a hand up toward the heights. 'Something queer or the dogs wouldn't be acting like this.'

THE NEXT DAY

"We were off early the next morning, and in a few minutes had begun our ascent. It was very difficult work. But we toiled steadily. We arrived on a wide ledge which ran off to the left, towards what appeared to be the entrance to a gap through the range. That it was a gap seemed plain enough from below; as to how far it extended back into the mountains we had had no means of knowing—unless we had gone forward to reconnoiter. I had felt so confident, however, of getting through this way, that this had not been done. I know it should have been done, but it wasn't.

"There is nothing so trying as suspense. And I confess I began to worry. Perhaps, after all, we should not have trusted to chance.

"Two hours of hard work brought us to the mouth. And, now that we were there, we started and didn't know what to make of it.

"'By the great Hercules,' said Thompson, 'it doesn't go clear through! Look how the walls come together and how the peaks on either side end by hugging each other.'

"Thompson, indeed, had given no bad description of the prospect.

"At this instant, however, one of the dogs broke into sharp whining. His look I found fixed, it seemed, high up on the rocky mass on our right.

"Before I could turn my look up there, Hampden cried out:

"'Oh, Lord, look at *that!*'

"I am afraid that, as I looked up, I exclaimed and took a step or two backward and crouched as though to shield myself. There was something driving down out of the heavens and directly toward us. At that moment, my startled senses could not give the object its true size or shape; it seemed of monstrous size, and certainly it was driving down upon us with the speed of an arrow. *It dropped.*

"Had one of those winged devils in Doré's pictures for Dante's Inferno launched himself down at us in this fashion from off that icy cliff, the sight of him could scarcely have been more startling and astonishing.

THE BIRD

"The apparition was so sudden and unexpected—no wonder our senses played us tricks; no wonder they magnified, distorted; no wonder they made the thing monstrous. Suddenly a great pinion shot out from either side of the driving object, and the next moment, with a dull rustling that was like a roar, a great bird went rushing past, barely twenty feet above our heads.

"It fetched up on the instant, came circling back and began to wheel round and round above us.

"'Look out!' cried Bogardus. 'He's going to drop again!'

"So, indeed, it seemed. And I could have sworn that the thing had his eyes fixed on me.

"Thompson had rushed to his sled to get a rifle, Hampden to his sled to get the other. Save for our knives and axes, these two rifles were the only weapons that we had. In all likelihood, if we had taken along more weapons, my story would have been very different.

"But thus it was that those poor loyal comrades of mine were doomed men—doomed to the horror in the palm-trees.

"Only two rifles! And we were soon to find ourselves in a place where a dozen would have been none too many!

"I thought the bird was going to drop upon me. This might have been only fancy on my part, but certainly his looks were anything but benevolent. But he changed his mind and began to rise.

"Thompson fired and missed. Miss again. Thompson flung forth a savage oath and clicked another cartridge into the chamber. The bullet went straight to the mark this time, and down the great bird tumbled into the snow.

"I was the first to reach it, and it struck savagely at me with a vicious beak. The next moment, however, it sank inert, and in a few seconds the strange creature was dead.

"Its wing spread was found to be eight feet; it was of a brown color; and, under each wing—mark this well—there was a white line!"

The explorer look at us with an expression I did not understand.

"Perhaps you wonder why I lay so much stress on that white line under the wings."

"That," Frontenac told him, "is just what I was wondering."

Captain Livingstone drew forth a pocketbook, opened it and took out a sheet of note paper.

"This," said he, reaching the paper to Frontenac, "is from Shackleton's *The Heart of the Antarctic*. Read it, I think it will show why."

Frontenac already was reading. On looking up, as he finished, he said:

"Strange! Very strange!"

And that was all that he said. But it was quite enough to show that Darwin Frontenac had been greatly impressed.

A QUOTATION
Without a word he handed the paper over to me. This is what I read, Shackleton's entry being for December the 5th:

"I was still badly snow-blind, so stayed in camp whilst Marshall and Adams went on to spy out a good route to follow after lunch was over. . . . The most remarkable thing they reported was that as they were walking along a bird, brown in color with a white line under each wing, flew just over their heads and disappeared to the south. It is, indeed, strange to hear of such an incident in latitude 83° 40′ South. They were sure it was not a skua gull, which is the only bird I could think of that would venture down here. . . ."

I confess I was puzzled not a little.

"It is true, as I afterwards learned, Shackleton (unless I misread him) thought the bird was really a skua gull. I think it extremely unlikely, however, that the men who saw the creature could have been deceived, especially when it passed 'just over their heads.' Supposing the bird Marshall and Adams believed was a strange one really was a skua, is the mystery any the less a mystery? The fact remains that the bird was traveling toward the Pole!

"Shackleton thought the incident a strange one; but, as to the strangest thing of all about it, he makes no comment whatever. Not a single word elicited by the mysterious fact that the bird was flying south!

"Then there is the skua Scott saw in latitude 87°. Scott doesn't even tell us what direction the bird took. In fact, he thought it was merely following his party.

"Amundsen was the only one who was truly impressed by this mysterious flight. Here is what he says."

The captain handed another paper to Frontenac, who, in turn, passed it on to me. The note was copied from Amundsen's *The South Pole*.

"As we were leaving this old friend [the beacon in latitude 84° 26′] and setting our course as it advised, to our unspeakable astonishment two great birds—skua gulls—suddenly came flying straight towards us. They circled round us once or twice and then settled on the beacon. Can anyone who reads these lines form an idea of the effect this had upon us? It is hardly likely. They brought us a message from the living world into this realm of death—a message of all that was dear to us. I think the same thoughts filled us all. They did not allow themselves a long rest, these first messengers from another world; they sat still a while, no doubt wondering who we were, then rose aloft and flew on to the south. Mysterious creatures! they were now exactly half-way between Framheim and the Pole, and yet they were going farther inland. Were they going over to the other side?"

"Well," the captain said when I had returned the paper to him, "that was where we were—on the other side. And I believe it was toward this very region that those skua gulls of Amundsen's and that strange bird seen by Shackleton's men were flying. Where could those creatures have been going if it wasn't toward the place there beyond the mountains?

THE PASS

"We had, all things considered, done a good day's work; but we pushed on for two miles more before we camped. It was bitterly cold, the temperature having fallen to 22° below zero. Also there was the heavy dampness in the air which made the frost even more bitter.

"The walls had closed in on us, their bases at this place being separated only five hundred feet. What was there before us? Certainly the eyes could give but little certain information in answer to that. Well, we should learn on the morrow. And certainly, too, the surface here was extremely difficult to pass. That night we were awakened more than once by the booming of the glacier. The sound was a deep, unearthly thing, and, until one became accustomed to it, it gave one a shiver. Something of the kind, however, we had heard on some of the other glaciers.

"Once, too, that night the dogs set up a sudden, fierce whining and howling that brought all of us out of our sleeping-bags into the bitter outside air. The dogs kept looking up the chasm, but we could discover nothing. Thompson declared he saw something black and without any particular shape, move up in the cut but the others thought he must have been deceived.

"I use the word night, but, of course, that word is not, strictly speaking, applicable. For here, though hidden by the mountains, the sun never set. The place in which we were camped was in deep shadow, gloom even, but the sunlight shone cold and bright on the mighty mountain masses above us.

"We were up early. It was still bitterly cold. I thought of going forward first to see for certain what was ahead, instead of thus blindly moving on with the dogs and sleds; but at last decided to push on without further investigation. For some time, almost three hours, the going was terrible. We were rising steadily, and the walls were now only two hundred feet or so apart. The rock masses, towering before us higher and higher, were almost free of snow. They were masses black and terrible.

"We were, indeed, making our way into one of the most remarkable passes in all the world. It was, as Thompson remarked, as if some cosmic giant had driven a wedge into the rocks and split them asunder.

"It was a little after three o'clock when we passed the highest point, eight thousand four hundred feet. The end of the day's march, however, found those great walls still towering above us. We had descended near a thousand feet, though, and had great hopes for the morrow.

THE JOURNEY CONTINUES

"If we had only known what was before us!

"The actions of the dogs were now a greater puzzle than ever. They sniffed the air constantly and gazed down the chasm. We had much discussion and speculation.

"We were to learn, and soon at that.

"I roused the party a little after five and by seven o'clock we were pushing on once more. This, the great day, was the eleventh of December. Despite the hard work of the last few days, both men and dogs were in fine fettle, and, when the surfaces would permit, we went along at a swinging gait.

"This, unfortunately, was not often or for any great stretch; as a whole, the surface of the glacier continued miserable for travel.

It grew worse as the descent grew steeper. Consequently the crevasses and pressure-waves and ridges gave us more trouble. The only consolation was that we were going down hill.

"Another difference we noticed, though at the time I thought nothing of it, for atmospheric changes are anything but unusual in that strange land.

"For some days the air had been clear, so clear that it seemed to sparkle like wine. But a curious haze was over everything now. It seemed to lift or move aside at times, then suddenly it would close in again. These movements produced changes in the appearance of objects that were simply astonishing. One minute a mountain pass would have a certain form, and then, perhaps five minutes later, one could scarcely believe that he was looking at the same object.

"This haze became thicker as we advanced. Indeed, ere long the eye could no longer, save for fleeting moments, make out those heights on either hand, though the chasm walls had now sunk to a comparatively low altitude.

"Height of noon camp five thousand feet. Haze thicker and more tricky than ever. Thermometer had risen to minus 2° Fahrenheit. We pushed on eagerly, wishing the haze would lift. But the haze did not lift. Instead, we suddenly plunged, as it were, into a dense fog. We could not see a hundred feet ahead. Had Scylla and Charybdis or ten thousand Cyclops been lying in wait we would have been none the wiser. Yet move on we must, and move on we did, literally feeling every foot of the way.

"Those were terrible hours that followed. There is no need, however, to dwell on them. I shall leave that to the imagination. It was trying, dangerous business, this groping forward—blindfolded, as it were—into the unknown. But I was determined to keep at the journey until something brought us to an utter standstill, for, if we stopped and waited for the fog to lift, we might have had to stay there for days.

"At length we suddenly became aware that sounds no longer came back in echoes. What had become of the chasm walls? Had we at last issued from that great canyon. Where were we?

EXPLORATIONS

"Thompson went off to the right, Hampden to the left. The aneroid gave us an altitude of four thousand two hundred feet. Since the noon halt, we had descended nearly a thousand feet. The temperature had risen to 6° Fahrenheit. At last, in about twenty minutes, Thompson returned. Nothing, he reported, but snow and ice and fog in that direction. A few minutes, and Hampden came back with the report that he had bumped into a granite wall.

"So on we went once more. I was forerunner—foregroper, rather, for that was what I was doing. Suddenly the fog thinned. I thought I even caught a glimpse of blue sky. Then the vapor closed in once more, denser it seemed than ever. Five minutes, and again the fog thinned out. This time there was no mistake: I did catch a glimpse of blue sky. But almost instantaneously the blue was blotted out, and once more I was groping my way on through gray darkness.

"How long it was I do not know. Perhaps it was no more than five minutes; perhaps twenty. Suddenly, however, the fog thinned, and the next moment I stepped out of it, as through a curtain, and stood in bright sunshine. Before my eyes a view the like of which no discoverer ever set eyes upon, greeted me.

"I am not, I believe, in any sense of the word, nervous or excitable. But it was all I could do to keep from crying out at what I saw. The next moment, however, a thought came that sobered me, at the same time filling my mind with a doubt that was simply terrible. Was it all only a mirage or a dream?

"So I said nothing, just stood there and gazed and waited for the others to come.

"Hampden was the first. As he stepped out into the sunlight and saw it, he started, fetched up and stared like a man transported to a sight of fairyland. Then he gave a loud shout or cry—I don't know which it was, perhaps it was both—that brought the others to our sides as fast as they could come."

8
THE GARDENS OF PARADISE

"'That,' I told Hampden, 'is just what I have been wondering myself.'

"The others were gazing in astonishment and in awe.

"'A dream?' said Thompson. 'No, it isn't a dream, because I have just pinched myself and proved that I was never wider awake in all my life.'

"'It *is* a dream,' said Wilkie, 'a dream that is *true*.'

"'It is Paradise,' murmured Hampden. 'Yes, Captain Livingstone, it is Paradise that you have discovered—great Lord, here in the very heart of this frozen continent!'

"And he reached out his hand and wrung mine. Then they all broke out cheering; and the other three pressed forward to shake my hand, and they all said that I had made the greatest geographical discovery of modern times and that they thanked God that they had been fortunate enough to be there with me.

"I am afraid that I became rather foolish then—yes, I admit it: try as I would, I couldn't keep the tears from my eyes. All I could do was, curse myself roundly for a silly old femmelette.

"'Look at the dogs!' said Thompson. 'The blamed beggars! I know now why they sniffed and sniffed and acted so darned mysterious.'

"The dogs were looking and looking, and there was a great waving of tails in celebration of our wonderful discovery.

"'Paradise,' I said. 'That is it, Hampden: its name is Paradise—the Gardens of Paradise.'

"'It certainly looks it,' said Bogardus.

"And it certainly did.

"Perhaps, indeed, the contrast added to its loveliness, but I am by no means sure that this was so. For days, for weeks, we had been toiling through an indescribable waste of snow and ice and barren rock, and then suddenly to step out of that fog curtain and see this! No marvel, forsooth, that we had wondered if it all wasn't only a dream!

"The air was not perfectly clear. At first sight, it seemed so, but soon one noticed that there was a strange dreaminess over everything, so to speak. It wasn't a haze. I don't know what it was. It reminded me, more than anything else, of these strange and wonderful effects that one sees in some of the greatest paintings of Turner. And yet it wasn't *that*, either. Also, everywhere the air seemed to be without movement. And the cloud effects! They were not grand or gorgeous, 'tis true, but they had a beauty that no painter has ever yet succeeded in placing on canvas. They were clouds like those that must float over fairyland.

"We did not look out upon the scene but down upon it, rather. I may liken the Gardens of Paradise to the bottom of a huge bowl, a deep plate would be better, the lofty, terrible mountains—running away in a great majestic arc, there to the right and to the left, until they were lost in the distance—forming the sides and the rim. This grand depression, however, must not be conceived of as a circular one. It was oval, rather—that is, this part of it over which our eyes could range. There was no telling, though, what form it took away over there in the northeast—we had come out upon the southwestern edge—or to what distance this wonderful and mysterious land might extend in that direction.

"Before us, the ground—the snow, I should have said—fell away, now in gentle undulations, now in broken swells and jagged pitches. And down there, probably two miles from the spot where we stood, the snow suddenly ended. There trees grew, in scattered and ragged patches—looking like pines, like weary, brooding sentinels. Down the ground sloped, down to great clumps and masses of trees and down and down until every swell and hill and plain was a mass of lovely green. Here and there streams were to be glimpsed, and there, off to the left, almost hidden amongst the swelling, rounded hills—a formation characteristic of these Gardens of Paradise—a lake mirrored back the blue and mauve and gold of the Antarctic sky.

"And there, far away, in the very midst of all this green and blue and dreamy, weird beauty, a great mountain towered aloft—its flanks for some distance up dark with trees and jutting rock, and then suddenly the region of perpetual snow. The summit of this great peak was lost in the clouds. The crowning one was of a curious shape, something like a mushroom, and it shone with colors so bright (and they seemed to flicker a little) that we wondered if that mass and color were not due to volcanic fires.

"Yes, there they rolled away for mile on mile, rolled on for league on league—the Gardens of Paradise. Altogether, a stranger and lovelier sight the eye of man has never gazed upon, nestling, as they do, in all their luxuriant and tropical beauty, there in the very heart of this frozen, desolate, lifeless Antarctic—in the midst of a land of unnamable loneliness, desolation and icy horror.

"Yes, and see them! There they were plain as plain could be in our powerful glasses. Look, there were palm-trees!

"'Palm-trees!' Thompson exclaimed. 'Captain,' said he, 'do you see any bananas?'

"I told Thompson that we might find things down there stranger than bananas and handed him the glasses so that he could see those palm-trees for himself.

"'I'm not surprised,' said Thompson. 'I'm beyond that now. I wonder, though—'

"He waved a hand towards the Gardens of Paradise.

"'Eden,' said he, 'had its serpent. I wonder if this Paradise has got one, too.'

"'We'll soon learn that,' I told him.

"'What I don't understand,' said Bogardus, 'is how on earth those trees and everything can *be*. Be!' said Bogardus. 'Reason tells me that the thing is impossible—absurd. And yet there they are! See 'em!'

"Hampden gave him an odd look.

"'Then so much the worse for reason,' Hampden told him. 'For, after all, what is there so very strange about it?'

"'Strange?' echoed Bogardus, staring.

"And I confess that I stared at that myself.

"'Why,' said Bogardus, 'the heat, for one thing. Here we have warmth and vegetation, even palm-trees, and all roundabout, for hundreds and hundreds of miles, nothing but snow and ice. Well, bless me, Harmer, if that isn't strange, then I don't know what on earth the word strange means.'

"'Oh, the thing is strange all right,' Hampden told him. 'That wasn't just my meaning. What I meant was that there is nothing mysterious about it. There is the warmth of Summer Haven; this is on a grander scale, that is all. Both are simply due to volcanic fires.'

"'Yes,' said Bogardus, 'but how does it come that this warmth lingers here and trees are growing? Why doesn't the cold air keep coming in, the way it does there at Summer Haven?'

"Hampden smiled a little and pointed up towards the mountains.

"'There's the reason. They rise up all around, a veritable wall—at any rate, as far as we can see. This wonderful basin is mountain-locked. Virtually, the only way the heat can escape is by radiation and convection.'

"'How beautiful and simple!' exclaimed Bogardus. 'I thought of those mountains forming a wall all around; but all the same it strikes me as a mighty queer thing, let me tell you. And here's something else:

"'Look at those streams, look at all this snow that must be melting and sending down water all around and all the time. Why isn't the basin filled to the brim? And suppose that the water flowed out, what then? It would be frozen as fast as it flowed, and keep piling up and up.'

"'It would,' said Hampden, 'but you see that it doesn't. The water flows away to the sea by some underground channel, that is all.'

"'How simple and beautiful!' exclaimed Bogardus. 'And how warm it must get going through these rocks! And tell me something: how is Captain Livingstone going to make the world believe this? I've got a good big enlarged tintype of them whooping and hollering when he begins to tell them about those palm-trees that he discovered far inside the Antarctic circle.'

"'Won't we be there,' demanded Thompson, 'to back him up if any of those gents waxes skeptical?'

'Pooh!' said Bogardus. 'They'll say that we all got moonstruck or something or were all lunatics to begin with.'

"'There are the cameras,' put in Hampden. 'Photographs will convince them if nothing else will.'

"'Photographs? Not those birds. They'll say that the pictures are fakes.'

"'Oh, cheer up, Trophonius,' smiled Hampden. 'The world isn't so bad as you think it is.'

"'Cheer up? Oh, I'm cheerful!' said Bogardus. 'I know something of the world, too. And you mark my words: Captain Livingstone is going to have a time of it when he gets back and begins to tell about these things.'

"'There are the cameras,' said Hampden. 'Photographs will convince the last Doubting Thomas of them all. And so we'll begin right now.'

"And he did. He got out his camera and photographed us there in the place of discovery and photographed the mountains and the Gardens of Paradise.

"And then we started down, all eager to reach the snow-line, to walk on grass and hear once more the sounds of running water.

"Alas, why can't man see into the future? Because, I suppose, it wouldn't be the future if he could. There we were hurrying down the snow towards the Gardens of Paradise; but—if we had only known what was going to happen down there!"

9

THE HORROR IN THE PALM-TREES

"I scarcely know how to tell it—this horror and mystery that awaited us. Certainly I have no desire to minimize any part of it, if for no other reason because you should know truly what awaits any man who makes his way into the Gardens of Paradise.

"Perhaps you will not go, Mr. Frontenac. But something tells me that you will. Yes, of one thing I feel certain: if I am any judge of a man, the very danger itself and the mystery that lurks there will draw you on—to what, God in Heaven only knows."

The expression on Frontenac's face never changed; not a lineament moved.

Alas, I thought, Captain Livingstone's judgment of the man before him was a judgment only too true!

"But," the explorer continued, "to get on with my story—to tell you of that horror there in the palm-trees and the discovery that was to follow, the strangest and most wonderful discovery of them all, of my poor frozen Sleeping Beauty there in her bed of crystal. And then—well, my tale is ended then.

"We went down fast enough, as can easily be imagined. The temperature was swiftly rising. There were curious minglings of the warmer air with the cold. The cheek would be warm one moment and chilled the next. These things we had known, though in a far less marked degree, at Summer Haven, and the boys had dubbed these warm and cold mixtures 'atmospheric highballs.'

"Near the edge of the snow, we halted; here the dogs and the sleds were to be left for the time being, whilst we men hurried down into Paradise. Into Paradise—great Heaven!

"Never were the details of a halt gone through with greater despatch. While the men were about these things—much to the disgust of the dogs, who wanted to go into Paradise as well as their masters—I went on, only stopping long enough to get one of the rifles.

"'Better bring along the other,' I told them. 'There's no telling, you know—no guessing what we may run into. We may need them both.'

"A few moments, and I had stepped off the snow and was treading my way down over lichen; a little space, was crushing through pretty daisy-like flowers, which covered the ground in all directions like a gorgeous carpet. I came to shrubs, stunted and savage-looking; to dwarf fierce-looking trees of a species of pine—a species that I had never seen before. The trees became larger and larger, were swiftly losing that fierce look, and soon other trees were growing amidst the pines—willows, maples, yes, and there was that wonderful tree, the madrona, for all the world like the madronas that grow here along your Puget Sound.

"Suddenly I became aware that it was insufferably warm, so halted and began to peel off. While I was thus getting rid of my zero togs, the others arrived, and then their clothes too began to fly. When we had finished, we had a good laugh at our appearance, which certainly was a singular one. But, though our costumes were anything but conventional, we were now comfortable, and that, believe me, was some consolation.

"Down there before us, the wood had an almost semi-tropical appearance. We moved on towards it. Of a sudden Hampden stopped and gazed intently at the ground off to our immediate right. The next moment he was moving that direction. We saw him stoop and place his palm to the earth.

"'What's going on now?' Thompson queried.

"'Come here,' was Hampden's answer, 'and see what you think of this.'

"We went: the ground was deliciously warm. And so we found it for some acres in extent, and how much farther it extended we did not know.

"'No wonder there are palm-trees!' exclaimed Thompson, 'with all this heat coming up! The whole valley must be like this, more or less and most probably mostly more.'

"'At any rate, there's a place that's more,' Hampden told him, pointing to a great space that was almost destitute of vegetation. 'The ground is so hot there that only a few shrubs can stick it out.'

"'That's so,' Bogardus said. 'You can see the heat waves boiling up from the ground.'

"'And there!' put in Wilkie. 'Look at that spring gushing up, gushing a regular full-grown creek. The water looks boiling hot.'

"We went over to this stream and found the water at so high a temperature that it was all one wanted to do to keep the hand immersed in it for even a few moments.

"'Warmth!' exclaimed Hampden. 'No wonder this great basin is covered with forest, some of it tropical, no wonder it is the Gardens of Paradise, with the ground radiating all this subterranean heat and the sun pouring down throughout the whole of the twenty-four hours, and that for months on end.'

"'Except,' said Wilkie, 'when the mountains hide him.'

"'I can see it now,' mused Bogardus. 'But it seems to me a strange thing that there is so tremendous a store of heat. One can't imagine how much is lost even in a single day, and yet here it has been going on for thousands upon thousands of years. Seems to me that the supply ought to be exhausted. At any rate,' said Bogardus, 'it will be some day.'

"Hampden smiled a little at this.

"'And so will the heat of the sun itself be exhausted—some day.'

"'It must be a mighty queer place, this, in the winter,' Bogardus added, 'when for months the sun never shines at all.'

"Hampden nodded.

"'A gloomy, weird place indeed it must be then.'

"'But,' said Thompson, 'still warm.'

"'Of course. But it must be a strange place truly when the long and terrible night settles down upon it.'

"Thus we talked and speculated as we moved on, going deeper and deeper all the while into this wonderful place. Insects were about us. Now and again great gorgeous butterflies were seen. We could hear birds singing, but as yet none had been seen.

"And then it happened—our fatal mistake. Our little party separated. I have never forgiven myself for permitting this. But how was I to know? Everything seemed so calm and peaceful, so safe. Indeed, what could there be here in these woods that could harm a man armed with a modern repeating rifle? I thought of these things, for, though I didn't fear anything at the time, yet I was reluctant to see our party go different ways.

"Had there been any grounds for fear, I would not have hesitated to speak as a commander, and that would have ended the matter then and there. Would to God that I had! As matters stood, however, as I had nothing but vague misgivings, misgivings that I could not explain even to myself, that exercise of authority would have seemed czaristic to my companions, and, indeed, so it would have seemed to myself also. So I merely suggested that it might perhaps be well for us all to stick together. But this made no impression upon them. Thompson (he was carrying the rifle), Bogardus and Wilkie continued to gaze longingly towards that vale, over to the right, where palm-trees grew. So I acquiesced, and off the three went, whilst Hampden and I started on in the direction of that mirror-like sheet of water we had seen nestling in the midst of the hills.

"'Be careful!' I admonished after them.

"Thompson raised the rifle and with a smile tapped it significantly. The next moment he and the two others had vanished from sight—never to be seen by us again. What we did see—the horror of that who could ever forget?

"We journeyed on, Hampden and I, steadily and with no little caution, now and again stopping to examine some strange plant or tree or flower. A strange, weird stillness and silence lay upon everything. At times leaves would move in a current of air, but there seemed to be something ghostly about those movements and the low rustling that accompanied them. It was as though they gave token of the presence of spirit things there in the air about us— things stealing about and following us with some sinister purpose.

It was as if, in some mysterious way, warnings of some terrible impending danger and mystery were being borne to the senses.

"I fought against this uncanny, unaccountable feeling, but I could not conquer it. Instead, it seemed to get its hold all the tighter upon me gripping, as it were, with the tentacles of an octopus. I called myself a crazy femmelette, an unmitigated fool and cursed myself for an idiot in good whacking fashion; but it all was of no use. That horrible sense of something impending, something *watching* and yet unseen—that horror had me, and I could not shake it off.

"Yet, though I was thus so mysteriously and powerfully affected—and, as I have said, I truly believe that I am by no means a nervous man—I did my utmost to prevent any sign of what I felt being seen by Hampden. Whether I succeeded in this or not, I can not say. But I do know that Hampden too was in the grip of that viewless, but none the less terrible, thing that I have likened to an octopus.

"But there was not a moment's hesitation. We talked and acted (at any rate, we tried to) as though we were having the gayest time in the world—all this, however, without any effect upon our caution and watchfulness.

"'All the same,' said I to myself, 'you ought to be ashamed of yourself. Like a kid—a big, an overgrown kid afraid of the dark!'

"The next instant Hampden came to a sudden stop, his hand closing on any arm and gripping it like a vise.

"'Listen!' he exclaimed in a whisper.

"We listened, but all I could hear was a ghostly rustle of leaves and the mournful drone of insects.

"'What was it?' I asked at last—my own voice too a whisper.

"'I don't know.'

"'A shot from Thompson's rifle, most likely.'

"'No!' Hampden declared. 'Whatever it was, if it was anything—whatever it was, it wasn't that!'

"We listened for a time.

"Then I queried:

"'If it was anything?'

"'Yes,' returned Hampden: 'if it was anything. For I'm not sure that the sound was a real one. My brain might have tricked me. But, whether real or imaginary, that sound I heard or thought that I did—well, whatever it was, it wasn't the report of a rifle.'

"I smiled a little at this but without letting Hampden know it. I thought his nerves were getting on the jumps. Certainly I had heard nothing whatever myself. But I did not smile afterwards when I thought of this incident.

"Did Hampden really hear something, or was it only a trick of his senses? We never learned, and now we never shall. I have my belief, however, and that is that the sound was a real one—that at that very moment the horrible tragedy had begun.

"Let me hasten on to the awful end, for I shudder to think of it, let alone to tell it.

"Hampden and I went on for perhaps a half hour longer. Evidently the lake was farther away than we had thought it. Also, we had to acknowledge that we were not sure just where we were. I don't mean by this that we were lost, that we would have any trouble in retracing our steps. What I mean is that we were no longer certain of the lake's precise direction. So we would go back and explore the Gardens of Paradise at some more opportune time.

"At length we stood again in that spot where our companions had left us. This was a long hill or ridge. Up this ridge we proceeded and in a few minutes had stepped out into the large open space above. We were perhaps two-thirds of the way across this spot—only a few stunted shrubs grew there—when Hampden stopped as though struck by a bullet and gave the strangest, most horrible cry that I had ever heard in all my life.

"The next moment I saw it. I don't know whether I cried out, too, or not, but I do know that I turned very sick at the sight.

"There, not fifty feet from the spot where we stood, lay a head—a severed human head!"

10

BY A GREAT CLAW

The explorer leaned forward in his chair. I saw a shudder pass through him. He covered his eyes with his hand.

I turned my look to Darwin Frontenac. His eyes were fixed on Captain Livingstone, and they shone with a light that was almost a glitter, whilst the expression on his lean features was so eager and keen that, I experienced something like a sudden shock.

"And," he said after waiting some moments for the other to go on, "you saw there a severed human head?"

"Yes; that is what we saw."

Again Captain Livingstone lapsed into silence.

Darwin Frontenac queried

"Was that *all?* Was there nothing else—no body there?"

"None. We looked all around, but there was no sign of the body anywhere. There was nothing but the head and a great quantity of gore, as though the body had been completely drained of its blood."

"Strange!" Frontenac muttered.

"We went to it and saw—how horrible it is to see the picture again!—that the head was Wilkie's."

"One moment, Captain Livingstone," said Frontenac. "How had the head been severed?"

The captain looked at him inquiringly.

"I mean," said Frontenac, "had it been cut from the trunk, or had it—?"

"Cut. How else could it have been done?"

"With a sharp instrument or—?"

"I don't know," Captain Livingstone said, "that any *instrument*, any *weapon* had been used to cut it off. Such a thing might have been used, but it is my idea that it was probably something very different."

"You interest me exceedingly, Captain Livingstone What, then, is your explanation?"

The explorer gave a significant gesture. "I have no explanation," he said.

"You interest me more than ever, Captain Livingstone!"

Frontenac looked at the other keenly, searchingly for a few moments, then said:

"Was the cut a clean one, or was the flesh torn and jagged?"

"Torn and jagged—horribly so. And across one cheek were marks that seemed to have been made by a great claw."

"Claw?" Darwin Frontenac exclaimed.

He sprang out of his chair and began to walk back and forth before us, his manner somewhat abstracted.

"You are sure, Captain," said he stopping, "that it wasn't a *hand?*"

"A hand! Great God, no! I tell you, it was the mark of an enormous claw!"

11
SLEEPING BEAUTY

For some moments Darwin Frontenac stood like one plunged in profound thought.

"Very strange!" he muttered at last, not aware, evidently, that he was speaking aloud. "A claw. An enormous claw. Now, I wonder if it were possible that—"

For a little space longer he stood there, then suddenly came out of his abstraction; he returned straightway to his chair and seated himself once more.

"Captain Livingstone," said he, "I never heard or read a stranger story than this you have told.

"The body, you say, was nowhere to be found?"

"No; it was gone."

"Any sign of a struggle?"

"None whatever. There were a few marks on the hard ground, but they were faint, and we could make nothing of them."

"Was there no sign to show in what direction the thing had carried the body away?"

"We could see none. The thought may seem a fantastic one, but how can we be sure that the *thing* moved on the ground?"

Darwin Frontenac leaned forward.

"Then," he suggested, "you think it possible that—"

"I do not offer any explanation, Mr. Frontenac. It all is an utter mystery to me.

"I told you," he went on, "that there was nothing but the body there. We thought so, but at last I found this, some thirty or forty feet from poor Wilkie's head."

He drew another paper from his pocketbook. It was a sheet from a note-book, and one edge of it was very ragged, as though it had been torn out in great haste, and the whole badly soiled. This he handed to Frontenac, who read it a second time and yet a third and then, without any comment, reached it over to me, the dark contraction of his brows, however, speaking more plainly than his lips could have done.

This is what I read, some of it so hastily written that it was barely legible:

"Go. Don't risk a single hour here—a single minute. Would need more men—many rifles. We had no show. There was no warning. Don't know, but it seemed to drop on us. Killed Thompson and Bogardus instantly. No chance to use rifle. I was badly wounded but got away. As I crawled saw it taking their heads clean off. Badly hurt—don't think can go farther—escape. Fear am followed. (The words that succeeded seemed to have been written in frenzied haste.) Think I see—God have mercy—it's coming now."

What, in God's name, was coming then—when he wrote those last words, even as his doom was upon him?

There was a deep silence in the room. It would be difficult to say how powerfully I was affected by this hasty, meager scrawl. And yet, after all, it was not so much what it told—it was what it didn't tell—it was what the poor doomed man would have told but could not.

One saw him there, alone, sorely wounded, overshadowed by a death horrible beyond all words, and yet, in those last awful moments, trying to leave a warning to the others—a warning to his kind and companions.

I thought I saw in this poor Wilkie a personification of that type, that brave man and true, that is the ideal of the race. So long as it has such sons, whatever its failings and sins and madness, all will be right in the end. When that noble (at times terrible) breed dies out, Heaven pity us all, for we shall sorely need it then.

I read Wilkie's message again and yet again, then reached it to Frontenac, who had extended a hand for it.

Once more he read it, then gave it back to the captain.

"I wonder," Frontenac said, "why it was torn out."

"I have often wondered at that myself, Mr. Frontenac."

"Did you find the book?"

"No; all we found was the pencil he had used.

"We were in a dilemma now. What was to be done? Go see if we could find Thompson and Bogardus, said I. To this Hampden was opposed, and I had to acknowledge that he could put forth the best of the argument.

"'It would be a foolish risk, Captain Livingstone,' he said. 'And for nothing. If we could hope to help them, it would be altogether different. But we can't. They're beyond that now. Look at what Wilkie says:

"'As I crawled saw it taking their heads clean off.'

"'What you say,' I told him, 'is true, but no one can say that I was afraid to go and recover the body of a comrade and friend.'

"'Very well,' said Hampden at last, 'if you are bound to go down there, I'll go, too. I can't see you go alone. But I tell you this: I think the chances are that we shall never come back, and so this wonderful discovery of yours will be lost to the world.'

"'I know that. Yet I am going.'

"'Then so am I,' Hampden said. 'I think this is what we ought to do first, though: go up to the sleds and get an ax. Not the best weapon in the world, but it is all there is, and I may be able to do something with an ax. Not much though, I fancy, seeing that Thompson never got a chance to fire a single shot and that the others couldn't get a hand on the rifle. Remember, Captain, what Wilkie says:

"'*It seemed to drop on us.*'

"I remembered that. There wasn't a single word on that horrible paper that I. didn't remember—that wasn't seared on my brain. But all I said was:

"'Let's get that ax.'

"So we started up, Hampden carrying Wilkie's head. The hair on it was rather long, and so he carried it by the hair—a horrible sight to see."

"One thing, Captain Livingstone," said Frontenac: "could the dogs be seen from that open spot where you had come upon Wilkie's head?"

"Oh, no. We had left them in a little hollow; you couldn't see them until you were right close."

"Did they bark or howl, make any sound that might have attracted attention to them?"

"None that we heard."

"I see," said Frontenac.

"Well," the captain went on, "Hampden got the ax (and a knife) and we started down again. We knew, of course, the direction that the three had taken on parting, but they had left no trail to guide us. We had but little difficulty, however, in finding the place of the tragedy, for Wilkie had *crawled*, all the way out, and the signs he had left were not hard to follow.

"Yes, there at last we stood, Hampden and I, in that place where the horror had dropped down upon them.

"There were palm-trees all about, but the spot itself was beneath the branches of a great cypress. The thing easily could have lain hidden up there, and we had no doubt whatever that it was from one of those branches that it had dropped. But what was it? There was nothing to throw any light on that. There were marks of a struggle, but it was plain that that struggle had been a very brief one. And what we had found in that spot where poor Wilkie had been killed, that we found here also—blood that showed the bodies had been completely exsanguinated and the heads of the two victims."

"The bodies were gone?" exclaimed Darwin Frontenac.

"Gone. There was the blood and the heads of our poor companions and that mark there on the trunk of the tree, and that was all—that mark, again, left by some enormous claw."

"The rifle?"

"Gone. So we came away, carrying their poor severed heads, or, rather, 'twas Hampden carried them, and this he did as he had the others—by the hair.

"'Twas little enough truly that we could do for our comrades now, but that little we would do. Perhaps at that very moment—I shuddered to think of it—their bodies were being feasted upon. But we could give their heads burial, and we did, raised a cross over the grave, and then we left that cursed place.

"There is no need to detail our return through that great defile. We had to abandon two of the sleds and the provisions that they carried. We did not leave them there, though, but found a good spot and made a depot, and there they are for any explorer who may follow. It was hard work, too, to handle so many dogs, but we did it and won steadily back along that terrible way we had come, taking with us the strangest story an explorer ever had to tell.

"Little did we dream that a discovery was to follow even more strange and wonderful than those wonderful and terrible Gardens of Paradise.

"At Discovery Depot, we went over to the talus where Hampden had made his great find. The fragment of pillar was too heavy for us to take away, but we carefully broke off a piece, though this seemed something very like sacrilege; if photographs couldn't convince them, certainly this stone with its harpies and palm-trees ought to do it.

"As I stretched out in my sleeping-bag that night, Hampden was sitting up in his, and he was still examining that sculptured fragment—or, rather, staring at it. I watched him for a time, for the brooding interest that he took in those figures—well, I couldn't help wondering.

"'What,' said I at last, 'do you find so fascinating? Is it the palm-trees or the harpies?'

"'The harpies,' Hampden told me. 'Did you notice—*their claws?*'

"I sat up in my bag and stared at him.

"'Hampden, what on earth do you mean?'

"That brooding look was gone from his face now, and, before ever he spoke, I knew what the answer would be.

"'Mean? Why do you think that I *meant* anything? Look at them, Captain. They are in more ways than one a striking piece of work—those claws.'

"I knew, though, what had been in Hampden's mind, and I cursed myself for a fool because I could not drive that thought from my own.

"It was on the 23rd of December that we left this camp, and two days later, on Christmas, came the discovery.

"It was in latitude 84° 25'. We were now near that great plain, the mountains, though, still towering up on every hand, very tumbled and jagged, and our way lying along a glacier that filled one of the deep valleys. We had swung over very close to the mountains on the right in hopes of finding a better way through the pressure ridges and the terrible sastrugi.

"The surface had looked better off in this direction, but, now that we were there, we found once more that things are not always as they seem. We were having a terrible time of it. It was mid-afternoon. The sun was shining clear and bright, the sky nearly cloudless. It was in one of our frequent halts, and I was leaning against the sled as we rested—or, I should have said, against the load on the sled—and was, as a man will do when he is doing nothing, studying the sides of a kind of gorge in the mountains.

"In a way (though I did not notice this at the time) this deep place was rather peculiarly situated, for into the greater part of it the sun's rays could never shine. In other words, the temperature in there could never rise to the melting point. You will see in a moment why I so particularly draw attention to this circumstance.

"Only here and there were the rocks themselves visible; snow and ice covered everything. There was the sunlit snow rising up all around, and the gorge itself in deep shadow. At first, what with the strong contrast, those depths, though masses of snow and ice themselves, seemed almost black. But, as I continued to gaze up into it, the obscurity that involved everything, these seemed to thin out and pass away like mist. I could make out masses and hollows that a few moments before had been totally invisible.

"A dark spot in particular claimed my attention. I didn't know why and don't know why yet, for I wasn't looking for anything, never dreamed that there might be something up there to find. In fact, as for these things that I was actually looking at, I wasn't *thinking* of them at all.

"I have said it was a dark spot, but there were, in fact, two, the darker (and smaller) one being above. Thus I went on with my examination, but certainly my thoughts, as I have remarked, were elsewhere—or, rather, it was as if I was thinking of two things at the same time, though that, I believe, is absurd. I soon perceived what it was: there had been a rock-slide up there and a recent one, too, if appearances were to be trusted. And that *very* dark spot—it appeared black no matter how hard I peered—what was that black thing there above?

"It seemed—it must be—yes, there could no longer be any doubt: it was the mouth of a cave!

"My thoughts were now any place but elsewhere! Still, so I thought the next moment, what was there in the discovery of this cavern mouth to call forth any great interest, any expectation whatever?

"'A cave,' said I, ''tis only a cave.'

"'Yes,' a little voice seemed to whisper in my ear, 'but, remember, sometimes things are found in caves.'

"Caves had been found in the Antarctic, but nothing had ever been found in them. Well, for the matter of that, explorers before us had never found geysers in the Antarctic, or sculptured stone, or Gardens of Paradise, with their palm-trees, their birds and flowers and that horror which had left the mark of its great claw. So there was no telling. Certainly it would do no harm to go and see.

"I got out my powerful glasses and examined the spot. This brought Hampden up alongside.

"'What's so interesting there?' he queried, gazing up.

"I handed him the glasses.

"'Tell me what you see?'

"'I see,' Hampden said, 'that the rock has slipped away up there. I should say, too, that the slip is a recent one.'

"'And that dark thing above. What is that?'

"'That is the mouth of a cave.'

"'Just what I thought. And I am going up and take a look inside that cave.'

"And here came a strange thing. Well has it been said that man is compounded of contradictions. I would never have expected to find Hampden showing no interest whatever in a moment such as this. Yet such was the case.

"'No flowery climb,' he observed, 'and the chances are that you will find nothing in that cave but emptiness.'

"'Well,' I told him, 'I'll have the satisfaction of being sure, at any rate.'

"And so off I went, leaving Hampden leaning against the sled and watching me in that listless, half-vacuous manner that, considering the man's constitutional restlessness and curiosity, surprised me not a little.

"The going was pretty difficult, almost as much so in that gorge as amongst the pressure-waves and pressure-ridges and the sastrugi of the glacier.

"At last I stood at the foot of the slide, and there I stopped to take breath and make a survey of things.

"A great mass of rock had given way, and clearly this had occurred but a short time before. This broken mass had taken the form of a talus and gave access, steep but not so very difficult if one were careful, to the mouth of the cavern. My examination led me to the opinion that the cave, before the rock had given way, had been completely concealed or that, at any rate, the entrance had been a very small one then.

"Now, however, it had an entrance wide and dark and yawning, and up I started to get a look into it.

"I had got up to the entrance and had just stopped to look around when my eyes fell on a sight, there not more than a yard distant, so shockingly unexpected and strange as to cause me to cry out and start so violently that my hold slipped and I lost my balance and thought, for a sickening instant, that I was going to go plunging down backwards.

"But I got a grip and recovered my balance and looked again.

"Though I could look into the cave, I was not yet on a level with the floor; my head and shoulders only were that high. The cavern floor itself was a mass of ice some feet in thickness. When the rock had given way, this ice had been cracked clean across, the part broken off going down, of course, with the avalanche. This ice was not clear like that formed from water but had the whitish appearance of snow-ice. And yet it wasn't like snow-ice, either. It was transparent rather than translucent, and yet it was neither.

"And now, gentlemen, I will tell you what I saw.

"There, incased in that ice even as that fish was that you brought in and thawed out; there, plain and yet as though seen through a misty glass, the face within six or eight inches of the edge; there in that terrible bed of cloudy crystal—there lay the body of a girl, or, rather, of a very young woman!"

12
"SHE ISN'T DEAD!"

"The sight, as you can easily imagine, was a shocking one truly. It gave me quite a turn. It was, however, though terribly so, a beautiful one, too. For she looked so fair and sweet and lovely.

"She lay on her back, the right knee drawn up a little, the left hand on her breast, her face turned towards me.

"Yes, so lovely and lifelike she looked that I could have imagined that she was only sleeping—if it had not been for the marble stillness of her bosom and that terrible look in her eyes.

"I had moved up farther and put my face close to the ice. I moved this way and that and at last was gazing straight into her eyes. I thought that they were blue, but of this could not be sure, for the pupils were extraordinarily dilated, giving the eyes a look that was horrible to see."

The explorer paused; he was looking at Darwin Frontenac in a strange manner.

"Belladonna, perhaps," said Frontenac.

"That was my thought, even then as I looked into them.

"And can any one imagine how powerfully the sight of that poor girl, my poor Sleeping Beauty—how powerfully that terrible and yet beautiful sight affected me? I do not think so, and I shall not attempt to describe it.

"For a time my thoughts were in a kind of daze. At first I couldn't grasp the full meaning of it all. Whence had she come? How long had she lain here in her bed of crystal, in the heart of this frozen, desolate land?

"Then of a sudden the answer came, the sudden full realization of the wonderful and awful truth; and I dropped my head to the ice and for some moments leaned there motionless, for the thought—or, rather, the multitude of thoughts that came rushing into my mind—overwhelmed me.

"For this girl had been here for thousands upon thousands of years, suffering no bodily change whatever in the course of those untold, awful ages. Here she lay when Alexander led his Macedonians forth to the conquest of Asia, when Hannibal threatened the might of Rome, when Achilles and Hector fought before the walls of Troy, ere the first king ascended to the throne of the Egyptians or the Chaldaeans.

"Why, here she lay, even as I saw her now, in the day of the Man of Neanderthal, he of Spy and the Man of Piltdown. Yes, back through the mists and darkness of the prehistoric ages, and back and back, and yet she lay here sleeping then—even in those dim days when, as the saying has it, the world was young. Sometimes I wonder if it hasn't always been old.

"For a long time—how long I did not know and do not know now—I stood there looking, then started back.

"I found that a remarkable change had come over Hampden. That listless, half-vacuous manner was gone; what I saw was just the opposite.

"'What on earth, Captain,' he called out as I was coming up, 'did you find up there?'

"'How,' I asked him, 'do you know that I did find something?'

"He tapped the glasses.

"I was watching. I thought once, just as you got to the top, that you were going to fall over backwards. It looked as though you got something of a shock.'

"I did not answer until I stood before him.

"'Hampden,' I then said, 'a stranger sight than the one that met my eyes at that moment no man on this earth has ever seen!'

"He made an exclamation and stared at me.

"''Tis so,' I told him. 'And God only knows what else may be there in that cave. We must explore that place. We make camp right here and now; then get your camera, and we are off.'

"I knew that, as a speedy affair, the making of this camp would be a record-smasher; but the thing was done, and we were off for the cave, sooner than I had expected.

"'Now, I warn you, Hampden,' I said as we went along, 'that you are going to get a shock too, when we reach that cave. So be prepared.'

"'But why on earth won't you tell me what it is?'

"'No; you must wait and see.'

"Were I to live to be a very, very aged man (which, of course, I shall never do) the picture which memory has of that look which came to Hampden's face when at last he stood there and saw her could never fade in even the slightest detail—when at last he was there before that bed of ice and saw my poor Sleeping Beauty.

"For a long time he stood and just looked, and then at last he spoke.

"'Poor little kid!' is what he said.

"And I saw tears in his eyes, and I knew that there were tears in my own.

"'One would think,' I said, 'that she is only sleeping.'

"'Sleeping!' exclaimed Hampden.

"He moved up close to the ice as I had done and gazed eagerly in upon the still face. Of a sudden he became excited. I could see his hand trembling. The face he turned toward me was bright with some powerful emotion and yet dark with horror.

"'Sleeping!' he exclaimed a little wildly. 'Great God, Captain Livingstone—'

"'In Heaven's name,' I asked after waiting a moment or so, 'what is it?'

"'God in Heaven,' Hampden cried, *she isn't dead!*'"

13
"THAT YOU WILL AWAKE HER!"

"I made an exclamation and gazed at him in indescribable astonishment, wondering if I had heard him aright.

"'Not dead?' I exclaimed.

"'Not dead! Captain Livingstone—oh, the poor little kid!'

"'Come, Hampden,' said I. 'What on earth are you talking about?'

"'I know what I am talking about, Captain. I said what I believe, and I say it again: This poor girl isn't dead!'

"'That's absurd!' I exclaimed. 'There she is in solid ice! She can't breathe!'

"I stared at him in speechless amazement. I became suddenly alarmed. What had come over Hampden?

"'Breathe!' exclaimed Hampden. 'If she could have breathed—or if the air had risen above the freezing point—then she would have died. The ice, the ice!' cried Hampden, beating it with his hand. 'That is what saved her!'

"'Saved her? Yes, it has saved her body from decay, from returning to the elements whence it came. Anyone will grant you that. Saved her? Man, it was the ice that killed her.'

"'No! Saved her! Saved her body and soul! Yes, the soul—the soul too! Captain Livingstone, her soul is still there!'

"I was now really alarmed, but worse (so I thought it) was to follow.

"'Come, come Hampden,' I said, 'let us consider this matter carefully, soberly. Here she is in solid ice; here she has been lying—just as we see her now—for thousands of years, and yet you say she is still alive!'

"'Captain Livingstone,' said he very earnestly, 'I didn't say she is *alive*.'

"'Heaven help us! A moment age you said that she isn't dead, and now you say that she isn't alive. I wish, Hampden, that you would tell me plainly what you really mean.'

"'I have told you. I said that this girl is not dead; that is what I meant. I said she isn't alive: that, too, is what I meant. In other words, she is *neither alive nor dead*—if you know what that means. That is why she doesn't have to breathe.'

"'If I know what that means. I'm afraid, Hampden, that I do not know what that means. To be perfectly frank with you, I will say that I wish you would stop talking nonsense.'

"'You think then,' he said, and he said it pretty testily, 'that I am touched in the head? Well, after all, the fault is largely my own. I should have explained, seeing that you are not aware of the scientific possibilities that one may—'

"'There, there, Hampden,' I interrupted, 'we will just let those scientific possibilities be for the present, and we will concern ourselves with facts—plain, palpable facts.'

"He said nothing to this.

"'In the first place,' I said, 'do you realize how old—how very old!—our Sleeping Beauty must be, how long she has been lying here in this ice?'

"'I think I do. When she lived, this Antarctic land had a warm climate, perhaps even a tropical one, and then suddenly the Great Cold fell—suddenly, instantaneously, as the great Cuvier believed.'

"'And she has been lying here through all the ages that have followed: you have not forgotten that?'

"'Forgotten it? How could I have forgotten that she has been here for ages?'

"'Thousands of years: probably a hundred thousand years, Hampden; and yet you say she is not dead!'

"'Think of the time, Captain Livingstone? For time alone can never touch her, there in her bed of crystal. Ten million years, a hundred million, a thousand million years, and she would be even as we see her now—if ice that holds her in were never disturbed. Age could follow age, eon follow eon, through all the eons of the coming eternity, and yet time alone could never lay its stain upon her or loose the soul from her body!'

"'If the soul is still there!'

"'Yes: if the soul is still there—as I truly believe that it is.'

"'I see, though,' he added, 'that I must explain.'

"And this he proceeded to do. I listened intently, doing my level best to understand, but I can see now that I understood but very imperfectly.

"He began with estivation and hibernation, taking great pains to show how they differed from the artificial suspension of vitality. Catalepsy came next, and of this mysterious condition he told me some very strange and terrible things. Then he went on to describe the effects of certain drugs, of belladonna, mandragora, chloral hydrate and others—how they could produce the perfect semblance of death.

"'And,' said Hampden, 'if the subject, while in that condition of seeming death, were frozen, he could be kept in that state for years, for hundreds of years—thousands. In fact, there is no limit to the time in which a body could be kept in that condition—of seeming death, remember.'

"'And yet,' said I, 'not alive!'

"'And yet not alive. That is the thing that must be firmly grasped and fully understood, that the body, whether that of a fish, a frog or a human being—it doesn't matter what—is neither alive nor dead.'

"'I'm afraid,' I told him, 'that I can't see that.'

"And I'm afraid, Mr. Frontenac, that I don't see it now.

"'It's just like that mathematical-point business,' Hampden said: 'the mathematical point is nothing at all, and yet there it is. And so it is with the body when animation is completely suspended, as is the case with this poor girl here before us: the soul is not dead, neither is it alive, and yet it is there!'*

"And other things he told me—of frogs and fishes, for instance, being frozen and restored to perfect life.

"I asked him if he had ever seen this thing done. No; he never had, but he had read about it.

"'I'm afraid,' I told him, 'that I am something of a Doubting Thomas, after all. I would like to see that.'

"'There can be no doubt about it,' Hampden said.

"And yet there was doubt about it, for I—in my ignorance and cocksureness—doubted it, just as the world was to doubt me. So it goes, so it goes. And not only that, but I doubted, so to speak, Hampden himself. For I couldn't get the idea out of my thick skull that the sight of Sleeping Beauty had—why, how, I couldn't imagine—affected poor Hampden's head. God forgive me. I see now how wrong I was.

"'But,' I objected, 'a human being is not a frog or a fish.'

"'Don't you see, Captain Livingstone; don't you see?' said Hampden. 'The girl was drugged, and, while she lay here insensible, in that state of seeming death, the Great Cold fell and she

---

* "If change be essential to our idea of life, it may be asked what is the condition of a seed, which may remain unaltered during a period of many centuries; vegetating at last when placed in favorable circumstances, as if it had only ripened the year before. Such a seed is not alive: for it is not performing any vital operations. But it is not dead, for it has undergone no disintegration; and it is still capable of being aroused into active life, by the application of the appropriate stimuli. The most correct designation of its state seems to be dormant vitality. The condition of an animal reduced to a state of complete torpidity and inaction is precisely analogous; into such a condition, the frog may be brought by cold, and the wheel-animalcule by desiccation."—Dr. Carpenter.

was frozen, incased in ice. And so she has remained (not dead and yet not alive) through all the ages that have followed.'

"'Suppose,' I queried, 'that she had not been drugged? Would the cold alone, in that case, have produced this condition of suspended vitality, as you declare it to be?'

"'I don't know,' said Hampden, 'but I am afraid that, if she had not been drugged, the cold would have killed her.'*

"'And how do you know that the cold didn't kill her, anyway—even though she lay here drugged?'

"'Of course. I don't *know*; I can only say what I *believe*.'

"'And not only that, but how do you know that the belladonna, or whatever it was that they gave her, didn't kill her before ever her body was frozen?'

"'I don't know *that*, either,' Hampden returned. 'I can only base my belief upon appearances and on what I think very possible and even probable. That is the foundation for my belief that she was not dead then—that she is not dead now.'

"'Well,' I said, 'let us say that this poor girl isn't dead—mind you, I don't say that I believe it; but let us say that it is so. Let us say that she is only sleeping. Heaven knows, she looks like one only asleep. There is nothing, I mean, corpse-like in the appearance of the body. But what then? She is only sleeping; but death itself could be no more terrible than this sleep of hers. Your boasted science is helpless here. Science can never awake her.'

"'No,' Hampden answered. 'This is a sleeper that no man on earth can ever awake. If she was a cold-blooded creature, it could be done. But as it is, she is doomed to the ice—to everlasting sleep (so we may call it because we have no better word) or a death foul and terrible, terrible, above all, because the very act of restoring her to life would, after all these thousands of years, mean her death.'

* ". . . It may be doubted whether a healthy warm-blooded animal suddenly and equally frozen through all its parts is dead, although it is not recoverable."—Dr. Richardson.

"Now, however, we know that Hampden was wrong! Your wonderful discovery, Mr. Frontenac, has shown that there is hope—granting always, that is, that she was not dead when the body was frozen, incased in ice. That, so I believe now, we may easily regard as possible.

"And so now you see why I have come to you, Mr. Frontenac, and why I have told you my story.

"And something tells me that I have not come in vain, that you will go and find her, that—great Heaven, the terrible wonder, the awful thoughts it gives a man—that you will *awake her!*"

14
FRONTENAC ANSWERS

I know that it gave me a terrible wonder—awful thoughts. To awake her! Her sleep had lasted for thousands of years, perhaps three hundred thousand, and now to awake her! What strange things (when she had learned our language) she could tell! What a story to listen to! Three hundred thousand years! What was the slumber of Rip Van Winkle, Epimenides or the Seven Sleepers to that? And, besides, all that was fiction, whilst this—but *was* it real?

Here suddenly came other thoughts—thoughts the very antipodes of those others.

Real? What on earth had come over me? Shades of the great Munchausen, come and listen and turn green with envy! What a weaver of spells was this Captain Stanley Livingstone, with his tales of palm-trees near the Southern Pole—palm-trees, forsooth, and in a land where the temperature in December and January, in the very midst of the Antarctic summer, is below freezing. And butterflies and birds and flowers, and a monster that cut off men's heads and left the mark of an enormous claw!

A sensible man, when he had done as well as that in the line of fiction and fairytales, ought, in common reason, to use a little restraint and rest there on his laurels. But not so our worthy Captain. He must needs cap it all with a real marvel. And so this Sleeping Beauty. Sleeping Beauty! That was wonderful enough, but to be sleeping in a bed of solid ice! Hocus-pocus, abracadabra, hokum and bunk! Whoever heard of a girl sleeping in a bed of ice? And only for a quarter of a million years or so!

Heavens, what a necromancer was our worthy Captain when he could bring me—yes, even me—under his spell, when he could make me believe (as I certainly had done) this wild story of his—a yarn that no man could believe in for a moment without a total abnegation of common-sense.

But, at this very moment, still other thoughts came. Was I not a little precipitate here, just a little bit too cocksure? Who was I to say what could or could not be? The Gardens of Paradise, and within the Antarctic circle! A strange place truly. Why, the thing was repugnant to commonsense. But hold on a minute. What, after all, was this boasted common-sense of ours? Was it a counselor to be implicitly trusted—a psychic queen, as it were, who could do no wrong? It certainly was not, as easily could be shown by a thousand instances.

The discoverer of the Yellowstone Wonderland, for example, had been branded as a liar by this wonderful common-sense.

"After his return to St. Louis," Chittenden tells us, "Colter evidently talked a great deal about his adventures, and in spite of the fact that such men as General Clark and the others we have mentioned (James, Brackenridge and Bradbury) esteemed his accounts worthy of record, he succeeded in making himself rated by the general public as an unmitigated prevaricator. His stories were generally discredited; their author became a subject of jest and ridicule, and the region of his reputed discoveries was long derisively known as 'Colter's Hell.'"

Well, as the discoverer of the Yellowstone Wonderland had been treated, so had the man who sat before us.

"James Bridger," to quote Chittenden again, "celebrated hunter, trader, and guide, whose name and career are part of the pioneer history of the West, was thoroughly familiar with the region now comprised in the Yellowstone Park. His personal knowledge of it dates back as far as 1830. He often visited it, not like Ferris in a single locality, but in all its parts, and was well acquainted with its wonderful features. In his efforts to disseminate the knowledge he had acquired, he was as persistent as Colter had been before him, and with little better success. He tried to get his descriptions before the public, but no periodical or newspaper would lend itself to his service. The editor of a leading western paper stated in 1879 that Bridger had told him of the Yellowstone wonders fully thirty years before. He prepared an article from his descriptions and then suppressed it, 'because a man who claimed to know Bridger told him he would be laughed out of town if he printed any of "old Jim Bridger's lies."' In later years this editor publicly apologized to Bridger for having doubted his statements."

At the present day one is totally at a loss to account for incredulity like this—for the ridicule that was heaped upon a man simply because he said he had gone to the headwaters of the Yellowstone and there he had seen a geyser!

Well, hadn't it always been so? Men like Colter and Bridger have always been branded as fakers; but your Sir Kenelm Digbys—ah, what wonderful men are your Sir Kenelm Digbys!

"Even as late as 1623," says Dr. Cheadle, "Sir Kenelm Digby, the Admirable Crichton of his time, produced a sympathetic powder which was to cure wounds even when the patient was out of sight. This powder had extraordinary success, and its efficacy was almost universally acknowledged."

There is common-sense for you! And it is a great consolation to know that there is little likelihood the supply will ever fail us.

This celebrated powder, by the way, was simply pulverized ferric sulphate.

I remembered, too, that, when the first Ornithorhynchus was brought to Europe, those wise fellows the naturalists, sat up and stared and then turned to common-sense for an explanation of the outré phenomenon before them, with this result: those wise old owls solemnly came to the conclusion that it was nothing but a clever hoax, that some joker had taken a duck's bill and stuck it onto the animal! Very clever, but he couldn't fool them!

Also, when they heard that someone somewhere in Africa had seen some kind of creature with a neck tremendously long, those same wise naturalists said they knew that *ex Africa semper aliquid novi*, for the ancients had so written, but—well—ahum, nothing so strange as often was to be found in the human encephalon, these strange things being known as illusions, hallucinations and delusions.

Not so very long ago common-sense prescribed the heart of the poor nightingale for those suffering from loss of memory, and for thousands of years, convinced mankind that the earth was flat as a pancake.

When Scheiner (to whom some attribute the discovery of the spots on the sun) informed the provincial of his order that the great luminary, the Eye of the Universe, was suffering from ophthalmia, this was the answer he received, dictated, of course, by our old friend common-sense:

"I have several times read my Aristotle all through from beginning to end, and I can assure you that he mentions not a syllable about it. Go, my son, tranquilize yourself, and be assured that what you suppose to be spots on the sun are nothing but specks in your eyes or flaws in your glasses."

It is easy enough to smile at this, at such blind submission to the authority of the great Stagirite—just as easy, in fact, as it is to forget that most of us, after all, are pretty good Aristotelians in more ways than one.

Your scientist is a great admirer of common-sense. Indeed, Huxley says somewhere that science is nothing but organized common-sense. Ahum, let us see what this common-sense really is. In former times, when a man spoke of stones falling down out of the sky, your scientist, this votary of common-sense, gave a smile of pity and said something about superstition and old wives' tales. It was not until the shower of meteoric stone at L'Aigle in Normandy, in 1803, that scientists realized that stones actually do fall from heaven. The French government sent Biot to investigate this old wives' tale that had come out of Normandy, and his report made it impossible for even the most devout worshiper of common-sense to doubt any longer.

And there you have it: up to the year 1803, common-sense declared the thing absurd and, ever since, that it is absurd to suppose it absurd. Can you beat it?

Well, I can.

Our boasted common sense often leads to near disaster. Tesla, Watt and Columbus are among those who succeeded only after fighting it.

Common-sense used to tell the scientist that, as a spherical body of incandescent gas loses heat, it must needs grow cooler and cooler, that the more heat it loses, the colder it must become; and then along came Lane and (quoting common-sense, who a moment before had said just the opposite) proved to that scientist that such a body, instead of growing cooler, in fact becomes hotter and hotter—that the more heat it loses, the hotter it gets!

What do you think about that?

We are told (by common-sense) that resistance retards the speed of a body, of course. For once common-sense, we say, is right. But common-sense hasn't finished yet. For right around common-sense turns and informs us that, if a body traveling round the sun—a planet or a comet—encounters a resisting medium, its speed, instead of being retarded, is accelerated—that the more resistance such a body encounters, the faster it must go!

Can you beat that? I can.

Common-sense tells us that molten metal is very hot and that it will burn a man. Yet a man can thrust his hand into a stream of metal as it flows from the furnace and draw the hand out again without even a blister. I have seen it done. All that man did—it was Darwin Frontenac—before thrusting his hand into that molten stream, was to dip it into a pail of water.

So what, after all, is common-sense but a sort of psychic Great Mogul? And, like all moguls, great or small, he sometimes cuts some mighty queer capers. For instance, sometimes at midday he gravely remarks that it is midnight. And what do we do then? Do we try to show his majesty that, instead of being midnight, it is in reality noonday? Not we. For he is the Great Mogul—and we? We are worshiping subjects (alias Aristotelians) and we all exclaim, our voices raised to accents ecstatic:

"Behold the moon and the star!"

I thought of these things and of many more, and then the Captain broke the silence and my train (or jumble) of thought—for which, I have little doubt, you will be rather thankful.

"Yes," said he, "to awake her!"

He was gazing earnestly, wistfully at Darwin Frontenac. Frontenac's eyes were fixed on the other, the expression in them keen and yet strangely vacuous, but he did not break the silence.

"To awake her!" murmured Captain Stanley Livingstone. "Once I would have thought such an idea wild as the wildest fancy of poet or romancer; but now I believe that it is a sober possibility."

"It is," Frontenac nodded, a glitter in his gray eyes, "if the girl's condition be indeed one of suspended animation, if life had not quitted the body before it was frozen."

"I believe, Mr. Frontenac, that it had not, that Hampden was right, that my poor Sleeping Beauty is in that strange state which is neither life nor death."

"It is very possible," Frontenac said. "But one can't be sure of that until—"

"Until?" queried the Captain, leaning forward.

"One can't be sure, Captain. Remember, the girl had been drugged."

"I remember that, Mr. Frontenac. But she isn't dead: she can't be dead! A dead body could never be so lifelike in appearance."

Frontenac made no response.

"There is one thing, though," said the discoverer: "suppose that the drug they gave her would have proved fatal if the cold had not fallen; in that case, if you awake her, will the poison continue its work and kill her, kill her after all these thousands of years?"

"No," Frontenac answered: "my antidote will neutralize the belladonna, mandragora or whatever it was they gave her—if I can awake her!"

"Then, Mr. Frontenac," the other exclaimed, "you are going to go down there and get her?"

Frontenac smiled a little.

"Exploring, Captain, is rather out of my line."

The other waved a hand airily.

"Don't hesitate a moment because of that. Did you learn to swim before ever you went into the water? Never fear, Mr. Frontenac, you will be an explorer before you get back."

"If I ever do!"

"You will get back to the world. You'll go down there better prepared than I was. You'll know what you are going to meet."

"I'm afraid that I don't. All I know is that it is a thing with an enormous claw."

"Oh, well," said the Captain, "you know that it is *there*, which is more than I did.

"And," he added, "as for experience, I understand that you have been in the Arctic."

Frontenac waved a hand deprecatingly.

"I was never very far from the ship. I was only a scientist, not an explorer, though I may truly say that it would have been the other way around if my own wishes could have been followed."

"And I," said the Captain, "am only an explorer, not a scientist. Experience, Mr. Frontenac, is, of course, a great thing, but not so great as it is often held up to be. It isn't everything, by any means. And, besides, experience is very apt to put a man into a rut. He is often sure, certain, absolutely positive that this thing can be done and that that thing can't when, as a matter of fact, he doesn't know anything about it at all. That's the one bad thing about experience. It is the new men, as a rule, who do the new things."

"I have long believed that. But here is another thing: I have my work here to do; nothing has been farther from my mind than that I should ever go forth as an explorer. And another thing, Captain: I am no longer young."

The Captain stared, then a smile moved those weather-beaten features.

"You are not yet old, by a good many years."

"Alas, I am; I'll soon be forty."

"Forty!"

Captain Livingstone laughed.

"Now," said Frontenac, "if I were as young as my friend McQuestion here, if I were (as he is) a regular, genuine, dyed-in-the-wool, blown-in-the-glass sourdough, a member of the great Order of Icicle Muckymucks as well as that of the Muckluck

Tillicums, if I could live for a whole week on a snowflake and simply feast upon a rabbit-track—if all that were only so, I wouldn't hesitate for a single moment. But, as it is—"

"As it is?" the Captain suggested.

"As it is, not being qualified to become an Icicle Muckymuck, to say nothing of a Muckluck Tillicum, what can I do?"

"Well, Mr. Frontenac," the explorer smiled, "your moment is up."

He turned his look to me.

"Are you going to go with him, Mr. McQuestion?"

"*Is* he going?"

The Captain turned his look back to Darwin Frontenac.

For some moments there was a deep silence, then Frontenac spoke.

"Yes, I will go, Captain Livingstone; I will get your Sleeping Beauty and awake her if I can—if that thing there in the Gardens of Paradise doesn't get me within the reach of its claws."

15
ANOTHER MONSTER—THE DOOR

Captain Stanley Livingstone came to his feet and reached out his hand; Frontenac too arose and extended his own; and the captain pumphandled away at him in fine fashion.

"I knew, Mr. Frontenac, that you would do it!" he exclaimed, the puffed and livid features working with strong emotion. "I knew that you would awake my Sleeping Beauty!"

As for myself, my astonishment was very great. This was not like Darwin Frontenac. I had thought that he would give this matter—one of the strangest and wildest things, certainly, that had ever been presented to any man—long and careful attention. And now look! Frontenac had already answered—answered before the explorer had even finished his story!

"And you, Mr. McQuestion?" the captain said. "Are you going to go, too?"

"Really the thing is so unexpected, so strange. I must have time to think it over—that is, if Darwin wants an Icicle Muckymuck like me along."

"You know nothing would please me more, old *tillicum!*"

"Well, I must think it over."

"Of course," the captain nodded. "Of course."

The two resumed their seats.

"I found her," said the captain, "but am a doomed man; I shall never see her again."

A strange look came over his visage. His lineaments moved in a wan, melancholy smile.

"I am getting up in years, and, if the truth must be told, I am, after all, something of a hardened old sinner, and yet—"

That smile slowly left his face, and for a time he was silent—a strange, rugged, pitiable figure.

"And yet, gentlemen, sometimes I think that—yes, I sometimes think that I love that girl."

Darwin Frontenac's look was suddenly keen and questioning, then as suddenly was what it had been a moment before.

"Yes, it is so," said the captain, burying his face in his hands. "I could never forget her. Call me an old fool—call me what you will! She was so sweet, so lovely there in her bed of crystal—a sight so sad that I wept to see her lying there. But I shall never see her again. My aneurism may burst at any moment."

Darwin Frontenac glanced in my direction. I saw in his eyes only wonder and awe. The captain raised his head from his hands. That wan, sad smile—a thing I could never describe—passed over his features once more.

"An old fool's weakness, gentlemen," he said, giving a melancholy wave of his hand. "I don't know why I have told you this. Heaven knows, I never intended to tell it to any man. But what, after all, does it matter? I shall never see her again. But you will see her, Mr. Frontenac, and you, too, I fancy, Mr. McQuestion. Yes you will see her there in her tomb of ice—perhaps on a day see her smiles and hear her laughter. Perhaps you—both of you—will love her too.

"Poor little kid! as Hampden said. You will be good to her, Mr. Frontenac, I know. Yes, she will never regret that you awoke her, or you regret it, either. In a way, she will be your daughter, unless, that is—a thing which I think not unlikely—she becomes one even dearer still."

It was Frontenac now who smiled. He made no response, however.

"But," said the captain, "who can say what will be? All that is in the future.

"As for the expedition, today would have found us almost ready to put to sea—perhaps, indeed, actually under way—if it hadn't been for this hellish aneurism of mine. I had known for some time that there was something wrong. I thought, though, 'twas nothing serious and that it would pass away, as so many other things had done. But it did not pass away. It got worse instead of better. And so finally I went to a doctor. I demanded the truth: he gave it to me. I went to another and yet another; it was the same thing. It was quite a shock at first, gentlemen. For a time I tell you I felt mighty bad. But I brought my philosophy, such as it is, to bear upon the matter, and I soon resigned myself to my fate.

"But what to do about the expedition? Things were rapidly nearing completion. Nunatak—maybe you have heard of Nunatak in Alaska, Mr. McQuestion? His real name is an odd one truly—Louis Louisiana."

"Oh, yes."

"A fine man," said the captain. "They say that he is one of the best, perhaps the very best musher in all the Northland. He is as tall as a bean-pole, skinny as a poker, and one eye is black and the other is blue. Ever meet him up there?"

"No. I've seen many a man up North with one eye or both eyes black and blue, but I never saw a man, there or any other place, with one eye blue and the other black. I remember hearing of this Nunatak, though."

I turned to Frontenac.

"Ever hear of a man with peepers like those before?"

"Oh, yes. Never saw such an one, though."

"As I was going to say," the explorer went on, "there was everything almost ready and Nunatak on his way down from the North with the dogs—genuine Eskimo dogs, from the Tinnanannomook country—and now, like a bolt from out the blue, came this sentence of death!

"What was to be done? Should the *Multnomah* sail anyway—the expedition to go on under the second in command when the aneurism finished me? I didn't know what to do. And, while I was trying to decide, I read of your discovery, Mr. Frontenac, and I made up my mind to come to you and tell you what I had never told any man—the whole of my story. Thank God, I did come! I shudder to think, though, how near I was to backing out, for I was afraid you might regard it all as nothing but a fairy tale.

"I suppose, however, that the *Multnomah* will be ready to cast off by the time that you can get your affairs in shape. When I decided to come to you, and tell you my story, the first thing I did (on the chance that you might believe me) was to draw up papers that would forestall any hitch or difficulty in case I should be bumped off before the expedition got away. There is no telling; I may live for months, and, again, I may go at any moment. However, I have fixed matters so that, if I die this minute, things can go on as smoothly as though nothing had happened.

"Your discovery, Mr. Frontenac, will make at least one change necessary: you will, I suppose, want a freezer on the *Multnomah?*"

"By all means."

"I didn't think that you would awake her down there."

"Of course not."

"That's what I thought. So there will have to be a freezing-room to bring her back in."

"Just so. And there are the dogs," Frontenac reminded him. "How many?"

"About one hundred."

"The freezer must be large enough to hold all those dogs, with some additional space. For we will *kill* them, pile them up in the freezer and thaw them out when we reach Summer Haven. That will be much better than having them crowded about the decks, to say nothing of the saving in food."

"By Joe!" the other exclaimed. "I never once thought of that."

"However," Frontenac said, "these details can be taken up later. I am anxious, Captain, to hear the rest of your story. Did you find anything else at that cave or in it?"

"We did, in it, as you shall soon see.

"We had come prepared (so I thought) to explore it, and at least we started in. For the first few yards, the roof was so low that we could not go upright. Then suddenly the walls drew apart and the roof went sloping up to form a great vault. There was now no ice underfoot or anywhere. The place grew larger and larger as we advanced until at last, standing in the middle point, we could barely make out the wall on either side. It was a strange, weird scene, and it gave a man some solemn thoughts to be entering this place which human foot had never trod for so many thousands of centuries.

"I was carrying the light, and I had stopped and raised it high above my head in order to get a good look roundabout when a sharp exclamation broke from Hampden. I looked, and I think that I exclaimed, too. At any rate, I know I started and a strange feeling came over me. There, off to the right and some distance ahead, were two burning eyes, gleaming in the darkness with a greenish, hellish fire.

"Even as my look fell upon them, their dull fire faded; then suddenly they had vanished.

"'The light!' said Hampden. 'Raise the light again!'

"I did so, and there were the two eyes burning once more.

"Hampden laughed.

"'Only the light shining on patches of mineral.'

"'Of course,' I said, moving towards them. 'At first I thought—but there can be no live thing in this place.'

"'Hardly,' Hampden laughed.

"We had gone some distance when I stopped again.

"'We had better be careful,' I told him.

"I pointed back towards the entrance, or in that direction in which I thought the entrance ought to be, for we were now encompassed by pitchy darkness.

"'We don't want to get lost in this hole.'

"Hampden treated this suggestion lightly.

"'Not much danger of that,' he told me.

"But I was not so confident on that score.

"'See,' I remarked, 'how the things send out arms in all directions.'

"Some of these were so large that I didn't know whether we were following the main cavern or not. Hampden, though, said that there was no ground for uneasiness, and so we went on, slowly but steadily, deeper and deeper into this strange and awful place.

"The temperature of the cavern had risen in a remarkable manner, how much we had no means of knowing, for we had no thermometer with us.

"I clearly perceived that a thorough exploration of this great cavern was, at the present time, simply impossible; we had not come prepared for that. And what would a thorough exploration bring to light? A man could not even imagine that. The Antarctic had turned so many theories and beliefs upside down and inside out * that there was no telling what might be found here.

"Certainly I never imagined anything so strange as what we did find.

"The credit goes to Hampden, poor fellow. For I had come to a stop, my mind made up to turn back at that point.

"'Just five hundred feet more,' said Hampden.

"'Not another inch,' I told him.

"But Hampden was a persistent fellow, and the result was that he got his five hundred feet.

"'One hundred and seventy paces,' said I. 'Unless we find something then, not a foot farther. This place is like an oven.'

"'One hundred and seventy,' said Hampden. 'And here's the first.'

"I never saw longer paces in all my life. I believe Hampden's legs must have been made of rubber.

"At last came the hundred-and-seventieth stride—I believe Hampden had managed to make it eight hundred feet—and there we halted.

* "The temperature of the sea-water is all the year round several degrees lower than the freezing point of fresh water, yet the growth of animal life is so vigorous that at moderate depths the entire bottom is covered and hidden under a dense carpet of rooted animals, and among these hunt and grub great numbers of active and predaceous fish and other locomotive animals. And all the time the temperature of their bodies is just about that of the water in which they live; that is to say, they are below freezing point, a temperature which has been supposed to be fatal to all life."—*Antarctic Days*, Murray and Marston.

"'Well,' I queried, 'satisfied now? Here we are, and we have found nothing.'

"Hampden did not answer. I found his eyes fixed on a point ahead and at some distance above the cavern floor. I looked, too. I could see nothing but a black mass of wall, but that was because a moment before the light had shone in my eyes.

"'Oh, Lord,' exclaimed Hampden, 'look at that!'

"A form took shape up there on that black mass of wall—a figure vague, monstrous, horrible.

"For some moments we stood there staring. The light that struggled to it was so feeble, however, that we could not be sure just what that thing was which we saw.

"We moved slowly on towards it.

"'A bat!' I exclaimed.

"'No!' said Hampden, whose eyes were better than mine. '*A harpy!*'

"I fetched up in my tracks, and a shiver went through me.

"'Again!' Hampden cried.

"'I wonder why a harpy,' I said. 'That thing at first gave me the creeps.'

"A few moments, and we were within five or six yards of the wall. There we halted and stood gazing up at the sculptured monster. The figure, cut out of the living rock, was a colossal one, being thirty feet in height and fully fifty in width. It was perched upon a heap of (sculptured) human skulls, the wings were outspread as though it was about to launch itself down upon us, and the expression of the face (a face of striking but repellant beauty) was fierce and terrible beyond all description.

"What was that? I blinked and looked again. That carven horror up there above had held our look; we had seen nothing else. But now I saw it.

"There, right before our eyes, right under that carven monster, was—a door!"

16

DEATH TAKES HIM

"As we moved toward it, Hampden said:

"'I see now what that harpy was for.'

"I stopped and looked at him.

"'What was it for?'

"'To warn people to keep away—to keep out.'

"I laughed.

"'It probably worked in those old superstitious days; but it will take more than that harpy up there, horrible though it is, to keep me out.'

"'I think, though,' said Hampden, 'that the door will.'

"And it did. The entrance we found about four feet in width by seven in height and closed by a mass of solid rock. That this stone was a door and not a sealing slab, we both believed. But how did it work? We pushed and shoved and threw ourselves against it, but it never budged.

"'A man might as well try to move Mount Rainier,' Hampden said.

"'And no doubt,' I remarked, 'a fellow could open it with a push of his little finger—if he only knew the secret.'

"'Of course,' said Hampden, 'but we don't know it.'

"'We might find the secret.'

"We made a long and careful search all around, but at last we had to give it up in despair.

"'What on earth,' Hampden said, 'is on the other side of that door?'

"That is a question I have asked myself a thousand times since. What secret has that harpy been guarding there in that awful darkness through all those ages. What will that man see who at last moves the stone slab and enters the passage? The answer I shall never know. But I believe, Mr. Frontenac, that on a day you will know it.

"And that is what we found, and we found nothing more, there in Sleeping Beauty's Cavern.

"Nothing daunted by this close call, for it really was that, Hampden was anxious to go in again; but I wouldn't hear of it.

"'Why,' Hampden cried, 'there is no telling what else there is in that cave!'

"'That is very true,' I told him; 'but what we want to do is not to run any risks but to get our story to the world.'

"Hampden was terribly put out about it; but I remained firm and adamant.

"We were nearing Depot Number One when it happened. The sky was dark and gloomy, but Hampden and I were in gay spirits. Certainly the prospect seemed a bright one. A few days more, and we would be back at Summer Haven. And then it came, like a bolt from out the blue, and I was left all alone, a man shaken and wretched.

"Hampden was leading. The surface seemed almost level and firm as a floor, and we were swinging along at a smart pace. My look was not upon him at the instant it happened. There was a cry, and I looked up and saw Hampden make a wild effort to turn and save himself, the rear end of the sled tip up, and the sled slip forward and vanish, dragging the dogs down after it. For an instant I thought that Hampden had gone down, too. But no, there he was clinging to the edge of the crevasse and crying wildly for help.

"I rushed forward. I saw with horror that Hampden was slipping, that he was sinking lower and lower. The snow and ice that he was clinging to were giving way. Would the edge hold till I reached him? I got to within thirty feet of him, and then it broke. One loud, terrible cry was heard, then utter silence—or, if any other

sound came up from that frightful place, I was not aware of it in the horror of that moment.

"I went to the edge and looked down—into an abyss that seemed fathomless, from which not the faintest sound came up.

"I cried out Hampden's name and cried it again and again, but never any answer came—never the faintest sound.

"How long I stayed there, I do not know. It is an awful feeling to have a man snatched from you like that—a feeling that I hope to God neither of you will ever know.

"At last, however, I left that cursed spot, and I did not make camp until I had reached the depot, nearly twenty miles distant from the scene of the tragedy.

"And that is why I have no photographs of the Gardens of Paradise or of Sleeping Beauty to show you. All had been on Hampden's sled, together with that piece which we had broken off the sculptured pillar, and now all were gone.

"There is little more to tell. It was awful making my way through that terrible loneliness, but there was one consolation: I would soon be home.

"It would be impossible to describe the joy that I felt when at last I gained the summit of the ridge to the north of Mount Theodore Roosevelt and Mount Woodrow Wilson and looked down on Summer Haven.

"There, far, away, was the hut and the *Multnomah* moored in her little cove. For some time I stood there looking upon that strange and familiar scene. Everything was so peaceful, so dreamy and lovely. It was a joy to see the old place again, and yet I knew sorrow too as I stood there and gazed upon it, for of the brave and loyal men who had gone with me into the Unknown, not a one was with me now.

"Many thoughts came to me as I stood there and not a few questions that I wished could be answered. Well, some of them would be answered when I reached the hut. So I spoke to the dogs, and once more we were in motion.

I had got within a quarter of a mile of the hut before they discovered me. There was a great waving of arms and some cheering, and they started towards me.

"'Where are the others?' was the first question they asked.

"I started to tell them. And now I saw for the first time that thing which was to embitter the rest of my days. Never could I forget that look which came to their faces when I mentioned the palm-trees. I had, of course, often wondered how my story would be received. I had never blinked the fact that there would be difficulties; but now, for the first time, I fully saw what really awaited me. The realization came with something like a shock. I had counted on the photographs removing any doubt that might linger. But there was not a single photograph to show them, all had been lost, with poor Hampden.

"Not a word did I say about Sleeping Beauty, or the cave, or that mysterious door over which that carven horror holds its eternal vigil; but I did try to give them a plain, accurate, convincing account of all the rest. It was not long, though, before I saw clearly that the effort was useless. Instead of overcoming their incredulity, I was, it was very clear, only strengthening their conviction—formed at the very first—that what I had gone through had turned my brain.

"At length they began to humor me. That was too much and the bitterest of all, and I gave up in anger and fierce despair.

"The rest you know, or you can easily imagine it.

"And so, now my story is done. What is to follow, no living man can say; and I shall never know it. But I do know that you will see wonderful things, and terrible ones too in all likelihood, before the word finis is written.

"I pray God to watch over you, Mr. Frontenac, and bring you safe through it all!"

17

THE "MULTNOMAH" SAILS

"Well, Bond," said Darwin Frontenac as we seated ourselves after seeing Captain Livingstone into his car, "what do you think of it?"

"No man ever told a stranger story—if, that is, what he told us is true."

"It is true, Bond."

"Do you mean to tell me you believe that that girl, incased in solid ice—if there is such a girl at all—is alive?"

"No."

"Then why—?"

"Just a moment," said Frontenac, uplifting a finger. "What I said was that I do not actually believe that she is alive. That, however, is not tantamount to saying that I believe she is dead. No man can say whether she is or is not. What I do believe is simply this: that it is very probable indeed that the poor thing is not dead."

"And you believe that you can awake her?"

"I have every reason to feel confident that such will be the result—that is, supposing always that she be not dead."

"After all these thousands of years!" I exclaimed. "One hundred, two hundred, three hundred thousand years! But how do we know, after all, that she has been there for so many ages, that she has been lying there ever since the Great Cold fell?"

"We don't know it but I think we shall find Captain Livingstone's inferences fully justified. We know that thousands upon thousands of years have rolled over this old globe of ours since the snow and ice gathered about the Poles. We know that the climate there was a warm one in Miocene times; therefore the cold must have fallen in the Pliocene. That it came suddenly, instantaneously, as the captain (with the great Cuvier) believes it did, is a matter upon which one may be permitted to entertain some doubts. On the other hand, certain considerations incline me to the belief that the captain may be right. But the point is simply this: Sleeping Beauty could not have lived there *after* the land was mantled in snow and ice; ergo she must have been there *when* that awful curse fell upon the Antarctic."

"Unless," I proffered, "the Gardens of Paradise once extended much farther than they do today and some of the survivors of the awful cataclysm had sought a refuge there."

"I thought," said Frontenac, "that that would be your suggestion. I think it unlikely, though, that such was actually the case. I incline to the belief that, instead of being much larger, the Gardens of Paradise were at one time even of less extent than they are today. For the cold of the Antarctic, bitter though it is now, was once far more terrible."

"We must wait—wait until you awake the sleeper."

"Until I awake the sleeper!" he murmured.

He turned his face towards me, and never shall I forget that look which I saw upon it.

"Bond," said he, "I wonder, supposing that I do awake her—I wonder if she will thank me for it or live to curse both me and the hour."

I remained silent, wondering.

"But," he added, "we should regard the matter in its purely scientific aspect, and then we find it one of extraordinary interest, to say nothing of its possibilities. Sentiment is all very well in its place—as are thorns and roses."

"Why the gloomy thoughts?" I queried. "Why so suddenly look at the dark possibilities? Remember, you may awake for some man a sweetheart—perhaps, indeed, your own fond lover."

Frontenac smiled at that, and then he laughed a little.

"I always knew that you were a poetical son of a gun, Bond, where the ladies are concerned, but I never dreamed you had it so bad as that."

"Well, now," I replied, "looking at the matter in a sober light, what is there so terribly romantic, so terribly poetical, so awfully absurd in my suggestion? The girl is young; she is (if the captain's eye is to be trusted) a very lovely Sleeping Beauty indeed; and do you think for a moment that there will be no lover?"

"I think that the lover will come. Oh, I know that—just as well as I know that it won't be I."

"Oh, indeed! Just wait till you awake her, wait till you see her a living, breathing woman in all the charm of her loveliness."

He smiled a little but made no response to this. What he said was:

"Do you know, Bond, what, in all the captain's strange story, gave me the greatest surprise?"

"The palm-trees?"

"The palm-trees? Fiddlesticks! Come again," said Frontenac. "And, that reminds me: did you know that Nordenskjold thought he might find an oasis in the heart of Greenland?"

"I didn't know that."

"Well, he did."

"Did any scientist ever look for icebergs in the Sahara? But to come back. The severed head of Wilkie—and the mark of that enormous claw?"

"Once more," said Frontenac.

"Sleeping Beauty herself?"

"Not even Sleeping Beauty herself."

"What a queer way you have of looking at things! Then it must have been that mysterious door there in the cavern?"

"You're a mighty good guesser, Bond."

"What on earth was it?"

"His telling us that he had fallen in love with that girl!"

"A strange love certainly," I said.

He was silent for some moments, then asked:

"Going to go with me to get Sleeping Beauty, Bond?"

"I must think the thing over."

"Of course. But I fancy I know what your answer will be."

"This thing you're entering upon," I reminded him, "isn't going to be a honeymoon."

"I haven't forgotten that. A honeymoon is only the end of a dream, but this—this," said Darwin Frontenac, "is the find of a century. And the captain got only a glimpse, so to speak. There is no telling what other things may be down there."

"That is very true. I'm not particularly anxious, though, to get decapitated."

"The mystery," he smiled, "makes the adventure—well, piquant."

"Piquant? Heaven help us!"

"Well, 'tis so," said Frontenac. "And the risk gives it pep."

"Pep? I think you'll call it something else when that thing in the palm-trees starts work on your jugular."

He smiled faintly, but he made no response; a silence ensued.

Of course, he could get Sleeping Beauty without running *that* fearful risk; but I knew better than ever to make such a suggestion to Darwin Frontenac!

Why is danger, mystery the fascinating thing it so often is? I have often wondered about it but never have found any real explanation. It doesn't matter how terrible, how horrible it may be, there are always men simply *crazy* to go. Its subtle, fierce power enshadows the fascination even of woman: sweethearts, wives are left behind, and with glad hearts the men go forth, in their ears (and hearts) the sweet, terrible song of the siren.

Why do they go? I wish I knew!

And I ought to know, too, for (though there was neither sweetheart nor wife in my case) I am one of those fools myself!

The next day Frontenac and I, accompanied by Captain Livingstone, went to see the *Multnomah*. It was about half past nine when we arrived at Pier 12, on the south side of which the famous ship was lying. A few moments, and we had issued from the warehouse and the whole of the vessel was in view. I say the whole of the vessel, but this (with the usual point of view in mind) is not strictly correct, for the tide was low, and we were looking not at the *Multnomah* but down upon her decks.

And the first thing that struck me was that the *Multnomah* was one of the queerest-looking tubs that I had ever set eyes on. Yes, that is what she reminded me of at the first glance—a tub. This was due to her unusual beam—she was only three times as long as she was wide—and to her bow-like stern. The *Multnomah* was not built on the lines of a yacht but for service—the fierce buffets and dangers of the terrible Antarctic seas.

A gangplank was out—up, rather—and in a few minutes we were on the deck. There we met the first mate—Mr. Ben Rainier, a man of powerful physique and a visage so grim that it would have been repellant but for the strange intellectual cast of some of the features.

"Well, Mr. Rainier," said the captain, "I have good news for you: the expedition is now a sure thing."

"I am glad to hear that, Captain Livingstone," said the mate, not the slightest change of expression, however, on his face. "I felt all the time that those doctors—"

"It isn't *that*," the captain told him. "The doctors knew. I am doomed. Mr. Frontenac takes command of the expedition. I go along, of course—until you dump me over the side with a sack of coal at my feet."

"This is sad news, Captain Livingstone," said the mate, still not the faintest change on that strange visage. "This is indeed sad news. Perhaps, however, things are not so bad as they seem; perhaps, after all, those doctors—"

The captain gave a melancholy wave of the hand.

"It wouldn't do me or anybody else any good to blink, Mr. Rainier," he said. "A man should never blink facts, no matter how disagreeable the facts may be. If he does, he is liable to get a wallop right between the eyes during one of the blinks."

"That is true," said Mr. Ben Rainier.

"No, I have had my day; and, now that I am finished, I am not going to shed any tears over my end. Instead of weeping over the inevitable, I thank God that my work—and work that I could never dream of doing myself—is to be carried on by Mr. Frontenac."

The mate turned his impassive visage towards my companion.

"This is sad news and glad news," he said. "The glad news is that our commander is to be Mr. Frontenac."

For my part, I couldn't help wondering if the mate really was glad.

"We of the Northwest," he added, "are proud of you, Mr. Frontenac—proud of your fame and that we are your neighbors, so to speak."

"Just wait till the expedition returns!" said the captain. "Great though Mr. Frontenac's fame is now—well, wait till then! Your pride will know no bounds. My one great regret in all this business is that I shall not be here to share that pride."

Then it was, for the first time, that thought I saw a change in that visage of Mr. Ben Rainier; I thought that a questioning look came into those yellow eyes of his, but even of this I could not be sure.

He remained silent, thinking no doubt that the captain would explain.

What the captain said was:

"Well, gentlemen, I will show you over the ship."

The *Multnomah* was a three-masted fore-and-after, with two square topsails on the foremast; her length one hundred and thirty-two feet over all, on the water-line one hundred and fifteen. Her beam, for a vessel of that length, was a most unusual one, being no less than thirty-eight feet and ten inches. She had a depth of eighteen and, when heavily laden, a draught of fifteen feet and a displacement of nine hundred tons. The sail area was about two thousand three hundred and eight square yards, and she had, for auxiliary power, a two hundred and twenty-five horse-power Diesel engine. By means of this motor, the *Multnomah*, when heavily laden, could move through the water at the rate of some five or six knots per hour. This was no great speed, truly, but it was a great thing for all that.

It is strange the way we sometimes arrive at momentous decisions—some of the circumstances that influence us being so subtle as to baffle analysis. In my case, when I stepped onto the

Multnomah's deck, I was, as regards this strange quest, uncertainty itself. Long before we left the ship, however, my mind was made up. I would go. I would go and see Sleeping Beauty in her bed of ice, see that mysterious door over which the great harpy held guard and enter the wonderful, the awful Gardens of Paradise.

Why this sudden dissipation of all doubt and uncertainty? Why this sudden, irrevocable decision, the consequences of which no man could even imagine? I did not know. I am not sure that I know now.

However, I said nothing about this at the time; indeed, it was not till the day following that I told Darwin Frontenac.

He gripped my hand, and his gray eyes gleamed in a way that thrilled me.

"I knew all the time, Bond, old *tillicum*," he said, "that you would go! I can't tell you how glad I am to learn that at last you know it yourself."

"When do we start?"

"The captain tells me that we ought to get away within the month. The *Multnomah* could sail before that, as soon as the freezer"—this was to be built in the fore-hold—"is done if it wasn't for the delayed arrival of some of the supplies, due, of course, to the hitch in his plans."

"Well," I said, "a week would give me plenty of time to get my affairs straightened out."

"A week?"

Frontenac gave a sound like a groan.

"A month will be none too long for me."

Swiftly now days followed on the heels of days.

Great had been the interest excited by Frontenac's discovery; and, when the big headlines informed the world that he was to head an expedition to the Antarctic, that interest became a very great interest indeed. And, in addition to its enhancement, there was that element of mystery about the whole enterprise.

What had Captain Stanley Livingstone told Darwin Frontenac? That was the question which was being asked everywhere. Of course, but three men knew—the captain, Frontenac and myself.

And *that* was our secret.

So the interviewers, in despair, left us and hied themselves to Professor Archimedes Bukink—who, it probably will be remembered, was the man that had really set this whole thing going.

The professor was wholly in the dark. He did not despair, however, but brought reason to bear upon the matter; in other words, he proceeded "with the greatest diffidence, in view of the great paucity of data," to propound an hypothesis. This celebrated hypothesis of Archimedes Bukink was, 'tis true, rather vague, but, like quite a few things that are vague, it had not a little truth in it.

It was something like this:

Imprimis, the professor wished it clearly understood that the matter was an utter mystery to him. In the second place, he had nothing substantial whatever on which to bottom a single conjecture. Nevertheless, he did conjecture, though, of course, "with the greatest diffidence." And his conjecture was that It, the great mystery It, was in some way connected, though in what way he had not the slightest conception, with Darwin Frontenac's amazing discoveries in suspended animation.

Frontenac, the newspaper lowered in his hands, looked at me, and there was a faint smile in his eyes, a smile of amusement and of anger that smoldered.

"The confounded bag-pipe on two legs!" he exclaimed. "Can you imagine how so shrewd a fellow as Bukink sometimes shows himself to be, can be such a colossal, unmitigated, infernal fool?"

I couldn't.

"But," I queried, "what does it matter? He can never guess the truth."

"I wasn't thinking of that," said Frontenac.

Swiftly the days passed, and nearer and nearer drew the day of sailing. Once we motored up into the mountains to see the dogs. The captain had sent the animals to a high altitude, nearly five thousand feet, to save them as much as possible from the summer weather. Up there we met Mr. Louis Louisiana, known as Nunatak—he with the one eye blue and the other eye black.

It was about a week before the *Multnomah* sailed that I got (after a manner of speaking) the surprise of my life.

"It has been my opinion all along," Darwin Frontenac told me, "that the expedition ought to have a scientist along—to study things geological and biological."

"And so," said I, wondering at that pause of his, "you have got a biologist and a geologist?"

"No. I have been more fortunate: I have got a biologist and geologist."

"Oh! Killing two birds with one stone. And the accomplished gentleman is who?"

"Professor Archimedes Bukink."

"What?"

"Just so," smiled Frontenac.

"But—that is, I thought—great Jupiter Ammon, after all the things you've said, after all the names you have called that man! You said he was a fool, an ass, a nincompoop, a bonehead, a fuddle cap—"

"I did. I said he was all that and more, and I say it again."

"And yet—"

"And yet," said Frontenac, "Archimedes Bukink is anything but a fool when it comes to geology and biology."

"But the man's utter lack of discretion?"

"I haven't forgotten that, Bond. We must guard against it, that is all. We mustn't let the old calliope know things—things, that is, that we don't want advertised from the house-tops."

"Well, what on earth will it be next? But isn't Bukink getting up in years?"

"He's far from senile yet. No, his years won't matter. He'll encounter no hardship, anyway; his habitat will be Summer Haven. And, besides (though, of course, a man doesn't want cripples along in an enterprise like this) I incline to the captain's belief that, when it comes to these things, the wonders of youth have been not a little exaggerated."

"It may be so. I hope your choice will not turn out a bad one."

"Furthermore, Bond, I am really greatly indebted to Granny Bukink—though I would never, never tell him so."

"Indebted?"

"Just so. For look you! Had it not been for Archimedes, I should, in all likelihood, never have heard the captain's story!"

"And, in all probability," I could not help saying to myself, "we'll wish, every one of us, before this wild business is ended, that you never had!"

On the fourteenth day of the month (September) Nunatak arrived with the dogs. The next day the animals—splendid creatures, every one of them—were *killed* and piled up in the freezer, to be thawed out and resuscitated on our arrival at Summer Haven.

There were one hundred dogs—one hundred and two, to be precise—but the killing was not a long affair. Frontenac stood at the entrance to the freezing-room and, as a dog was brought forward, he made an injection in the animal's neck. On the instant, down it dropped, as though a bullet had gone crashing into its brain. Without more ado, the animal was lifted up and taken inside, and another dog was brought forward. And so it went, almost with the regularity of clock-work. Dog after dog received his injection—the fluid used was a vivid scarlet—down he dropped, to all appearances as dead as a doornail, was piled up in the refrigerator, and another followed.

It was a strange sight—a terrible thing to see. It gave Nunatak quite a turn, especially when he went into the freezing-room after the *killing* was over and saw the frozen bodies piled up one on top of another, the eyes fixed in a glassy, horrible stare.

"The poor brutes!" said Nunatak, unable to keep the tears from those strange eyes of his. "You've fixed them now!"

"They're all right," Frontenac assured him. "They are only sleeping, so to speak. And they'll be fixed so that the pitching of the ship, however violent, cannot budge them."

"Sleepin'!" echoed the musher. "Yes, they're sleepin'—sleepin' the sleep that we'll all find ourselves in some day. Sleepin'! Yes, they're sleepin'. They're dead, that's what they are, every one of them, dead as so many pickled mackerel, as you'll find when you try to wake them up. I guess I know a dead dog when I see one!

"Lord help us!" he added. "What is this here old world of ours comin' to, anyway?"

The next day, at ten minutes to five in the afternoon, the last line was cast off, and the *Multnomah* began to back out into the fairway. A great crowd had gathered, and we certainly received a rousing send-off. Even the face of Captain Livingstone lighted up. This, however, was but for a few moments. A black cloud suddenly cast its shadow across his features.

A few moments, and we had cleared the pier and were out in the stream. The engine was reversed; the *Multnomah* lost sternway, stood still for a few seconds, then began to move forward. The ship's head swung away, over until we had the West Point light a point or two on our starboard bow, when the helmsman steadied the wheel and held her there.

We were off—off at last on our strange quest! How strange that quest really was, only three men knew—*thought* they knew.

Sunrise found us off the Dungeness light, with all canvas set (save the square fore-topsails) and the wind on our starboard beam. The motor was still going, however, for the wind was a light one. But, as the day advanced, it increased to a fresh breeze, when the engine was stopped and we went along under canvas alone, the ship slowly rising and falling now to the long swells coming in from the sea.

18

THE KILLERS

We were running through the great Strait of Juan de Fuca, that inlet once so mysterious and fabled—and completely missed, by the way, by the celebrated Captain Cook. To the north, stretched the dark wooded hills of Vancouver Island; to the south, lay the Washington shore, its hills, too, dark and wooded, the mountains striking in their somber beauty, with the summit of Olympus (the Santa Rosalia of the Spanish captains) rising above all, eight thousand feet aloft.

It was one of those days of blue sky and cloud, of bright, crispy sunshine and sudden shadow. There seemed to be something threatening in the air. One moment the sea would be a dark, wondrous blue in the sunlight; the next moment everything would be involved in shadows somber and awful

Shorter and shorter grew those intervals of sunlight, denser the clouds and deeper the gloom.

And, when at length we had Tatoosh on our lee beam, the dark masses closed in over the last spot of blue, the hue of the sea, under the gloom cast by the unbroken canopy of cloud, turning leaden and sinister.

This I thought no auspicious omen; but neither the captain nor any of the watch seemed to pay any particular attention to this change, in which, so it seemed to me, there was something ominous.

There had been no change, however, in the wind, which was still blowing from the north in what seamen term a fresh breeze—in other words, twenty-eight or thirty miles per hour.

The patent log had been over for some time now, the reading having been noted (and recorded) on the *Multnomah's* passing that point directly north of Tatoosh light. This the captain called *taking the departure*, and it was then that the dead reckoning began.

The ship's course (true) was south-southwest. But one other vessel was visible, a bark, hull-down, in the southern board, close hauled on the starboard tack.

The day was drawing to a close. Suddenly the cloud-curtain lifted far in the west. A dull streak of light appeared along the horizon. It became brighter and brighter—a vivid yellow. The yellow turned to orange, and, in that streak of garish light, suddenly appeared the upper limb of the sun—its color the dark, terrible red of blood. Slowly it sank into the black waters, and I likened it to some monstrous evil eye slowly concealed by a lid even more evil and monstrous.

The light lingered for a few moments, dull and wrathful; then the cloud curtain settled down again.

The gloom rapidly deepened, and then of a sudden a dense obscurity settled on the sea, as the rain which the dark sky had long threatened began to descend with great violence. A few moments, and one could not see more than fifty fathoms.

A NEAR COLLISION

Immediately the *Multnomah's* fog-horn began its melancholy sounding—three blasts in succession.

Came at length the sound of another horn, that of the bark. And thereafter we heard it at pretty regular intervals—one blast being sounded.

Then, after a longer interval, two blasts came.

"On the other tack!" exclaimed Captain Livingstone. "The damned fool, is he going to lay across our forefoot?"

And then suddenly we saw her, nearly dead ahead and almost upon us—a shadowy, uncertain mass, her port light gleaming angrily through the driving rain, the starboard one shining as though with ghostly fire.

The *Multnomah's* helm was put up, bringing the wind almost dead astern. As for the stranger (who had the right of way) he put his helm down, bringing the ship's head into the wind until, for a moment, I thought that she would be taken aback. But she fell off again, and in a moment the ships were driving past, so close that some of the spray thrown up from the other's bows fell upon our decks.

"You blink-blanked fool!" cried Captain Livingstone, shaking his fist at the receding vessel.

It had been a close call.

"Must be full of hop or hootch!" the captain ejaculated.

The stranger had disappeared into the gloom. Came again the melancholy sounding of his fog-horn.

"Snort away," said the captain, "and see if old Flattery will heed your warning."

"He'll have to go some," Ben Rainier remarked, "to weather the cape on that tack."

Morning found a clear sky and the *Multnomah*, her course still south-southwest, logging six knots, the wind from the northwest.

As soon as the sun had risen a dozen degrees or so above the horizon (for below that the correction for refraction is uncertain) Captain Livingstone took a time sight and azimuth. Of course, dead reckoning gave him the ship's position with a high degree of exactitude. For instance, when he made his observation, about half-past seven, the *Multnomah* had, since taking her departure, sailed ninety-five knots. Her course being south-southwest, she had made good eighty-eight miles of southing and thirty-six miles (nautical) of westing. With these data it were a simple matter to mark the ship's position upon the chart and say:

"There she is!"

But Stanley Livingstone did not do things that way.

This morning observation gave him his longitude. At midday, he took another sight—the meridian altitude of the sun. From this he obtained his latitude. It was an easy matter to obtain the noon longitude from the longitude given by the morning sight, and so he had the *Multnomah's* precise position at noon. At this point a new departure was taken. Another observation was made in the afternoon.

And so it went, day after day, none of this work ever being omitted when it was possible to take an observation.

And, as I watched this poor doomed man carrying on his work thus, I would think what a strange thing a human being is, after all, and often a lump would rise in my throat. He might at any moment drop to the deck a corpse. He knew it. But he would go on with his work to the last. It would be no weakling that would fall when Death smote him in the breast; it would be Stanley Livingstone, master to the end of the good ship *Multnomah*.

But, if I could have peered into the future, visioned the killers, seen the awful end that fate had in store for this man already doomed—well, it had been a merciful stroke had Death burst the captain's aneurism and stretched him dead at our feet.

What, with the possibility that Captain Livingstone might drop dead at any moment. I would often wonder how we should find things when Mr. Ben Rainier, the first mate (his place in turn taken by the second mate), became captain. Of course, Frontenac was commander of the expedition, but Mr. Ben Rainier would be master of the *Multnomah*—and would things go on as smoothly then? Near the thirteenth parallel of north latitude, we lost the anti-trades and entered the calms of Cancer. Then came the great north-east trade, and at length the belt of the equatorial calms or the doldrums.

This region of equatorial calms, however, is not so tranquil a place as the name implies. We had frequent squalls, some of them accompanied by deluges of rain, and once we found ourselves in a storm in which the wind seemed to be doing its level best to blow from three directions at the same time.

Just north of the equator, we fell in with the southeast trade.

It was on the 21st of October, at three o'clock in the afternoon, and in longitude 127° W., that the *Multnomah* crossed the line.

We lost the southeast trades about the thirtieth parallel of south latitude, passed through the calms of Capricorn and caught the

"brave west winds," which sent us along through the roaring forties toward the wild and tempestuous seas of Cape Horn.

WE SEE OUR FIRST ICEBERG

We saw our first iceberg near the fifty-second parallel. It was eight
or nine hundred feet long and much worn—sculptured into fantastic towers and pinnacles.

The sight brought strange, sad thoughts of Sleeping Beauty—
far away in the midst of that unutterable desolation and silence.
Poor little kid!

The days were long, the sun rising about four o'clock. Indeed—
the sun's declination now being about 20°—twilight, when the
weather was fair, lingered throughout the night.

It was now that I noticed it for the first time—a curious phenomenon and one that I had never seen mentioned in a single
scientific book: the moon (and, indeed, every other celestial
object) had turned upside down!

On the 12th of December we passed Cape Horn. The weather was beautiful, the wind from the west-northwest, and the *Multnomah* sailed in close to this weather-beaten and dreaded promontory.

Frontenac had got the cinematograph-camera ready, and some truly wonderful views were obtained of this gloomy and terrible place—gloomy even with the sunshine flooding sea and land.

Banks of cumuli gathering in the southwest told us that our beautiful weather was not going to last long.

The *Multnomah* bore away to the eastward. A number of icebergs were in sight, enhancing the somber aspect of the desolate scene.

And, sure enough, morning found a gale from the southwest howling through our rigging, a tremendous sea running and the air so thick with rain, mist and sleet that often our horizon was within the radius of a hundred yards. Bergs were known to be about us in various directions, and this knowledge, what with our circumscribed horizon, was one by no means conducive to rosy thoughts and speculations.

The wind hauled round to the west and finally to the northwest; by midnight the gale had blown itself out.

When the sun came up, which he did about three o'clock, the *Multnomah* was standing on her course, with everything set save her topsails.

Squalls were of frequent occurrence during the day. Many birds were about the ship—albatrosses, cape pigeons, Antarctic and snowy petrels. Several bergs were seen, and in the afternoon two big rorquals passed within a quarter of a mile of us. The rorqual, by the way, is said to be the largest mammal that has ever existed. The sight of these enormous creatures was a stirring one. It threw Professor Archimedes Bukink into a scientific ecstasy. Out came notebook and pencil, and Bukink proceeded to slap down his observations in whirlwind fashion. He got so excited, however, that he made notes that neither himself nor any one else could make head or tail of. They were about as decipherable as so many Maya hieroglyphics.

"Oh, well," said the professor, "I must fall back upon my visual impressions and imbibe comfort from the certitude that my cacography will be calligraphy on the next occasion when I am favored with the opportunity of making observations upon *Balaenoptera Sibbaldi*."

Some days passed and brought us near that meridian on which Captain Livingstone planned to enter the pack.

ISLANDS OF ICE

It was seldom that we did not have at least one berg in sight, and sometimes there were dozens. Some bergs were of great size, were, in fact, ice-islands. One measured three miles and a half in length, its height three hundred and eighty feet. It was greatly worn, sculptured into obelisks, pinnacles, towers and great castles, the fantastic forms giving the mass the appearance of a *ghost* city adrift upon the waters.

Captain Livingstone had seen bergs more than five hundred feet in height. Reports of masses much higher than this, however, are on record.

"One of our most celebrated and talented naval surveyers," says Findlay, "informed me that he had seen icebergs in southern regions 800 feet high. The *General von Geen*, August 6th, 1840, passed an iceberg 1,000 feet high."

And this in latitude 37° 32′ S.

It was on the afternoon of the 22nd of December (corresponding, of course, to the 21st of June in northern latitudes) and in latitude 60° 15′ S. that we entered the ice. A fine breeze was blowing from the northwest at the time, and the *Multnomah* thrust the brash aside as though it were so much thistledown. But this was too good to last long. An hour, and we were in the pack itself. The engine was going now, the ship pushing her way through toward a lead running to the southeastward. It was a tussle, but we got there, and the *Multnomah* went gliding down that lane like a sea bird.

There was hardly any swell here; an eerie silence had fallen, broken only by the soft rustle of the ice. There was an indescribable, ghostly something in that sound.

After about an hour's run, the lead closed. The *Multnomah*, however, drove straight ahead into the ice. Twice she was brought to a complete standstill; but each time her powerful engine drove her on, the third time clean through into open water again.

The sun disappeared about nine o'clock, down in the southwest. A dead calm had fallen. It was a strange, weird scene, and one beautiful beyond description in the wonderful colors of sunset.

Ten o'clock found us hemmed in by great floes—the *Multnomah* at last indeed at a standstill. There was nothing to do but wait for an opening. One might occur in an hour, in five minutes, in twenty-four hours, or a week. For these movements of the ice are as uncertain and unaccountable as the proverbial operations of the feminine mind. The phenomenon, it seems to me, must, in a large measure, be due to the action of wind or current, or more frequently of both. Undoubtedly, too, the tides play an important part. In this instance, the wind could have had nothing whatever to do with it: the ice opened up about one o'clock, and at that time there wasn't a breath of wind, nor had there been for hours.

Rainier was officer of the watch, and he at once sent the *Multnomah* into the opening—conning the ship from the crow's-nest. Though so near the noon of night, it really was not night; rather, it was ghostly day. The sun was less than ten degrees below the horizon, the sky clear, and so a strong twilight flooded the pack.

Yes, that was what it was—not night, but a day; meet for the wanderings of disembodied souls. And yet here were we making our way through this ghostly scene, to wrest from the Unknown some of those grim secrets over which she had held vigil from age unto age—secrets strange and wondrous; weird, horrible things.

When I came on deck at four o'clock, the end of the middle and the beginning of the morning watch, the *Multnomah* was ploughing her way through mushy drift. Floes were all about, however; a number of bergs in sight, two of these monstrous things; while the strong blink to the southward showed us that we should, in all likelihood, ere long have a dense pack to contend with.

The sun was, of course, risen—a blood-red ball of fire low to the horizon down in the southeast-by-east. A wind was springing up from the southwest, and the sky had a chill and angry look.

At seven o'clock, Captain Livingstone took a sight, the sun then being on the prime vertical or exactly east of us, his altitude twenty-seven or twenty-eight degrees.

The prospect by this time was not a rosy one. The *Multnomah* was threading her way through a sinuous lead. A mile or two, though, and we would be at the end, the way then barred by floes jammed together. Open water was visible to the south but could we get through?

Well, the ship did get through, after much ramming and jamming.

And scarcely had she glided out into the open water when a great mass broke the surface within a hundred feet of our starboard bow.

"There she blows!"

It was a rorqual. A short distance off, another object appeared, an object from which projected a long fin-like dagger.

"Killer!" said Captain Livingstone.

"And there's another!" said Frontenac, pointing.

"And another," I said.

"By Heaven," the captain exclaimed, "they're after him!"

A BATTLE BETWEEN TWO GIANTS OF THE SEA

Of these vicious creatures I had both heard and read some strange and terrible things. Here is one from the great Cuvier himself: we are told that the killer "is a cruel enemy to the whale, which it attacks in troops, tormenting it till it opens its mouth, when they devour the tongue."

What a heartless, soulless, horrible thing Nature is, after all!

The rorqual had taken the alarm, but it was too late. There was a rush, a great disturbance by his head, and a killer had got him by the lower jaw. The whale lashed himself about, turning the sea into a caldron of blood-streaked foam. He threw his head twenty feet into the air, but the killer kept his hold like a bulldog.

Came another rush, another and another; the killers were on him now! Of what followed I can give no adequate description. Fierce as had been the struggle of the whale, it was as nothing to that which followed. It was a horrible and yet a wonderful thing to

see. And matters suddenly assumed a rather unpleasant aspect: the combatants were drawing in toward the *Multnomah*, and we could not swing away from them, because already, on the port side, we had the ice close aboard.

The rorqual was a giant even for a rorqual; our estimates placed his length at over one hundred feet. And it was an amazing and awful sight to see the huge creature throw himself—the three killers clinging to his jaws—clean out of the water. But he could not shake them off, and, as he fell, two more of his enemies threw themselves upon him and gripped and slashed with their terrible teeth.

The *Balaenopter* was doomed. Already his struggles were growing weaker; the sea for yards was red with his blood.

At length he lay rolling sluggishly, like a monstrous log.

Came a sudden outburst. The huge beast threw himself half out of the water. Foam and bloody spray showered upon our deck. Then came a shock—a shock under which the *Multnomah* shivered from stem to stern and heeled over until the water came bubbling in through the port scuppers.

It was a breathless, appalling moment; but the most vivid memory of that wild scene is not the terrible things that flashed into my mind or the great laboring body of the whale alongside, but of Professor Archimedes Bukink in pursuit of his notebook!

I honestly believe that he was not in the least alarmed, that he was so engrossed in the scientific aspect of the business (whatever that was) as to be utterly unconscious of the dire possibilities it presented.

For my part, I expected to see whale and killers land on top of us or that monstrous tail sweep the deck.

Back came the *Multnomah* on her roll to starboard. And up rose the great back of the whale. I thought that the monster was going to come crashing through the bulwarks and onto the deck. But, at the very instant that this horror seemed inevitable, a frightful convulsion flung the body away from us. A few moments, and the *Multnomah*, to my profound relief, had got clear. And it was well that she had. For the whale flung himself back again. Up into the air he rose, his mouth wide open, foam and blood flying in all directions. Down he came smashing against the floe, shattering and cracking the ice as though it were glass, crushing one of his enemies against the sharp edge and killing him almost instantly.

"Hooray, old fellow!" shouted Frontenac. "Do it again!"

But that was the last great effort that the *Balaenopter* made to free himself from those clinging horrors. It was patent that his strength was ebbing swiftly now. Already the tragedy had entered upon its final phase.

The *Multnomah* was standing steadily on through the lead, much to the surprise and chagrin of Archimedes Bukink, who wanted the ship to return to the scene of the combat—or at least stand by so he could witness the end.

"What for?" the captain roared.

"For science," quoth the professor, nothing daunted by the vehemence that the other had displayed.

"Whereupon Captain Livingstone said that science could go to the periœci of Paradise.

And that (so we thought) was the last of the killers.

One of them, by the way—the second to appear—had his great dorsal fin cut off to a mere stump. We could tell that fellow if we saw him again. At the time, though, I never thought of that.

I hasten now to the awful end.

19
SUB-FIN

There were times when the *Multnomah* made but very little headway during the whole of the twenty-four hours. Indeed, once we did not gain a single foot; we lost. We encountered heavy hummocked pack that day; there was nothing to do but wait for the ice to open; and, while we waited, the current carried us back for some miles.

At other times, though, we made sixty or seventy miles of southing during the twenty-four hours; and once—that was on the 2nd of January, and we were in open pack—the ship made a run of a little over one hundred miles.

On the 8th of January, about nine o'clock in the morning, the *Multnomah* crossed the Antarctic circle. We made a fairly good run that day and had the sun at midnight.

Each day now found the sun at the noon of night a little higher above the horizon and a little lower in the northern sky at midday. Had we been at the Pole itself, we should, of course, have had the sun—save for his change in declination, and that would have been imperceptible without an instrument—riding as high in the heavens at midnight as at noon.

But we weren't at the Pole, and we were not bound for the Pole. Instead, we were bound for things—but, there, did we really, after all, know what we were bound for?

We had seen numbers of penguins—emperors and adelies. As yet, but a single skua gull had been sighted. Seals had at times been rather plentiful—most of them crab-eaters, the others

Weddells. Once Frontenac had spotted a Ross seal. This we had been anxious to secure as a specimen, for this animal is now becoming pretty scarce; but the creature had got away, much to the chagrin of Archimedes Bukink. Some sea-leopards had appeared—creatures graceful in a certain sinister, snaky fashion. Numbers of whales, too, had been in sight—a few of them humpbacks. The humpback, it is to be feared, is doomed to early extinction. There had been very few killers—no more than three or four.

As we drew near the seventieth parallel, a strong water sky appeared in the south. The open pack became very open pack; finally the *Multnomah* was moving through drift ice, and, hooray! at last she was in open sea!

To the southward, and to the east and the west, not a single cake of ice was to be seen anywhere. It had a curious magical quality—this sudden change. There was a placid swell in this open water, and there was positively something exhilarating in the gentle rise and fall of the *Multnomah's* deck. A fine breeze was blowing, and so off went the engine, and away the ship went gliding on the wind.

The sky was almost cloudless, the sea a deep, wonderful blue. Many snowy petrels were about us. In all directions, whales were blowing. The scene was animated, a beautiful one. It made a man breathe deeply, for the very joy of it, and tell himself:

"It is a wonderful thing, after all, this hard old world of ours, and life is good!"

And I wondered what this scene, at the moment so beautiful, but at other times so gloomy and dreary and terrible, had been like when Sleeping Beauty lived and perhaps loved—if, indeed, there had been any sea at all here then!

But all things must end; after a run of a hundred and fifty miles through this wonderful open sea, came the pack again.

In latitude 74° 45′, the *Multnomah* encountered close pack, some of it hummocky, extending as far as the eye could reach. Until the ice opened, progress was simply out of the question. So the ship was moored to a floe, and the game of watchful waiting was on.

Thirty or forty bergs were in sight. One of them, a mile or so on our starboard beam, had a height of over four hundred feet. It was much worn and towered up out of the waste of ice like a great ruined castle.

A day passed, but there was no change in the ice that barred our way to the south, though some of the leads behind us had closed, others had opened up and even new ones had appeared. The only living things in sight were some penguins, emperors, several of which were shot.

Then, in the afternoon of the second day, came the horror.

About three o'clock a seal was discovered off to the westward, a mile or so distant, and Frontenac and I started off in hopes of getting the creature, he carrying the rifle. I had no weapon of any kind.

A boisterous game of football, on the floe to which the *Multnomah* was moored, was in progress at the time. Shortly after quitting the ship, we passed Captain Livingstone.

He was sitting, probably fifty feet from the edge of the floe, his chin was resting on his left hand, and he was gazing away to the southward with a strange and abstracted look.

Of what was he thinking? In all likelihood, I told myself, of that poor girl he had found down there in her bed of crystal.

He neither saw our approach nor heard it, and we, for our part, did not choose to disturb his reverie.

We passed within twenty feet of the man, but he never knew it. That picture often rises before my eyes—the dark seated figure, immovable, sitting in the very shadow of sadness and doom, gazing away to the south.

"Poor chap!" said Darwin Frontenac. "I wish I knew his thoughts."

"I am glad," I told him, "that mine aren't of the same cast."

"'Tis no pleasant thing truly," he returned, "to know that you are carrying an aortic aneurism in your breast; but there are worse fates."

At this point I find a hiatus in my recollection; I too had fallen into a profound reverie.

"Perhaps you—both of you—will love her, too."

These words were being murmured in my brain when I was suddenly brought back to my immediate surroundings by the voice of Darwin Frontenac.

"What was that?" I queried.

He regarded me for a moment in quizzical fashion.

"Somnambulating, Bond?" he smiled.

"I was thinking. But what was it that you said?"

"I said that our crab-eater is gone."

I looked; there was certainly no seal in sight.

"So it seems."

"Yes," he smiled, "it seems so. He may, however, be hidden by one of these hummocks. We might as well go forward and make sure."

We went forward, to the edge of the lead, but our seal had vanished. A few moments, and we began to retrace our steps.

Again I fell into a reverie—out of which I was jerked by a sharp exclamation from Frontenac.

"Look there!" he cried, pointing.

We were within a hundred yards of the captain, who sat in the very same posture as when we had passed him. Within a few yards of the edge of the floe, a big fin, shaped like a curved dagger, was sinking from sight.

"Killers!" I exclaimed.

There were three of those terrible creatures.

"And look at that!" I cried. "See that stub of a fin! That fellow was one of those that attacked the whale!"

"I recognized the brute!" muttered Darwin Frontenac.

"And see," said I, "they're sounding, too. They are going under the ice, heading in the direction of—"

"Good God!" burst from Frontenac. "They're after the captain!"

He gave a loud cry. That seated figure slowly turned its head.

"Look out!" yelled Frontenac, starting forward. "Killers!"

I followed.

Captain Livingstone came to his feet. The movement, however, was a slow one; it was clear that he had not caught the dire import of Frontenac's warning.

"Killers!" Darwin yelled. "They're after you!"

THE END OF CAPTAIN LIVINGSTONE

The captain started from the spot instanter, heading in our direction. He had taken but three or four steps, however, when the first killer struck.

The ice cracked and heaved, and the man went down flat. In a moment he was up again, but at that very moment the second killer came crashing up, breaking clean through.

The captain disappeared. In a moment, though, as the ice settled, we saw him once more. For the third time he arose. Then it was that the third killer struck.

We were now close, and—how I shudder to think of it, let alone to write it down—we saw that hideous stub fin appear, then we saw the great jaws close on Stanley Livingstone's body.

That scream the man gave—oh, if I could only forget that sound! The killer reared his head high in the air, holding his victim in his mouth as a cat holds a mouse; then he began to sink from sight.

With a cry of horror, Frontenac threw the rifle to his shoulder. The next instant, the sharp report rang out. If the bullet struck the killer, it did so innocuously. It is my belief that it went wild.

The next instant, a second head came up and seized upon the man.

Then the killers were gone with their victim.

Remained only the smashed ice and those horrid stains of scarlet.

20

SUMMER HAVEN AND A NEW CAPTAIN

It was on the 20th of January that we sighted land. We were running through open pack that day and through a thin fog (lifting now and then) that rendered our surroundings dim and ghostly. But, along in the afternoon—it was about four o'clock—the fog suddenly vanished, when was heard the welcome and thrilling cry:

"Land ho!"

Captain Ben Rainier, from his dead reckoning, had placed the ship's noon position at forty miles from land. Since then, keeping a sharp lookout, we had made twenty-four miles of southing, and there lay the land right where it was supposed to be, distant some fifteen miles.

I say land, but not a spot of land itself was to be seen anywhere. There, however, was the snow that covered it, rising in high rounded masses, and in the background two mighty, majestic peaks towered up, indistinct of outline, lovely as some Turnerian vision and yet grim as terrible sentinels, too.

"Mounts Theodore Roosevelt and Woodrow Wilson," said Captain Ben Rainier.

By seven o'clock we were off the entrance to Multnomah Pass, but here we were held up by pack ice, and it was not until eight in the morning that we got through.

A few minutes then, and we were standing into the entrance. Dark volcanic rock was now visible in places. Then came the first turn and that remarkable mass of rock which Captain Livingstone had named Multnomah Castle.

"Seems like coming home again!" said Ben Rainier. "Poor Captain Livingstone, how he wanted to see this place again before he died!"

Came the second turn, the third, and a few minutes later the *Multnomah* was gliding out into the placid waters of Summer Haven.

Ana there of a sudden rose the column of boiling water from Hero's Fountain, the steam from it ascending to a height of a half mile or more.

At length I went forward and stood beside Nunatak, who was gazing upon the strange scene with a curious, wistful eagerness and in utter silence.

"Well," I queried, "what do you think of it?"

"Think of it! I was just tellin' myself what a queer place this old world of ours really is."

He waved a hand to the southward and said in a lowered voice:

"And *this* is nothin' to what is down *there* somewheres!"

"Nothing."

"'Tis my idee," Nunatak added, "that of all livin' men none but yourself and Frontenac there knows what Cap Livingstone found in that place."

"None," I told him.

"And a fine pickle this we are in now!" he ejaculated.

"How so?"

"How so? Why, here we are with this long mush before us, and the Lord only knows what at the end of it, and all our dogs dead in that cursed freezer—dead as so many dried herrin's."

I laughed.

"You wait and see."

"I don't have to wait. I've already seen, ain't I? You tell me this, McQuestion: did you ever see Frontenac bring a dog in that fix back to life again?"

"I never have. But I saw him resuscitate a fish—a fish incased in solid ice."

"A fish! If 'twas some humans, now, that I could name, I could entertain some hopes in the matter; but a dog ain't a fish. No, McQuestion, they're dead, them dogs is; they're dead as sardines. The boss is a fine gink, and all that, and a regular *hyas tyee* when it comes to brains; but I'll never be able to forgive him for what he done to them poor dogs."

"So you believe that, if we are to get south, we'll have to tug the sleds ourselves?"

"That's just what we will have to do, unless—"

"Unless what?"

Nunatak leaned closer, and his manner became gravely esoteric.

"Shoot!" I told him.

"Unless," he whispered, "we can harness up a team of these here seals."

"It won't be long," I returned, "before you see all those dogs scampering around the landscape as peppy as they ever were at their peppiest."

"I'll see a canned oyster playin' a tambourine first! I know. When a dog's *memaloose*, McQuestion, he'll never do any more scamperin' around any landscape nor snowscape—unless, that is, it's in them happy huntin'-grounds.

"But look at them geysers. See them spout—like a school of whales. The Valley of Ten Thousand Smokes is a sight for a man to see; but this Summer Haven, I have to admit, sure has got it beat.

"And now, speakin' of our mush after them same palm-trees, and the good Lord only knows what else, I sure do hope, McQuestion, that this here Cap Rainier don't have charge of the provision-supply."

"Why so?"

"Why so? So's we won't have no dearth of *muckymuck*, that's why. Close! Why, that feller is so parsimonious with supplies that, if he owned the air, he wouldn't let a catbird whistle!"

The ship stood steadily on, drawing in slowly towards the western shore. At length we opened the *Multnomah's* little cove; not far away was the hut, a strange sight and one melancholy too in this deserted and desolate spot. There was but very little snow on these hills, which rose in long gentle swells like waves. And, towering above all, there in the south, were those mighty peaks—twin Rainiers, each rising fifteen thousand feet into the sky, the beauty of them wonderful, grim and awful.

WE DROP ANCHOR

The *Multnomah* turned into the cove. The engine stopped, an anchor was let go, and the ship swung round to her cable and became stationary.

Here we were at last, and the long, long voyage was ended! But the adventure was not ended. Indeed, this was, after a manner of speaking, only the beginning. What awaited us there in the south? What tales would we have to tell on our return—the terrible Gardens of Paradise explored, Sleeping Beauty, in her block of ice, on one of the sleds? If, indeed, we did not leave our bones down there!

But what was the use of addressing questions to Fate? Did she ever give answers? Never any at all. We must wait. Time only would tell—slow, cruel, inexorable Time. Patience was our only consolation. And in the meantime work—work conducive to strength of body; and thoughts—thoughts conducive to strength of heart and strength of sort.

For surely we should need it all.

21

"I WISH THAT HE HAD!"

A boat was at once lowered, and Frontenac, Rainier, Nunatak and myself were rowed ashore and went up to the hut.

"Just as we left her," said Ben Rainier.

"I shouldn't think," Nunatak remarked, "that visitors would be very frequent in these here parts."

"All the same," Rainier answered, "it wouldn't have surprised me at all if we had found somebody here. I thought some fellow would come—well, to see if our descriptions were exaggerated. Nothing, you know, in all Antarctic history, surprised people more than the discovery of this Summer Haven."

"How about the palm-trees?" queried Frontenac.

Captain Ben Rainier had taken a key from a nail above the entrance to the hut; this he had been on the point of inserting in the padlock. But now he turned and looked at Darwin Frontenac earnestly.

"That was different," he said. "We had proof of this discovery. Do you, after all, actually believe that Captain Livingstone actually did find palm-trees down there?"

"Why not?"

"Palm-trees within the Antarctic circle. I'm afraid that I can't believe that."

"Here's Summer Haven."

"Summer Haven," returned Ben Rainier, "isn't palm-trees."

"How," Frontenac asked, "do you explain the severed heads of Wilkie, Thompson and Bogardus?"

"I don't believe that their heads were cut off at all. I don't believe that Captain Livingstone knew any more about what became of those men than I know. In short, it is my belief that those severed heads, the palm-trees and all the rest of it, no matter what the rest of it was—all that, delirium!" said Ben Rainier.

"We shall see!" said Darwin Frontenac.

Busy were the days that now succeeded, the novelty of our surroundings rendering those days very interesting ones.

Frontenac, Archimedes Bukink, Nunatak and myself moved into the hut forthwith; the others preferred the *Multnomah*.

On the third day a big killer whale—he must have been thirty feet in length—rose near the ship, which apparition elicited from Nunatak some solicitude on the score of Mr. Orca Gladiator's health: the change from the icy waters of the sea to this warmth of Summer Haven might, quoth Nunatak, "give the poor critter pneumony."

THE DOGS BROUGHT TO LIFE

It was on this day, too, that Darwin Frontenac began the resuscitation of the dogs. I was the only witness of the actual restoration itself, which was by no means so simple and easy a matter as the suspending of the vital functions had been.

And never shall I forget that look on Nunatak's face when I brought the first dog up on deck, Skookum by name—the creature as bright-eyed and frisky as though he had just been aroused from a natural snooze.

The musher stared, rubbed his blue eye and stared again, rubbed his black eye and stared harder than ever.

"Can it really be!" he exclaimed. "Is it really you, Skookum—after bein' dead for so long?"

He dropped to his knees, hugged the dog to him and rocked him back and forth, murmuring endearing swear words.

"And I thought that he couldn't do it! Yes, Skookum, old *tillicum* (partner), I thought that Frontenac had murdered you and all the rest, that you was all as dead as so many canned lobsters. But I'll never doubt the boss no more. He can do anything. He's goin' to find them same palm-trees, that everybody thought was so many pipe-dreams, and the good Lord only knows what else besides. I'll head with him for hell itself—and may be that's where we are goin', Skookum—and I'll never ask a single question but just mush along after."

The others were crowding around, gazing at the dog in wonder and perhaps in awe.

I left them and returned to Frontenac.

On being removed from the freezer—five were taken at a time, after the revivification of Skookum—the dogs were placed in another room, the temperature of which stood at thirty-two degrees Fahrenheit. It was slowly increased. At the end of an hour it was fifty degrees. Frontenac now used his antidote. This was a bright purple fluid, its appearance unpleasantly oily, and it was injected into the neck. I tasted this stuff, at Frontenac's suggestion and assurance that it was perfectly innocuous. It had an indescribable, sweetish taste—the strangest imaginable. There was no effect whatever that I was aware of, except a slight tingling on the tongue.

"Weak stuff, after all," I remarked.

Darwin Frontenac smiled a little.

"That's because you are warm."

"Warm?"

"Just so. If your body was cold like these, the effect, I fancy, would be powerful enough—though, of course, you wouldn't be aware of that."

"Then the warmth neutralizes it?"

"I suppose one could put it that way."

"Why, then, did you bring them here? They were colder there in the freezing-room."

"Because the action of the antidote alone will not raise the body to a blood temperature. And, besides, raising the temperature of the body is not its real function, though a very important one, I admit. It's real action—and without that action recovery from a state of suspended animation would be impossible—is upon the blood."

"But," I said, "the blood is not circulating. As far as any vital process is concerned, the animal is as dead as a doornail. How, then, can this antidote be absorbed, permeate the whole circulatory system?"

"I think," Frontenac returned, a smile somewhat esoteric on his lean features, "that a little reflection will give you the answer to that."

For some time after the injection of the antidote—twenty or thirty minutes—there was no perceptible change whatever in the body. But, though not perceptible, a great change was taking place—a change that, at the expiration of the time mentioned, began to make itself manifest. The eyes began to lose that weird, horrible glassiness, the limbs their terrible rigidity. And at length the heart—so long stilled—began to beat and the animal to breathe.

A few minutes, and the animal would yawn and stretch himself, then get up and move around as though nothing untoward had happened to him.

That first day fifteen of the dogs were restored to life, so to speak. The next twenty-five, the day following thirty-two, and the fourth day saw the last body taken from the freezing-room.

Then I would think of Sleeping Beauty, and strange, indeed, were the thoughts that came to me at such moments. Was she really in that strange state that men called one of suspended animation? Was her soul locked up within her body there in her tomb of paleocrystic ice, or was it a corpse that was imbedded there? Poor little kid! For a time we were exploring around and recovering our land legs, which I was very glad, certainly, to get under me once more. And for a time our plans were uncertain. Should we lay down depots, then go into winter quarters here at Summer Haven, or should we at once begin our march for the Gardens of Paradise and winter there? There was much to be said on both sides, and much discussion did we have upon the subject. To pass the winter among the palm-trees—if, that is, we could keep our heads on our shoulders—would, from a scientific point of view, and, indeed, from any other, be an experience replete with extraordinary interest.

But, on the other hand, there was our lack of experience to be con-sidered and the uncertainty with regard to the supply of food. To take grub along sufficient to tide us through the winter was out of the question. Could we depend upon providing the necessary food-supply after reaching that wonderful and terrible place? It was Frontenac's belief that we could. Such, too, was my own.

However, the decision which we reached was to get down depots as far to the south as we could, go into winter quarters at Summer Haven and start for the Gardens of Paradise in the spring.

So now came the depot journeys. Three times we left Summer Haven, our faces to the south. On the third journey—"mush" in the vernacular of Louis Louisiana—we got our depot twenty miles or so beyond Captain Livingstone's Depot Number Three.

"Everything so far," said I, "is just as poor Livingstone described it."

"And so," said Darwin Frontenac, "will be everything else. The fate of the discoverer seems to be a hard one—Columbus in chains, Galileo on his knees, our Captain Stanley Livingstone a man pre-viously, cruelly wronged."

Nunatak turned his face to the southward, and his gaze was a strange and wistful one.

"Palm-trees!" he murmured. "I wisht, now, that I knowed everything that poor Cap Livingstone found down there."

"So do I," Frontenac said, a wan smile passing athwart his lean face. "Bond and I know what he *saw*."

"Well," the musher queried, giving the other a quizzical look, "didn't he *see* what he *found*?"

"Not in every instance," was Frontenac's answer. "I wish that he had!"

During the return journey came our first experience with the dreaded blizzard of the Antarctic. It burst upon us in the early hours of the morning, and it did not subside till near midnight. It was rather snug in our tent, occupied by Frontenac, Nunatak and myself, and in the other tent, too; but I found the inaction pretty trying. It is anything but pleasant to sit on (or in) one's sleeping-bag for hours at a stretch whilst storm-demons howl like spectral maniacs and pull and tug at your shelter.

The only thing one can do in such circumstances is to read or write. As for writing, I brought my journal entries forward, right up to the moment. As for reading, it so chanced that there was but a single volume at hand—*Narrative of A. Gordon Pym*. For two hours or so I perused its grisly pages, then tossed the little red volume over to Nunatak and wished him joy. It so chanced (I assure you it was an accident) that the book came down right on Nunatak's nose, but Louis Louisiana didn't mind a little thing like that.

As for Frontenac, he was writing, writing, Goodness only knows what he was always writing about.

As is usual, the thermometer rose during the blizzard—from minus 30° to minus 10°. When we turned out the next morning, the weather, though the sun was not risen yet, was smiling brightly upon us. Nunatak was of the opinion, however, that her smile was "kinda vampish."

And Nunatak was right. For, in the early afternoon, the sky, the snowscape, and the gloomy mountains began to turn dark and sinister, and ere long we were again in the midst of a tearing blizzard.

On the succeeding morning, however, the weather had cleared, and we were under way at an early hour. We were now some hundred and twenty miles from the hut—which, by the way, was situated in latitude 77° 45'. Nothing worthy of note, however, occurred during the remainder of that journey—though some extraordinary mirage effects were seen. Our surroundings at times assumed so strange and fantastic an aspect that one fancied he was looking upon the work of some viewless cosmic magician.

In the Antarctic things are certainly not always what they seem. And in this, I believe lies the explanation of those supposed discoveries there of lands and mountains that never existed where they were seen.

Amundsen gives a striking instance of the strange effects produced by atmospheric anomalies in those regions.

"I remember," he says, "our astonishment on the return journey [from the Pole] on finding the whole landscape completely transformed! If it had not been for Mount Helmer Hanssen, it would have been difficult for us to know where we were. The atmosphere in those regions may play the most awkward tricks."

We were learning that.

Right glad were we when we drew up at the hut—glad that the work was done and gladder still that we had done so well.

On the 26th of April the sun left us, to be seen no more for four months. At midday, though, he came up very close to the horizon, and there was then (if the sky was not overcast) a strong glow along the skyline in that direction, and the rays would light up the lofty heights of Mount Theodore Roosevelt and Mount Woodrow Wilson. But the sun was rapidly increasing his northern declination, and soon even those awesome heights were no longer touched by his rays at noon. Twilight now reigned throughout most of the twenty-four hours; for a brief interval around midnight there was darkness, the sun, at the noon of night, being twenty-seven or twenty-eight degrees below the sensible horizon and some degrees farther, of course, below the apparent one.

The long, long night had come; but it must not be imagined that we had settled down to a life of idleness and boredom. Far from it. Much was to be done, and we were doing much. Frontenac had things on a routine basis. There was none of that pernicious system of depending upon volunteers—pernicious in that the willing ones do more than their share, whilst the slackers grin up their sleeves.

It is a regrettable fact, but none the less is it a fact because it is regrettable, that it is almost impossible to gather together a body of men, however inconsiderable in size, without finding when the test comes that you have a shirker amongst them; and fortunate is that leader who finds that he has no more than one.

Such individuals, I was sorry to discover, we had with us; but Darwin Frontenac saw to it that the shirkers did not shirk. Every member of the. expedition had his routine work to do, and that work was done.

I say every member, but there was one exception, and that single exception was Professor Archimedes Bukink. He was the only one of us who was monarch of his hours. He could spend them studying the flaming of the wondrous aurora australis—first seen on March the 25th—counting the hairs on the legs of some microscopic inhabitant of Summer Haven or doing whatever his heart listed. And my opinion of the worthy Bukink; as I watched him, began to go up a few pegs. There were some busy men there at Summer Haven, but the busiest man of them all, I do verily believe, was Archimedes Bukink.

"I am mighty glad, Bond," Frontenac once said to me, "that we didn't head straight for the Gardens."

"Why?"

"Because, amongst other things, I grieve to find that in several instances my judgment of the men was lamentably at fault. Had we set out on our march straightway, Rustad would have been one of the party."

"I have wondered about *that* myself."

"The remark," said Darwin Frontenac, "is a supererogatory one, but I can't help saying that Rustad has proved himself utterly unworthy his place in the expedition, to say nothing of being a member of the southern party. His true place is upon a soap-box.

"Mistakes may be made," he went on, "Without anything awful ensuing; we have made them, and undoubtedly we shall make more. But there must be no mistake with regard to the personnel of the southern party."

This was the first time I had heard him speak so gravely, and needless to say it gave me something to think about. I had all along regarded in a very sober light that adventure for which we were now so impatiently waiting; it was only at this moment, however, that I began to realize how very seriously it was regarded by Darwin Frontenac himself.

The days passed, some of them swiftly enough, some of them dragging. They became weeks, months. And then at last, on the 19th of August, there was the sun peeping above the northern sky-line at noon! To see this great event, we had ascended to the summit of one of the hills, whence was to be had a view of the distant sea-horizon, in this case ice-horizon, for the sea was completely frozen over. Only the edge of the great glowing disk was visible, and that but for a very few moments. Great was our rejoicing, notwithstanding.

The sun had returned! He was rapidly decreasing his northern declination, at the rate (roughly) of a degree in every three days; that start for which we had so long been waiting (whilst preparing) was not far away now. A few weeks, and we would be heading south—south, towards Sleeping Beauty and the Gardens of Paradise.

Paradise? There seemed, at any rate to me, something of mockery in that name which Captain Livingstone had chosen.

Paradise? I prayed God, deep in my heart, that it would not prove abhorrent to us as hell's foulest corner.

Came at last *the* day—the 14th of September. This was an early start, but Frontenac was anxious to get to the valley of the palm trees at the earliest date possible, so as to have time for a thorough exploration of that strange region (unless, indeed, it should prove of greater extent than we had reason to believe it), and the return to Summer Haven whilst it was still possible to take the *Multnomah* through the pack.

In our plans there must needs be ample allowance made for delays, and even then there was no telling. No man living could say what might occur. It was a case where what seemed to be time enough might easily prove a time all too short, indeed. And, leaving these things aside, the ice conditions in that sea through which the *Multnomah* would have to force her way are the most terrible to be found anywhere in the Antarctic. The possibility of spending another winter, and it was a possibility that we must not blink, was not a pleasant one certainly to contemplate. And there was the possibility, too, that we might get away from Summer Haven only to find (supposing our return a late one) the *Multnomah* beset.

So we must, at all hazard, get an early start for the Gardens of Paradise and be on the return march as soon as was consistent with the full achievement of our purpose.

Well, we had done all that it was humanly possible to do. Now was the time for action—to see what the Fates had in store for us.

The sun rose above the white eastern hills that morning about twenty minutes past seven. I do not know that I have ever seen a sunrise more lovely than that was. All the colors of the rainbow were in the sky and shone again the placid waters of Summer Haven.

"A happy omen!" said I to Frontenac, waving a hand in the direction of that prismatic wonder.

"Yes," he smiled. "The Parcae are, so to speak, smiling upon us, Bond."

I nodded at this pleasant conceit of his. Well did I know, however, and that from bitter experience, how fickle, treacherous, heartless the Parcae really are. But that unpleasant thought, of course, I kept to myself.

Well, we shook hands all around.

"Mush!" cried Louis Louisiana, cracking his long whip.

And we were off!

There were seven of us—Frontenac himself, Louis Louisiana, Wilbur Addison, Richardson Watson, Ole Hansen, Thomas Loomis and myself.

At first Frontenac had planned to take a larger party than this. "Would need more men—many rifles."

Such were the words of Wilkie, written even as his doom was coming upon him. If he could only have set down what that thing was which he saw!

Much deliberation had we had upon the matter—Frontenac, Nunatak and myself—and the result had been Frontenac's decision (which Nunatak and I, all things considered, thought a wise one) that the southern party should be small.

As is usual in such cases, however, there was much to be said on both sides. The element of doubt and uncertainty would rear its head no matter which decision was reached. When it came to the march itself, the advantages were, of course, altogether on the side of the small party. But, when one thought of the Gardens of Paradise and the horror that lurked there—well, matters then assumed a very different aspect, indeed.

Seven men! Captain Livingstone's band had consisted of five (including himself) and its fate had been one awful to contemplate. We should have but two men more; but here entered a factor—and a very important one, too—that at first sight, if the eye were kept on numbers alone, might be overlooked. Forewarned is forearmed. And we had been forewarned. We did not, 'tis true, know what that horror was there in the palm-trees, but we knew that that horror was there, and we would be on the lookout for it and prepared to meet it when it came; whereas Captain Livingstone and his men had never dreamed of the existence of that monster with the enormous claw or of anything like it.

"That knowledge alone," said Darwin Frontenac, "doubles our band. Seven men who know that there is danger and are prepared to receive it when it comes are equal to at least fourteen who are walking right into a trap, so to speak. Though there will be only seven of us, we will, as compared with poor Livingstone's party, number fourteen men."

"That is very true," Nunatak nodded. "And I was just thinkin' what a wonderful savin' there'll be thataway in grub."

"In grub?"

"In grub," quoth Louis Louisiana, "though we'll number fourteen men, and maybe more, there'll only be seven tummies to feed."

"Quite so," Frontenac nodded. "And each of us will be well armed, which was not the case with the others."

"Only seven of us," Nunatak interposed. "Too bad the *other* seven of us can't tote shootin'-contraptions."

"Each man," Frontenac went on, "will have a rifle and two revolvers. And it is upon those revolvers, I fancy, that we shall depend when moving through the gloom of the trees. The revolver, of course, is a better weapon at close quarters than the rifle. That thing with the claw, you'll remember, Bond, dropped so suddenly upon them that they couldn't fire even one single shot with the rifle."

"I remember that. And perhaps it would have been the same thing had the weapon been a revolver."

"Not if each man had had such a weapon."

"You know," I said, "one of the strangest things about that horrible business is why not one of them could get in a single shot."

"I wish," Darwin Frontenac answered, "that that was the only strange thing about it."

He had given the men a careful and detailed account of all that had happened there in the Gardens of Paradise and had ended with a few hints relative to the grisly possibilities that awaited us. This, however, had not produced the faintest sign of the most fleeting hesitation. His words, on the contrary, only made those brave fellows more than ever anxious to go.

Of Sleeping Beauty he had not uttered a single syllable.

There were six sleds; in other words, each man (except Frontenac) had his sled and team of dogs. Each sled—and load, that is—weighed about 900 pounds. There were 90 dogs, 15 in each team. And on one of those sleds we would bring back a stronger load than any vehicle made by man had ever carried—Sleeping Beauty in her coffin of ice.

Coffin! Why, each sled, even now, what with the black provision cases, had an unpleasant semblance to a coffin.

As for instruments, the principal ones were the following: Four thermometers, three aneroids, three hypsometers, five chronometer-watches, two sextants, three artificial horizons and one cinematograph-camera.

That day we made 17 miles and had, I believe, 17 dog fights. I had never seen creatures so surcharged with life as those animals were.

"As full of pep," quoth Nunatak, "as ninety sticks of dynamite."
And his remark, forsooth, was a most apposite one.

"But it won't last," the musher added, somewhat ruefully. "It'll
be taken out of them, and then we'll wisht that they was peppy
once more."

Swiftly now day followed day, and steadily we moved on, deeper
and deeper into this terrible region. Though I say steadily, I would
not be understood as meaning that there was no interruption whatever in our progress. Once, in fact, we were held campbound for
two days by a blizzard. Other delays were met with, too, though
slight ones. In no instance besides the one just mentioned did we
lose so much as a single day, which, all things considered, was
really a remarkable run of luck.

Our camp at the end of the march on the 11th of October was,
by dead reckoning (the sky had been overcast for 48 hours)
exactly on the parallel of latitude 84°. We were now at the southern edge of that great plain of which Captain Livingstone had
spoken and were about to enter the mountains again. Strange
thoughts and feelings came to me as I stood and gazed away into
those tumbled masses before us. According to Captain Livingstone,
Sleeping Beauty lay in latitude 84° 25'—in other words, she was
distant now only 25 geographical miles.

I suppose that Frontenac must have known what I thought and
felt, for he came and stood beside me and, after a few moments,
during which he, too, gazed away to the southward, he said:

"A good day's march would take us to her, Bond."

"That's what I was thinking. I have my doubts, though, that
tomorrow's march will be 25 miles."

"I have mine, too. But it won't be long now before we see her."

"Good God," I exclaimed, "what a horrible place to lie in from
century to century, from age to age and age again!"

"Yes," said Darwin Frontenac; "a horrible one, truly."

And I thought that, as he stood there gazing at that frozen,
terrible waste of snow and rock, the poor girl, for the first time,
became an object other than one of mere scientific interest. And,
when he spoke, I saw my thought become a certitude.

"Poor little kid!" is what he said.

During the whole of the following day, the going was very difficult, but we succeeded in making good 14 miles of southing. This was according to dead reckoning, for we had not yet succeeded in getting a single glimpse of the sun. The next morning, however, he broke through the dark curtain and soon was scattering the clouds in all directions. A meridian altitude gave our latitude as 84° 21'. By dead reckoning, it was 84° 17', which speaks well indeed for the accuracy of our sled-meters.

Only four miles now from Sleeping Beauty.

And by two o'clock we had reached the spot.

Keen and eager were the looks which Frontenac and I sent as we opened that gorge in the mountains. The others, wholly unconscious of the interest that was attached to this place, continued steadily on, the negotiation of the difficult route engrossing their attention.

Frontenac and I halted.

"There it is, Bond!" said he, pointing, then raising the binoculars to his eyes. "There's the cavern mouth, though pretty well filled, it appears, with snow."

For some time we stood there looking and wondering, then pushed on after the others. A half mile or so beyond the place, a level spot, comparatively speaking, was reached, when we halted and made camp—a proceeding, it was patent, that puzzled the others.

Frontenac, however, offered not a single syllable of explanation.

Straightway he, Nunatak and myself headed for the cavern, the musher carrying a spade. It was plain that that spade intrigued Nunatak, but not a word of explanation was vouchsafed him, whilst he did not suffer curiosity to elicit from him the slightest query.

As we were drawing near, he suddenly stopped and stood, peering up.

"Looks mighty like a cave up there," he observed.

"That's what it is," Frontenac told him, "probably the most wonderful cavern in all the world."

Nunatak made no response.

The next moment we had started up. Frontenac was the first to reach the entrance; a few seconds, though, and I was beside him.

"Not a sign of her, Bond," he said, in a low voice.

"It's the snow—the snow!" I exclaimed excitedly.

"Of course."

He turned his head and looked down.

"The spade, Nunatak," he said. "Hurry up with that spade!"

"Ain't I hurryin'?" came the aggrieved answer of the musher. "Do you think, boss, that I'm a spider?

"I uster to think," he went on, "that I was a musher; but the way you fellows sailed up this here place showed me that I was a turtle. If it hadn't been for these crampons, I'd sure enough have broke my neck."

Frontenac and I had started to scoop off the snow with our mittened hands. A few moments, though, and Nunatak was nearing the top. I reached down for the spade; as I straightened up, it was seized by Frontenac, who began to remove the snow with feverish haste, careful, though, not to dig into the ice.

At this Nunatak could no longer restrain his curiosity—which, indeed, had suddenly become something very like astonishment.

"What," he exclaimed, "are you lookin' for?"

Scarcely had the last word left the musher's lips when an exclamation broke from Darwin Frontenac.

I bent forward to see, my heart beating heavily.

Frontenac dropped the spade and began to dust the snow from the ice with his mitts.

Suddenly he paused—exclaimed again— pointed.

"Look!" he cried. "Look, Bond! *There she is!*"

23
THE SUDDEN VOICE

I had already seen her—or, rather, her head and shoulders, for that was all of the sleeper that, as yet, was visible.

Frontenac dropped to his knees, put his head close to the ice-front and peered in at the girl's face.

Nunatak thrust himself forward to see, his swift movement threatening for a moment to destroy my equilibrium and precipitate me off the spot.

The next instant an exclamation of wonder and horror burst from his lips.

"What awful thing is this?" the musher cried.

To that neither of us made any response. Darwin Frontenac raised his head and turned his look up to me.

"Her eyes," he said. "Look at her eyes, Bond."

I bent forward and looked—looked straight into the eyes of the sleeper. They were no more than eight inches from the edge of the ice. They were wide open; the long dark lashes were as natural as though it were air and not this paleocrystic ice that incased them, and the pupils were extraordinarily dilated. The iris seemed blue, but whether that was the actual color or not, I could not tell.

"It is horrible!" I said, shuddering. "Horrible!"

"It is wonderful, Bond!" said Darwin Frontenac, bending forward once more. "It is wonderful!"

"I'd say," came the voice of Nunatak, "that McQuestion is right; 'tis an awful sight to see. And 'tis a mystery, too; how on earth did this poor creature get here?"

"She," I told him, "has been here always."

"Always?"

"Ever," I explained, "since the snow and ice fell upon the Antarctic."

He stared at me for some moments.

"What you talkin' about, McQuestion?" he exclaimed.

"I know what I am talking about. Look at her dress; it is almost tropical. She has been here for thousands upon thousands of years. No man living can say how long this poor girl has been lying here—here in her coffin of ice."

"Coffin!"

The next instant Nunatak's hand had closed on my arm with convulsive strength.

"A coffin!" he cried. "McQuestion, tell me this: Do you think that she is like them poor dogs was before he woke them?"

I nodded.

"The probability," I told him, "points in that direction."

He turned his look to Darwin Frontenac, who had arisen and was once more removing snow, so as to obtain a view of the sleeper's whole person.

"And," the musher said, "you are goin' to wake her up, boss—wake her up just like you did them poor dogs?"

Frontenac paused, and for a moment or two looked at the other with a curious, abstracted expression on his lean face.

"Such, Louis, is my hope," she said, "Yes, I am going to awake her."

"But—"

"Well?"

"Even you, boss, can't waken dead people. This purty darlin', her heart is still and frozen; the poor girl is dead."

"She may be, Louis, and she may not be. No one can tell that—now."

"I can, boss."

"A man," Darwin Frontenac added, "can only balance probabilities and base his belief on the result. That is what I have done, and my belief is that the girl, though entombed in this mass of solid ice, is not a corpse."

"She's dead!" said Louis Louisiana. "You awoke them huskies, but you'll never awake this sleeper, boss."

"That," Frontenac answered, a wan smile passing athwart his features, "is just what you said about those dogs, because they lay there stiff and frozen."

"I guess you're right, boss," said Louis Louisiana.

He turned slowly and sank down upon the ice at Sleeping Beauty's feet.

"Great Lord," he said, "what will it be next?"

Soon Frontenac had finished. He stood there leaning on his spade and looking down on the sleeper.

"What you goin' to do?" queried the musher. "Goin' to cut—?"

He broke off and, turning quickly around, peered into the dark mouth of the cavern.

"What's the matter?" I asked.

"I thought that I heard somethin'—in *there*."

"What?"

"I dunno what. It sounded like a voice."

"A voice?" said Darwin Frontenac.

He laughed.

"Probably an echo of your own."

"I suppose so," the musher said. "That must have been what it was—that or just plain imagination.

"But, as I was about to say," he added, "are you goin' to cut out a block of this ice; a block with the girl inside of it, and take her up to the *Multnomah?*"

"Just so. We'll disturb nothing here, though, until we come back from the Gardens of Paradise."

"That's as I figgered it. You'll take her to the *Multnomah* and then you'll awake her—if she ain't dead."

"I'll awake her," said Frontenac, "when we get back to Seattle. There are, of course, other reasons why I would never awake this girl here in the Antarctic; but most surely I would never do it unless there was a woman at hand."

"Of course," Nunatak nodded; "I was unthoughtful there."

Frontenac smiled wanly.

"It wasn't the only point, Louis; on which you were unthoughtful."

He sent his look into the cavern. A few moments, and he turned to Nunatak and said:

"Louis, I wish you to return to camp and get those two lanterns. You wondered, I believe, why we were taking along those lanterns."

"I did, boss; but I see now why you brought them."

"And bring that twine, also, Louis. There are two miles of it on that spool."

"Aye, aye, boss. Anything else?"

"Yes; ask the others if they care to come and see the sleeper—and the inside of this cavern."

Louis Louisiana sent a curious look into the low, dark entrance.

"Somethin' in there, boss?"

"Of course. God only knows what. There's a door in there."

"A door! Goin' to open it, boss?" Frontenac laughed.

"According to the descriptions given by Captain Livingstone, we'd have to have drill or dynamite to see what is beyond that door."

"Then we ain't goin' to see what's behind it."

"And," Frontenac added, "see that none of the dogs follow; fasten them up, every one of them."

"Great poodles, boss! What's the idee?"

Darwin Frontenac moved a hand toward the sleeper.

"There's no telling. If they saw her, they might dig her out."

"I was untoughtful again. 'Twouldn't be puppy-play, that," said the musher; "but they might do it all the same—dig her out and strip her bones, even though she is froze like a rock."

"We'll take no chances, Louis."

"That all, boss?"

"All, I believe," nodded Frontenac.

The musher turned to descend.

"Just a minute, Nunatak," I said. "I want to get a couple of photographs."

These taken, Louis Louisiana started forthwith for the camp.

Frontenac lapsed into brooding silence. I moved up to the ice once more, dropped on my knees and gazed in upon that lovely, awful face—so plain and yet with a strange mistiness about it, so to speak, something like the image upon the ground glass when the focusing of the camera is not quite perfect. And, as I knelt there and looked upon the sleeper, strange, weird, fantastic thoughts and feelings came to me. I could not keep the tears from my eyes. And those words of the man who had found her echoed and reechoed through gloomy, awful corridors in my brain:

"Perhaps you—both of you—will love her, too."

Frontenac laid a hand on my shoulder. I raised my head; his look was upon the sleeper's face, a strange, indescribable expression in his eyes.

"Poor little kid!" he said.

At length came Nunatak and the others. The scene rises before me as I write as vivid as though it had been yesterday—the sleeper there in her bed of cloudy crystal, the men clustered together before the ice and looking in upon her in wonder and in awe.

"Well," said Frontenac, at last, "now that you all have seen her, we will cover her with snow again, then enter the cave. There is a door in that cavern, a massive door of solid rock. We know no more than that, save that the cavern is an extensive one. A full exploration, with the limited time at our disposal, is, in all probability, out of the question."

We were a long time in finding the door, over which that awful carven harpy holds eternal guard; and much we marveled that Captain Livingstone and Hampden had ever succeeded in finding their way out of this terrible labyrinth.

But at last we stood before that mysterious door. What was beyond it?

And that terrible figure up above, more striking by far than the great sphinx of Egypt—why had those men of that dim, nebulous past carved that frightful monster there?

It was a strange scene truly, and one to give a man some eerie thoughts and feelings. There was the mysterious door, the Gorgon figure above it, works of an antiquity so remote that even the imagination grew weary as it moved through those gloomy vistas which— vista beyond vista, and on and on, age to age succeeding—stretched back toward it; and there, standing before this handiwork of an unknown people, we seven men of the modern world, seekers after strange things, enigmas, horrors.

Well, this was one of them—one of all three.

The lanterns cast deep shadows, shadows that assumed monstrous proportions as they stretched away to involve themselves in that Stygian gloom.

Sometimes (as one of the lanterns, or both of them, moved) the shadows would sway, quiver, glide this way and that, rush over floor, lofty vault or walls like disembodied, nameless things.

To show how weirdly and powerfully the scene affected the mind, I felt myself thinking of the men who had designed these things, of those whose hands had fashioned that harpy out of the living limestone rock, pierced the wall and closed the entrance with that massive door of granite—wondered if their spirits ever visited this spot, lingered and watched in this cavern of Erebus. And, so powerful was this thought, I found myself glancing into the shadows and blackness, as though seeking spectral forms and eyes.

We went up to the door and pressed upon it; we might as well have pressed against the wall on either side.

"Funny thing, it seems to me," said Louis Louisiana.

"What," queried Frontenac, "is a strange thing?"

"That there is so little dust hereabouts this door, boss—considerin', that is, that these things have been here for millions of years."

"Millions? You mean thousands of years, Louis."

"Well, thousands, then. Thousands or millions—I don't see as it makes much difference either ways."

"You forget Captain Livingstone and Hampden. See all the dust they removed from the entrance."

"Oh, I ain't forgot that, boss. And here's 'nother thing: I was wonderin'—"

"Well?"

"I was wonderin', boss, if somebody—I mean some *thing*—hasn't been here before us."

"Livingstone and Hampden were here before us."

"That ain't what I meant, boss. I meant before us but *after* Cap Livingstone."

Darwin Frontenac turned quickly, turned so that he stood squarely facing the musher.

"What *do* you mean?" he demanded.

The next instant, however, Frontenac's expression, his whole manner, changed; he laughed a little, as though ashamed of a momentary weakness.

"Maybe you think that I'm *pelton*, boss; but how do you explain that?"

The musher was pointing toward a mark on the cavern floor. Frontenac stepped forward and bent over the impression. The rest of us, too, moved toward the spot.

"Well," queried Nunatak, and there was a tone of triumph in his voice, "what is your explanation, boss?"

"A very simple one, Louis; this mark was left by the foot of Captain Livingstone or Hampden."

"No, no!" said the musher. "Look at it close, boss. It's different!"

He appealed to me. I bent over it. Surely Frontenac was right. But, as I continued to gaze upon that blurred impression, a doubt crept into my mind. I called myself a fool, though, for even permitting that doubt to enter my brain, to say nothing of letting it linger there. Some man, some thing here after Captain Livingstone and his companion! Why, the thought was preposterous. How, in the name of reason, could any—?

Came a sudden sound behind us—a hollow, horrible voice.

24

"AH-CONE-CAWN-GA"

We straightened up and whirled to the direction whence had come that sudden, mysterious, horrible sound. For a few seconds, what with the strong light we had had in our eyes, nothing was visible there in the dense darkness.

"Good God," exclaimed Loomis in accents of horror, and his words came in echoes from the gloomy walls as though spectral beings had rolled them back in fell mockery and fiendish gloating, "what was that?"

"Surely," came the quiet voice of Darwin Frontenac, "it was a human being that spoke."

"If so," Nunatak said, "such a human as no man of us ever heard before."

The next instant he gave a sharp exclamation and began stabbing the air with a crooked finger.

"Look, look!" he cried. "Them it comes! See it! What did I tell you?"

The creature was now visible—a quasi-human, fearsome figure.

"Stand together, men," came a hollow voice, that of Hansen. "This is no man! 'Tis something from hell itself!"

The creature's visage could be made out now, though indistinctly—a death's head in which eyes burned with a fierce, smoky, smoldering fire.

"'Tis a human being, boys," said Darwin Frontenac, "a man like ourselves—a man, though, from hell itself."

There could no longer be any doubt, and each of us, I believe, was more relieved than he would have cared to acknowledge. It

was a human being—such a man, though, as I never had seen in all my life.

He was naked save for a ragged cloth about the loins. A kind of moccasin—now, however, worn and cut to ribbons—incased his feet. His head hung forward, swaying, as he advanced, from side to side with a reptilian motion. The cheeks were hollow, the eyes sunk deep in the sockets; face and body were horrible with dust and gore; the skin was drawn tight over the bones, rendering his appearance skeletal, fearful.

Straight toward us he came—this swaying skeleton that yet was living. His lips were drawn back from the teeth in a fixed and fright-ful grin. He kept muttering and mumbling—the sounds seeming to issue not from the mouth, but through the very walls of the chest.

On he came until he was within a dozen feet of us. Then he halted and made to raise his right hand on high, his wild, burning eyes fixed on Darwin Frontenac, that horrible voice, now raised to a high pitch, sounding all the while.

But of a sudden the hand was arrested. It began to sink; the fierce light left his eyes; the grinning face seemed to set in a corpselike rigidity, and the man came pitching forward into the arms of Frontenac.

Frontenac let him sink to the floor, and we turned him onto his back.

"Sheer exhaustion," said Darwin, his hand over the man's heart, "and starvation."

"Memaloose?" asked Nunatak.

"No; the heart still beats, though sluggishly."

"One thing," Nunatak said, "he has been spared the terrors of thirst. He must have got water, else he could never have come to this pass. He would have been dead long ago."

Frontenac pointed to a skin bag (or bottle) at the man's side, carried by a strap passing over the right shoulder.

"A third full," he said, prodding the bag—which gave forth a gurgling sound as it moved—with his finger.

"Funny," said Nunatak, "that he didn't eat the skin. I guess he preferred starvation to thirst. But where did he get the water?"

Frontenac took up the bag, removed the stopper and wet the man's forehead.

"He has been badly wounded here," said Frontenac, indicating the right side of the head. "Must have got it in a fall."

"And there," I said, pointing to the victim's right side. "Clean through the ribs."

"And them ain't the only places," Nunatak remarked. "He is bruised and cut from the top of his head clean to the soles of his feet."

"Poor fellow!" said Frontenac. "'Tis a wonder that he's alive."

"I fear me," said Nunatak, "that he ain't goin' to be alive very long."

"I fear that, too, Louis. But food may do wonders. So go back at once to the camp—thanks to this string, you can go straight to the entrance and in to us again—so go back to camp, Louis, and bring—"

Frontenac paused and turned his look from the musher's face to that of the Antarctican. The eyelids were twitching, the lips writhing back in that horrible grin and the left hand began a spasmodic twitching.

"Coming to," said Watson.

"Or," Nunatak observed, "about to quit this here old Vale of Sorrer."

The eyes of the victim opened. I now saw, for the first time, that those eyes were blue—a bright, wonderful cerulean; yes, wonderful even through that horror which filled them.

He began to speak, his look fixed on the face of Darwin Frontenac.

"He is repeating something," Frontenac said. "Listen to that."

We listened for some moments to that strange verbal repetition.

"What is it?" Frontenac asked.

"*Ah-cone-cawn-ga*," I told him.

The others nodded.

"That," concurred Nunatak, "is the very word that he's sayin'."

"Or," Frontenac suggested, "words."

"*Ah-cone-cawn-ga!*" said the Antarctican once more, for the first time looking me in the face.

"If," Nunatak exclaimed, "he could only *tell* us!"

The victim suddenly raised himself into a sitting position; almost as suddenly, though, he collapsed back into Frontenac's arms. It was patent that the man's will was in a grim struggle. He raised his skeleton arm and pointed, his lips moving in what, for a moment, I thought was a smile—yes, a joyful smile. The next moment, however, I believed it to be a look of fear and horror. I raised my eyes in the direction indicated by his skeleton finger, and a shiver ran through me as they lighted upon that monster above the door.

"*Ah-cone-cawn-ga!*" said the Antarctican.

The hand dropped to the floor as though the arm had been snipped from the body; the head sank forward, then rolled sidewise in horrible fashion as Frontenac let the corpse sink down to the cavern floor.

25
THE HEAD

Ah-cone-cawn-ga! Much speculation was elicited by that word—
or words. What had the Antarctican tried to tell us? *Ah-cone-cawn-
ga!* What did it mean? Was it a thing, a place, a human being,
or what was it? Well, wondering about it could never give us the
answer; nevertheless we kept wondering and wondering.

"There is one thing that I can't help regarding as significant," I
told them. "I can't say, though, that it makes the thing any clearer.
In fact, it makes it more mysterious than ever."

"I think," Darwin Frontenac observed, "I know what you mean.
The last time he spoke that word (or words) he pointed towards
the harpy: you think, Bond, that Ah-cone-cawn-ga has *something*
to do with *that* up there?"

"It seems to me that the suggestion is not altogether a fanciful one."

"Same here, McQuestion," concurred Nunatak. "What did he
point towards that awful figger for?"

But Darwin Frontenac shook his head in marked dissent.

"There is, of course, no use guessing what he meant to tell us;
but we can regard it as almost certain, it seems to me, that, whatever it was, it had no connection at all with that harpy. Why, he
had never even set eyes on that thing!"

"Just the same he might have known when he saw it. This may
not be the only one."

"I don't believe," Frontenac answered, "that the poor devil even
knew what he was pointing at, that he saw the monster at all—even
when he was looking at it."

I admitted that this might have been the case—which, however, was by no means tantamount to saying that I believed it had indeed been so.

In this mysterious business, only one thing was incontrovertible, and this was that the man had come from the Gardens of Paradise. It was possible, probable perhaps, that he had not come from that part seen by Captain Livingstone; but that the man had come to this awful spot from some part of that wonderful valley was so clear that no man of us, for one moment, entertained the slightest doubt on that point.

Here, then, was another route into Paradise. No thermometer here in these underground ways dancing a minus jig, doing the can-can, or taking a snooze at 30° or 40° below. No glaring white here to blind you; no pressure-waves or pressure-ridges to cross or go around; no terrible sastrugi; no crevasses hundreds of feet in depth add treacherously concealed by a film drawn from edge to edge.

These thoughts, however, did not throw me into a transport of joy. The fact is that as I considered the possibility thus so suddenly presented, the greater became my uneasiness.

The absence of the things mentioned before (and others) was, of course, simply wonderful by way of contrast; but, on the other hand, my imagination (and I do not think that I am in any sense a very imaginative man) had not the least difficulty in picturing things in this subterranean place that would positively make me long to hug a sastrugus, and shed tears of joy at the very thought of a crevasse.

To endeavor to get into the Gardens of Paradise by this subterranean route! Suppose we should find this wonderful idea regarded with favor by Darwin Frontenac? Well, I certainly hoped that we shouldn't.

We photographed ourselves, the door, the monster on guard above it and the dead man, whom we at last carried off and lay in a vault in the cavern wall. We had removed the water-bag and his belt. There was a beautiful sheath attached to the belt; the weapon, however, had been lost. So we laid him down there in that tomb chamber which Nature herself had hollowed out of the crinoidal limestone rock—a tomb noble enough for any earthly potentate; and there we left him—the mummified body or the white bones to startle, perhaps, some future explorer and touch his proud, brave heart with the sad lesson of mortality's glittering dreams and the fearful end that awaits it.

I believe I have forgotten to mention that at this point where the door is situated, the great gallery makes a sharp turn to the right. It was from this direction that the Antarctican had come to us. This reminds me, too, by the way, that Nunatak expressed the belief that he actually had heard a voice that time at the entrance; we others, however, were of the opinion that the musher had certainly been deceived.

We now quitted the spot, moving in that direction whence the Antarctican had come. Twenty minutes or so elapsed, and then Addison announced that all the string was reeled off the spool. This meant that, since quitting the door, we had advanced half a mile.

There had been no noteworthy change in the form of the cavern. On we went, leaving marks to guide us in our return. We could not dream of trusting to our footprints, for half of the time there weren't any; there were long distances where not the faintest impression remained on the hard floor to mark our passage across it.

Another twenty minutes passed, and then there was a change. We had seen but few stalactitic or stalagmitic formations, and these only small ones; but now we suddenly entered a grotto, the beauties and marvels of which were such as to surpass any description that I could ever pen—or, indeed, any other man.

In all directions, stalactites were hanging, some of them as slender and symmetrical as the masts of a noble ship. In many places stalactite had met stalagmite, forming pillars—some of them thirty feet in diameter—of a beauty that the human hand never has fashioned. There was a group of columns that gave forth a musical sound when struck sharply by the hand, and upon these, after some practice, Frontenac actually succeeding in playing *Yankee Doodle*. The wonders of the place had, apparently, not suffered the slightest change during all those ages since the cessation of the sinter-bearing water-drip which had formed them.

I have said that this was a grotto, but it was, in fact, a perfect labyrinth of grottoes. So entranced were we by the beauties and marvels of the place that we clean forgot to leave marks to guide us back. When we remembered, it was to discover that we were lost.

Lost! We made light of it but I am convinced that, in his secret heart, the discovery was an alarming one to every man. I know that it was so in my case. Visions of a fate similar to that which had befallen the Antarctican began to flicker and flash before my eyes; and, when three whole hours had passed and our extrication from this most wonderful but most fearful place was apparently as remote as ever, I began to curse that very moment when we had advanced beyond the harpy and the door.

Another hour passed—an hour such as I do not wish ever to go through again—and then suddenly, on our emerging from a long winding gallery, a loud shout went up, to be echoed and reechoed from the lofty walls. No marvel that we shouted, for we found ourselves approaching that very spot in which we had deposited the spool!

In our advance, we had not noticed the mouth of this gallery to which we owed our escape from that maze of caverns and grottoes. Little wonder, though, that we had not seen that entrance. Forsooth, almost as much must have been missed as had been seen.

The experience had certainly been an unpleasant one; but, now that we stood safe, I was very glad indeed that we had got lost. For now we knew what it would mean to attempt the attainment of the Gardens of Paradise by these underground ways. What with this pleasant cogitation, I was constrained to remark that this subterranean route to Paradise would, I supposed, be very fine—if one could only find it; but that I preferred the sastrugi and the crevasses. This elicited from Frontenac a wan smile and a response to the effect that we had no one to blame but ourselves for what had befallen us—that, if we had only left marks, there would never have been a moment's uncertainty as to our position.

"Alas," thought I, "of what use is experience if a man will not profit by it?"

It was midnight when we stood again at the entrance, in the biting cold. A sound, mournful, fiercely sad, filled the air; the dogs were having a concert—old Ole Bull no doubt, as usual, leading. Strange, mysterious creatures! Why do they raise their voices thus, in a lament so weirdly sad and so fearful? There, in that lugubrious, savage howling, is encompassed, it seems, the sorrow and the travail of life, and the horror and the mystery that wait upon its end. Mysterious beings! Have they knowledge of cosmic arcana that even man never has glimpsed—or, having glimpsed, has only budded upon them cobwebby castles in the halls of which he finds himself entangled as some weak insect caught in the web of the spider; or sunless, horrible dungeons in which his soul wallows in cold obstruction and in foul despair?

The sun was low behind the southern mountains. His declination was now about 8° south, and so, if the apparent horizon had been coincident with the sensible—in other words, if the place had been an extensive plain—we should have had the sun, at this midnight hour, some three degrees above the skyline.

The air was without the slightest movement. The sky was clear, fleecy clouds hanging motionless in the blue immensity that arched over us. In the south, the sun turned the blue of the heavens—almost an azure—to amethyst and chrysoprase, primrose, gold and scarlet. The mountains were involved in deep violet shadows, here and there a peak burning with blood-red fire. It was a strange and wonderful scene; beautiful, in a way a terrible one, too.

Frontenac, as we made our way campward over the sastrugi of the glacier, was blind to all this beauty of sky and savage landscape. Sleeping Beauty's Cavern, its marvels and mysteries—it was of these that Frontenac was thinking.

"As for its physical properties, there are two things, Bond," said he, "that strike me as very remarkable. One is the high temperature of the cavern—51° Fahrenheit at the door—the other that there is only the gentlest indraught of air at the entrance.

"Why should there be a hurricane there?"

"A little reflection upon the phenomena presented by the equilibrium and the motion of elastic fluids," said he, "will show that there ought to be a very strong indraught."

"But there isn't," was my sage observation.

"But why isn't there? Something queer about that cave, Bond. It is a fact well known that great caverns breathe. Take the Mammoth Cave, for instance. In summer the cave *exhales*, the air moving with the force of a gale at the Iron Gate, about three hundred feet from the mouth. But, when the temperature of the outside air falls below that of the cavern, the mean of which is 54°, then it *inhales.*

"However," he added, "there can be no doubt that temperature alone is not, in every instance, an adequate explanation. In other words, sometimes some of the phenomena presented by the respiration of caverns are inexplicable."

"Well," I told him, am not going to lose any sleep trying to figure out why that zephyr at the mouth of the cave isn't a typhoon. Certainly I am not going to try to explain the respiration of a cavern (of which I know nothing whatever) when scientists (who know all about everything) can't explain that simple phenomenon, an ice-cave—one of those caves in which there is a lot of ice in summer, but in which not a single particle is to be found in winter."*

"Perhaps," he smiled, "we'll find something in there tomorrow for the explanation of which you would be glad to give a whole year of your life."

* "One of the largest of these natural icehouses is in the Carpathian Mountains, near the village of Selitze, and is resorted to, in mid-summer, to supply the wants of the villagers. At that season the roof is covered with immense icicles, and the drops falling on the sandy floor are instantly congealed. On the approach of winter the icy mass begins to dissolve; and, by Christmas, it is gone, leaving the cavern dry and warm till spring returns!"—Hovey.

In my secret soul, I groaned aloud. "Then our exploration of that labyrinth of Erebus is not yet ended?"

"'Tis my hope," he made answer, "that we shall see much more than we have."

Which meant that I couldn't hope (though wishing mighty hard) that we shouldn't.

Nine o'clock the next morning found us at the entrance once more. We had one of the sled-meters with us, so that there would be no guess-work about the distances traversed. We passed the monster and the door, then the spool and entered that maze of grottoes. We saw to it this time, you may be sure, that we did not get lost. On we went through that wonderful place. No pen could describe the beauties that we saw there. We were in fairyland. The formations took a thousand-thousand shapes, some of them indescribably fantastic, others terrible as spectral figures lurking about tombstones.

There were columns slender and fluted, as beautiful as those of a Grecian temple. We saw ribbons, festoons, curtains, flowers (oulopholites), trees, animals, birds, fountains, waterfalls, angels, demons, Gorgons, serpents, gnomes, dragons.

Some of the sinter was translucent; and at last we found some columns that were as transparent as glass!

Whilst the others were standing there examining and admiring the first of these, I moved forward—to be brought up by a sight so strange and horrible that, for a few moments, I could scarcely believe the testimony of my senses.

My exclamation brought the others to the spot instanter.

Pointing to the column before me, I cried: "I don't know whether it is a dream or a picture by Doré; but—isn't that a human head?"

26
THAT FORTUNE HAS WARNED US

Yes, that was what we saw; as I am a living and honorable man, there was a human head in that pillar of sinter-glass!

We gazed in upon the object in indescribable amazement and in horror. The skin, the color of which was a dirty brownish-yellow, was drawn tight to the bones, the whole head having a dry and withered look; there could be no doubt, however, that this strangest relic of mortality upon which the eye of man ever lighted was that of a white man.

"And look at that!" exclaimed Frontenac, pointing to the next column. "There is another one!"

The moment succeeding Nunatak ejaculated:

"And there's the third!"

"Another!" said Hansen.

"And two more there!" Loomis added. A few minutes, and still another was found, making seven altogether of these strange, grisly objects.

As for the physical agencies which had brought about this singular phenomenon, the rationale was a simple one: the heads had been placed upon the stalagmites, and the drip of the acidulated water had done the rest; the deposit of crystal sinter had incased them. And there they were like insects preserved in amber.

But why had those old Antarticans done so strange a thing?

"If the whole body," said Frontenac, "had been placed under the drip, there would have been no mystery at all about it. But why only the head?"

179

"Maybe, boss," observed Louis Louisiana, "the Fiend hisself might be able to answer that question. What horrible things human bein's really are—a lot of them 'tany rate! Probably, now, this is just the pleasant little joke of some robber or priest or tyrant."

"Probably," I suggested, "Sleeping Beauty will be able to throw light upon the matter."

"'Tis not impossible," Frontenac said.

"But these objects must have been old even in her day. The heads were, of course, placed upon the stalagmites, yet not a one of them is in a stalagmite now; sufficient time elapsed for the formations to meet and form these pillars. In her time they must have been even as they are today, for, in the falling of the Great Cold, the drip ceased."

"Still," I proffered, "there might not have been much space, when the heads were placed there, between stalactite and stalagmite."

"That is, of course, true. Still I think that they must, when she was born, have been here for a long time. I think it unlikely that Sleeping Beauty ever saw them. Perhaps, indeed, she never even heard of them."

"We shall see."

"Unless," he said, "the girl is, after all a corpse."

"I don't know," muttered Nunatak, "that they would be any the more wonderful we knowed why the thing was done."

We found nothing, more in that place, which we called the Hall of the Heads.

Our sled-meter showed four and one-half miles at this spot. We figured that we went about three miles from the entrance in bee-line.

On we went. For a half mile or so, the going was very difficult. The floor was strewn in all directions with fallen stalactites. In some places, even columns had fallen.

Our hypothesis was that an earthquake had produced this havoc. The meter was useless here, and so Nunatak, who had been trailing the instrument, slung it onto his back. Two hands were none too many for the negotiation of this scene of confusion and ruin. On issuing from it, we entered a low, wide gallery, the walls and the roof of which were almost as smooth and regular as though fashioned by the hand of man. There was not a vestige of sinter anywhere; there had been no water-drip here.

"I should not be surprised, though," I said, "to find the formation of dripstone still taking place. We know that there is water somewhere in this cavern."

"Perhaps," Loomis suggested, "a river flowing from the Gardens of Paradise."

"It is not impossible. But my idea was that there probably are fissures in which the warm air of the cave meets the ice and melts it."

"But there would be no dripstone formed," Frontenac said, "because the water would not be acidulated."

"By George, I forgot about that!"

"Do you know," I asked him some moments afterward, "what I was thinking?"

"Nothing awful, I trust."

"I have been thinking, for some time now—I can't keep the con-founded idea out of my head! But I have been thinking what a beau-tiful fix we would be in if something were to happen to our lights."

"Nothing can happen to our lanterns," Darwin Frontenac an-swered lightly.

"You speak as though an accident were simply a thing impos-sible. And, besides, last night I had a dream—"

"That, I suppose," he put in, "you would have me believe was not all a dream, that Fortune has warned us. For Heaven's sake, no oneirocritics, Bond! Spare us that!"

"Oh, well," said I, "'tis the same old story: a prophet is ever without honor in his own country."

That gallery was exactly one mile and a quarter in length. It opened into a great chamber, almost a perfect circle and with a diameter of fully one thousand five hundred feet. The formations here were beautiful beyond anything that we had heretofore seen.

And here it was that the first turn of fortune came.

High up in one wall, with grotesque stalactites hanging about it, was a curious hole, which Nunatak must needs peek into. Good-ness only knows why that particular opening should have intrigued him in a manner so remarkable. But thus it was. And so up he went, climbing carefully, for the ascent was a rather difficult one, whilst we sat on a fallen stalactite and watched him.

He had reached the very top and had just straightened up to look in when it happened. Something gave way beneath him; he clutched at a stalactite to regain his equilibrium; the stalactite dropped from the roof, smashing three more loose as it fell, and down came stalactites and a mass of fragments with our poor musher in the midst of them all.

We cried out in horror—I noticed with a sinking of the heart that no sound had broken from the victim—and rushed forward. Poor Nunatak! Our poor comrade was dead!

As we fetched up, however, he reared his tall form from out the debris, shook the dust from his clothes and calmly remarked that he had come down much faster than he had come up!

Whilst we were rejoicing in his escape, a sudden thought came to me: "The lantern! Where is the lantern?"

At last we found it—or, rather, what had been it. For the thing which we found, under one of the stalactites, looked about as much like a lantern as a pile of ashes in the grate resembles the stately tree that was consumed there.

I looked at Frontenac with that exultation which the true prophet feels when the dire calamity predicted has at last fallen upon the sinful and (above all) heedless people.

As for Frontenac, a barely discernible smile touched his lean face, and he quoted these words of Byron's:

> "Of all the horrid, hideous notes of woe!
>   Sadder than owl-songs on the midnight blast,
>   is that portentous phrase, 'I told you so.'"

"Well," said I, "I *did!*"

"Be an optimist, Bond," Frontenac laughed. "It won't happen again."

"As though that is the only thing which can happen!"

"Curse the curiosity," exclaimed Nunatak, "that took me up to that confounded hole! I do actually believe 'twas an evil spirit that led me to do it.

"And yet," he added, "I wisht that I had got a peek!"

Frontenac smiled a little.

"We won't risk *this* light, Louis," he said

I wondered if this loss of one of our lights would mean (as I sincerely wished it would) that here was the end of our advance. We had, of course, only one light now—and if something were to happen to that?

However, not the slightest hesitation was evinced by our leader, whilst none of the others showed any disposition whatever to even suggest that it might be expedient to turn back now. Nor, alas, did I! How often have I bitterly regretted that I suffered my false pride to keep one silent! true, it might not have done any good; but on the other hand, had I spoken, I might have prevented that horror which even now makes my blood run cold.

But I did not!

And so at last we quitted that great chamber, my soul oppressed by vague but nonetheless terrible fancies and fears—as if, indeed, I had, in some unaccountable manner, sad prescience that some horrible tragedy was imminent.

27
WHAT HAPPENED

It was not long in coming.

A quarter of an hour passed, and then it was that we stepped out into the fatal chamber.

It was as though we had entered a grotto in the heart of a great jewel, so beautiful were the formations that everywhere met the eye.

We had scarcely entered the place when Frontenac drew up with an exclamation for silence.

A faint musical tinkling was heard.

"What is it?" someone whispered, the voice, I thought, evincing a superstition, some nameless dread.

"Listen!" said Frontenac.

At this moment I became aware of another sound.

"Drip, drop!" it went. "Drop, drip!"

"Over there!" Frontenac said.

He started. We followed. Loomis was beside him, carrying the light.

What was that mysterious tinkling, at every moment now becoming more distinct?

Then suddenly the explanation flashed into my stupid brain, even as Nunatak exclaimed:

"Water!"

"Of course," was Frontenac's answer. "What did you think that it was?"

"For a few moments," the musher said, "I sure, half thought that 'twas fairies or spirits or somethin'."

"Bad spirits?" Frontenac queried.

"Yes, boss; schemin' devils."

"Spectral sirens, as it were."

"Regular spirit witches, boss."

And thus they had their little joke at the expense of those eerie fancies which the mysterious sounds had conjured up. Little did a man of us dream what a horrible thing this discovery was to prove.

"There she is!" said Frontenac.

And there it was—a tiny stream of water issuing from a point high up in the wall and falling, with that curious metallic, musical tinkle, into a large semi-circular basin, whence it escaped in a gentle flow to disappear on the instant into an orifice in the cavern floor.

"Wonder," said Nunatak, "if 'twas here that that poor devil of an Antarctic feller got his water."

Not a sign was found, however, to show that any human being had ever visited the pool.

We had turned to quit the spot when a remark from Nunatak caused Frontenac and me (we were just behind Loomis, who, it will be remembered, was carrying the light) to stop and look back. It was to this fortuitous circumstance, there cannot be the slightest doubt, that we—Frontenac and I at any rate—owed our lives.

Loomis paused for a moment, then moved forward.

Came a cry, a sudden rending, crackling—utter blackness

A shriek, despairing, horrible, arose, as though from the depths of a pit.

Came a horrible rumble, silence, and then a sound as though produced by a great mass plunging into water at an appalling depth.

"Great God!"

The voice, which I recognized as Hansen's, was aquiver with horror.

"What was it?" I cried.

"*Don't move!*"

The words were Frontenac's, and they cut through the blackness like a knife.

"As you value your lives, don't move an inch!"

"What was it?" I asked.

"The floor!" said Frontenac.

"It give way!" cried Nunatak. "I saw it goin'—then everything was black."

"The light!" I cried. "The light! The lantern is gone!"

"Yes," the musher said. "The lantern is gone. And poor Loomis is gone. We can never get out to the mouth of the cave in this darkness. And, before the end comes, we'll wisht to God that our bones was down there with poor Loomis's."

I shuddered with horror as I thought of the fate that awaited us in this fearful place. It was not of Loomis that I was thinking—though I *did* think of him, poor fellow—but of the loss of the lantern. And, before you set me down as a selfish heartless brute, remember that I was not thinking of a simple little fabrication of glass and metal, worth at most but a few dimes and pennies, but of the lives of six human beings.

For to even dream of ever reaching the entrance without a light—why, it were the wildest madness. We were doomed men—doomed to the horrible fate (if not to a worse one) which had befallen that poor being from Paradise.

Came a sharp scratching sound; a sudden light burst out—the feeble light of a match in the hand of Frontenac. And I noticed that that hand did not show the slightest tremor.

"Look!" he exclaimed.

But there was no need to tell us to do that; we were looking—at that hole in the floor, yawning, dark, frightful as must be the deepest pit in hell's blackest corner.

I shrank back, for I was within two yards of the edge.

The opening was roughly elliptical in shape, the major axis probably fifteen feet, the minor ten or twelve. As the light was growing dim, a mass on the opposite side, one weighing perhaps two hundred pounds, broke off and disappeared. The next instant we were in darkness once more. Frontenac was counting. He had reached six when the sound came up from those fearful depths.

"Great Heaven!" he exclaimed. "Four hundred feet!"

He struck another light, then stretched out on the floor, flat on his stomach, and looked over the edge.

"For God's sake, Darwin," I cried, "be careful! That may be undermined, too!"

He called out Loomis's name, but the only answer heard was the mocking echoes of his own voice.

He called again and again—many times, the mournful echoes metamorphosed by my horror-chilled senses into exultant, demoniacal laughter.

"There can be no hope," I said. "Poor Loomis was dead before ever he struck."

"Lucky feller!" came the voice of Nunatak, the words sounding in my ears like the croaking of some sinister specter.

Frontenac raised his head and turned his look upon the musher's pale visage. But he said nothing. As he was thus looking back, the match burned to thumb and finger, and he dropped it into the pit.

Pitchy blackness rushed in upon us again.

"Yes," came the voice of Frontenac from the darkness, and it was as though he was speaking to himself, "the lantern is gone!"

Frontenac struck another light, as did Hansen.

"There is no danger in this spot," Frontenac assured us; "the floor isn't undermined here."

"Too bad 'twasn't!" Nunatak muttered.

"So," Darwin said, "our minds may rest easy on that score at any rate."

"Wretched consolation, that," I told him.

"Who would have dreamed, he went on, "that this tinkling, innocent-looking little stream had hollowed so fearful a pit, only a mere shell of floor remaining to conceal the horror underfoot? Probably, though, when it began its work, the stream was a large one. And, of course, the work was done before ever the Great Cold fell. For then the supply of carbonic acid ceased, and it is the acid and not the mechanical action of the water—though the latter does play a part—that destroys the rock."

"What does it matter how it was done?" queried Nunatak bitterly. "It has dragged down as fine a man as ever went out on a trail, and it has entombed us all here in the heart of Sleepin' Beauty's Cavern! Why think about formin' theories?"

We were again in darkness.

"No man," I said, "must ever have set foot upon that spot in those ancient times."

"Who can say?" returned Frontenac. "A more probable inference, it seems to me, is that the floor over the pit was firmer then."

189

"Why," came the voice of Watson, "couldn't we tell that the place was hollow? Why, for instance, didn't we hear the sound of the falling water?"

"Hear it?" Frontenac ejaculated. "Why, it is spray; mist long before it reaches the bottom."

"And why," came the voice of Louis Louisiana, "didn't we bring along one of the dogs. If we only had one of them dogs! He would lead us out if the darkness was ten times as black as it is."

"Yes!" said Frontenac bitterly. "But we didn't bring a dog."

I asked:

"Darwin, what's to be done now?"

"Start for the entrance, Bond."

"Start or stay," came the voice of Nunatak, "what difference does it make? 'Tis human nature, though, to keep on goin' to the very end, and so I say:

"Mush!"

"Same here," said Addison.

"Ditto," came the voice of Watson.

"Them's my sentiments," Hansen said.

There was a brief silence.

"There's the water," suggested Frontenac. "We'll renew our supply, and we'd better each take a good pull at that spring."

We did.

"All ready, boys?" Frontenac sang out at last.

"Ready!"

"Then here we go!"

He struck a light and started. Only a few steps had been taken, however, when he stopped and, looking back at us, said:

"Really we ought to make a few tests before leaving this hole—"

"Tests!" I exclaimed.

"With the object," said he, "of securing as close an approximation as possible—for the result, of course, could be nothing more than an approximation—of the depth of that pit."

"The pit! Cursed be the moment," I cried, "that we entered this hellish grot!"

"Amen!" said Nunatak.

"Oh, well," Addison philosophized, "it might have been worse."

"If it had," the masher growled, "it would have been the worst."

"You croaking bird of ill-omen, Louis!" Frontenac said, a faint glimmer of a smile on his face.

Scarcely had he uttered the last word when he clapped a hand to his head fiercely and cried out. But that was not all: the next instant our leader—he the self-contained, the man of iron nerves—was laughing and dancing, his tall form and lean features presenting a strange, eerie, maniacal appearance in the expiring light of the match.

"Great Heaven, Darwin," I cried in amazement and distress, "what is it?"

Suddenly the light went out.

But I had seen enough to send an icy chill to my heart. The one horror that my tortured brain had never conceived—that was this fearful thing which had fallen:

Frontenac was mad!

29
"WHO WILL BE THE NEXT?"

I heard a muttering in the darkness, and my blood ran cold at the sound.

Suddenly he burst out:

"Blockhead, oaf, dolt, fool! Oh, fool—imbecile and idiot of inconceivable asininity! Thick-skulled, double-domed, triple-damned lunatic!"

I cudgeled such brains as I had left in hopes they would conceive some remark that might mitigate this sudden, fearful madness which had seized upon poor Frontenac, and with this result:

"There, there, Darwin! You mustn't take on this way—really you mustn't, old fellow. Our case may be a desperate one, but, after all, it is not hopeless."

My words were succeeded by the most intense silence I ever had experienced in all my life. Horrible thoughts writhed and coiled in my skull, writhed and coiled like a tangled mass of vipers. This terrible silence—what did it mean? What was to follow? What effect had my words produced upon the brain of the madman?

A laugh was the answer—a laugh, long, loud, pealing, merry.

"Really, Bond, I believe you thought that I had gone clean off my head—completely, utterly and absolutely off my noodle!"

"Off your noodle! Good Heaven, is it any wonder if I did? You called yourself a double-domed, triple-damned lunatic—whatever that is! I don't know, but I certainly do know that you certainly acted like one. What on earth did you carry on like that for?"

His merry laugh rang out again.

"Old *tillicum*," (partner), said he, checking himself, "this is the delightfulest thing I have known in many a long day, I do assure you! I wouldn't have missed it for the world!"

And off he went again.

"Explain the little matter, boss," came the voice of Nunatak, "so's the rest of us can enjoy the little joke, too."

A flush burned my cheeks, a flush of fierce, insensate anger—anger at Frontenac because of his actions of a lunatic and at myself for having suffered my senses to distort and magnify in so absurd a manner what I had seen and heard.

"Well," said I, somewhat testily, I regret to have to admit, "elucidate!"

"We're saved!" Frontenac said.

"Saved? What are you talking about?"

"That's what we are."

"What on earth do you mean?"

"Just what I said. Why, there is our reserve supply of oil—right here in this can in my pocket!"

"What good is that," I wailed, "when the lantern is gone?"

"Bond, Bond! I see I wasn't the only lunatic, after all, in this bright and intelligent audience."

"Hooray!" roared Nunatak. "All we need now is a wick!"

"Of course," Darwin said. "And to manufacture a wick will be no formidable matter. Then a hole in the stopper, and presto! a real, regular, genuine lamp to light our way back to the entrance!"

It was magical—our swift rush from the black depths of despair to these iridescent heights of hope, exultation.

Blockheads, dolts! Why had none of us thought of that before?

In the light of a piece of woolen stuff that had been dipped into the oil, Frontenac made a hole in the stopper, whilst Nunatak, with a speed and deftness for which I should not have given him credit, fashioned the wick. A few minutes, and there it was—a light, feeble though it was, that shone bright and beautiful as Hope's own lamp.

Regarding the matter soberly, however, 'twas a far cry indeed from the bright lanterns with which we had entered, to this primitive flame, and terrible were those galleries and chambers through which we had to make our way. Indeed, had it not been for the marks left and the careful notes made during our advance, the outlook, even now, would have been a black one.

We moved over to the edge and stood looking into the blackness of the pit.

"Poor fellow!" said Darwin Frontenac. "'Tis a horrible tomb—but, then, so is a tomb of marble.

"Let us start. No, we will see how deep this pit is."

"How," Nunatak asked, "are you goin' to do that, boss? We ain't got no line to sound it."

"'Tis easy, Louis, though we can't claim any great accuracy for the result."

Frontenac stretched himself out on the floor, looking over the edge, his chronometer watch in his hand. I took a similar position beside him, holding a fragment of rock over the abyss.

"Good Lord," burst out Louis, "maybe that rock'll hit poor Loomis!"

"I think it unlikely," Frontenac returned. "The sounds told us that the pool down there is a deep one. The depth of it may be hundreds of feet. Anyway, it won't hurt the poor fellow any if it does hit him.

"Ready, Bond?"

"Ready."

"Now!"

"Six," said he when the sound came up.

A dozen trials were made, and they gave a mean of exactly six seconds. In that time, a body would fall five hundred and seventy-nine feet *in vacuo*. But this abyss was not a vacuum. Also, there was the time it took the sound-waves to ascend. After allowing for the resistance of the air and the fraction of a second required for the sound to reach us—quantities, of course, that could not be known with precision—the result obtained by Frontenac was a depth of "just about four hundred feet."

We lost no time in quitting that fearful place. Slowly and carefully we made our way back. Several times we were brought up in uncertainty, but in every instance our careful notes put us right again. At length, there was the spool; we were indeed safe now. There would have been no difficulty whatever in reaching the entrance, from this point, in utter darkness, thanks to the string. Not that there was any likelihood of our being compelled to do so; the flame of the lamp was as bright as ever. At the harpy and the door we stopped and for a time stood gazing upon these strange, mysterious objects, which we were probably beholding for the last time. The halt, however, was a brief one, for by this time we were pretty well satiated with marvels and mysteries. It was six o'clock when we stood once more at the entrance, having been in that terrible but certainly most wonderful, underground world for nine hours.

That night the ghost of poor Loomis came to me in my dreams. Three times it came. In every instance the horror of the thing awoke me. And every time the figure asked the same question:

"Who will be the next? Why won't you tell me who will be the next?"

Morning found it blizzing fiercely. One could not see a dozen feet. All day the blizzard raged, all night and all the day following. On the morning of the third day, however—this was the 18th of October, the weather was clear and calm, and we got underway at an early hour, Frontenac driving Loomis's team.

Of the ninety dogs with which we had pulled out from Summer Haven, we had lost eight. One had been pitched upon by comrades, killed and eaten upon the spot. On another occasion, Skookum (the first dog resuscitated) would have met the same fate had we not flown to the rescue. His end, however, was virtually the same; poor creature was so badly slashed and torn that his sufferings were ended by a blow an ax. He was then fed to his cannibalistic brethren. Two had deserted; these we never heard of again. Three had almost literally died in harness. The deaths of these animals were a mystery upon which the post mortem, performed by Frontenac, shed no light whatever. The eighth had sickened and received the mercy of a bullet in the brain.

That day we made but eight miles. However, after due consideration, I have decided not to enter into a detailed description of

the days that now followed, interesting though some of them
certainly were. Our journey from Sleeping Beauty's Cavern to the
valley of the palm trees was much like those made by other
Antarctic travelers, and I am anxious to get on to the Gardens—
where our experiences were such as are to be found in the wild
pages of a romanticist or in a spirit-shaking nightmare rather than
those of the world of reality, strange though that world may sometimes be.

30
PARADISE

With regard to things meteorological, we had, up to this time, a phenomenal run of luck. But now we encountered adverse conditions. It was no unusual thing to find the thermometer down in the minus forties. Winds blew, fierce and bitter, bitter and fierce as the passions of mankind and for a whole week blizzard followed blizzard with a regularity that was amazing and certainly was most maddening. What with these vicissitudes of fortune, we did not reach those mountains that barred the way to the southward until the 1st of November. Our camp that night was in latitude 86° 9'. From this point the way led to the eastward, towards that great defile which would take us through the mountains to the Gardens of Paradise.

The next day I had a very close call. Suddenly the snow sank beneath my feet, dropped, and there I was with my skiffs bridging the fearful profundity of a crevasse.

All the others, their dogs and sleds, my own too, had crossed this very spot, and here it had broken on my gliding onto it, and I was by no means the heavyweight of the party. The situation was an appalling one. I have never heard of a man being in one precisely analogous. I durst not move a foot, and the blue depths over which I stood turned me giddy and sick. In front the skiis were supported by a mere crust of snow and ice, and, for all I knew, things were even worse behind. All I could do was cry out. This, it is scarcely necessary to say, I lost no time in doing. Even this threatened to destroy my equilibrium. They heard me and turned, and back they all came flying, Frontenac and Addison in the lead.

"Steady, Bond, steady!" Darwin cried as he came up. "We'll have you safe in an instant!"

"Be careful!" I warned. "The edge there is only a crust!"

They were careful.

"Make her safe, boys!" sang out Nunatak. "We'll tail onto you two, so's if he slips or somethin', you won't have to let go or all go down together."

This was done. Then Frontenac reached out a hand and grasped my right, Addison my left; there was a pull, and I shot across to safety.

Frontenac gave a deep respiration.

"I thought, Bond, that you were a goner that time."

As for Nunatak, that worthy grinned from ear to ear and remarked:

"A feller sure must be stuck on acrobatics, I'd say, when he'll straddle a crevasse in that-away fashion."

That day, what with the terrible surface encountered, we made only five and one-half miles. The next, the 3rd, we did better, we made ten miles, which brought us to the base of the mountains. It was hereabouts that Captain Livingstone saw the skuas. But not a vestige of life had we discovered. It was on his march to this spot, too, that Livingstone's dogs began that mysterious sniffing. We had the same phenomenon, though in our case there was, of course, no mystery at all about it.*

---

* "'What on earth is Uroa scenting?' It was Bjaaland who made this remark, on one of these last days, when I was going by the side of his sledge and talking to him. 'And the strange thing is that he's scenting to the south. It can never be—' Mylius, Ring and Suggen showed the same interest in the southerly direction; it was quite extraordinary to see how they raised their heads, with every sign of curiosity, put their noses in the air, and sniffed due south. One would really have thought there was something remarkable to be found there."—Amundsen: *The South Pole*.

At this camp was left Frontenac's sled. Four thousand feet above us, six thousand above the level of the sea, was the entrance to that way riven through the very heart of the mountains. Captain Livingstone was less than a day in reaching that spot; how he did it has always been a mystery to me. We were almost a day and a half in reaching the entrance. It was in this spot, it probably will be remembered, that they killed that strange bird, that bird like the one seen by Shackleton's men, brown of color and with a white line under each wing.

We gazed up at those black-ice-burdened cliffs, but there was no creature up there to launch itself down upon us.

Our camp that night was deep in the defile, lofty, awful masses towering high above us.

Noon of the next day, the 6th of November, we were at the highest point, about eight thousand four hundred feet above the level of the sea.

That afternoon we descended a little over two thousand feet. The wonderful valley was very near now; but it was getting late, and haze and fog obscured our surroundings, and so we decided to camp. A good rest, and then into the fog and on to Paradise!

Morning found us enveloped in a fog so dense that objects were sometimes invisible at a distance of only twenty feet. No use staying for it to lift, however. So we started. It was mighty unpleasant traveling like this—groping our way through this gray obscurity. But grope we did, and on and on—with thoughts of crevasses and other possibilities to keep us pleasant company.

On and on, slowly, steadily. Hours passed. Then suddenly, as Captain Livingstone had done, we stepped, one after another, out of the fog as through a curtain, and there were the Gardens of Paradise!

31
WE ENTER

I shall not attempt to describe the thoughts and feelings that came to us as we stood there and gazed out upon that strange and lovely scene. I believe every man of us, so lovely was it, likened it to a vision of fairyland. But it was not fairyland, despite its beauty and the strange wonder of it all, for 'twas the abode of a frightful monster—the abode of monsters, rather. Somewhere, too, perhaps up there in the invisible northeast, was a race of men—a race of white men. And where human beings are—well, there is not fairyland, however wonderful the land, and the human beings themselves, may be.

Ah-cone-cawn-ga! Ah-cone-cawn-ga! What was the meaning of that word syllabled by the Antarctican upon our wondering minds? Would it be ours to rent the veil and see? Or would it remain (for us) one of the mysteries of this mysterious land?

Everything visible was just as Captain Livingstone had described it. Our view, however, was not so extensive a one as his had been, for a haze, with a strange quality of dreaminess for which we could not account, obscured distant objects, completely concealing, of course, what lay beyond them. The great mountain that rose up in the midst of the valley—named Mount Wilkes by Captain Livingstone—loomed ghostly and evanescent. There, off to the left, was the lake, glittering like a great jewel in the rays of the Antarctic sun. Yes, and there they were—there were the palm-trees!

It was our belief that we had come out at a point somewhat to the left of the place where Captain Livingstone stepped through the fog-curtain; and, on consulting his map, this was found to be the case. The distance proved to be about two miles.

We found the grave—torn open. It was plain that this had been done long before, in all likelihood, I thought, immediately after the departure of Livingstone and Hampden. The cross lay shattered amongst the flowers, and not far off a skull was found. A careful search everywhere revealed nothing more. The skull—we had no means of knowing whether it was that of Wilkie, Thompson or Bogardus—we buried again and placed another cross the head of the grave. A solemn, sad business this, the first to befall us on our arrival at Paradise—one that enhanced that foreboding which enveloped my very soul in its gloomy shadows.

This sad office performed, we started down, leaving one of the men, Watson, to his colossal chagrin and disgust, to guard the camp. We were, of course, no longer in our zero togs. A good idea of what our divestiture meant will be furnished by the remark that I was now wearing one pair of socks instead of seven!

As for weapons, each of us had a rifle, two revolvers and a goodly supply of ammunition.

It was a strange thing to be moving, here in the very heart of the frozen Antarctic, beneath the branches of stately trees. The sheen of sunlight upon the foliage and moss overhead—some of the moss hung from the great branches in long festoons—was most beautiful. No less beautiful was the sun-blaze on the mass of vegetation that clothed the ground. Awful, too, were those dense shadows all roundabout us.

As we advanced deeper and deeper into the place, the flora assumed a character more and more tropical. Gorgeous flowers, many of them parasitical, were passed. Came the almost continuous drone of insects. Creeping, crawling, flying things were everywhere. Great butterflies flitted in the sunlight and in those gloomy forest depths into which we sent so many searching glances.

And this mention of butterflies renders apropos one of the curious entomological discoveries made by Frontenac in these Gardens of Paradise: a butterfly with a "terebrant mouth," as he chose to express it. In other words, this is the first (and the only)

butterfly known with a boring mouth; all the others are purely suc-
torial. The only exception, amongst the great order of the *Lepi-
doptera*, previously known, is that of some Australian moths—
Ophideres, I believe—these insects, like *Papillilarius frontenacci*,
having boring mouths.

Our objective was the scene of the tragedy. This, thanks to
Captain Livingstone's careful directions, we had no difficulty in
finding.

Yes, there we stood at last in that very spot where it had dropped
upon the three victims.

"Look at that!" suddenly exclaimed Frontenac.

He was pointing toward the trunk of the great cypress There it
was, faint but unmistakable—the mark of a great claw.

I felt a shiver run through me and the blood turn cold in my
veins.

"Can it be possible," I said, "that the thing which left this mark—?"

"Well, Bond?" Frontenac queried. "Captain Livingstone suggested the possibility that it did not have to move on the ground."

"Bosh! The suggestion is not worthy a second thought. It is
preposterous, utterly preposterous. Of course, the thing might be
arboreal; but that isn't what Livingstone meant."

Of a truth, it was a dark, mysterious and terrible business that
now faced us.

32
"IT WAS WHITE, HORRIBLY WHITE!"

We examined the spot carefully, thinking that we might find the rifle which the unfortunate men had carried; in the horror of that moment, the weapon easily might have been overlooked by Captain Livingstone and Hampden. But we did not find it; nothing whatever was discovered. What had it done with that weapon?

We advanced deeper into the forest, moving, you may be sure, with every sense on the *qui vive*. Not long after we left the scene of the tragedy, the sunlight suddenly disappeared (doubtless the great orb had moved behind one of the mountain peaks) and the woods turned gloomy and awful. Through openings in the dense foliage overhead were caught glimpses of lovely sky of the deepest blue; but this only enhanced the sombre, weird gloom which pervaded the depths of this mysterious forest.

Minute followed minute; an hour passed. The forest suddenly turned more sombre and weird than ever. A silence had fallen, heavy, portentous. Not even the call of a bird broke the stillness now.

"What's goin' on?" queried Nunatak, glancing curiously, apprehensively into the gloom that every moment was deepening about us. "It looks like night was closin' in, but there can't be any night here in Paradise."

I raised my look to the dark canopy of leaves overhead. The openings gave glimpses of a dark and wrathful sky. Came a blinding flash, succeeded in three or four seconds by a fearful rolling roar. There was a sporadic spattering on the leaves overhead. A little space, and the wind began to sigh and moan up there. In the depths where we stood, however, there was as yet not the faintest movement of the air. Another flash, and again the thunder roared and rolled. Then came the rain. A few moments, and it was coming through that roof of leaves in a dripping deluge.

"Why in thunder," said Nunatak with a most aggrieved air, "ain't it snow? A feller would think 'twould be snow and not this here rain that'd make an Oregonian webfoot sit up and stare."

"Why, Louis," asked Frontenac solemnly, "is a hen?"

We were seeking a place of shelter, keeping as far as possible from a tree-trunk, when Addison gave a sharp exclamation. He was pointing fiercely, a tense expression on his features.

"Look at *that!*"

There, in the dense gloom and the rain and the mist, was a moving object, vague, spectral—a moving white thing that in an instant had vanished.

We stood staring, uncertain, wondering, whilst the lightning flashed, the thunder roared and the dripping, streaming deluge descended about us, but the object was not seen again.

"What was it?" said Addison, his voice a whisper.

Nobody answered. That was the very question that each of us was asking himself.

"My God!" Addison exclaimed suddenly.

Frontenac looked at him interrogatively, keenly.

"Did you notice," Addison asked, "the strange color of it? It was—it was white, horribly white!"

A bitter smile passed athwart the lean face of our leader.

"Suppose it had been pink or purple or vermilion?"

"White," Addison murmured, "horribly white!"

"Think it was a ghost, Wilbur?"

"I wish somebody would tell me what it was. One thing I do know: it wasn't human."

"I see you have turned supernaturalist."

"Well, what was the thing?"

"I haven't the faintest idea," Frontenac told him. "Another little mystery for us to solve.

"And no time like the present moment," added our leader, starting toward that spot in which the white object had shown itself and so suddenly, mysteriously had vanished.

"I say, boss," protested the musher, "maybe you're walking right into a trap."

Frontenac never paused, made no response.

"Well," said the musher resignedly, "I guess it's a case of foller-the-leader."

Ere he ceased speaking, he was moving along in Frontenac's footsteps, finger on the trigger (twigger he called it) of his rifle; the rest of us, too, got in motion.

There was a sudden growl of wind, and the next instant we were fetched up in our tracks by a sound loud and fearful, like a moan drawn from some monster in mortal agony.

"What's that?"

The voice was Hansen's.

Frontenac was moving forward again. He glanced back, and, through the gloom, I saw a smile glimmering in his features.

"Only," he said, "a tree rubbing against another."

A few moments, and he slowed up and began looking all around.

"Must have been right about here," he said.

"A fellow," observed Hansen, "would need a searchlight to find any signs in this dark hole."

It was indeed a gloomy, awesome place that we had got into.

Suddenly Frontenac exclaimed, turned sharp to the left. The next instant he had halted and, heedless of the dripping flood in which he stood, was bending over some object or impression.

"There you are!" said he, glancing up at us and pointing with his rifle. "There is the mark of Wilbur's ghost."

Nunatak was beside him now and bending over the spoor. As we came up, the musher raised his tall form, a grin spreading over his face until I feared it was going to engulf his ears.

"If all our mysteries," said he, "would only prove no more terrible than this one! 'Tis only the mark of some kind of a deer critter!"

33
THE HEADLESS MONSTER

And such indeed it was! And the dark, fearful thoughts that the glimpse of a creature so harmless had sent rushing into our minds! What a tricky, untrustworthy thing the human brain is, after all Something of mystery, a fear, and behold—fearsome thoughts, monsters, ghosts, psychic Gorgons, hydras and chimeras dire!

The lightning soon ceased, but it was fully an hour before there was any diminution in the rain. Once started, though, the change was a rapid, a most striking one. Through the openings overhead the deep blue of an unclouded sky suddenly appeared again; the gloom about us thinned, lifted, crept away into the secret places; and suddenly they came, the bright rays of the sun, gleaming and flashing on tree-trunk and foliage, enhancing, however, the sombre gloom of the forest depths.

"Well, boys," said Frontenac, "I think we might as well head for camp."

To this no one offered any objection. We had not cleared up the fearful mystery of these woods; but that had not been our purpose, this first journey into the forests of Paradise being a mere excursion, so to speak, not an expedition of discovery.

The return to camp was not marked by any incident especially worthy of notice. Watson, however, had something to show us— a bird (which he had shot) brown of color and with a white line under each wing.

"Just like," said he, "the one killed by Livingstone's party, and the one seen by Shackleton's men on the other side of the Pole, in latitude 83° 40'. That bird was headed south, in this direction; maybe, for all we know to the contrary, 'tis the very one that they saw."

We had seen a number of birds in the forest, but none like this creature, which, by the way, had a wing spread of four feet.

The next day was passed in making ready for our expedition into this mysterious and weird land, and in looking around. In the afternoon, Frontenac and I went off with the object of finding the depot left by Captain Livingstone. We had a time of it, for a dense fog enveloped the place, but find it we did at last. There was no telling; the supplies here might come in mighty handy. All the others were shown the spot. Nothing, however, was touched. All we did was clear away the snow, which was not near so deep as we had expected to find it.

We were now about to enter upon the grim work of the expedition. The exploring party was to set out the next morning, the 9th of November. What awaited it? Success, failure, disaster, or something of all three?

The party was to consist of Frontenac, myself and two others. Our leader found himself unable to make a choice, and so the men drew lots. Nunatak and Watson made the lucky draws. Addison and Hansen were bitterly disappointed, of course, but accepted the result without a murmur. Frontenac was at some pains to impress upon them the necessity of taking no chances whatever, no matter how tranquil and safe everything might seem.

"Whatever happens," said he, "one of you must always be on guard."

Also, he placed in their hands written instructions—which covered one or two rather unpleasant possibilities.

"No man can say what awaits us in there," and he waved a hand towards the Gardens of Paradise. "You will, as directed in this paper, remain here until the 15th of December. If we are not back by that date, you will know that something has gone wrong. Under no circumstances, though, will you make any effort whatever to ascertain our fate. You will start at once for Summer Haven. You will, following as closely as possible the instructions given you in this paper, hew out Sleeping Beauty—leaving her, of course, incased in the ice—and take her with you to the *Multnomah*. Before sailing, I made provision against the contingency that I might be lost: the great secret is carefully down on paper, in a vault in Seattle, and another will awake the girl in case I do not return.

"And now the die is cast. We have done all we can with a prospective regard to success and safety. The rest is in the hands of the Fates."

We got away the next morning at eight o'clock. Each man carried a supply of food sufficient to last him two weeks; then there were our arms and ammunition and other things—which shows that we were not traveling as light as we could have desired.

If we only had one (at least) of the dogs. With such a creature along, warning would be certain in case danger (from any living thing) was near. But, alas, the dog might betray our presence at a

moment when such intelligence would spell irrevocable and hor-rible disaster.

We headed straight into the Gardens. An hour passed, another, still another, and nothing had happened. A half hour more, and then we stepped out into a trail—one evidently, however, not much trodden. Was it that of an animal or—? There was no spoor to give us the answer to that question. The trail ran at right angles to the route we had been pursuing. Which way should we go? To the right or to the left? The right, we decided.

Fifteen or twenty minutes passed, the while we continued our steady, cautious advance. Then suddenly the trail issued into a clearing—a great sylvan chamber rather, for the branches formed an almost unbroken camp overhead—and there, before our aston-ished eyes, was the headless monster.

34
A MYSTERY NO LONGER

The monster upon which we had so suddenly come here in the depths of this Antarctic forest was nothing more or less than a granite colossus. It was a seated female figure, forty feet in height, and, though headless, there was something indescribable and terrific about it. A thing most strange was this: we had reason to believe that this fearful goddess—for the figure of a goddess we took it to be—had never had a head at all! We were at a loss to account for a circumstance so very singular, but that was our belief—that this colossal granite figure had always been acephalous.

I thought of those heads in Sleeping Beauty's Cavern, there in the pillars of sinter-glass, and I thought of the beheadings of Thompson, Bogardus and Wilkie, and I wondered if there was not some dark and fearful nexus between this figure, sitting here through unnumbered centuries, and those grisly sinter columns and the severed heads of the unfortunate explorers.

We thought it highly probable, too, that there had never been a time, since that day the sculptors ceased work upon it, that this deity had wanted worshippers. Certainly the condition of the great idol itself, after all the ages that had elapsed, and that of the place in which it stood, were such as to strongly substantiate this belief. Whether, however, that had been so or not, there could be no doubt that she had her worshippers *now*. But what manner of beings were they? Strangely enough there was nothing to throw any light whatsoever upon that. But we were soon to have the answer.

"Well," said Frontenac at last, "we have seen all there is here, so let's go on."

So we quitted that fearful sylvan cathedral, following a well-beaten path but one so dark that I could not help likening it to a cavern—and I had had enough of caverns to last me for many a long day! The path led to the northeastward—the very direction in which we wanted to go.

We had gone perhaps a mile, and then came the discovery. The trail dipped into a little hollow, through which flowed a sluggish stream. Frontenac, who was leading, came to an abrupt stop, exclaimed and pointed to the ground with his rifle. There, in the soft black earth, was a footprint—but such a footprint as no man of us had ever before looked upon!

"Great guns!" exclaimed Nunatak, straightening up and glancing about into the gloom of the trees, "like a grizzly's!"

There were many marks, coming and going, the marks of huge feet—quasi-human feet with enormous claws.

"What on earth," said Watson, "can they be—the things that left these marks?"

"Giants!" Nunatak muttered. "Giants—or somethin' worse. I tell you, fellers, I sure do wisht that I had another gun!"

Our leader laughed.

"You've got one more weapon now, Louis, than your two hands can manage."

"If only," said Louis Louisiana, "I had practiced up some on pulling twiggers with my toes! I seed a feller once who could do it, and I have an idee 'twould come in handy here."

"And," I said, "'tis such things that worship that horrible colossus. I would rather imagine the scenes that take place there before that figure than be a witness of them."

"Human grizzlies!" muttered Nunatak, gazing at one of the great footprints. "Giants! Monsters! Bear-men!"

"There certainly," Darwin nodded, "is something strikingly ursine about the appearance of this spoor. Bear-men! Well, who knows, Louis?"

"Surely," I exclaimed, "you don't actually think that—?"

"I didn't say that I thought it, Bond. This only is certain: we'll soon *know*."

We soon did know!

We had gone about a mile farther and had just stopped to examine a plant with long tendrils that moved like live things when touched—reminding me most forcibly of the tentacula of an octopus. Frontenac had just thrust his rifle forth and touched one of the arms, which on the instant had closed about the barrel and now held it in the grip of a vice.

"That thing ain't a plant!" exclaimed Nunatak, his voice touched with horror. "It's *alive!*"

"It's an animal," said Watson, "even though 'tis rooted to the ground."

"A land devil-fish!" Nunatak ejaculated. "Ugh!"

Scarcely had the last word left his lips when a movement, off in the forest, as though a shadow passing, whirled me around.

"Look there!" I cried. "It's coming!"

There was very little undergrowth here. In this respect, it might have been a scene in some beautiful park. And, coming down an enshadowed, sun-flecked aisle of the forest, coming straight towards us, was—*it!* There at last, no more than a hundred feet distant, was the mystery! Fearful the apparition which was approaching—but, thank God, the mystery of Paradise was a mystery no longer!

35
WHAT WE SAW

Frontenac tore his weapon from the grip of the octopus-plant. The musher flung forth a savage oath and raised his rifle to his shoulder.

"Not so fast, Louis!" said Darwin, thrusting up the muzzle of the other's weapon. "Hold your fire, boys. Let's see what it does."

At that instant the thing stepped into a stream of sunlight, and there it paused, a monster clothed in golden fire, and stood regarding us with stolid interest. It was now some fifty feet distant.

"Your camera, Bond!" whispered Frontenac, keeping his eyes on that fearful apparition. "Try a shot with that."

I did, while the others stood with upraised weapons, fingers on triggers.

Suddenly I whirled. What was that! Surely a sound had come from behind. Was the place full of them? But nothing was to be seen there or anywhere else—only that figure standing there before us framed and clothed in the fire of the sun.

And that thing which we saw? Imagine the biggest grizzly bear that you ever heard of. That will be a creature terrible enough, I know. But now imagine it turned into a thing half human, and you will have a faint—a *very* faint—idea of the monster which stood before us. Yes, as I hope to see Heaven, that is what it was—a human grizzly, a huge bear-man!

Evidently there was that about us which was somewhat of an enigma. I wondered if it was our standing thus resolutely and facing him. Undoubtedly he thought that we were unarmed.

There was a belt round the bear-man's middle; from this belt he suddenly whipped out a great knife—a weapon of flint—and, with a most horrible roar, started towards us.

"Now, Bond, now!" cried Fronton. "We'll take care of him! Get a picture!"

I snapped just as the monster gave another roar. At that instant, too, Frontenac fired. The bullet went right into the open mouth and out the back of the head, and down the bear-man fell and in a few moments was still.

"Great Heaven," I exclaimed as we stood looking down on the great form, almost as terrible in death as it had been when living, "this is the thing that beheaded Livingstone's men!"

"And this here feller," said Nunatak, "intended to do somethin' very similar to us, I reckon. Wonder if they got that decapitating stunt from the goddess back there."

"I thought of a big ape," Darwin Frontenac said, "but certainly in none of my hypotheses was there ever even the ghost of a bear-man." He pointed to the feet.

"There's the great claw, about which we have done so much wondering, which made the mystery so fearful. Evidently—look at the hands—the creatures never go on all fours, are true bipeds."

"Why should they go on all fours?" queried Louis Louisiana. "They're bears, but ain't they human like us?"

"Not like us, Louis."

"I mean as regards their brains they're human. By the great Harry, I'll say we're in Paradise!"

At length we resumed our advance.

"Probably," said Watson as we moved, along the trail of the bear-men, "we'll wish, before we're done with these woods, that we had eyes in the back of our heads."

I was wishing that already!

It was late in the afternoon when we came to the edge of a large open space and saw the camp of the bear-people. It was at the farther side, by a little stream, and consisted of a half dozen huts, made of woven branches and roofed with long leaves like those of the pandanus.

A fire was burning, and there were a half dozen figures about it. Three of these were children. The others, which we took to be females, were cooking the evening meal—that is, two of them were; the third stood looking on, holding an infant in her arms, for all the world as any human mother would do.

As we stood, screened by the foliage, looking out upon this strange scene, two bear-men suddenly came into view, one of whom was carrying some dark object.

"What the deuce," said Nunatak, "has the feller got?"

"Turtle," answered Frontenac, the binoculars to his eyes.

For a long time we remained watching these strange beings. There was nothing terrible about them now—though how terrible they could be, that we knew full well. In fact, the scene was merely singular, at times almost comical, reminding us most forcibly of a chapter from some storybook for children.

When our curiosity had been satisfied, we quitted the place, striking out into the pathless forest. After traveling for about two miles, we halted in a fine park-like spot, where we proposed to pass the night—if I may use that word, for here the sun, though at times hidden by a mountain peak, never set at all. The night, then, passed uneventfully, each man taking his two-hour turn as guard.

We were off early next morning, the 10th, steering a course that would take us to the eastern flank of Mount Wilkes. But *there* it did not take us, for, after traveling for about three hours, we found further progress in that direction barred by a great swamp. We turned to the left and at length came to what we thought was the edge of the morass; but the firm ground proved to be only a peninsula, and so, after advancing four miles, we had to retrace our steps. Goodness knows how much headway we made in all our wandering that day; perhaps, indeed, we did not advance one single foot.

The next day, however, about five o'clock in the afternoon, we reached the base of the mountain, where we camped. We had turtle for supper and could have had venison too. There was one consolation in the midst of all those evils which might befall us: there was no danger of our starving to death here in the Gardens of Paradise.

"Which same," remarked Louis Louisiana, "reminds me of the feller who shouted as he tumbled into the nest of yaller-jackets:

"'Thank God, they ain't hornets!'"

36
ANOTHER!

We resumed our journey about eight o'clock; this was the 12th of November. When we halted at six in the afternoon, we had made good but eight or ten miles. And that, considering the difficulties with which we had had to contend, was regarded as a very good advance. The mountain-side was gashed by ravines and gorges, the bottoms of them strewn with boulders, rock fragments and masses of all shapes and sizes. Countless streams came foaming and cascading down from the snow-fields high above us. Wherever a. root could get a hold—and that was everywhere except upon the absolutely naked surface of the rock—trees were growing, forming in some places an almost impenetrable tangle. And through all this we had to make our way, for things were even worse higher up, while below stretched impassable swamp.

The day following things were no better; if anything, they were worse. By mid-afternoon, however, we were well around on the northeastern side, and we now ascended to a height of a thousand feet or so to see what lay before us. Our reconnaissance was not a particularly gratifying one. A haze drew its veil over distant objects, whilst the expanse of country over which the eyes could range was in no essential feature different from that which lay behind us. I may mention, though, that glimpses were had of a fair-sized stream, the course of which seemed to be a particularly erratic one, and that the swamp which had given us so much trouble evidently ended hereabouts.

Our camp that night was at the base of Mount Wilkes, and here was seen the shadow of the first of those evils which a malign destiny was to loose upon us—though at the time we did not know that a shadow had fallen.

We noticed that Watson had an unnatural look; especially was the expression in his eyes a strange one. On our asking him if anything was wrong, he made light of it, saying that he did feel "kind of queer in the head"—how queer we all were to learn, soon and to our sorrow—but that he would be all right in the morning.

But in the morning Watson was not all right. He declared that he was, however, and so we started, but it was not without grave misgivings. We set out at seven o'clock. About nine our march came to an abrupt end. Then it was that Watson suddenly stopped, sank upon a log, his hands pressed to his temples and said he guessed he was sick, after all. The attack was as swift as mysterious. A few minutes, and a strong man lay as helpless as a babe. Nothing in our medicine-kit gave him the slightest relief. We could do nothing but stand there and watch the man suffer.

"It's my head," said Watson. "It's as though augers were boring into my brain."

Shortly after midday the victim became comatose. This we thought the precursor of death. For forty-eight hours he lay, save for his feeble breathing, like a dead man—then suddenly opened his eyes and quietly asked what time it was! In six or eight hours he was almost wholly himself again.

Great was our joy at this miraculous recovery of poor Watson, but, alas, that joy was soon damped. It suddenly became patent that this insidious and most mysterious malady (it certainly was not a fever) had laid its fell hand upon another victim. This was Louis Louisiana. And, just as he was recovering, it seized me, and then came Frontenac's turn. Thus a whole week was lost, and there is no necessity for me to dwell upon what a serious thing for the success of the expedition that loss might prove to be. Also, the possibility must not be blinked that it might bowl us over again. And suppose all of us were seized at the same time and just

suppose that a bear-man were to come waddling into the scene—
well, it would be *bon soir et bonne nuit* then with a vengeance!

It was on the 22nd that we got under way once more. In the
afternoon we crossed two trails of the bear-people; but we did not
linger at those points. We had no desire whatsoever to follow those
trails, to see where or to what they led. *That* mystery had been
solved; our purpose now was to clear up the mystery of that race
of real men, white men, men like ourselves.

It was about half past four when we reached that stream which
I mentioned some pages back. Fifteen or twenty minutes afterwards, we discovered the canoe, its bow drawn far up on the sandy
shore. Trees overhung the water, out for a distance of fifteen or
twenty feet, their branches, which bent down until they touched
the surface itself, forming an almost impenetrable screen of foliage before the spot.

"Look!" whispered Louis. "See them tracks in the sand! Another
of them grizzlies—maybe more!"

That last word had scarcely left Nunatak's lips when a bear-
man leaped out from behind a tree-trunk and, with a blow of his
club, smashed Watson's head like an eggshell.

37
MALIGN FATE

The whole thing must have happened in two seconds. Back went the club for another blow as the bear-man sprang at Frontenac. We fired, the three of us, almost simultaneously, and down the great brute went on his face, Frontenac springing aside to avoid the pitching body.

But he was not dead, this fearful assailant. Up he rose, still clutching that terrible club; but he swayed upon his feet, and the eyes that glared upon us had a wild and glassy look. Bang! and the bear-man fell dead, a bullet from Nunatak's rifle through his brain.

"I wonder," the musher exclaimed, glaring about a little wildly, "if the brute was alone."

"Alone," said Frontenac. "There are no tracks there in the sand but his."

We carried the body of Watson to a spot deep in the forest, where we dug a grave, loosening the earth with our hatchet and our knives and scooping it out with our hands. And there we buried our poor comrade, and at last we came back.

As for the body of the bear-man, we rolled that down the bank and into the river.

It was getting late, but we had no desire to camp at or near that cursed spot. So we got into the canoe—there were two paddles in it—shoved it through the wall of foliage and were on our way down the stream.

But we did not go far. A half hour or so, and we put our craft into a spot where she lay completely hidden by the leaves, and there we passed the night, each man taking the watch for three hours.

At eight o'clock the next morning, the 23rd, we shoved out into the stream and resumed our journey.

The river was very sinuous here, the current rather sluggish.

I transcribe the following from my journal, *verbatim et literatim*:

"Nov. 23d.—Horrible discovery this afternoon, though we had speculated anent the possibility of this very thing. A little after 11 a.m. came to a large village of bear-people. Remained hidden, however, and watched. Not fear, for we believe a few bullets would tame these creatures, but Frontenac was adverse to spilling of blood. Almost as loath to kill one of these brutes as he would be to shoot a human being. About 2 p. m. three large canoes arrived, from down the stream. Much excitement in village and great celebration. We now saw a horrible sight—three human bodies were taken out of the canoes, one that of a woman and everyone *headless*. Wish I had not seen what followed—the cooking, the carving and the feasting. Evidently these creatures regard human flesh as the greatest of delicacies. Certain features of the reception accorded the canoe party—it was well armed with bows and arrows—lead us to believe that the expedition had been one of great hazard. But—where did they get those victims?

"Believe we got some remarkable photos with telescope-camera. We lay low until all was quiet in village, then got into canoe and passed down unperceived. Writing this at 11:30 p.m. Place in shadow, but sky a deep blue and mountains on other side; grand in sunlight.

"Frontenac has just voiced a curious thought: do these bear-people *hibernate* during the long Antarctic night?

"Nov. 24th.—I began to wonder if a malign fate has not loosed bane-hounds upon our trail. At 9 a.m. halted to get some sleep, for had had none for over 24 hours. Louis felt queer in head again. We feared another attack of *gimletitis*—as he has dubbed that fearful malady. And of a truth the pain could scarcely be more excruciating if fiends were driving a hundred gimlets into the brain. And sure enough it bowled him over. As I write this, at 10 p.m., he lies like a dead man. What can this fearful seizure be? Is it caused by something in food, the water, the bite of some insect or some noxious exhalation from the warm earth? We have no means of knowing, but we do know that things are beginning to look pretty bad for us.

"This afternoon Frontenac shot a deer—a lovely little creature, its skin snow-white and beautifully ocellated, like the tail of a peacock or wings of an argus-pheasant. Thank Heaven, hunger is not one of the evils that beset us here!

"Nov. 25th, 9 p.m.—Louis still like a dead man. Fear it has me now.

"Nov. 28th.—It stretched me out. And now Frontenac is down. This is horrible. We have been out from camp twenty days now, and on the 15th of December Addison and Hansen are to start for Summer Haven. I wonder—but what is the use of wondering?

"Nov. 29th.—This afternoon Frontenac opened his eyes. Is himself again now, though in low spirits over the way things have turned out. It is indeed a bitter disappointment. Our bolt is shot. This is our farthest. Somewhere before us—we wonder how near, how far—is the mystery of *Ah-cone-cawn-ga*, as we call it. But we dare not risk it. Men cannot fight this thing which has brought our purpose to such wreck. Our outlook as it is dark enough truly. We have but two weeks in which to get back to camp—and the journey out has taken three! To advance were madness. Can we make it back in time, or are we doomed to remain in this awful place for years—for the rest of our lives? God knows. But, if the latter, our lives may not be at all like Methuselah's.

"Yes, bitter is our disappointment, whilst we shudder to think of the possibilities that are closing in upon us.

"I have said that this is our farthest, but this is not strictly correct. A mile or so distant, rises a great rock, perhaps 700 or 800 feet in height. In the morning we are going to proceed to this rock and from its summit look out over that region which the Parcae have forbidden us to enter. Even this delay worries me, for every single hour is precious now.

"Nov. 30th.—Another day of horror. Even Frontenac, the man of iron, is shaken.

"We proceeded to the great rock and up to its summit—a rounded mass of naked granite. Weather glorious. Air very clear—clearest we have ever seen it in this valley. Country very hilly and much broken. Mountains drew in until the valley was very narrow. The region up there had a strangely convulsed appearance—the mountains presenting an aspect gloomy, wild and savage, and finally losing themselves in dense vapor. There was something very strange about that vapor—something uncanny. Could make nothing of this most amazing phenomenon, though we studied it carefully through our powerful glasses. It rose in great billows, which swelled out and *burst* and descended in long curving lines like the spray of fountains. Long arms, twisting, swaying, would start out from it and vanished with the suddenness of auroral fires. And from the heart of it shot and leaped and quivered a greenish, a ghostly, a fearful radiance.

"''Tis awful!' cried Nunatak. 'Great Powers, what *can* it be?'

"Frontenac groaned.

"'So near!' he said. 'So near to that—and we have to go back!

"'Unless,' he added, glancing at us wistfully, 'we'd care to cast in our lot with the Antarcticans—for I have no doubt we could reach their country—until other explorers come.'

"It didn't take Nunatak and me long to annihilate that suggestion!

"Frontenac left a record of our visit, and then, after a last, long look towards that mysterious northeast, we turned and started back. The rock we called Rock Disappointment.

"The canoe was abandoned. Course of river so erratic that we could make better time on foot. It was along about 3 o'clock that it happened. Nunatak was leading. Reached up to move aside a branch and the next instant staggered back with an awful cry, as though he had been stabbed. About his left wrist was wound a serpent, a vivid green and with red spots upon it, its fangs buried cheep in the flesh. Nunatak whipped out his knife and slashed it across that coiled horror, badly cutting his knuckles and wrist. I can't set down what followed. Poor Louis! Well, in a half hour it was over. We could not stay there by the grave, so pushed on to

this spot, a distance of three miles or so. What malevolent thing is
this that dogs our steps? I am beginning to think of viewless
entities, spectral shapes—there, there, I mustn't let my mind go
like that! If I do, we—at any rate, I—shall never get back at all!"

But we did get back. A different route was chosen, one passing
on the other side of Mount Wilkes, and it was well for us that we
steered such a course. Had the return been made on our outbound
trail, we could never have made it in time—if we had made it at all!
To our surprise, not a single bear-man was seen, which means that
not a single ursine aborigine, to use a phrase of Frontenac's, saw
us. If one had, we should have known it soon enough—our first
warning perhaps an arrow between the ribs. Gimletitis met us,
however, and stretched us out, one after the other, and for a time I
abandoned hope. But even that fell enemy could not make it
disaster. I shudder, though, to think how near he came to doing
so. For it was on the 15th itself, at four o'clock in the afternoon,
that we reached camp. This was, of course, the day that Addison
and Hansen were to set out on the long journey to Summer Haven;
but, hurrah! they were still there! They had no intention, the loyal
fellows, of disobeying the orders of their chief; but—Frontenac had
not mentioned any hour, and they were not going to start until
11:59!

We were surprised to learn that they had not seen even the
ghost of a bear-man.

"And the dogs," said Addison, "had some glorious concerts, too.
Funny the grizzlies didn't pay us a visit."

For two days we remained there, Frontenac and I doing nothing
but rest—in other words, doing nothing but nothing.

"I wonder," I said, "if that infernal gimletitis will bowl us over
any more."

"I expect it will," returned Frontenac, "but that the severity—a
feeble word that—of the attacks will be found to diminish swiftly
and that the attacks themselves will ere long cease."

And so it proved.

It was on the 18th that we started, in the early morning. As we
were about to enter the fog, we stopped and for a space stood

looking out over the Gardens of Paradise. A solemn moment, that. Gladness was ours and sadness too. That weird land; our poor comrades, Watson and Louis; the terrible quasi-human creatures whose home it was; those headless forms we had seen lifted out of the canoes; that swelling, bursting vapor and its greenish, ghostly, fearful radiance—but I cannot set them down, those thoughts that came thronging into my mind, those feelings that gripped my heart.

We turned, started the dogs, and in a few moments everything was hidden by the fog.

It was on the 28th of January, at half-past three in the afternoon, when we reached Summer Haven. Never can any feature, even the slightest, of that scene which followed lose its vividness in my memory—that scene before the hut when Frontenac undid the lashings on his sled, threw off the canvas covering, and they saw Sleeping Beauty lying there in the block of ice.

"Poor little," said Archimedes Bukink; "oh, the poor little kid!"

He made no attempt to hide the tears that dimmed his eyes. His is a kind soul, is Bukink's.

The next day the *Multnomah* was fighting her way northward through the pack. We arrived at Seattle on the 15th of May.

38
HE WAKES THE SLEEPER

That very day Frontenac sent a telegram to his sister, Mrs. Charlotte Marshall, who lived down in Portland, urgently requesting that she come up and come prepared to stay for some weeks at least.

"I must have someone here," said he, "to look after this poor Sleeping Beauty, and Charlotte is the one woman in the world. Ever meet Charlotte, Bond?"

I never had.

"You'll fall in love with Charlotte," said Frontenac. "Everybody does. She's a dear, a brick—I suppose, what with these days of unequal rights, I ought to say a brickette. Ten years older than I am, but I'll swear she looks five years younger, and I hardly think that I greatly resemble old Rip Van Winkle. Yes, I won't wake Sleeping Beauty until Charlotte comes—if she doesn't come for ten years!"

But Mrs. Marshall came, and, as will be seen in a moment, it was, indeed, a most fortunate thing that she did. If she had not—well, I shudder every time I think of it. It chanced, however, that she was out of town at the time, so it was not until the 18th that Frontenac received an answer to his wire:

"Will arrive 19th," it read, "5:45 train."

At 5:30 the next day, Frontenac swung his car to the curb before the station, and we descended to await the arrival of the train from Portland, due in fifteen minutes and, wonderful to relate, on time.

Frontenac had said I would fall in love with his sister; I did—thanked God she was to be there at the awakening of the sleeper.

226

"Darwin, Darwin," she cried as she clung to him and kissed him, "you foolish boy to go down to South Poles and awful places, and before we could come back even to say good-bye! You must never, never go on such an awful expeditions again!"

Frontenac said 'twas very unlikely that he ever should.

"And," said she as we were going up to the auto, "what is this weird story about a girl in ice?"

In a few words he told her. She exclaimed, stopped and looked at him in sheer amazement.

"Then it *is* true?"

"Yes, it is true. I wish we could have kept it a secret, though— from the public, I mean."

"And—and you are going to *awake* her?"

"Yes, I hope to awake her."

"My Heaven! But she must be—surely, Darwin, the girl is dead! There in solid ice!"

He explained, succinctly but clearly.

"But," said his sister, "how can she breathe?"

"Of course, she is *not* breathing."

"I don't mean that. I mean if you *awake* her. In ice! Her lungs must be full of ice, too."

"Oh, no, Charlotte. She was not immersed in water but was covered with snow, and how could snowflakes have got into her lungs?"

"Oh!" said she. "It is all so strange, so awful, so wonderful—I can't begin to understand it."

Immediately on our arrival at Frontenac's house, Mrs. Marshall exclaimed, in low and awe-struck tones:

"Where is she? Let me see her, Darwin."

So we went to the freezing-room, and she saw her.

"Oh, the poor, poor darling!"

For some moments she stood there, then burst into tears and left the chamber—a place as awful, she said, as a tomb.

That very night it was, about two o'clock, that it occurred—one of the most mysterious things in all this strange and weird business: an attempt was made to steal Sleeping Beauty!

It seems certain that the ghouls would have succeeded, too, had it not been for Mrs. Marshall. She found herself—most fortunately, as it proved—a victim to a terrible insomnia, and, as she lay thinking and wondering, it seemed that a low, inexplicable sound suddenly mingled with the sighing of the wind in the trees. Yes, there it was again—a sound low, metallic, mysterious! She arose and (leaving the room dark) stole to the window and looked out.

The night was cloudy, and there was no moon, but it was not so dark as to conceal those figures—there were four—at the entrance to the freezing-chamber. Even as her eyes fell upon them, they vanished, and she knew that they had forced the door and entered. Instantly she gave the alarm—whereupon, of course, the thieves dashed for their automobile (waiting out in the road) and made their escape. Who they were, what purpose lay behind this ghoulish business, that has remained an utter mystery—a mystery, I fancy, which even Mr. Sherlock Holmes himself would say is "really unique, Watson, from some points of view."

A guard was at once posted, armed with a repeating rifle—none other than that weapon which Frontenac had carried in the Gardens of Paradise.

"And guarded the place is going to be," Darwin told me, the next day, "until I awake her. But that won't be long—only this day and to night."

"You are going to awake her tomorrow?"

"Tomorrow, Bond. And I hope my old *tillicum* (partner) will come over."

"I shall be here—most certainly I shall come. What time?"

"Be here at nine. Only two others are to see it—Charlotte and my old friend, Dr, Hollister. It was to him, you know, that the secret was to pass in case I failed to return from the forests of Paradise. No, *three* others—a nurse, too. Yes, a nurse ought to be present. And this time tomorrow, Bond? I wonder—"

I made no response. For a long time there was silence.

The next morning I arrived right on the stroke of nine.

How can I describe what followed? I cannot do so; I can only *tell* it.

A few minutes after my arrival, Dr. Hollister came, and with him the nurse. We at once went out to the room wherein lay the sleeper—Frontenac, his sister, Dr. Hollister, the nurse, Miss Brewster, and myself. The temperature of the chamber we found above the freezing-point. Already the ice which incased Sleeping Beauty was melting. Frontenac began chipping it away, in which occupation he was ere long joined by Dr. Hollister, It was not a great time, therefore, before the girl lay a dripping figure before us—her hair, however, still ice-incased.

Her nostrils were now rubbed with that bright-purple liquid, so unpleasantly oily in appearance; then her face, neck and bosom. The temperature of the room was rising steadily, steadily but very slowly; at last, the thermometer reached 98°, and then it rose no more. Then it was that Frontenac injected the antidote— that bright-purple stuff—into the neck. Oh, that wait which followed! Twenty minutes, thirty minutes—forty! Sleeping Beauty still lay rigid, corpse-like.

Dr. Hollister had drawn a chair to her side, and there he sat waiting, his stethoscope to her bosom—that bosom as still as marble.

"The change—the change at last! Her eyes! *Look at her eyes!*"

And her cheeks! Surely—yes, into the cheeks of the sleeper a faint color was creeping.

Frontenac placed his hands to her sides and began a gentle compression—in imitation of the expiratory and inspiratory movements of breathing.

"Her heart!"

It was Dr. Hollister who spoke.

"It beats?" Frontenac cried.

"It beats! The pulsation weak—but—stronger—stronger!"

Frontenac's hands ceased to perform those respiratory movements.

Look!

The girl's breast slowly rose, fell and rose again!

She stirred, sighed, closed her eyes. The pupils were contracting; the eyes were blue. From time to time she opened them, to close them quickly as though the light were painful.

Then suddenly she turned her head, raised her look to Frontenac's face *and spoke!*

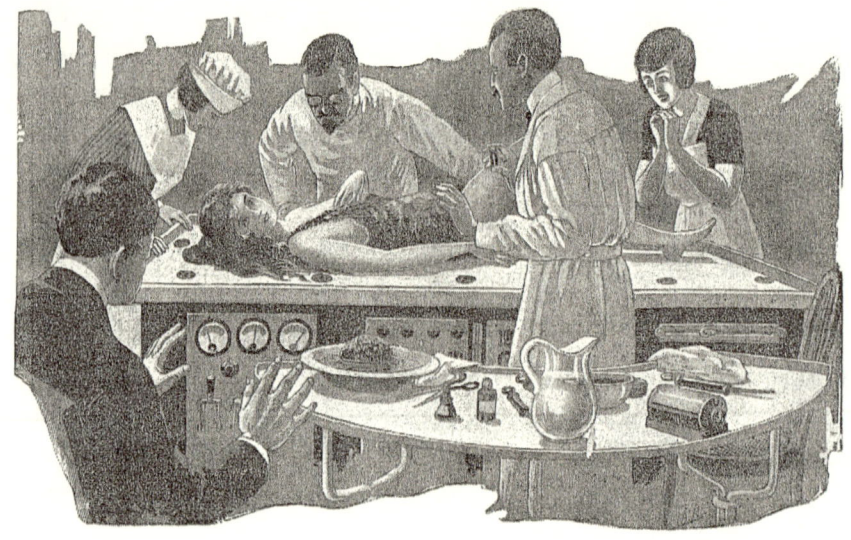

Three weeks have elapsed since then—since Frontenac awoke the sleeper. For four or five days, Sleeping Beauty was a very sick girl. The change that occurred at the expiration of that time, however, was a most remarkable one: a day or two, and she had wholly recovered.

The thing that seemed to astonish her the most, and which was a poignant distress to her, was that no one could understand a single syllable that she uttered. How often the poor girl has broken off and burst into a flood of tears! Only one thing have we learned, and that is her name—Zandara, which I think a very beautiful one. For her part, she soon knew the names of all about her and the names of many objects. And the way she says Darwin Frontenac! It is, as his sister declares, simply adorable. Zandara's acquisition of English promises to be a most rapid one; before so very long, therefore, we shall know what occurred down at the mouth of that cavern unnumbered centuries ago.

What the poor girl thinks has happened, that, of course, no one knows. One thing only is certain: that no inkling of the wonderful, the awful truth has ever entered her mind.

I have often wondered what the effect upon her will be when at last she learns, as learn she must; and I wish that that time was here, and I dread to see it come.

A few days since, Frontenac showed Zandara some of the photographs that we took down there—none of those, however, in which there is snow or ice, anything to tell her of the fearful change which has taken place in the Antarctic.

She was delightfully excited when shown the bear-men. It is clear that she knew of those strange beings.

On beholding the harpy and the door, Zandara manifested extreme agitation, and, when she turned her questioning eyes up to Frontenac's face I saw in them a look of sheer horror.

In time we have every reason to believe, light will be thrown upon *that* mystery; perhaps, indeed, the darkness which now involves everything there will be wholly dissipated. But when she saw a photograph showing one of those heads in the pillars of sinter-glass—then a most astonishing thing happened: Sleeping Beauty burst into rippling, merry laughter!

Why did she do so strange a thing?

But patience—time. Time will give us the answer—the answer to that question and to questions more interesting.

IN AMUNDSEN'S TENT

IN AMUNDSEN'S TENT

"Inside the tent, in a little bag, I left a letter, addressed to H. M. the King, giving information of what he (sic) had accomplished. . . . Besides this letter, I wrote a short epistle to Captain Scott, who, I assumed, would be the first to find the tent."

Captain Amundsen: *The South Pole*

"We have just arrived at this tent, 2 miles from our camp, therefore about 1½ miles from the pole. In the tent we find a record of five Norwegians having been here, as follows:

Roald Amundsen
Olav Olavson Bjaaland
Hilmer Hanssen
Sverre H. Hassel
Oscar Wisting
16 Dec. 1911.

"Left a note to say I had visited the tent with companions."

Captain Scott: his last journal

"Travelers," says Richard A. Proctor, "are sometimes said to tell marvelous stories; but it is a noteworthy fact that, in nine cases out of ten, the marvelous stories of travelers have been confirmed."

Certainly no traveler ever set down a more marvelous story than that of Robert Drumgold. This record I am at last giving to the world, with my humble apologies to the spirit of the hapless explorer for withholding it so long. But the truth is that Eastman, Dahlstrom and I thought it the work of a mind deranged; little wonder, forsooth, if his mind had given way, what with the fearful sufferings which he had gone through and the horror of that fate which was closing in upon him.

What was it, that *thing* (if thing it was) which came to him, the sole survivor of the party which had reached the Southern Pole, thrust itself into the tent and, issuing, left but the severed head of Drumgold there?

Our explanation at the time, and until recently, was that Drumgold had been set upon by his dogs and devoured. Why, though, the flesh had not been stripped from the head was to us an utter mystery. But that was only one of the many things that were utter mysteries.

But now we know—or feel certain—that this explanation was as far from the truth as that desolate, ice-mantled spot where he met his end is from the smiling, flower-spangled regions of the tropics.

Yes, we thought that the mind of poor Robert Drumgold had given way, that the horror in Amundsen's tent and that thing which came to Drumgold there in his own—we thought all was madness only. Hence our suppression of this part of the Drumgold manuscript. We feared that the publication of so extraordinary a record might cast a cloud of doubt upon the real achievements of the Sutherland expedition.

But of late our ideas and beliefs have undergone a change that is nothing less than a metamorphosis. This metamorphosis, it is scarcely necessary to say, was due to the startling discoveries made in the region of the Southern Pole by the late Captain Stanley Livingstone, as confirmed and extended by the expedition conducted by

Darwin Frontenac. Captain Livingstone, we now learn, kept his real discovery, what with the doubts and derision which met him on his return to the world, a secret from every living soul but two—Darwin Frontenac and Bond McQuestion. It is but now, on the return of Frontenac, that we learn how truly wonderful and amazing were those discoveries made by the ill-starred captain. And yet, despite the success of the Frontenac expedition, it must be admitted that the mystery down there in the Antarctic is enhanced rather than dissipated. Darwin Frontenac and his companions saw much; but we know that there are things and beings down there that they did not see. The Antarctic—or, rather, part of it—has thus suddenly become the most interesting and certainly the most fearful area on this globe of ours.

So another marvelous story told—or, rather, only partly told—by a traveler has been confirmed. And here are Eastman and I preparing to go once more to the Antarctic to confirm, as we hope, another story—one eery and fearful as any ever conceived by any romanticist.

And to think that it was ourselves, Eastman, Dahlstrom and I, who made the discovery! Yes, it was we who entered the tent, found there the head of Robert Drumgold and the pages whereon he had scrawled his story of mystery and horror. To think that we stood there, in the very spot where it had been, and thought the story but as the baseless fabric of some madman's vision!

How vividly it all rises before me again—the white expanse, glaring, blinding in the untempered light of the Antarctic sun; the dogs straining in the harness, the cases on the sleds, long and black like coffins; our sudden halt as Eastman fetched up in his tracks, pointed and said, "Hello, what's that?"

A half-mile or so off to the left, some object broke the blinding white of the plains.

"*Nunatak*, I suppose," was my answer.

"Looks to me like a cairn or a tent," Dahlstrom said.

"How on earth," I queried, "could a tent have got down here in 87° 30' south? We are far from the route of either Amundsen or Scott."

"H'm," said Eastman, shoving his amber-colored glasses up onto his forehead that he might get a better look, "I wonder. Jupiter Ammon, Nels," he added, glancing at Dahlstrom, "I believe that you are right."

"It certainly," Dahlstrom nodded, "looks like a cairn or a tent to me. I don't think it's a *nunatak*."

"Well," said I, "it would not be difficult to put it to the proof."

"And that, my hearties," exclaimed Eastman, "is just what we'll do! We'll soon see what it is—whether it is a cairn, a tent, or only a *nunatak*."

The next moment we were in motion, heading straight for the mysterious object there in the midst of the eternal desolation of snow and ice.

"Look there!" Eastman, who was leading the way, suddenly shouted. "See that? It *is* a tent!"

A few moments, and I saw that it was indeed so. But who had pitched it there? What were we to find within it?

I could never describe those thoughts and feelings which were ours as we approached that spot. The snow lay piled about the tent to a depth of four feet or more. Near by, a splintered ski protruded from the surface—and that was all.

And the stillness! The air, at the moment, was without the slightest movement. No sounds but those made by our movements, and those of the dogs, and our own breathing, broke that awful silence of death.

"Poor devils!" said Eastman at last. "One thing, they certainly pitched their tent well."

The tent was supported by a single pole, set in the middle. To this pole three guy-lines were fastened, one of them as taut as the day its stake had been driven into the surface. But this was not all: a half-dozen lines, or more, were attached to the sides of the tent. There it had stood for we knew not how long, bidding defiance to the fierce winds of that terrible region.

Dahlstrom and I each got a spade and began to remove the snow. The entrance we found unfastened but completely blocked by a couple of provision-cases (empty) and a piece of canvas. "How on earth," I exclaimed "did those things get into that position?"

"The wind," said Dahlstrom. "And, if the entrance had not been blocked, there wouldn't have been any tent here now; the wind would have split and destroyed it long ago."

"H'm," mused Eastman. "The wind did it, Nels—blocked the place like that? I wonder."

The next moment we had cleared the entrance. I thrust my head through the opening. Strangely enough, very little snow had drifted in. The tent was dark green, a circumstance which rendered the light within somewhat weird and ghastly—or perhaps my imagination contributed not a little to that effect.

"What do you see, Bill?" asked Eastman. "What's inside?"

My answer was a cry, and the next instant I had sprung back from the entrance.

"What is it, Bill?" Eastman exclaimed. "Great heaven, what is it, man?"

"A head!" I told him.

"A head?"

"A human head!"

He and Dahlstrom stooped and peered in. "What is the meaning of this?"

Eastman cried. "A severed human head!"

Dahlstrom dashed a mittened hand across his eyes. "Are we dreaming?" he exclaimed.

"'Tis no dream, Nels," returned our leader. "I wish to heaven it was. A head! A human head!"

"Is there nothing more?" I asked.

"Nothing. No body, not even stripped bone—only that severed head. Could the dogs—"

"Yes?" queried Dahlstrom.

"Could the dogs have done this?"

"Dogs!" Dahlstrom said. "This is not the work of dogs."

We entered and stood looking down upon the grisly remnant of mortality.

"It wasn't dogs," said Dahlstrom.

"Not dogs?" Eastman queried. "What other explanation is there—except cannibalism?"

Cannibalism! A shudder went through my heart. I may as well say at once, however, that our discovery of a good supply of pemmican and biscuit on the sled, at that moment completely hidden by the snow, was to show us that that fearful explanation was not the true one. The dogs! That was it, that was the explanation—even though what the victim himself had set down told us a very different story. Yes, the explorer had been set upon by his dogs and devoured. But there were things that militated against that theory. Why had the animals left that head—in the frozen eyes (they were blue eyes) and upon the frozen features of which was a look of horror that sends a shudder through my very soul even now? Why, the head did not have even the mark of a single fang, though it appeared to have been *chewed* from the trunk. Dahlstrom, however, was of the opinion that it had been *hacked* off.

And there, in the man's story, in the story of Robert Drumgold, we found another mystery—a mystery as insoluble (if it was true) as the presence here of his severed head. There the story was, scrawled in lead-pencil across the pages of his journal. But what were we to make of a record—the concluding pages of it, that is—so strange and so dreadful?

But enough of this, of what we thought and of what we wondered. The journal itself lies before me, and I now proceed to set down the story of

Robert Drumgold in his own words. Not a word, not a comma shall be deleted, inserted or changed.

Let it begin with his entry for January the 3rd, at the end of which day the little party was only fifteen miles (geographical) from the Pole.

Here it is.

Jan. 3.—Lat. of our camp 89° 45′ 10″. Only fifteen miles more, and the Pole is ours—unless Amundsen or Scott has beaten us to it, or both. But it will be ours just the same, even though the glory of discovery is found to be another's. What shall we find there?

All are in fine spirits. Even the dogs seem to know that this is the consummation of some great achievement. And a thing that is a mystery to us is the interest they have shown this day in the region before us. Did we halt, there they were gazing and gazing straight south and sometimes sniffing and sniffing. What does it mean?

Yes, in fine spirits all—dogs as well as we three men. Everything is auspicious. The weather for the last three days has been simply glorious. Not once, in this time, has the temperature been below minus 5. As I write this, the thermometer shows one degree above. The blue of the sky is like that of which painters dream, and, in that blue, tower cloud formations, violet-tinged in the shadows, that are beautiful beyond all description. If it were possible to forget the fact that nothing stands between ourselves and a horrible death save the meager supply of food on the sleds, one could think he was in some fairyland— a glorious fairyland of white and blue and violet.

A fairyland? Why has that thought so often occurred to me? Why have I so often likened this desolate, terrible region to fairyland? Terrible? Yes, to human beings it is terrible—frightful beyond all words. But, though so unutterably terrible to men, it may not be so in reality. After all, are all things, even of this earth of ours, to say nothing of the universe, made for man—this being (a god-like spirit in the body of a quasi-ape) who, let in the midst of wonders, leers and slavers in madness and hate and wallows in the muck of a thousand lusts? May there not be other beings—yes, even on this very earth, of ours—more wonderful—yes, and more terrible too—than he?

Heaven knows, more than once, in this desolation of snow and ice, I have seemed to feel their presence in the air about us—nameless entities, disembodied, *watching* things.

Little wonder, forsooth, that I have again and again thought of these strange words of one of America's greatest scientists, Alexander Winchell:

"Nor is incorporated rational existence conditioned on warm blood nor on any temperature which does not change the forms of matter of which the organism may be composed. There may be intelligences corporealized after some concept not involving the processes of ingestion, assimilation and reproduction. Such bodies would not require daily food and warmth. They might be lost in the abysses of the ocean, or laid up on a stormy cliff through the tempests of an arctic winter, or plunged in a volcano for a hundred years, and yet retain consciousness and thought."

All this Winchell tells us is conceivable, and he adds:

"*Bodies are merely the load fitting of intelligence to particular modifications of universal matter and force.*"

And these entities, nameless things whose presence I seem to feel at times—are they benignant beings or things more fearful than even the madness of the human brain ever has fashioned?

But, then, I must stop this. If Sutherland or Travers were to read what I have set down here, they would think that I was losing my senses or would declare me already insane. And yet, as there is a heaven above us, it seems that I do actually believe that this frightful place knows the presence of beings other than ourselves and our dogs—things which we cannot see but which are watching us.

Enough of this.

Only fifteen miles from the Pole. Now for a sleep and on to our goal in the morning. Morning! There is no morning here, but day unending. The sun now rides as high at midnight as it does at midday. Of course, there is a change in altitude, but it is so slight as to be imperceptible without an instrument.

But the Pole! Tomorrow the Pole! What will we find there? Only an unbroken expanse of white, or—

Jan. 4.—The mystery and horror of this day—oh, how could I ever set that down? Sometimes, so fearful were those hours through which we have just passed, I even find myself wondering if it wasn't all only a dream. A dream! I would to heaven that it had been but a dream! As for the end—I must keep such thoughts out of my head.

Got under way at an early hour. Weather more wondrous than ever. Sky an azure that would have sent a painter into ecstasies. Cloud-formations indescribably beautiful and grand. The going, however, was pretty difficult. The place a great plain stretching away with a monotonous uniformity of surface as far as the eye could reach. A plain never trod by human foot before? At length, when our dead reckoning showed that we were drawing near to the Pole, we had the answer to that. Then it was that the keen eyes of Travers detected some object rising above the blinding white of the snow.

On the instant Sutherland had thrust his amber glasses up onto his forehead and had his binoculars to his eyes.

"Cairn!" he exclaimed, and his voice sounded hollow and very strange. "A cairn or a—*tent*. Boys, they have beaten us to the Pole!"

He handed the glasses to Travers and leaned, as though a sudden weariness had settled upon him, against the provision-cases on his sled.

"Forestalled!" said he. "Forestalled!"

I felt very sorry for our brave leader in those, his moments of terrible disappointment, but for the life of me I did not know what to say. And so I said nothing.

At that moment a cloud concealed the sun, and the place where we stood was suddenly involved in a gloom that was deep and awful. So sudden and pronounced, indeed, was the change that we gazed about us with curious and wondering looks. Far off to the right and to the left, the plain blazed white and blinding. Soon, however, the last gleam of sunshine had vanished from off it. I raised my look up to the heavens. Here and there edges of cloud were touched as though with the light of wrathful golden fire. Even then, however, that light was fading. A few minutes, and the last angry gleam of the sun had vanished. The gloom seemed to deepen about us every moment. A curious haze was concealing the blue expanse of the sky overhead. There was not the slightest movement in the gloomy and weird atmosphere. The silence was heavy, awful, the silence of the abode of utter desolation and of death.

"What on earth are we in for now?" said Travers.

Sutherland moved from his sled and stood gazing about into the eerie gloom.

"Queer change, this!" said he. "It would have delighted the heart of Doré."

"It means a blizzard, most likely," I observed. "Hadn't we better make camp before it strikes us? No telling what a blizzard may be like in this awful spot."

"Blizzard?" said Sutherland. "I don't think it means a blizzard, Bob. No telling, though. Mighty queer change, certainly. And how different the place looks now, in this strange gloom! It is surely weird and terrible—that is, it certainly looks weird and terrible."

He turned his look to Travers.

"Well, Bill," he asked, "what did you make of it?"

He waved a hand in the direction of that mysterious object the sight of which had so suddenly brought us to a halt. I say in the direction of the object, for the thing itself was no longer to be seen.

"I believe it is a tent," Travers told him.

"Well," said our leader, "we can soon find out what it is—cairn or tent, for one or the other it must certainly be."

The next instant the heavy, awful silence was broken by the sharp crack of his whip.

"Mush on, you poor brutes!" he cried. "On we go to see what is over there. Here we are at the South Pole. Let us see who has beaten us to it."

But the dogs didn't want to go on, which did not surprise me at all, because, for some time now, they had been showing signs of some strange, inexplicable uneasiness. What had got into the creatures, anyway? For a time we puzzled over it; then we *knew*, though the explanation was still an utter mystery to us. They were *afraid*. Afraid? An inadequate word, indeed. It was fear, stark, terrible, that had entered the poor brutes. But whence had come this inexplicable fear? That also we soon knew. The thing they feared, whatever it was, was in that very direction in which we were headed!

A cairn, a tent? What did this thing mean?

"What on earth is the matter with the critters?" exclaimed Travers. "Can it be that—"

"It's for us to find out what it means," said Sutherland. Again we got in motion. The place was still involved in that strange, weird gloom. The silence was still that awful silence of desolation and of death.

Slowly but steadily we moved forward, urging on the reluctant, fearful animals with our whips.

At last Sutherland, who was leading, cried out
that he saw it. He halted, peering forward into the
gloom, and we urged our teams up alongside his.

"It must be a tent," he said.

And a tent we found it to be—a small one supported by a single bamboo and well guyed in all
directions. Made of drab-colored gabardine. To the
top of the tent-pole another had been lashed. From
this, motionless in the still air, hung the remains of
a small Norwegian flag and, underneath it, a pennant with the word "Fram" upon it. Amundsen's tent!

What should we find inside it? And what was the
meaning of that—the strange way it bulged out on
one side?

The entrance was securely laced. The tent, it was
certain, had been here for a year, all through the long
Antarctic night; and yet, to our astonishment, but
little snow was piled up about it, and most of this
was drift. The explanation of this must, I suppose,
be that, before the air currents have reached the
Pole, almost all the snow has been deposited from
them.

For some minutes we just stood there, and many,
and some of them dreadful enough, were the
thoughts that came and went. Through the long Antarctic night! What strange things this tent could tell
us had it been vouchsafed the power of words! But
strange things it might tell us, nevertheless. For what
was that inside, making the tent bulge out in so unaccountable a manner? I moved forward to feel of it
there with my mittened hand, but, for some reason
that I cannot explain, of a sudden I drew back. At
that instant one of the dogs whined—the sound so
strange and the terror of the animal so unmistakable that I shuddered and felt a chill pass through
my heart. Others of the dogs began to whine in that

mysterious manner, and all shrank back cowering from the tent.

"What does it mean?" said Travers, his voice sunk almost to a whisper. "Look at them. It is as though they are imploring us to—keep away."

"To keep away," echoed Sutherland, his look leaving the dogs and fixing itself once more on the tent.

"Their senses," said Travers, "are keener than ours. They already know what we can't know until we see it."

"See it!" Sutherland explained. "I wonder. Boys, what are we going to see when we look into that tent? Poor fellows! They reached the Pole. But did they ever leave it? Are we going to find them in there dead?"

"Dead?" said Travers with a sudden start. "The dogs would never act that way if 'twas only a corpse inside. And, besides, if that theory was true, wouldn't the sleds be here to tell the story? Yet look around. The level uniformity of the place shows that no sled lies buried here."

"That is true," said our leader. "What *can* it mean? What *could* make that tent bulge out like that? Well, here is the mystery before us, and all we have to do is unlace the entrance and look inside to solve it."

He stepped to the entrance, followed by Travers and me, and began to unlace it. At that instant an icy current of air struck the place and the pennant above our heads flapped with a dull and ominous sound. One of the dogs, too, thrust his muzzle skyward, and a deep and long-drawn howl arose. And while the mournful, savage sound yet filled the air, a strange thing happened.

Through a sudden rent in that gloomy curtain of cloud, the sun sent a golden, awful light down upon the spot where we stood. It was but a shaft of light, only three or four hundred feet wide, though miles in length, and there we stood in the very middle of it, the plain on each side involved in that weird gloom, now denser and more eery than ever in contrast to that sword of golden fire which thus so suddenly had been flung down across the snow.

"Queer place this!" said Travers. "Just like a beam lying across a stage in a theater."

Travers' smile was a most apposite one, more so than he perhaps ever dreamed himself. That place was a stage, our light the wrathful fire of the Antarctic sun, ourselves the actors in a scene stranger than any ever beheld in the mimic world.

For some moments, so strange was it all, we stood there looking about us in wonder and perhaps each one of us in not a little secret awe.

"Queer place, all right!" said Sutherland. "But—"

He laughed a hollow, sardonic laugh. Up above, the pennant flapped and flapped again, the sound of it hollow and ghostly. Again rose the long-drawn, mournful, fiercely sad howl of the wolf-dog.

"But," added our leader, "we don't want to be imagining things, you know."

"Of course not," said Travers.

"Of course not," I echoed.

A little space, and the entrance was open and Sutherland had thrust head and shoulders through it.

I don't know how long it was that he stood there like that. Perhaps it was only a few seconds, but to Travers and me it seemed rather long.

"What is it?" Travers exclaimed at last. "What do you see?"

The answer was a scream—the horror of that sound I can never forget—and Sutherland came staggering back and, I believe, would have fallen had we not sprung and caught him.

"What is it?" cried Travers. "In God's name, Sutherland, what did you see?"

Sutherland beat the side of his head with his hand, and his look was wild and horrible.

"What is it?" I exclaimed. "What did you see in there?"

"I can't tell you—I can't! Oh, oh, I wish that I had never seen it! Don't look! Boys, don't look into that tent—unless you are prepared to welcome madness, or worse."

"What gibberish is this?" Travers demanded, gazing at our leader in astonishment. "Come, come, man! Buck up. Get a grip on yourself. Let's have an end to this nonsense. Why should the sight of a dead man, or dead men affect you in this mad fashion?"

"Dead men?" Sutherland laughed, the sound wild, maniacal.

"Dead men? If 'twas only that! Is this the South Pole? Is this the earth, or are we in a nightmare on some other planet?"

"For heaven's sake," cried Travers, "come out of it! What's got into you? Don't let your nerves go like this."

"A dead man?" queried our leader, peering into the face of Travers. "You think I saw a dead man? I wish it was only a dead man. Thank God, you two didn't look!"

On the instant Travers had turned.

"Well," said he, "I *am* going to look!"

But Sutherland cried out, screamed, sprang after him and tried to drag him back.

"It would mean horror and perhaps madness!" cried Sutherland. "Look at me. Do you want to be like me?"

"No!" Travers returned. "But I am going to see what is in that tent."

He struggled to break free, but Sutherland clung to him in a frenzy of madness.

"Help me, Bob!" Sutherland cried. "Hold him back, or we'll all go insane."

But I did not help him to hold Travers back, for, of course, it was my belief that Sutherland himself was insane. Nor did Sutherland hold Travers. With a sudden wrench, Travers was free. The next instant he had thrust head and shoulders through the entrance of the tent.

Sutherland groaned and watched him with eyes full of unutterable horror.

I moved toward the entrance, but Sutherland flung himself at me with such violence that I was sent over into the snow. I sprang to my feet full of anger and amazement.

"What the hell," I cried, "is the matter with you, anyway? Have you gone crazy?"

The answer was a groan, horrible beyond all words of man, but that sound did not come from Sutherland. I turned. Travers was staggering away from the entrance, a hand pressed over his face, sounds that I could never describe breaking from deep in his throat. Sutherland, as the man came staggering up to him, thrust forth an arm and touched Travers lightly on the shoulder. The effect was instantaneous and frightful. Travers sprang aside as though a serpent had struck at him, screamed and screamed yet again.

"There, there!" said Sutherland gently. "I told you not to do it. I tried to make you understand, but—but you thought that I was mad."

"It can't belong to this earth!" moaned Travers.

"No," said Sutherland. "That horror was never born on this planet of ours. And the inhabitants of earth, though they do not know it, can thank God Almighty for that."

"But it is *here!*" Travers exclaimed. "How did it come to this awful place? And where did it come from?"

"Well," consoled Sutherland, "it is dead—it must be dead."

"Dead? How do we know that it is dead? And don't forget this: it didn't come here alone!"

Sutherland started. At that moment the sunlight vanished, and everything was once more involved in gloom.

"What do you mean?" Sutherland asked. "Not alone? How do you know that it did not come alone?"

"Why, it is there *inside* the tent; but the entrance was laced—from the *outside!*"

"Fool, fool that I am!" cried Sutherland a little fiercely. "Why didn't I think of that? Not alone! Of course it was not alone!"

He gazed about into the gloom, and I knew the nameless fear and horror that chilled him to the very heart, for they chilled me to my very own.

Of a sudden arose again that mournful, savage howl of the wolf-dog. We three men started as though it was the voice of some ghoul from hell's most dreadful corner.

"Shut up, you brute!" gritted Travers. "Shut up, or I'll brain you!"

Whether it was Travers' threat or not, I do not know; but that howl sank, ceased almost on the instant. Again the silence of desolation and of death lay upon the spot. But above the tent the pennant stirred and rustled, the sound of it, I thought, like the slithering of some repulsive serpent.

"What did you see in there?" I asked them.

"Bob—Bob," said Sutherland, "don't ask us that."

"The thing itself," said I, turning, "can't be any worse than this mystery and nightmare of imagination."

But the two of them threw themselves before me and barred my way.

"No!" said Sutherland firmly. "You must not look into that tent, Bob. You must not see that—that—I don't know what to call it. Trust us; believe us, Bob! 'Tis for your sake that we say that you must not do it. We, Travers and I, can never be the same men again—the brains, the souls of us can never be what they were before we saw *that!*"

"Very well," I acquiesced. "I can't help saying, though, that the whole thing seems to me like the dream of a madman."

"That," said Sutherland, "is a small matter indeed. Insane? Believe that it is the dream of a madman. Believe that we are insane. Believe that you are insane yourself. Believe anything you like. Only *don't look!*"

"Very well," I told him. "I won't look. I give in. You two have made coward of me."

"A coward?" said Sutherland. "Don't talk nonsense, Bob. There are some things that a man should never know; there are some things that a man should never see; that horror there in Amundsen's tent is—*both!*"

"But you said that it is dead."

Travers groaned. Sutherland laughed a little wildly.

"Trust us," said the latter; "believe us, Bob. 'Tis for your sake, not for our own. For that is too late now. We have seen it, and you have not."

For some minutes we stood there by the tent, in that weird gloom, then turned to leave the cursed spot. I said that undoubtedly Amundsen had left some records inside, that possibly Scott had reached the Pole, and visited the tent, and that we ought to secure any such memories. Sutherland and Travers nodded, but each declared that he would not put his head through that entrance again for all the wealth of Ormus and of Ind—or words to that effect. We must, they said, get away from the awful place—get back to the world of men with our fearful message.

"You won't tell me what you saw?" I said, "and yet you want to get back so that you can tell it to the world."

"We aren't going to tell the world what we saw," answered Sutherland. "In the first place, we couldn't, and, in the second place, if we could, not a living soul would believe us. But we can warn people, for that thing in there did not come alone. Where is the other one—or the others?"

"Dead, too, let us hope!" I exclaimed.

"Amen!" said Sutherland. "But maybe, as Bill says, it isn't dead. Probably—"

Sutherland paused, and a wild, indescribable look came into his eyes.

"Maybe it—*can't die!*"

"Probably," said I nonchalantly, yet with secret disgust and with poignant sorrow.

What was the use? What good would it do to try to reason with a couple of madmen? Yes, we must get away from this spot, or they would have me insane, too. And the long road back? Could we ever make it now? And what *had* they seen? What unimaginable horror was there behind that thin wall of gabardine? Well, whatever it was, it was real. Of that I could not entertain the slightest doubt. Real? Real enough to wreck, virtually instantaneously, the strong brains of two strong men. But—were my poor companions really mad, after all?

"Or maybe," Sutherland was saying, "the other one, or the others, went back to Venus or Mars or Sirius or Algol, or hell itself, or wherever they came from, to get more of their kind. If that is so, heaven have pity on poor humanity! And, if it or they are still here on this earth, then sooner or later—it may be a dozen years, it may be a century—but sooner or later the world will know it, know it to its woe and to its horror. For they, if living, or if gone for others, will come again."

"I was thinking—" began Travers, his eyes fixed on the tent.

"Yes?" Sutherland queried.

"—that," Travers told him, "it might be a good plan to empty the rifle into that thing. Maybe it isn't dead; maybe it can't die—maybe it only *changes*. Probably it is just hibernating, so to speak."

"If so," I laughed, "it will probably hibernate till doomsday."

But neither one of my companions laughed.

"Or," said Travers, "it may be a demon, a ghost materialized. I can't say incarnated."

"A ghost materialized!" I exclaimed. "Well, may not every man or woman be just that? Heaven knows, many a one acts like a demon or a fiend incarnate."

"They may be," nodded Sutherland. "But that hypothesis doesn't help us any here."

"It may help things some," said Travers, starting toward his sled. A moment or two, and he had got out the rifle.

"I thought," said he, "that nothing could ever take me back to that entrance. But the hope that I may—"

Sutherland groaned.

"It isn't earthly. Bill," he said hoarsely. "It's a nightmare. I think we had better go now."

Travers was going—straight toward the tent.

"Come back, Bill!" groaned Sutherland. "Come back! Let us go while we can."

But Travers did not come back. Slowly he moved forward, rifle thrust out before him, finger on the trigger. He reached the tent, hesitated a moment, then thrust the rifle-barrel through. As fast as he could work trigger and lever, he emptied the weapon into the tent—into that horror inside it.

He whirled and came back as though in fear the tent was about to spew forth behind him all the legions of foulest hell.

What was that? The blood seemed to freeze in my veins and heart as there arose from out the tent a sound—a sound low and throbbing—a sound that no man ever had heard on this earth—one that I hope no man will ever hear again.

A panic, a madness seized upon us, upon men and dogs alike, and away we fled from that cursed place.

The sound ceased. But again we heard it. It was more fearful, more unearthly, soul-maddening, hellish than before.

"Look!" cried Sutherland. "Oh, my God, *look at that!*"

The tent was barely visible now. A moment or two, and the curtain of gloom would conceal it. At first I could not imagine what had made Sutherland cry out like that. Then I saw it, in that very moment before the gloom hid it from view. The tent was moving! It swayed, jerked like some shapeless monster in the throes of death, like some nameless thing seen in the horror of nightmare or limned on the brain of utter madness itself.

And that is what happened there; that is what we saw. I have set it down at some length and to the best of my ability under the truly awful circumstances in which I am placed. In these hastily crawled pages is recorded an experience that, I believe, is not surpassed by the wildest to be found in the pages of the most imaginative romanticist. Whether the record is destined ever to reach the world, ever to be scanned by the eye of another—only the future can answer that.

I will try to hope for the best. I cannot blink the fact, however, that things are pretty bad for us. It is not only this sinister, nameless mystery from which we are fleeing—though heaven knows that is horrible enough—but it is the *minds* of my companions. And, added to that, is the fear for my own. But there, I must get myself in hand. After all, as Sutherland said, I didn't see it. I must not give way. We must somehow get our story to the world, though we may have for our reward only the mockery of the world's unbelief, its scoffing—the world, against which is now moving, gathering, a menace more dreadful than any that ever moved in the fevered brain of any prophet of woe and blood and disaster.

We are a dozen miles or so from the Pole now. In that mad dash away from that tent of horror, we lost our bearings and for a time, I fear, went panicky. The strange, eery gloom denser than ever. Then came a fall of fine snow-crystals, which rendered things worse than ever. Just when about to give up in despair, chanced upon one of our beacons. This gave us our bearings, and we pressed on to this spot.

Travers has just thrust his head into the tent to tell us that he is sure he saw something moving off in the gloom. Something moving! This must be looked into.

(If Robert Drumgold could only have left as full a record of those days which followed as he had of that fearful 4th of January! No man can ever know what the three explorers went through in

their struggle to escape that doom from which there was no escape—
a doom the mystery and horror of which perhaps surpass in grue-
someness what the most dreadful Gothic imagination ever conceived in its utterest abandonment to delirium and madness.)

Jan. 5.—Travers had seen something, for we, the
three of us, saw it again today. Was it that horror,
that thing not of this earth, which they saw in
Amundsen's tent? We don't know what it is. All we
know is that it is something that moves. God have
pity on us all—and on every man and woman and
child on this earth of ours if this thing is what we
fear!

6th.—Made 25 mi. today—20 yesterday. Did not see
it today. *But heard it.* Seemed near—once, in fact,
as though right over our heads. But that must have
been imagination. Effect on dogs most terrible. Poor
brutes! It is as horrible to them as it is to us. Sometimes I think even more. Why is it following us?

7th.—Two of the dogs gone this morning. One or
another of us on guard all "night." Nothing seen, not
a sound heard, yet the animals have vanished. Did
they desert us? We say that is what happened but
each man of us knows that none of us believes it.
Made 18 mi. Fear that Travers is going mad.

8th.—Travers gone! He took the watch last night at
12, relieving Sutherland. That was the last seen of
Travers—the last that we shall ever see. No tracks—
not a sign in the snow. Travers, poor Travers, gone!
Who will be the next?

Jan. 9—*Saw it again!* Why does it let us see it like
this—sometimes? Is it that horror in Amundsen's
tent? Sutherland declares that it is not—that it is

something even more hellish. But then S. is mad now—mad—mad—mad. If I wasn't sane, I could think that it all was only imagination. *But I saw it!*

Jan. 11—Think it is the 11th but not sure. I can no longer be sure of anything—save that I am alone and that it is watching me. Don't know how I know, for I cannot see it. But I do know—it is watching me. It is always watching. And sometime it will come and get me—as it got Travers and Sutherland and half of the dogs.

Yes, today must be the 11th. For it was yester-day—surely it was only yesterday—that it took Sutherland. I didn't see it take him, for a fog had come up, and Sutherland—he would go on in the fog—was so slow in following that the vapor hid him from view. At last when he didn't come, I went back. But S. was gone—man, dogs, sled, everything was gone. Poor Sutherland! But then he was mad. Prob-ably that was why it took him. Has it spared me be-cause I am yet sane? S. had the rifle. Always he clung to that rifle—as though a bullet could save him from what we saw! My only weapon is an ax. But what good is an ax?

Jan. 13th.—Maybe it is the 14th. I don't know. What does it matter? Saw it *three* times today. Each time it was closer. Dogs still whining about tent. There—that horrible hellish sound again. Dogs still now. That sound again. But I dare not look out. The ax.

Hours later. Can't write any more.

Silence. Voices—I seem to hear voices. But that sound again.

Coming nearer. At entrance now—now—

DROME

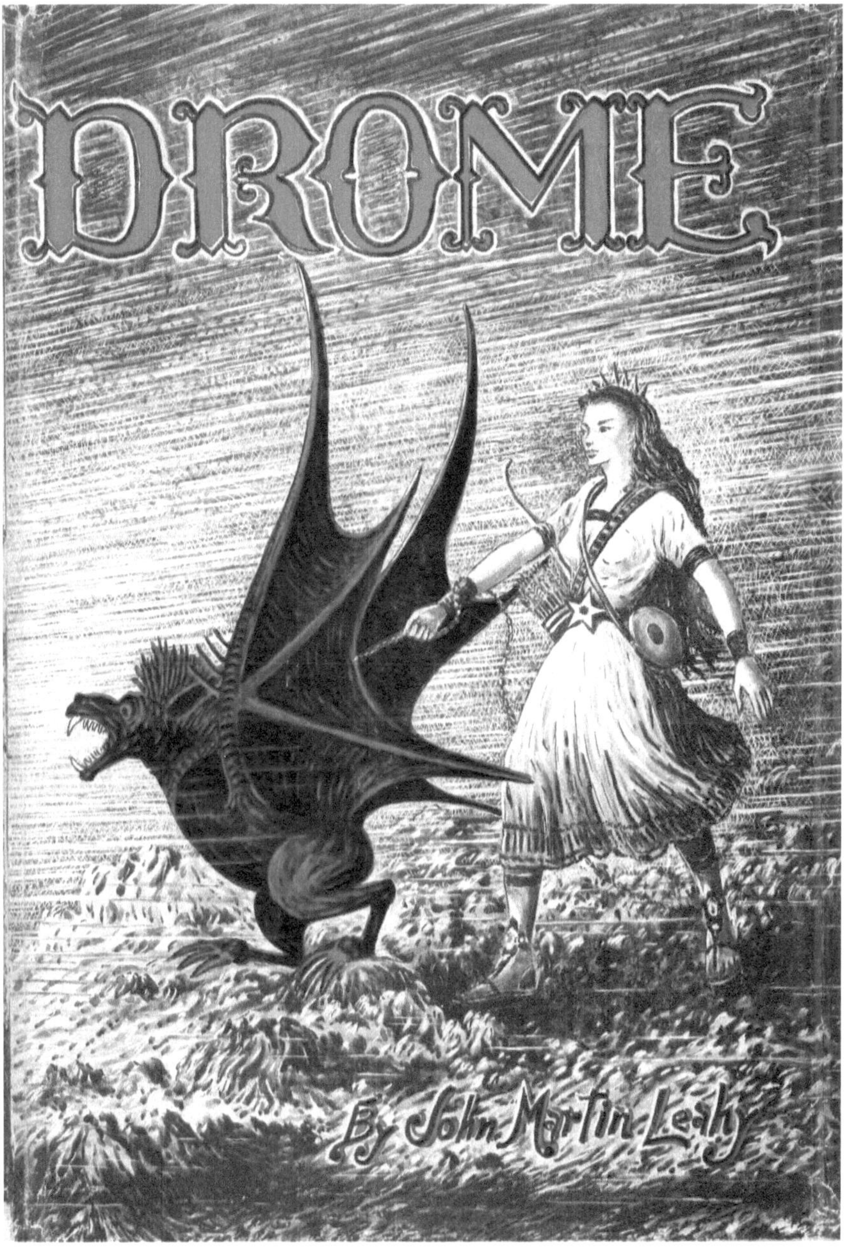
DROME
By John Martin Leahy

"For there is one descent into this region."—
Josephus: *Discourse to the Greeks Concerning Hades.*

PREFACE
BY DARWIN FRONTENAC

"But please to remember that although we can prove to our own satisfaction that some things really exist, we can not prove that any imaginable thing outside our experience can not possibly exist. Imagine the wildest impossibility you can think of; you will not induce a modern man of science to admit the impossibility of it as an absolute."—F. Marion Crawford: *Whosoever Shall Offend.*

On my return from the Antarctic, it was with surprise and grief that I learned of the very strange and wholly inexplicable disappearance of Milton Rhodes and William Carter. The special work of Rhodes was in a department of science very different from that to which my own pertains; but we were much interested in each other's investigations and problems, and, indeed, we even conducted some experiments together.

It will be quite patent, then, that, as the *Multnomah* made her way northward, I was looking forward with much pleasure anticipated to the meeting with my friend—with all that I had to tell him of our adventures and discoveries in the region of the Southern Pole, picturing to myself the astonishment that would most certainly be his on seeing some of the things brought from that mysterious region; above all, imagining his reaction when we would behold our poor Sleeping Beauty in her crystal coffin, in which she had lain (neither living nor dead, as I believe; or as my friend Bond

McQuestion has it, in a living death) from some awful day in that period men call the Pliocene.

And then to come back and find that Milton Rhodes had disappeared, and with him William Carter!

They had vanished as suddenly and mysteriously as though a secret departure had been made for the moon or Mars or Venus.

It was very little, I was surprised to learn, that any one could tell me. And that very little presented some very singular features indeed. This was certain: Milton Rhodes had planned to begin in a very few days a series of experiments (the exact nature of which was unknown) that would claim his close and undivided attention for weeks, possibly months, experiments that would keep him imprisoned, so to speak, in his laboratory. But he had not even begun those experiments; he had vanished. What had caused the sudden change? What had happened?

As for William Carter, he was about to start on a journey which would take him as far as Central America. Again, what had happened? What had caused *him* to give over all that he had purposed and go and disappear along with Milton Rhodes?

Here there was but one bit of light, but that light seemed to make the problem the more perplexing. The very day before that on which Rhodes and Carter got into the automobile and started for Mount Rainier, some visitor had come and had been received by Rhodes in the library, Carter being present at this meeting. Some of the concomitants of this visit had been a little unusual, it was remembered, though at the time no one had given that a thought.

It was believed that this man had remained there with Rhodes and Carter for a period somewhat extended. But who had this mysterious visitor been? It was, of course, held as certain that something told by this man to the scientist and his companion was the key to the mystery. But what had the visitor told them?

We knew that Rhodes and Carter had gone to Mount Rainier. But why had they so suddenly abandoned all their plans and gone to the mountain? On the mountain they had disappeared. More than that no man could tell.

And now we come to another enigma. Rhodes seldom drove a car himself. On this trip, however, he was at the wheel. The only other occupant of that car was Carter. And Rhodes had left with his chauffer, Everett Castleman, instructions over which I puzzled my head a good deal but without my ever becoming any the wiser. These instructions were somewhat extraordinary.

They were these:

If Rhodes had not returned, or if no word had been received from him, within a period of ten days, then Castleman was to go to Mount Rainier. He was to go to Paradise, and he was to go on the eleventh day. And he was to maintain a strict silence about everything appertaining to this whole proceeding. At Paradise he was to remain for another period. This was one of eight days. If, at the expiration of that time, neither Rhodes nor Carter had appeared, Castleman was, on the ninth day to take the car back to Seattle, and then the imposition of silence regarding that part which Castleman had played was at an end.

The mystery, of course, was what had become of Milton Rhodes and William Carter. Had some fatal accident occurred? Had they, for instance, fallen into a crevasse and perished? Or had they just gone off on some wild mountain hike and would they be returning any day?

As to this last hypothesis, those instructions given to Castleman should have shown its utter untenability.

And so the time passed. And Milton Rhodes and William Carter never came back. Week followed week. Month followed month. All hope was abandoned—had been abandoned long before the *Multnomah* entered Elliott Bay.

And that mysterious visitor? Why had he not spoken? Why had he not come forward and told what he knew? Where was he? Had he too vanished? Had he joined Rhodes and Carter on the mountain, and had the three vanished together? And what had he told them there in Rhodes' library on that fateful day?

Thus matters stood when one afternoon an automobile came gliding into my place, and there in it were Milton Rhodes and William Carter!

With respect to the mystery of their disappearance, I could for some time elicit from them no enlightenment whatever. Instead:

"Where is she, Darwin?" asked Milton Rhodes, looking about. "Let me see her! Let me meet her! Quick!"

"So you know about my Sleeping Beauty in the Ice?"

"Of course! The first thing that I did," he told me, "was to get a copy of *Zandara**. We've just finished reading it. And, if it hadn't been for what has happened to us, to Bill here and me, then I might have been inclined, Darwin old *tillicum*, to fancy that Bond had been romancing in that book of his instead of setting forth an account of actual adventure and discovery."

"But, Milton," I asked, "what in the world did happen?"

"We'll come to that soon, Darwin old top. What Bill and I want now is to see your Zandara."

"Well, you'll have to wait till she gets hack. That should be in an hour or so.

"But, again, what on earth happened? *Where* have you two been all this time?"

But I must not go on like this, or I will find that I am writing a book myself instead of a preface to William Carter's narrative.

You will see it mentioned in his Prolegomenon that his manuscript was to be placed in my keeping, to be given by me to the world when the time fixed upon had expired. All that I need say on that point is that the *raison d'être* of this prospective measure will be quite obvious to you ere you have read to the last page of *Drome*.

Save for three very brief footnotes, and to those my name is appended, every word in the pages that follow is from the hand of William Barrington Carter.

I hasten to conclude, that you may proceed to learn who that mysterious visitor was, what he told them, *where* Rhodes and Carter went—*where they are now*.

Seattle, Washington,
September 18, 1951.

* *Zandara* by John Martin Leahy, Fantasy Publishing Company, Inc., 1953. [Ed.: This book was never published.]

PROLEGOMENON

"Our world has lately discovered another: and who will assure us it is the last of his brothers, since the demons, the Sibyls and we ourselves have been ignorant of this till now?"

"Nostre monde vient d'en retrouver un autre: et qui nous rêpond si c'est le dernier de ses frêres, puisque les dêmons, les sibylles et nous avons ignorê cettui-ci jusqu' à cette heure?"—Montaigne.

"There is," says August Derleth, "an element of the unnecessary about even the most apparently needed introduction."

What with that element, and what with my own experience, as a reader, with introductions, it was my intention to write nothing in the species of a foreword to this my narrative of those amazing adventures and discoveries in which Milton Rhodes and I so unexpectedly and so suddenly found ourselves involved. I thought that I would most certainly have set down in the account itself everything that I should wish to write upon the subject.

But, now that my manuscript is finished, and now that the time draws on apace when it is to be placed in the keeping of our valued friend Darwin Frontenac, by whom, when the period fixed upon has elapsed, it will be given to the world, I feel that there are some points anent which it would be well to say a few words.

In the first place, apropos of the shortcomings, of which, in some instances, I am painfully sensible, of this work when viewed

269

through the glasses of the literary artist, I may say in extenuation that this is the first book that I have ever written—and certainly, by the by, it will be the last.

Whether the fact that this is an initial venture in authorship excuses my deficiencies as a craftsman with pen, paper and words, I cannot say; but, at any rate, it is an explanation.

Furthermore, far outweighing (so it seems to me) any artistic desiderata, is this: the following narrative does not come to you from any secondhand source or from any source even farther removed; it is written by one who was an eyewitness of, and an actor in, the scenes, adventures and discoveries described in it—an actor that, I do assure you, would at times have given much to be some place else.

Also, in the writing of this book, I placed above all other things the endeavor to attain the utmost accuracy possible; the style was, therefore, in a great measure, left to take care of itself. With old Anatomy Burton, though very likely he quoted,* I can say:

"I write for minds, not ears."

Too, more than once when disposing of difficulties obtruded upon me by the noncoincidence of thought with words, have I had in mind this observation of Saint Augustine:

"For there are but few things which we speak properly, many things improperly; but what we may wish to say is understood."

And, similarly, when reminding myself that I had not set out to produce a work of art but merely to put down upon paper a plain and straightforward account of actual happenings and discoveries, many a time did I think of these words of John Stuart Mill:

---

* This surmise of Mr. Carter's is correct. The above quotation is taken from a modernized *Anatomy of Melancholy*. Burton, though from what Latin writer he took the words I cannot say, wrote:

"*Animis haec scribo, non auribus.*"
                                        —Darwin Frontenac.

"For it is no objection to a harrow that it is not a plough, nor to a saw that it is not a chisel."

And so it should be no objection to this my account of our discovery of another world that it has not the charm of Dante's *Hell* or the delicate beauties of Kipling's *Gunga Din*.

In the second place, I wish that I could say more about that mysterious phenomenon the firedrake, Saint Elmo's fire, or whatever it should be called, light-cloudlet, light-cloud, light-mass, light-ghost—sometimes it looks likes luminous *mist*—but I know no more at this date about the origin of that most remarkable manifestation than I did after seeing the first "ghost," nor does Milton Rhodes himself, and Milton Rhodes, as everybody knows, is a scientist.

Of course, if people were like Trimalchio in the *Satyricon* of Petronius (and many people are) authors or scientists would not need to bother their heads about explanations, conjectures, theories, hypothesis or such sort when telling about strange phenomena or events; for, when some matter was being expounded by one of his guests, a gentleman by the name of Agamemnon, Trimalchio disposed of the whole business in this simple and summary fashion:

"If the thing really happened, there is no problem; if it never happened, it is all nonsense."

But, in the present instance—not to the Trimalchios, of course, but to any person with an iota of the scientific spirit in his encephalon—the fact is the very converse of this; for, if the firedrakes, the light-clouds, did not "happen," there would be no problem at all.

The Trimalchios, I have no doubt, would at once put the stamp of their approval upon this statement, which I lift from *Hudibras*:

> "But what, alas! is it to us
> Whether i' th' moon men thus or thus
> Do eat their porridge, cut their corns,
> Or whether they have tails or horns?"

But the light in that other world is not the only problem to the solution of which I wish that I had something to offer. There are many problems. Here is one: the "eclipses." These are sometimes truly awful.

For instance, just imagine yourself in a forest dense and mysterious, and, furthermore, imagine that one of those fearful carnivores the snake-cats, is stealing toward you, stealing nearer and nearer, watching for the chance to spring; imagine yourself in such a pleasant pass as that, and then imagine a sudden and total extinction of the light (which is what, for want of a better word, we call an eclipse) so that you yourself and everything about you are involved in impenetrable darkness. How would you like to find yourself in such a place as that and have that happen to you? Well, as you will see in its proper pages, that is just where we were, and that, and more too, is just what happened to us.

And *that* will give you an idea of what I mean when I say an eclipse can sometimes be awful indeed.

Why the light at times quivers, shakes, fades, bursts out so brightly, or why, slowly or all of a sudden, it ceases to be at all, is certainly an extremely curious and most mystifying business.

But

"To them we leave it to expound
That deal in sciences profound."

A possibility has occurred to Rhodes and me that is by no means conducive, what with the care and labor that I have expended in the endeavor to be accurate in the writing of this true history, to any feeling of happiness on my part. My companion in adventure and discovery is, however, pleased to entertain the idea that it would certainly be "funny." Funny?

That possibility is simply this: so very strange is the story which I tell in the pages that follow, many a reader may be disposed to set the whole thing down as fiction! And, indeed, many a reader may do just that!

Fiction, forsooth!

Well, if any one actually is of that opinion or belief when he has finished reading this book, all I can say is that I wish such a one had been with us there on that narrow bridge, the yawning black chasm of unknown profundity, on either side, when the angel and her demon so suddenly appeared there directly before us!

I have an idea that, if he had been there, he would have wished, and have wished as hard as he had ever wished anything in his life, that the whole business would turn out to be fiction or nightmare!

> "Why then should witlesse man so much misweene
> That nothing is but that which he hath seene?"

But I must hasten to bring this introduction to a close. Already I have exceeded the space that I had allotted for it, without even mentioning a number of things that I had in mind, and without having yet set down that which especially brought me to the decision to write anything prolegomenary at all.

And, now that I come to it, I feel hesitant. But this will not do.

In my whole narrative, there is, I am sure, but one single allusion, and that most brief—namely, *Amor ordinem nescit*—to my own heart-tragedy; and, as that allusion, even, is involved in obscurity, I will in this place and incontinently make it clear, and I do it by writing this:

I would rather have, though it were but for one single hour, Drorathusa as My Only than have for a lifetime any other woman I have ever known.

You will, I have no doubt, smile when you read this; you may think Eros has put me into a state very similar to the one in which the poor wight found himself of whom Burton wrote:

"He wisheth himself a saddle for her to sit on, a posy for her to smell to, and it would not grieve him to be hanged if he might be strangled in her garters."

Well, that busy little imp Venus's son (and he's as busy in that other world as he is in this) enjoys getting men and women into just such states of mind and heart. He moved even the rather cold-hearted Plato—I mean the great philosopher, not one of the poets so named, the philosopher who banished poets and Love himself from his Republic—the little imp moved even *him* to write:

> "Thou gazest on the stars, my Life! Ah! gladly would
>   I be
> Yon starry skies, with thousand eyes, that I might
>   gaze on thee!"

And I would rather have this heart-tragedy mine—have loved and lost Drorathusa—than never to have seen my lady.

"The heart has its reasons," says Pascal, "that reason can not understand."

Swiftly now the time draws on, on towards that final journey which Milton Rhodes and I are to make, and to make with glad hearts, that journey from which there is never to be a return, that journey back to another world, a world where there is no sun, no moon, no skies, no stars—a world where there is neither day nor night.

Vale.

William Barrington Carter

1
THE MYSTERIOUS VISITOR

The forenoon of that momentous August day (how momentous time, like unto some spirit-shaking vision, was soon and swiftly to show us) had been bright and sunny. Snowy cumuli sailed along before a breeze from the north. When the wind comes from that quarter here in Seattle, it means good weather. But there was something sinister about this one.

As the day advanced, the clouds increased in number and volume; by noon the whole sky was overcast. And now? It was midafternoon now; a gale from the south was savagely flinging and dashing the rain against the windows, and it had become so dark that Milton Rhodes had turned on one of the library-lamps. There was something strange about that darkness which so suddenly had fallen upon us.

"Too fierce to last long, Bill," observed Milton Rhodes, raising his head and listening to the beating of the rain and the roar of the wind.

He arose from his chair, went over to one of the southern windows and stood looking out into the storm.

"Coming down in sheets, Bill. It can't keep this up for very long."

I went over and stood beside him.

"No," I returned; "it can't keep this up. But, rain or sun, our trip is spoiled now."

"For today, yes. But there is tomorrow, Bill."

But, in the sense that Milton Rhodes meant, there was to be no tomorrow: at the very moment, in the midst of the roar and the rage of the elements, Destiny spoke, in the ring of a telephone-bell—Destiny, she who is wont to make such strange sport with the lives of men. I sometimes wonder if stranger sport any man has ever known than she was to make with ours.

"Wonder who the deuce 'tis now," muttered Milton Rhodes as he left the room to answer the call.

I remained there at the window. Of that fateful conversation over the wire, I heard not so much as a single syllable. I must have fallen into a deep reverie or something; at any rate, the next thing I knew there was a sudden voice, and Milton Rhodes was standing beside me again, a quizzical expression on his dark features.

"What is it, Bill?" he smiled. "In love at last, old *tillicum?* Didn't hear me until I spoke the third time."

"Gosh," I said, "this is getting dreadful! But—"

"Well?"

"What is it?"

"Oh, a visitor."

I regarded him for a moment in silence.

"You don't seem very enthusiastic," I observed.

"Why should I be? Some crank, most likely. Must be, or he wouldn't set out in such a storm as this is.'

"Great Pluvius, is he coming through this deluge?"

"He is. Unless I'm mighty badly mistaken, he is on his way over right now."

"Must be something mighty important."

"Oh, it's important all right, important to *him*," said Milton Rhodes. "But will it interest *me?*"

"I'll tell you that before the day is done. But who is this queer gentleman?"

"Name's Scranton, Mr. James W. Scranton. That's all that I know about him, save that he is bringing us a mystery. He called it a terrible, horrible *scientific* mystery."

"That," I exclaimed, "sounds interesting!"

It was patent, however, that Milton Rhodes was not looking forward to the meeting with any particular enthusiasm.

"It may sound interesting," he said; "but will it prove so? That is the question, Bill. To some people, you know, some very funny things constitute a mystery. Mr. James W. Scranton's mystery may prove to belong to that species. We must wait and see. Said that he had heard of me, that, as I have a gift (that is what he called it, Bill, a gift) of solving puzzles and mysteries, whether scientific, psychic, spooky or otherwise—well, he had a story to tell me that would eclipse any I ever had heard, a mystery that would drive Sherlock Holmes himself to suicide. Yes, that's what he really said, Bill—the great Sherlock himself to suicide."

"That's coming big!" I said.

Milton Rhodes smiled wanly.

"We haven't heard his yarn yet. We can't come to a judgment on such uncertain data."

"Scranton," said I. "Scranton. Hold on a minute."

"What is it now?"

"Wonder if he belongs to the old Scranton family."

"Never heard of it, Bill."

"Pioneers," I said. "Came out here before ever Seattle was founded. Homesteaded down at Puyallup or somewhere, about the same time as Ezra Meeker. It seems to me—"

"Well?" queried Milton Rhodes after some moments, during which I tried my level best to recollect the particulars of a certain wild, gloomy story of mystery and death and horror that I had heard long years before—in my boyhood days, in fact.

"I can not recollect it," I told him. "I didn't understand it even when I heard the man, an old acquaintance of the Scrantons, tell the story—a story of some black fate, some curse that had fallen upon the family."

"So that's the kind of mystery it is! From what the man said, though that was vague, shadowy, I thought that it was something very different. I thought that it was *scientific*."

"Maybe it is. We are speculating, you know, if one may call it that, on pretty flimsy data. One thing: I distinctly remember that Rainier had something to do with it."

"What Rainier?"

"Why, Mount Rainier."

"This is becoming intriguing," said Milton Rhodes, "if it isn't anything else. You spoke of a black fate, a curse: what has noble Old He, as the old mountain-men called Rainier, to do with such insignificant matters as the destinies of us insects called humans?"

"According to the old fellow I mentioned, that old acquaintance of the Scrantons, it was there, on Rainier, that this dark and mysterious business started."

"What was it that started?"

"That's just it. The man didn't know himself what had happened up there."

"Hum," said Milton Rhodes.

"That," I went on, "was many years ago. It was just, I believe, after Kautz climbed the mountain. Yes, I am sure he said 'twas just after that. And this man who told us the story—his name was Simpson—said 'twas something that Scranton learned on Kautz's return to Steilacoom that led to his, Scranton's, visit, to Old He. Not from Kautz himself, though Scranton knew the lieutenant well, but from the soldier Hamilton."

"What was it that he learned?"

"There it is again!" I told him. "Simpson said he could tell what that something was, but he told us that he would not do so."

"A very mysterious business," smiled Milton Rhodes. "I hope that our visitor's story, whatever it is, will prove more definite."

"Wasn't it," I asked, "in the fifties that Kautz made the ascent?"

"In July, 1857. And pretty shabbily has history treated him, too. It's always Stevens and Van Trump, Van Trump and Stevens. Why, their Indian, Sluiskin, is better known than Kautz!"

"But I thought," said I, "that Stevens and Van Trump were the very first men to reach the summit of Mount Rainier."

"Oh, don't misunderstand me, Bill," answered Milton Rhodes. "All honor to Stevens and Van Trump, the first of men to reach the very top of the mountain; but all honor, too, to the first white man to set foot on Rainier, the discoverer of the great Nisqually

Glacier, the first to stand upon the top of Old He, though adverse circumstances prevented his reaching the highest point."

"Amen," said I—as little dreaming as Kautz, Stevens and Van Trump themselves had ever done of that discovery which was to follow, and soon now at that.

For a time we held desultory talk, then fell silent and waited.

There was a lull in the storm; the darkness lifted, then suddenly it fell again, and the rain began to descend with greater violence than ever.

Milton Rhodes had left his chair and was standing by one of the eastern windows.

"This must be our visitor, Bill," he said suddenly.

I arose and went over to his side, to see a big sedan swinging in to the curb.

"Yes!" exclaimed Rhodes, his face beginning to brighten. "There is Mr. James W. Scranton.

"Let us hope, Bill," he added, "that the mystery which he is bringing us will prove a real one, real and scientific."

The next moment a slight figure, collar up to ears, stepped from the car and headed swiftly up the walk, leaning sidewise against the wind and rain.

"'Now is the dramatic moment of fate, Watson'," quoted Milton Rhodes with a smile as he started towards the door, "'when you hear a step upon the stair which is walking into your life, and you know not whether for good or ill'."

2
WHAT HE TOLD US

A few moments, and Milton Rhodes and his visitor entered the room.

"My friend Mr. Carter," Rhodes remarked to Mr. James W. Scranton as he introduced us, "has assisted me in some of my problems; he is my colleague, so to say, and you may speak with the utmost confidence that your story, if you wish it so, will be held an utter secret."

"For the present, I wish it to be a secret," returned Scranton, seating himself in the chair which Rhodes had pushed forward, "and so always if no discovery follows. If, however, you discover things—and I have no doubt that you will do so—why, then, of course, you may make everything public where, when and in whatsoever manner you wish."

"And so," said Milton, "you bring us a mystery—a scientific mystery."

"Yes, Mr. Rhodes. It is scientific, and I believe that it will prove to be something more. In all probability stranger than any which any man *on* this earth has ever known."

There was not the slightest change on Milton Rhodes' features, and yet I could have sworn that a slight fleeting smile had touched them. I turned my look back to our visitor, and I saw upon his face an expression so strange that I stared at him in something very like surprise.

What was it that this man was going to tell us?

Soon that expression was gone, though its shadow still rested on his thin and pale features.

"This mystery of which I have come to tell you," he said suddenly, "is an old, old one."

I glanced at Milton Rhodes.

"Then why," he asked, "bring it to me?"

An enigmatic smile flitted across Scranton's face.

"Because it is *new* as well. You will soon see what I mean, Mr. Rhodes. You will see why, after all these years, I suddenly found myself so anxious to see you that I couldn't even wait until this storm and deluge ended."

From the inside pocket of his coat he drew a leather-covered notebook, much worn and evidently very old.

"This," said he, holding the book up between thumb and forefinger, "is the journal kept by my grandfather, Charles Scranton, during his journey to, and partial ascent of, Mount Rainier in the year 1858."

Milton Rhodes glanced over at me and said:

"Our little deduction, Bill, wasn't so bad, after all."

Scranton turned his eyes from one to the other of us with a questioning look.

"Mr. Carter," Rhodes explained, "was just telling me about that trip, and he wondered if you belonged to the old pioneer Scranton family."

"This," exclaimed the other, "is something of a surprise to me! Few people, I thought, very few people, even knew of the journey."

"Well, Mr. Carter happens to be one of the few."

"May I ask," said Scranton, addressing himself to me, "how you learned that my grandfather had visited the mountain? And *what* you know?"

"When I was a boy, I heard a man—his name was Simpson—tell about it."

"Oh," said Scranton, and it was as though some fear or some thing of dread had suddenly left him.

"His story, however," I added, "was vague, mysterious. Even at the time I couldn't understand what it was all about."

"Of course. For, though Simpson knew of the journey, he knew but little of what had *happened*. And more than once did I hear my grandfather express regret that he had told Simpson even as much as he had. I suppose there was something, perhaps a great deal, of that I-could-tell-a-lot-if-I-wanted-to in Simpson's yarn."

"There was," I nodded.

"The man, however, knew virtually nothing—in fact, nothing at all about *it*. I have no doubt, though, that he did a lot of guessing. I don't believe that my grandfather, dead these many years now, ever told a single living soul all. And, as for all that he told me—well, I can't tell everything even to you, Mr. Rhodes."

A strange look came into the eyes of Milton Rhodes, but he remained silent.

Scranton raised the notebook again.

"Nor is everything here. Nor do I propose to read everything that is here. Just now the details do not matter. It is the facts, the principal facts, with which we have to do now. This record, if you are interested—and I have no doubt that you will be—I shall leave in your hands until such time as you care to return it to me.

"Now for my grandfather's journey.

"With three companions, he left the old homestead near what is now Puyallup, on the 16th of August, 1858. At Steilacoom, they got an Indian guide, Sklokoyum by name. The journey was made on horseback to the Sick Moon Prairie.* There the animals were left, with one man to guard them, and my grandfather, his two companions and the Indian—this guide, however, had never been higher up the Nisqually River than Copper Creek—set out on foot for the mountain."

"One moment," Milton Rhodes interrupted. "According to that Simpson, it was something that your grandfather heard from the soldier Hamilton, and not from Kautz himself, that led to his making this journey to Mount Rainier. Is that correct?"

* *Sick Moon: Old Moon* in the Chinook jargon.
—Darwin Frontenac.

"Yes; it is correct."

"May I ask, Mr. Scranton, what it was that he learned?"

Again that enigmatic smile on Scranton's face. He tapped the old journal.

"You will learn that, Mr. Rhodes, when you read this record."

"I see. Pray proceed."

3
THE MYSTERY OF OLD HE

"It was about three o'clock in the afternoon of the 24th," said Scranton, "that they reached the foot of the Nisqually Glacier, called Kautz Glacier by my grandfather. As for what followed, I shall give you that in my grandfather's own words."

He opened the book, at a place marked with a strip of paper, and read from it the following:

"August 24th, 10 p.m.—At last we are on the mountain. And how can I set it down—this thing that has happened? What I write here must be inadequate indeed, but I shall not worry about that, for a hundred years could never dim the memory of what I saw. I have often wondered why the Indians were afraid of Rainier; I know now. And what do I really know? I know what I saw, I know what happened; but only God in Heaven knows what it means.

"Got started early. Still following the river. Going very difficult. Crossed stream a number of times and once had to take to the woods. Reached the glacier about three o'clock—an enormous wall of dirty ice, four or five hundred feet in height, with the Nisqually flowing right out of it. Day had turned dark and threatening. Climbed the eastern wall of the canon. Clouds suddenly settled down—a fog cold and thick and dripping—and we made camp by a tiny stream, near the edge of the canon cut by the glacier. Soon had a good fire burning. And it was not long before it came—the shrouded figure and with it that horrible shape, 'if,' as old Milton has it in *Paradise Lost*, 'shape it might be called that shape had none.'

284

"At times the fog would settle down so thick we could see no farther than fifty feet. Then suddenly objects could be made out two or three hundred feet away. At the moment the fog was about us thicker than ever. We were sitting by the fire, warming ourselves and talking—White, Long and myself. All at once there was an exclamation. I looked at Long, and what I saw on his face and in his eyes brought me to my feet in an instant and whirled my look up in that direction in which he was staring.

"And there on the top of the bank, not more than thirty feet from us, stood a tall, white, shrouded figure, a female figure, and beside it, seemingly squatting like a monstrous toad, was that dark shape that had no shape. But, though shape it had none, it had eyes—big eyes that burned at us with a greenish, hellish fire.

"White snatched up his rifle and thrust it forward, but I stepped over and shoved the muzzle aside. When we looked up there again, the woman, for a woman, a white woman too, it certainly was—well, she was gone, and with her that formless thing with the hellish fire in its big eyes.

"'What was it?' exclaimed White.

"He rubbed his eyes and stared up there again, then this way and that, all about into the thick vapor.

"'Was it only a dream?'

"'It was real enough,' I told him. 'It was a woman, a white woman.'

"'Or,' put in Long, 'the spirit of one.'

"'I know one thing,' said White: 'she may be a flesh-and-blood creature, and she may be a spirit; but that thing that crouched there beside her was not of this world of ours!'

"He shuddered.

"'Not of this world of ours! Men, what *was* that thing?'

"That, of course, was a question that neither Long nor myself could answer.

"'If,' I said, 'it hadn't been for this fog! If we could only have seen them better!'

"Of a sudden White exclaimed:

"'Where's Sklokoyum?'

"'Not far,' I told him. 'Say—he was up there, up there where they came from. Come, let's look into this.'

"I sprang up the bank. They followed. A moment, and we were in that very spot where the woman and the thing had stood so brief a space before.

"'It was no dream, at any rate,' observed Long, pointing to the crushed purple flowers—a species, I believe, of aster.

"'No,' I returned; 'it was not a dream.'

"'Maybe,' said White, peering about, 'we'll wish, before this business is ended, that it all had been a dream,'

"Came a loud scream from above. Silence. And then the crash of some heavy body through the branches and shrubs.

"Sklokoyum!' I cried.

"White's hand closed on my arm with the grip of a vice.

"'Hear that?'

"I heard it. It was the voice of a woman or a girl.

"'She's calling,' said Long, 'calling to *it*.'

"'Great Heaven!' I exclaimed. 'It's after the Indian! Come!'

"I started up, but I had taken only a half-dozen springs or so when Sklokoyum came leaping, plunging into view. I have seen fear, horrible fear, that of cowards and the fear of brave men; but never had I, never have I, seen anything like that fear which I saw now. And Sklokoyum, whatever his faults, has a *skookum tumtum*—in other words, is no coward.

"Down the Indian came plunging. There was a glimpse of a blood-covered visage; then he was past. The next instant a shock, a savage oath from White, and he and the Siwash fell in a heap, went over the edge and rolled down the bank and clean to the fire.

"Long and I followed, keeping a sharp lookout behind us, and, indeed, in every direction. But no glimpse was caught of any moving thing, nor did the faintest sound come to us from out that cursed vapor, settling on the trees and dripping, dripping, dripping.

"Sklokoyum's right cheek was slashed as though by some great talon, and he had been terribly bitten in the throat.

"'A little more,' observed Long, 'and it would have been the jugular, and that would have meant *klahowya*, Sklokoyum.'

"The Indian declared that he had been attacked by a demon, a *klale tamahnowis*, a winged fiend from the white man's hell itself. What was it like? Sklokoyum could not tell us that. All he knew was that the demon had wings, teeth a foot in length and that fire shot out of its eyes and smoke belched from its nostrils. And surely it would have killed him (and I have no doubt that it would have) if an angel, an angel from the white man's Heaven, had not come and driven it off. What was the angel like? Sklokoyum could not describe her, so wonderful was the vision. And her voice—why, at the very sound of her voice, that horrible *tamahnowis* flapped its wings and slunk away into the fog and the gloom of the trees.

"Poor Sklokoyum! No wonder he gave us so wild an account of what had happened up there! And, said he, to remain here would be certain death. We must go back, start at once, Well, we are still here, and we are not going to turn back at this spot, though I have no doubt that Sklokoyum himself will do so the very first thing in the morning.

"The fog is thinning. Now and again I see a star gleaming down with ghostly fire. We came here seeking a mystery; well, we certainly have found one. I wonder if I can get any sleep tonight. Long is to relieve me at twelve o'clock. For, of course, we cannot, after what has happened, leave our camp without a guard. And I wonder if—what, though, is the good of wondering? But what is she, Sklokoyum's angel? And what is that *klale tamahnowis*, that demon? And where is the angel now?"

4
"VOICES!"

Scranton closed the journal on the forefinger of his right hand and looked at Milton Rhodes.

"Well," said he, "what do you think of that?"

Rhodes did not say what he thought of it. I thought that I knew, though I had to acknowledge that I wasn't sure just what I thought of this wild yarn myself.

After a little silence, Milton Rhodes asked:

"Is that all?"

"All? Indeed, no!" returned Scranton.

He opened the book and prepared to read from it again.

"This adventure that I have just read to you," he said looking over the top of the journal at Milton Rhodes, "took place in what is now known as Paradise Park—a Paradise where, as you well know, there is sometimes twenty-five feet of snow in the winter."

"Of course that was the place," Milton nodded, "for they had climbed the eastern wall of the canyon and had camped near the edge."

"And the one that followed," Scranton added, "on what we now call the Cowlitz Glacier. I believe, Mr. Rhodes, that you have visited Rainier a number of times?"

"Many times, Mr. Scranton. Few men, I believe, know the great mountain better than I do; and I never followed in the footsteps of a guide, imported or otherwise, either."

"Then, in all likelihood, you know the Tamahnowis Rocks in the Cowlitz Glacier."

"I have been there a dozen times."

"Did you ever, Mr. Rhodes, notice anything unusual at that place?"

"Nothing whatever. I found the ascent of the rocks themselves rather difficult and the crevasses there interesting, but nothing more."

"Well, it was there," said Scranton, "that what I am going to read to you now took place. Yes, I know that it was there at the Tamahnowis Rocks, though I myself never could find anything there, either. And now, after all these long years, once more it is in that very spot that—"

He broke off abruptly and dropped his look to the old record. Milton Rhodes leaned forward.

"Mr. Scranton," he asked, "what were you going to say?"

Scranton tapped the old journal with a forefinger.

"*This* first," he said. "Then *that*."

"The story begins to take shape," observed Milton Rhodes; and I wondered what on earth he meant. "Pray proceed."

Whereupon the other raised the book, cleared his throat with an ahem and started to read to us this astonishing record:

"August 25th.—I was right: the very first thing in the morning the Indian left us. Nothing could induce him to go forward, to remain at the camp even. The demons of Rainier would get us, said he, if we went on—the terrible *tamahnowis* that dwelt in the fiery lake on the summit and in the caverns in the mountain side, caverns dark and fiery and horrible as the caves in hell itself. Had we not had warning? One had come down here, even among the trees, and undoubtedly it would have killed us all had it not been for that angel. He, Sklokoyum, would not go forward a single foot. He was going to *klatawah hyak kopa Steilacoom*. How the old fellow begged us to turn back, too! It was quite touching, as was his leave-taking when he finally saw that we were determined to go on. Old Sklokoyum acted as though he was taking leave of the dead—as, indeed, he was. And at last he turned and left us, and in a few minutes he had vanished from sight.

"How I wish to God now that we had gone back with him!"

At this point, Scranton paused and said:

"The Indian was never seen again or even heard of again."

The account (which I am copying from the journal itself) went on thus:

"Fog disappeared during the night. A fairer morning, I believe, never dawned on Rainier. Sky the softest, the loveliest of blues. A few fleecy clouds about the summit of the mountain, but not a single wisp of vapor to be seen anywhere else in all the sky.

"Proceeded to get a good survey of things. From the edge of the canyon, got a fine view clear down the glacier and clear up it, too. Ice here covered with dirt and rock-fragments, save a strip in the middle, showing white and bluish. Badly crevassed. It must have been right about here that Kautz left the glacier. He climbed the cliffs on the other side, and then, the next morning, he started for the top. It seemed, to us, however, that the ascent could be made more easily on this side. But we were not headed for the summit; we had a mystery to solve, and we immediately set about trying to do it.

"We started to trail them—the angel and that thing with the big eyes that burned with a greenish, hellish fire. Where they had crushed through the flower-meadows, this was not difficult. At other places, however, no more sign than if they had moved on through the air itself. One thing was soon clear: they had held steadily *upward*, never swinging far from the edge of that profound canyon in which flows that mighty river of ice.

"The ground became rocky. No sign. Then at last, in a sandy spot, we suddenly came to the plain prints left by the feet of the angel as she passed there, and, mingled with those prints, there were marks over which we bent in perplexity and then in utter amazement.

"These marks were about eight inches in length, and, as I looked at them, I felt a shiver run through me and I thought of a monstrous bird and even of a reptilian horror. But that squatting form we had seen for those few fleeting moments—well, *that* had not been either a bird or a reptile.

"'One thing,' said Long, 'is plain: *it* was leading and the angel was following.'

"White and I looked closely, and we saw that this had certainly been so.

"'It appears,' Long remarked, 'that the fog didn't interfere any with their journey. They seem to have gone along as steadily and surely as if they had been in bright sunshine.'

"'I wonder,' White said, 'if the thing was smelling the way back like a dog.'

"'Back where?' I asked. 'And I see no sign of a down trail.'

"'Lord,' exclaimed Long, looking about uneasily, 'the Siwashes say that queer things go on up here, that the mountain is haunted; and, blame me, if I ain't beginning to think that they are right! Maybe, before we are done, we'll wish that we had turned back with old Sklokoyum.'

"I didn't like to hear him talk like that. He spoke as though he were jesting, but I knew that superstitious dread had laid a hand upon him.

"'Nonsense!' I laughed. 'Haunted? That woman that we saw and that thing—well, we know that they were real enough, and we knew that even when we didn't have these footprints to tell us.'

"'Oh, they are real, all right,' said Long. 'But real *what?*'

"A little while after that, we came to a snowfield, an acre or two in extent, and there we made a strange discovery. The trail led right across it. And it was plain that *it* had still been leading and the angel had been following. Of a sudden White, who was in advance, exclaimed and pointed.

"'Look at that,' he said. 'See that? Its tracks end here.'

"And that is just what they did! But the tracks of the angel went right on across the snow.

"'Where did the thing go to?' I wondered.

"'Perhaps,' suggested Long, 'she picked it up and carried it.'

"But I shook my head.

"'A woman—or a man either, for the matter of that—carrying that thing!' White exclaimed. 'She could never have done that. And you can see for yourself; she never even paused here. Had she stopped to pick the thing up—what a queer thought—we would have the story written here in the snow.'

"'Then,' said Long, 'it must have gone on through the air.'

"'Humph!' White ejaculated. 'Through the air! Well, Sklokoyum said that the thing has wings—the bat wings of the white man's devil!'

"'But,' I objected, 'Sklokoyum was so badly scared that he didn't know what he saw.'

"I wonder,' said White.

"Beyond the snowfield, the place was strewn in all directions with rock-fragments. It was comparatively level, however, and the going was not difficult. A tiny stream off to the right, a steep rocky mass before us. We were soon, having crossed the stream, ascending this. It was a steep climb, but we were not long in getting up it. At this place we passed the last shrub. We figured that we must be near an altitude of seven thousand feet now. Dark clouds forming. At times, in a cloud-shadow, the place would have a gloomy and wild aspect. No trail, though at intervals we would find a disturbed stone or faint marks in the earth. Our route lay along a broken ridge of rock. On our left the land fell away toward Kautz's Glacier [the Nisqually] while on the right, coming up close, was another glacier [the Paradise] white and beautiful.

"Ere long we reached a point where the ridge had a width of but a few yards, a small glacier on the left, the great beautiful one on the other side. And here we found it, found the trail of the thing and Sklokoyum's angel. They had come up along the edge of the ice on our left (to avoid the climb up over the rocks) crossed over the ridge (very low at this point) and held steadily along the glacier, keeping close to the edge. And in that dense fog! And just to the right the ice went sweeping down, like a smooth frozen waterfall. A single false step there, and one would go sliding down, down into yawning crevasses. How had they done it? And to where had they been going, in this region of barren rock and eternal snow and ice, through that awful fog and with night drawing on?

"There was but one way to get the answer to that, and that was to follow.

"And so we followed.

"And how can I set down here what happened? I cannot. I simply cannot. Not that it matters, for it can never, in even the slightest feature, fade from my mind. It may be that I shall find myself wishing that some of it would.

"Clouds grew larger, thicker, blacker. The change was a sudden, sinister one; there seemed to be something uncanny about it even. Our surroundings became gloomy, indescribably dreary and savage. We halted, there in the tracks of the thing and the angel, and looked about us, and we looked with a growing uneasiness and with an awe that sent a chill to the heart—at any rate, I know that it did to mine.

"White and Long wanted to turn back. Clouds had fallen upon the summit of Rainier and were settling lower and lower. Viewed from a distance, they are clouds, but, when you find yourself in them, they are fog; and to find our way back in fog would be no easy matter. However, so I objected, it would be by no means impossible. There would be no danger, I said, if we were careful.

"'There is that pile of rocks,' I added, pointing ahead. 'Let's go on to that at any rate. The trail seems to lead straight towards those rocks. I hate to even think of turning back now, now when we are so near.'

"Still, I noted with some uneasiness, my companions hesitated, their minds, I suppose, a prey to feelings for which they could not have found a rational explanation. All this, however, really was not strange, for it was truly a wild and savage and awesome place and hour.

"At length, in an evil moment, we moved forward.

"Yes, soon there could be no doubt whatever about it: the trail led straight toward those rocks. What would we find there?

"So engrossed were we that we did not see it coming. There was a sudden exclamation, we halted, and there was the fog—the dreaded fog that we had forgotten—drifting about us. The next moment it was gone, but more was drifting after. We resumed our advance. It was not far now. Why couldn't the fog have waited a little longer? But what did it matter? It could affect but little our immediate purpose; and, though I knew that it would be difficult, surely we could find our way back to the camp.

"The fog thinned, and the rocks loomed up before us, dim and ghostly but close at hand. Then the vapor thickened about us again, and they were gone. We were in the midst of crevasses now and had to proceed with great caution. How it happened none of us knew; but of a sudden we saw that we had lost the trail. But we did not turn back to find it. It didn't matter, really. The demon and the angel had gone to those rocks. Of that we were certain. And there the rocks were, right there before us. 'Tis true we couldn't see them now, but they were there.

"We went on. Minutes passed. And still there were no rocks. At length we had to acknowledge it: in the twistings and turnings we had been compelled to make among those cursed crevasses, we had missed our objective, and now we knew not where we were.

"But we knew that we were not far. White and Long cursed and wanted to know how we were ever going to find our way back through this fog, since we had failed to find the rocks when they had been right there in front of us. But it was nothing really serious; we would find that rock-mass. We started. Of a sudden Long gave a sharp but low exclamation, and his hand clutched at my arm.

"'What is it?' I asked in a voice low and guarded.

"'*Voices!*' he whispered.

5
"DROME!"

We listened. Not a sound. Suddenly the glacier cracked and boomed, then silence again. We waited, listening. Still not the faintest sound. Long, so White and I decided, must have been deceived. But Long declared that he had not.

"'I heard voices, I tell you! I know that I was not mistaken at all. I heard voices.'

"Again we listened.

"'There!' Long said suddenly. 'Hear them?'

"Yes, there, coming to us from out of the fog, were voices, plain, unmistakable, and yet at the same time—how shall I say it?—strangely muffled. Yes, that is the word, muffled. I wondered if the fog did that; but it couldn't, I decided, be the fog. One voice was silvery and strong, that of Sklokoyum's angel doubtless; the other deep and rough, the voice of a man. The woman (or girl) seemed to be urging something, pleading with him. Once we thought that there came a third voice, but we could not be sure of that. But of one thing we were sure: they were not speaking in English, in Spanish, French, Siwash or Chinook. And we felt certain, too, that it was not Scandinavian, German or Italian.

"'They are over there,' said Long, pointing. 'I am sure of it.'

"'No, there!' whispered White.

"For my part, I was convinced that these mysterious beings were in still a different direction!

"'Well,' I suggested, 'let's be moving. We won't get the solution of this queer business by standing here and wondering.'

295

"We got in motion, uncertain, though, whether we were really advancing in the right direction; but we could not, I thought, be greatly in error. Soon we came to a great crevasse. White leaped across it, and on that instant the voices ceased.

"Had they heard?

"We waited, White crouching there on the other side. Soon the sounds came again, whereupon White, in spite of my whispered remonstrance, began stealing forward. Long and I being less active, did not care to risk that jump, and so we made our way along the edge of the fissure, seeking a place to cross. This we were not long in finding, but by this time, to my profound uneasiness, White had disappeared in the fog.

"We advanced cautiously, and as swiftly as possible. This, however, was not very swiftly. See! There it was, the ghostly loom of the rocks through the vapor. At that instant the voices ceased. Came a scream, a short, sharp scream from the woman. A cry from White, the crack of his revolver, and then that scream he gave—oh, the horror of that I can never forget. Long and I could not see him, or the others—only the ghostly rocks; and soon, too, they were disappearing, for the fog was growing denser.

"We heard the sound of a body striking the ice and knew that White had fallen. He was still screaming that piercing, blood-curdling scream. We struggled to reach him, but the crevasses, those damnable crevasses, held us up.

"The sound sank. Of a sudden it ceased.

"But there was no silence. The voice of the woman rang out sharp and clear. And I thought that I understood it: she was calling to it, to that thing we had seen, down at the camp, squatting beside her, its eyes burning with that demoniacal fire—*calling it off!*

"Came a short silence, broken by a cry of horror from the angel. The man's voice was heard, then her own in sudden, fierce, angry pleading; at any rate, so it seemed to me—that she was pleading with him again.

"But what had happened to White?

"All this time—which, indeed, was very brief—Long and I were struggling forward. When we got out of that fissured ice and reached the place of the tragedy, the surroundings were as still as death. There lay our companion stretched out on the blood-soaked ice, a gurgle and wheezing coming from his torn throat with his every gasp for breath.

"I knelt down beside him, while Long, poor fellow, stood staring about into the fog, his revolver in his hand. A single glance showed that there was no hope, that it was only a matter of moments.

"'Go!' gasped the dying man. 'It was Satan, the Fiend himself. And an angel. And the angel, she said: *Drome!*"

"'Yes, I heard her say it. She said:

"*Drome!*'"

"There was a shudder, and White was dead. And the fog drifted down denser than ever, and the stillness there was as the stillness of the grave."

6
AGAIN!

What was that? The angel's voice again, seeming to issue from the very heart of that mass of rocks. A loud cry and a succession of sharp cries—cries that, I thought, ended in a sobbing sound. Then silence. But no. What was that, that rustling, that flapping in the air?

"Long and I looked wildly—overhead, and then I knew a fear that sent an icy shudder into my heart.

"I cried out—probably it was a scream that I gave—and sprang backward. My soles were well calked, but this could not save me, and down I went flat on my back. The revolver was knocked from my hand and went sliding along the ice for many feet. I sprang up. At this instant the thing came driving down at Long.

"He fired, but he must have missed. The thing struck him in the throat and chest and drove him to the ice. I sprang for my weapon. Long screamed, screamed as White had done, and fought with the fury of a fiend. I got the revolver and started back. The thing had its teeth buried in Long's throat. So fierce was the struggle that I could not fire for fear lest I should hit my companion. As I came up, the monster loosened its hold and sprang high into the air, flapping its bat wings, then it came driving straight at me.

"I fired, but the bullet must have gone wild. Again, and it screamed and went struggling upward. I emptied my revolver, but I fear that I missed with every shot, except that second one. A few seconds, and that winged monster had disappeared.

"I turned to Long. I have seen some horrible sights in my time but never anything so horrible as what I saw now. For there was Long, my companion, my friend—there he was raised up on his hands, his arms rigid as steel, and the blood pouring from his throat. And I—I could only weep and watch him as he bled to death. But it did not last long. In Heaven's mercy, the horror was ended soon.

"And then—well, what followed is not very clear in my mind. I know that a madness seemed to come over me. But I did not flee from that place of mystery and death; the madness, if madness it was, was not like that. It was not of myself that I was thinking; it was not of escape. It was as though a bloody mist had fallen upon the place. Vengeance was what I wanted—vengeance and blood, vengeance and slaughter. I reloaded my revolver, picked up Long's and thrust it into my pocket, then caught up White's weapon with my left hand and started for the rocks, shouting defiance and curses as I went.

"I reached that pile of stone, found the tracks of the angel and the man and of that winged beast; but, at the edge of the rocks, the tracks vanished, and I could not follow farther. But I did not stop there. I went on, clear around that pile, and again and yet again. I climbed it, clear to the summit, searched everywhere; but I could not find a single trace of them I sought. Once, indeed, I thought that I heard a voice, the voice of the angel—thought that I heard that cursed word *Drome*.

"But I can not write any more now. Why, oh, why didn't we listen to Sklokoyum and keep away from this hellish mountain? That, of course, would have been foolish; but it would not have been this thing which will haunt me to my dying hour."

7
"AND NOW TELL ME!"

Scranton closed the journal, leaned back in his chair and looked questioningly at Milton Rhodes.

"There you are!" he said. "I told you that I was bringing you a mystery, and I trust that I have, at least in a great measure, met your expectations."

There was silence for a moment.

"Hellish mountain!" said Rhodes. "Hellish mountain! Noble old Rainier a hellish mountain!

"Pardon my soliloquy," he added suddenly, "And I want to thank you, Mr. Scranton, for bringing me a problem that, unless I am greatly in error, promises to be one of extraordinary scientific interest."

Extraordinary scientific interest! What on earth did he mean by that?

"Still," he subjoined, "I must confess that there are some things about it that are very perplexing, and more than perplexing."

"I think I know what you mean. And that explains why the story has been kept a secret all these years."

"Your grandfather, Mr. Scranton, seems to have been a well-educated man."

"Yes; he was."

Milton Rhodes' pause was a significant one, but Scranton did not enlighten him further.

"On his return from Old He, did he tell just what had happened up there?"

"He did not, of course, care to tell everything, Mr. Rhodes, for fear he would not be believed. And little wonder. He was cautious, very guarded in his story; but, at that, not a single soul believed him. Perhaps, indeed, his very fear of distrust and suspicion and his consequent caution and vagueness, hastened and enhanced those dark and sinister thoughts and suspicions of his neighbors, and, indeed, of every one else who heard the story. There was talk of insanity, of murder even. This was the cruelest wound of all, and my grandfather carried the scar of it to his grave."

"Probably it would have been better," said Rhodes, "had he given them the whole of the story, down to the minutest detail."

"I do not see how. When they did not believe the little that he did tell, how on earth could they have believed the wild, the fantastic, the horrible thing itself?"

"Well, you may be right, Mr. Scranton. And here is a strange thing, too. It is inexplicable, a mystery indeed. For many years now, thousands of sightseers have every summer visited the mountain—this mountain that your grandfather found so mysterious, so hellish—and yet nothing has ever happened."

"That is true, Mr. Rhodes."

"They have found Rainier," said Milton Rhodes, "beautiful, majestic, a sight to delight the hearts of the gods; but no man has ever found anything having even the remotest resemblance to what your grandfather saw—has ever even found strange footprints in the snow. I ask you: where has the mystery been hiding all these years?"

"That is a question I shall not try to answer, Mr. Rhodes. It is my belief, however, that the mystery has never been *hiding*—using the word; that is, in its literal signification."

"Of course," Milton said. "But you know what I mean."

The other nodded.

"And now, Mr. Rhodes, I am going to tell you why I this day so suddenly found myself so anxious to come to you and give you this story."

Milton Rhodes leaned forward, and the look which he fixed on the face of Scranton was eager and keen.

"I believe, Mr. Rhodes, I at one point said enough to give you an idea of what—"

"Yes, yes!" Milton interrupted. "And now tell me!"

"The angel," said Scranton, "has come again!"

"Alone?"

"No; the demon is with her."

8

"DROME" AGAIN

Scranton produced a clipping from a newspaper.

"This," he told us, "is from today's noon edition of *The Herald*. The account, you observe, is a short one; but it is my belief that it will prove to have been (at any rate, the precursor of) the most extraordinary piece of news that this paper has ever printed."

He looked from one to the other of us as if challenging us to doubt it.

"What," asked Rhodes, "is it about?"

"The mysterious death (which the writer would have us believe was not mysterious at all) of Miss Rhoda Dillingham, daughter of the well-known landscape painter, on the Cowlitz Glacier, *at the Tamahnowis Rocks*, on the afternoon of Wednesday last."

"Mysterious?" queried Milton Rhodes. "I remember reading a short account of the girl's death. There was, however, nothing to indicate that there had been anything at all mysterious about the tragedy. Nor was there any mention of the Tamahnowis Rocks even. It said only that she had been killed, by a fall, on the Cowlitz Glacier."

"But there *was* something mysterious, Mr. Rhodes, how mysterious no one seems to even dream. For again we have it, that word which White heard the angel speak—that awful word Drome."

"Drome!" Milton Rhodes exclaimed. "That word again—after all these years?"

"Yes," said Scranton. "And you will understand the full and fearful meaning of what has just happened there on Mount Rainier when I tell you that knowledge of that mysterious word has always been held an utter secret by the Scrantons. No living man but myself knew it, and yet there it is again."

"This is becoming interesting indeed!" exclaimed Milton Rhodes.

"I was sure that you would find it so. And now permit me to read to you what the newspaper has to say about this poor girl's death."

He held the clipping up to get a better light upon it and read the following:

"The death of Miss Rhoda Dillingham, daughter of Francis Dillingham, the well-known painter of mountain scenery, on the Cowlitz Glacier on the afternoon of last Wednesday, was, it has now been definitely ascertained, a purely accidental one. Victor Boileau, the veteran Swiss guide, has shown that there is not the slightest foundation for the wild, fantastic rumors that began to be heard just after the girl's death. Boileau's visit to the Tamahnowis Rocks, the scene of the tragedy, and his careful examination of the place, have proved that the victim came to her death by a fall from the rocks.

"There was no witness to the tragedy itself. Francis Dillingham, the father of the unfortunate girl, was on another part of the rocks at the time, sketching. On hearing the screams, he rushed to his daughter. He found her lying on the ice at the foot of the rock, and on the point of expiring. She spoke but once, and this was to utter these enigmatic words:

"'Drome! She said, "Drome!"'

"This is one of those features which gave rise to the stories that something uncanny and mysterious had occurred at the Tamahnowis Rocks, as if the spot, indeed, was justifying its eerie name.

"Another is that Dillingham declared that he himself, as he made his way over the rocks in answer to his daughter's screams, heard another voice, an unknown voice, and that he is sure that he distinctly heard that voice pronounce that strange word Drome.

"Victor Boileau, however, has shown that there had been no third person there at the occurrence of the tragedy, that Rhoda

Dillingham's death was wholly accidental, that it was caused by a fall, from a height of about thirty feet, down the broken and precipitous face of the rocky mass.

"Another feature much stressed by those who see a mystery in everything connected with this tragic accident was the cruel wound in the throat of the victim. The throat, it is said, had every appearance of having been torn by teeth; but it is now known that the wound was made by some sharp, jagged point of rock, struck by the girl during her fall."

9
"TO MY DYING HOUR"

Scranton folded the clipping and placed it between leaves of the journal.

"There!" he said. "My story is ended. You have all the principal facts now. Additional details may be found in this old record—if you are interested in the case and care to peruse it."

Milton Rhodes reached forth a hand for the battered old journal.

"I am indeed interested," he said. "And I wish to thank you again, Mr. Scranton, for bringing to me a problem that promises to be one of extraordinary scientific interest."

"I suppose that you will visit the mountain, the Tamahnowis Rocks, as soon as possible."

Milton Rhodes nodded.

"It will take some time, some hours, that is, to make the necessary preparations; for this journey, I fancy, is going to prove a very strange one and perhaps a very terrible one, too. But tomorrow evening, I trust, will find us at Paradise. If so, on the following morning, we will be at the Tamahnowis Rocks."

"We?" queried Scranton.

"Yes; my friend Carter here is going along. Indeed, without Bill at my side, I don't know that I would care to face this thing."

"Me?" I exclaimed. "Where did you get that? I didn't say that I was going."

"That is true, Bill," Milton laughed; "you didn't say that you were going."

A silence ensued, during which Scranton sat in deep thought, as, indeed, did Milton Rhodes and myself. What did it all mean? Oh, what was I to make of this wild, this fantastic, this fearful thing?

"There is no necessity," Scranton said suddenly, "for the warning, I know; and yet I can't help pointing out that this adventure that you are about to enter upon may prove a very dangerous, even a very horrible one."

"Yes," Rhodes nodded; "it may prove a very dangerous, a very horrible adventure indeed."

"Why," I exclaimed, "all this cabalistic lingo and all this mystery? Why not be explicit? There is only one place that the angel could possibly have come from, this wonderful and terrible creature that says Drome and has a demon for her companion."

"Yes, Bill," Milton nodded; "there is only one place. And it was from that very place that she and her demon came."

"Good Heaven! Why, that supposition is absurd. The thing's preposterous."

"Do you think so, Bill? The submarine, the airplane, the radio—all were absurd, all were preposterous, Bill, until men got them. And many other things, too. Why, it was only yesterday that the sphericity of this old world that we inhabit ceased to be absurd, ceased to be preposterous. Don't be too sure, old *tillicum*. Remember the oft-repeated observation of Hamlet:

> "'There are more things in heaven *and earth*, Horatio,
>   Than are dreamt of in your philosophy.'"

"That is true enough. But this is different. This isn't philosophy or something in philosophy. This—"

"Awaits us!" said Milton Rhodes. "The question of prime importance to us now is if we can find the way to that place whence the angel and the demon came; for, so it seems to me, there can be little doubt that it is only on rare occasions, on very rare occasions, that these strange beings appear on the mountain."

"It is," Scranton remarked, "as, of course, you know, against the rules to take any firearm into the Park; but, if I were you, I should never start upon this enterprise without weapons."

"You may rest assured on that point," Milton told him: "we will be armed. The hazardous possibilities of this very strange problem that we are going to endeavor to solve justifies this infraction of the rule."

"Well," said Scranton, suddenly rising from his chair, "you are doubtless anxious to start your preparations at once, and I am keeping you from them. There is one thing, though, Mr. Rhodes, that I, that—"

He paused, and a look of trouble, of distress settled upon his pale, pinched features.

"What is it?" Milton Rhodes queried.

"I am glad that you are going, and yet—and yet I may regret this day, this visit, to my dying hour. For the thing that I have brought you is dangerous. It is more than that; it is awful."

"And probably," said Milton, "it is very wonderful indeed."

"But," Scranton added, "one should not blink the possibility that—"

"Tut, tut, man!" Milton Rhodes exclaimed, laughing. "We mustn't find you a bird of ill-omen now. You mustn't think things like that."

"Yet I can't help thinking about them, Mr. Rhodes. I wish that I could accompany you, at least as far as the scene of the tragedies; but I am far from strong. Even to drive a car sometimes taxes my strength. I doubt if I could now make the climb even from the Inn as far as Sluiskin Falls."

A silence fell, to be suddenly broken by Milton.

"Let us regard *that* as a happy augury," said he, pointing towards the southern windows, through which the sunlight, bright and sparkling, came streaming in: "the gloom and the storm have passed away, and all is bright once more."

"I pray Heaven that *it* prove so!" the other exclaimed.

"For my part, I shall always be glad that you came to me, Mr. Scranton; glad always, even—even," said Milton Rhodes, "if I never come back."

10

ON THE MOUNTAIN

It was a few minutes past three on the afternoon of the day follow-ing when Milton Rhodes and I got into his automobile and started for Mount Rainier. When we arrived at the Park entrance, which we did about half-past six, the speedometer showed a run of one hundred and two miles.

"Any firearms, a cat or a dog in that car?" was the question when Milton went over to register.

"Nope," said Milton.

There was a revolver in one of his pockets, however, and an-other in one of mine. But there was no weapon in the car: hadn't I got out of the car so that there wouldn't be?

A few moments, and we were under way again, the road, which ran through primeval forest, a narrow one now, sinuous and, it must be confessed, hardly as smooth as glass.

Soon we crossed Tahoma Creek, where we had a glimpse of the mountain, its snowy, rocky heights aglow with a wonderful golden tint in the rays of the setting sun. Strange, wild, fantastic thoughts and fears came to me again, and upon my mind settled gloomy fore-boding—sinister, nameless, foreboding terrible as a pall. We were drawing near the great mountain now, with its unutterable cosmic grandeur and loneliness, near to its unknown, which Milton Rhodes and I were perhaps fated to know soon and perhaps to know to our sorrow.

From these gloomy, disturbing thoughts, which yet had a strange fascination too, I was at length aroused by the voice of Rhodes.

"Kautz Creek," said he.

And the next moment we shot across the stream, which went racing and growling over its boulders, the pale chocolate hue of its water advertising its glacial origin.

"Up about two thousand four hundred feet now," Milton added. "Longmire Springs next. I say, Bill, I wonder where we shall be this time tomorrow, eh?"

"Goodness knows. Sometimes I find myself wondering if the whole thing isn't pure moonshine, a dream. An angel and a demon on the slopes of Mount Rainier! And they say that this is the Twentieth Century!"

Rhodes smiled wanly.

"I think that you will find the thing real enough, Billy, me lad," said he.

"Too real, maybe. The fact is that I don't know what on earth to think."

"The only thing to do is to wait, Bill. And we won't have to wait long, either."

When we swung to the grade out of Longmire, I thought that we were at last beginning the real climb to the mountain. But Milton said no.

"When we reach the Van Trump auto park, then we'll start up," said he.

And we did—the road turning and twisting up a forest-clad steep. Then, its sinuosities behind us, it ran along in a comparatively straight line, ascending all the time, to Christine Falls and to the crossing of the Nisqually, the latter just below the end of the glacier—snout, as they call it. Yes, there it was, the great wall of ice, four or five hundred feet in height, looking, however, what with the earth and boulders ground into it, more like a mass of rock than like ice. There it was, the first glacier I ever had seen, the first living glacier, indeed, ever discovered in all these United States—at any rate, the first one ever reported. Elevation four thousand feet.

The bridge behind us, we swung sharp to the right and went slanting up a steep rampart of rock, moving now away from the glacier, away from the mountain; in other words, we were heading straight for Longmire but climbing, climbing. At length the road, cut in the precipitous rock, narrowed to the width of but a single auto; and at this point we halted, for descending cars had the way.

The view here was a striking one indeed, down the Nisqually Valley and over its flanking, tumbled mountains, and the scene would probably have been even more striking than I found it had the spot not been one to make the head swim. I had the out side of the auto, and I could look right over the edge, over the edge and down the precipitous wall of rock to the bed of the Nisqually, half a thousand feet below.

The last car rolled by, and we got the signal to come on. This narrow part of the road passed, we swung in from the edge of the rampart, and I confess that I was not at all sorry that we did so.

Silver Forest, Frog Heaven, Narada Falls, Inspiration Point, then Paradise Valley, with its strange tree-forms, its beautiful flower-meadows, and, in the distance, the Inn on its commanding height, five thousand five hundred feet above the level of the sea; and, filling all the background, the great mountain itself, towering fourteen thousand four hundred feet aloft; the end of our journey in sight at last!

The end? Yes—until tomorrow. And then what? The beginning then—the beginning of what would, in all likelihood, prove an adventure as hazardous as it was strange, a most fearful quest.

Had I been a believer in the oneirocritical science, the things that I dreamed that night would have ended the enterprise (as far as I was concerned) then and there: in the morning I would have started for Seattle instanter. But I was not, and I am not now; and yet often I wonder why I dreamed some of those terrible things— those things which came true.

And, through all the horror, a cowled thing, a figure with bat wings, hovered or glided in the shadows of the background and at intervals, in tones cavernous and sepulchral, gave utterance to that dreaded name:

"*Drome!*"

11
THE TAMAHNOWIS ROCKS

It was very early—in fact, the first rays of the sun, not yet risen, had just touched the lofty heights of Rainier—when Rhodes and I left the Inn.

Besides our revolvers and a goodly supply of ammunition, there were the lights, an aneroid, a thermometer, our canteens, ice-picks; two pieces of light but very strong rope, each seventy-five feet in length; our knives, like those which hunters carry; and food sufficient to last us *a week*.

Yes, and there were the ice-creepers, which we should need in making our way over the glaciers, the Paradise and the Cowlitz, to that mass of rock, the scene of those mysterious tragedies.

We did not take the direct trail up but went over to the edge of the canyon that I—for this was my first visit to Mount Rainier—might see the Nisqually Glacier.

And, as we made our way upward through the brightening scene, as I gazed upon the grim cosmic beauty all about me, up into the great cirque of the Nisqually, up to the broad summit of the mountain and (in the opposite direction) out over the Tatoosh Range to distant Mount Adams and Mount St. Helens all violet and gold in the morning sun—well, that strange story which had brought us here then took on the seeming of a mirage or a dream.

"The mountain," said Milton Rhodes, as we stood leaning on our alpenstocks during one of our halts, "once rose to a height of sixteen thousand feet or more. The dip of the lava layers shows that. The whole top was blown clean off."

"Must have been some real fireworks," was my comment, "when that happened."

"See that line of bare rock there on the very summit, Bill, midway between Point Success up here on the left and Gibralter here on the right?"

"I noticed that," I told him, "and was wondering about it. Why isn't there any snow there?"

"Heat, Bill," said Rhodes. "Heat."

"Heat! Great Vesuvius, I thought that Mount Rainier was a dead volcano."

"Not dead, Pill, Only slumbering. Four eruptions are on record.* Whether Old He is to die in his slumber, or whether he is one day to awake in mad fury—that, of course, no man can tell us."

"To see it belching forth smoke and sending down streams of lava would be an interesting sight certainly," said I. "And I wonder what effect that would have on this Drome business—that is, if there is any such thing as Drome at all."

"Drome!" Milton echoed.

For some moments he stood there with a strange look of abstraction upon his face.

"Drome! Ah, Bill," said he, "I wish that I knew what it means. But come, we'll never reach the Tamahnowis Rocks if we stand here wondering."

And so we resumed our climb. We were the early birds this morning; not a living soul was to be seen anywhere on the mountain. But hark! What was that? Somebody whistling somewhere up

---

* "At this time (November, 1843) two of the great snowy cones, Mount Regnier and St. Helens, were in action. On the 23rd of the preceding November, St. Helens had scattered its ashes, like a white fall of snow, over the Dalles of the Columbia, 50 miles distant. A specimen of these ashes was given to me by Mr. Brewer, one of the clergymen at the Dalles."— Fremont.

there and off to the right. The whistles came in rapid succession, and they were loud and clear and ringing. I stopped and looked but could see nothing.

I should have explained that we had turned aside from the edge of the canyon, had crossed that little stream mentioned by grandfather Scranton and had begun to climb that steep rocky mass that he spoke of.

"What the deuce," said I, "is that fellow whistling like that for? It can't be to us."

"That," Milton Rhodes smiled, "isn't a man, Bill."

"Not a man?"

"It's a marmot," Milton told me.

"A marmot? Well," said I, "we live and we learn. I could have sworn, Milton, that it was a human being."

The ascent was a steep one, and we climbed in silence. The horse-trail, coming from the left, goes slanting and then twisting its way up this rocky rampart. On reaching the path, we paused for some moments to get our breath, then plodded on.

"I was thinking," said Milton Rhodes at last, "of what Francis Parkman said."

"What did he say?"

"'I would go farther for one look into the crater of Vesuvius than to see all the ruined temple in Italy.'"

"I wonder," I returned, "how far we shall have to go to see that angel that says Drome, not to mention her pretty demon."

Rhodes laughed.

"We are getting there, Bill; we're getting there—near the scene of the tragedies at any rate."

Ere long we reached the top. Here we passed the last shrub and in a little space came to a small glacier. The tracks of the horses led straight across it. But our route did not go thither; it led up over the rocks.

Suddenly, as we toiled our way upward, Rhodes, with the remark that Science had some strange stories to tell, asked me if I had ever heard of Tartaglia's *slates*. I never had, though I had heard of Tartaglia, and I wanted to know about those slates.

"Tombstones," said Milton.

"Tombstones?"

"Tombstones, Bill. What with the terrible poverty, Tartaglia, when educating himself, could not get even a slate, and so he went out and wrote his exercises on tombstones."

"Gosh!"

"And did you ever hear of Demoivre's death? There is a problem for your psychological sharks."

"I never heard of him. And how did the gentleman die?"

"He told them that he had to sleep so many minutes longer each day."

"And did he do it?"

"That's what he did, Bill."

"And," I asked with growing curiosity, "when he had slept through the twenty-four hours? Then what?"

"He never woke up," said Milton Rhodes.

Then he told me that queer story about Isaac Barrow, or, rather, about his father. When sent to school, at Charter-house, young Barrow raised the very deuce and raised it high; so much deuce, in fact, that dad Barrow, whilst praying, said that, if it should be the Divine pleasure to take from him any of his children, he could best stand the loss of Isaac.

And did I know what the heart of a man does when his head is cut off? I (who was wondering at his sudden turn to these queer scientific matters) said I supposed that the heart stops beating. But Milton Rhodes said no; the organ continues its pulsations for an hour or longer.

And had I heard of Spallanzani's very curious experiment with the crow? I never had, but I wanted to. Spallanzani, Milton told me, gave a crow a good feed and then chopped its head off. (That decapitation didn't surprise me any, for I knew that Spallanzani was a real scientist.) The body was placed in a temperature the same as that of the living bird and kept there for six hours. Spallanzani then took the body out, opened it and found that the food which he had given the bird was thoroughly digested.

"These scientists," was my comment, "are queer birds themselves."

Then he told me some strange things about sympathetic vibrations—that a drinking-glass can be smashed by the human voice (I knew that), that an alpine avalanche can be started thundering down by the tinkle of a bell; and so, as Tyndall tells us, the muleteers in the Swiss mountains silence the bells of their animals when in proximity to such danger. And he told me of that musician who came near destroying the Colebrook Dale suspension bridge *with his fiddle.**

Then came the strangest thing of all—the story of Vogt's cricket. The professor severed the body of a cricket (a living cricket, of course) into two pieces, and the fore part then turned round and *ate up the hinder!*

"Yes," Milton Rhodes said, "Science has some queer stories to tell."

"I should say that she has!"

"And maybe," he added, "she'll have a stranger one than ever to tell when we get back—that is, if we ever do."

We passed McClure's Rock, height about seven thousand four hundred feet; made our way along the head of a small glacier, which fell away towards the Nisqually; ascended the cleaver, at this point very low and along the base of which we had been moving; and there, on the other side and coming up within a few yards of the spot where we stood, was the Paradise Glacier, white and beautiful in the sunlight.

* "When the bridge at Colebrook Dale (the first iron bridge in the world) was building, a fiddler came along and said to the workmen that he could fiddle their bridge down. The builders thought this boast a fiddle-de-dee, and invited the itinerant musician to fiddle away to his heart's content. One note after another was struck upon the strings until one was found with which the bridge was in sympathy. When the bridge began to shake violently, the incredulous workmen were alarmed at the unexpected result, and ordered the fiddler to stop."—Prof. J. Lovering.

Milton Rhodes gave me an inquiring look.

"Recognize this spot?" he queried.

"I never saw it before, of course; but, yes, I believe that I do: this is the place where the angel and the demon crossed over, the spot where Scranton, White and Long found the tracks again."

"This is the place."

"And where," I asked, "are the Tamahnowis Rocks?"

"Can't see them from here, Bill. They're right over there, half a mile distant or so, probably three-quarters."

He moved down to the edge of the snow and ice; I followed.

"Now for the creepers," said Milton, seating himself on a rock-fragment. "Then we are off."

A few moments, and we had fastened on the toothed soles of steel and were under way again.

Suddenly Rhodes, who was leading, stopped, raised his alpenstock and pointed with it.

"There they are, Bill!"

And there they were. The Rocks of Tamahnowis—the Spirit, the Demon Rocks—in sight at last.

12
WE ENTER THEIR SHADOW

For a space we stood there in silence looking at that dark mass which reared itself up, like a temple in ruins I thought, in the midst of the crevassed ice. Then I said:

"Who, looking at that pile, would ever dream that there was anything mysterious and terrible about it, anything *scientific?*"

"The place," Milton Rhodes returned, "certainly has an innocent look; but looks, you know, are often deceiving. And how deceiving in this particular instance, that we know full well indeed. Besides Scranton, yourself and me, not a living soul knows how horrible was the death of that poor girl."

I made no response. Many were the thoughts that came and went as I stood there and looked at those Tamahnowis Rocks.

Of a sudden I noticed a slight smile in the eyes of my companion.

"Why the grin?" I queried. "This, I must say, is a sweet time for grins. I would suggest that, instead, you say your prayers."

Rhodes laughed. Then he pointed to my right hand. This, I now discovered, was resting on that pocket which held my revolver.

"I see," he said, "that you have your artillery very handy."

"Yes; and I notice that you have, too."

"I wish that I could have it even more so, Bill.

"You know, old *tillicum*," he added, his brows contracting and a shadow seeming to pass athwart his face and then to return and linger there, "maybe I'll wish that I hadn't dragged you into this wild, unearthly business. And yet I wouldn't care to face it without you beside me."

"*Dragged* me into it?" I exclaimed. "Now, look here: please, Milton, don't say that again."

"I hope, Bill, that I haven't —"

"Not a bit, not a bit. But I hope you will never talk like that any more."

He raised a hand and placed it on my shoulder.

"Pardon me, old *tillicum*," he said. "And yet, after all, I may regret it, for this business before us may prove a most terrible one—something even worse than that."

For a few moments there was silence, and then I said: "Well, let's *klatawah*."

"Yes," said he, turning and starting; "let's *klatawah*."

"And," he added, "do you know what that reminds me of?"

"I wonder."

"Of Sluiskin's appeal to Stevens and Van Trump, down there at the falls that now bear his name:

"'*Wake klatawah! Wake klatawah!*'"

"But," said I, "they went, and they *came back*. That's an augury."

"But," he answered, "if it hadn't been for those steam-caves up there in the crater, they might not have come back, might have perished on the summit that night in the bitter cold. And then the Siwash would have been a true prophet."

"Well, there may be something equivalent to those steam-caves somewhere in the place that we are going to. I don't mean, of course, *in* that pile of rock over there."

"Of course not. But that isn't what's troubling me; it's the possibility that we may be too late."

"Too late?" I exclaimed.

"Just so. It is only at long intervals—so far as we know, that is—that these strange beings appear on the mountain."

"Well?" I queried.

"Well, Bill, glaciers, you know, move."

"I know that. But what on earth has the movement of the ice to do with the appearance of this angel on Mount Rainier?"

But Milton wouldn't tell me that. Instead, he told me to think. Think? I did. I thought hard; but I couldn't see it. However, we were drawing close to the rocks now, and soon I would have the answer. I felt that pocket again. Yes, the revolver was still there!

"Look here!" said I suddenly.

Milton Rhodes, who was on the point of springing across a fissure, turned and looked.

"How does this come?" I wanted to know. "I thought that the Tamahnowis Rocks were on the Cowlitz Glacier?"

"This is the Cowlitz, Bill."

"But we haven't left the Paradise yet."

"Oh, yes, we have. There is no cleaver between them, no anything; at this place it is all one continuous sheet of ice."

"Oh, that's it. Well, the ice is pretty badly crevassed before us. Glad it isn't all like this."

We worked our way forward, twisting and turning. Slowly but steadily we advanced, drawing near and nearer to that dark, frowning, broken mass, wondering (at any rate, I was) about the secrets that we should find there—unless, indeed, we were too late. What had Milton meant by that? How on earth could the apparition of the angel and the demon be in any manner contingent upon the movement of the ice?

Well, we were very near now; we were so near, in fact, that, if there was any one, any *thing* lurking there in the rocks, human or monster (or both) he or it could hear us.

We would soon know whether we had come too late.

Ere long we had got over the fissures and were moving over ice unbroken and smooth. I wondered if this was the spot where, so many years ago, White and Long had been killed. But I did not voice that thought. The truth is that this terrible place held me silent. And, when we moved into the shadow cast by the broken, towering pile, the scene became more weird and terrible than ever.

A few moments, and we halted, so close to the rocky wall, precipitous and broken, that I could have touched it with outstretched hand.

How cold it seemed here, how strange that sinister quality (or was it only my imagination?) of the enveloping shadows!

"Well," said Milton Rhodes, and I noticed that his voice was low and guarded, "here we are."

I made no response.

The silence there was as the silence of a tomb.

13
"I THOUGHT I HEARD SOMETHING"

"What," I asked, "is the first thing to do now?"

"Find the spot where Rhoda Dillingham was killed. The snow-fall of the day before yesterday covered the stains, of course. I feel confident, however, what with the description that Victor Boileau gave me, that I shall recognize the spot the moment I see it. It's over there on the other side, Bill, in the sunlight."

"Why that precise spot?"

"Because I hope to find something there—something that Victor Boileau himself didn't see."

A cold shiver went through my heart. We were so near now. Yes, so near; but near to what? Or had we come too late?

"Now for it, Bill!" said Milton Rhodes.

He turned and began to work his way down along the base of the rock-wall. The ice now sloped steeply, and, from there to the end of the frowning mass of rocks, and for some distance beyond it, the glacier was fissured and split in all directions. The going was really difficult. Had we tried it without the creepers, we should have broken our necks. One consolation was that the distance was a short one. Why on earth had the artist brought his daughter to this awful place?

But, then, there had been nothing terrible about the scene to Dillingham, until the tragedy. As for the appearance of the rocks—yes, I had to acknowledge that—there was nothing intrinsically terrible about it: it was what one knew that made it so. Its sinister, its awful seeming would not have been there had I not known what had happened.

We made our way around the end of the rocky pile into the glare of the sunlight and started up the crevassed and split surface there. The slope, however, was not near so steep as the one we had descended on the other side. Sixty feet, and Rhodes stopped and said, looking eagerly, keenly this way and that:

"This is the place, Bill. There can be no mistake. Here are the two big crevasses that Boileau described. Yes, it was in this very spot, ten or twelve feet from the base of the wall, that the girl lay when her father came—lay dying, that terrible wound in her throat."

He began to scrape the snow away with his steel-soled shoes. A few moments, and he paused and pointed. I shuddered as I saw that stain he had uncovered.

"There. You see, Bill?"

"I see. Cover it up."

I ran my eyes along the base of the rocks; I searched every spot that the eye could reach on the face or in the shadowy recesses of the dark, broken mass, towering there high above us; I looked all around at the fissured ice: but there was nothing unusual to be seen anywhere.

"Where," I asked, and my tones were low and guarded, "did the angel, if the angel was here—where, Milton, could the angel and the demon have vanished so suddenly and without leaving a single trace?"

"There lies our problem, Bill. A very few minutes should find us in possession of the answer—if, that is, we have not come too late. As to the vanishing without leaving a single trace behind them, that no trace was found is by no means tantamount to saying that they left none."

"I know that. But where did they go?"

"Let us," said Rhodes, "see if we can discover the answer."

"I don't think," I observed, "that they could have gone *right into* the rocks: either Dillingham, as he made his way here to the girl, would have seen them, or Boileau would have found the *entrance* to the way that they took."

"At any rate," Rhodes answered, "we may take that, for the moment, as a working hypothesis, and so we will turn our attention now to another quarter. If we fail there—though, remember, ice *moves*, Bill—we will then give these rocks a complete and careful examination with the object of settling the question whether the great Boileau really did see everything that is to be found here."

"And so—" I began.

"And so?" he queried.

"Then they—or it—disappeared by way of the ice."

"Precisely," Rhodes nodded: "by way of the ice. And now you see what I meant when I reminded you that the ice here moves."

"Yes; I believe that I do, at last. Great Heaven, Milton, what can this thing mean?"

"That is for us to seek to discover. And so we will give our attention to these crevasses."

He moved to the edge of one of those big fissures that I have mentioned, the upper one, and peered down into the bluish depths of it. I followed and stood beside him.

"It couldn't have been into this one," he said.

"Impossible," I told him.

He moved along the edge of the crevasse, in the direction of the rocks. I went along after him, my right hand near that pocket which held my revolver.

"And," thought I bitterly to myself, "this is the Twentieth Century!"

"They could," said Rhodes at length, stopping within a few yards of the wall of rock, "have gone into the crevasse at this point. Yes, most certainly they could have done so."

"But where could they have gone to? There is no break in the wall here, not even a crack."

"Don't forget, Bill, that ice moves."

"If *that* is the explanation, we shall go back no wiser than when we came."

"Let us hope," he returned, "that it doesn't prove the explanation. I have no knowledge as to the rate of the ice-movement here.

The Nisqually moves a foot or more a day in summer. The movement here may be very similar, though, on the other hand, there are certain considerations which suggest the possibility that it may be only a few inches per diem."

"It may be so."

"However, Bill, this speculation or surmise will avail us nothing now. So let's give our attention to this other crevasse. And, if it too should reveal nothing—well, there are plenty of others."

"Yes," said I rather dubiously; "there are plenty of others."

"The unusual size of these two," he went on, "and this being the scene of the tragedy led me to think that it would not be a bad idea to start the examination at this point. The great Boileau—and I learned this with not a little satisfaction, Bill, though I may say 'twas with no colossal surprise—the great Boileau did not give even the slightest attention to any crevasse. He knew before ever he came up here, of course, that the girl's death had been a purely accidental one.

"However, let us see what we are to find in this other fissure."

We found it even wider than the one which we had just quitted. And scarcely had we come to a pause there on the edge of it, and within a few yards of the rock, when I started and gave a low exclamation for silence.

For some moments we stood listening intently, but all was silent, save for the low, ghostly whisper of the mountain wind.

"What was it?" Rhodes asked in a low voice.

"I don't know. It may have been nothing, of course. But I certainly thought I heard something."

"Where?"

"I can't say. It seemed to come from out of the rock itself or—from this."

And I indicated the crevasse at our feet.

14
THE WAY TO DROME

The depth of the fissure was here twelve or fifteen feet. A short
distance out, however, it narrowed, and at that point it was almost
completely filled with snow. I noticed even then, in that moment
of tense uncertainty, that it would be very easy for a person to make
his way down that snow to the bottom. A few steps then, and
he would be at the real base of that wall of rock. Yes, *that* would
explain it!

A strange excitement possessed me, though I endeavored to
suppress every sign of it. Yes, the angel and the demon—if the angel had been out upon the ice at the moment of the tragedy—could
have disappeared easily enough. 'Tis true, no tracks had been noticed there. That, however, was no proof positive that there had
been none. And perhaps, forsooth, there had been no tracks there
to discover. The angel might not have been out upon the glacier at
all, and the thing might not have left a single mark in the snow. It
could have disappeared without doing that. For I knew what had
killed poor Rhoda Dillingham.

Supposing, however, that this was indeed the secret, what then?
A great deal was explained, but as much remained inexplicable.
For where on earth, after reaching the bottom of the crevasse, could
the angel and the demon have gone? There was, so far as I could
see, no possible way of escape. There was a remarkable overhang
of rock there at the end, coming down within a yard or so of the
floor. But that was all it was, an overhang. It was not the entrance
to any subterranean passage.

326

Perhaps, if this was indeed the way, we had come too late; perhaps there had been an opening there, an opening that, what with the movement of the ice, was now wholly concealed.

I looked at Milton Rhodes, and on the instant I knew that he too had been noticing all these things. Had the same thoughts come to him also?

"Everything is still now," I observed. "That sound might have been only a fancy."

He nodded slowly.

"Or it might have been made by the glacier. No telling, though, Bill. It might have been real enough and something else. We mustn't forget that for one moment."

"I am not likely to do so. However, what do you make of this?"

"It may be the way to—the way to Drome. And it may, of course, be nothing of the kind. They easily could have vanished into this crevasse."

"And then where could they have gone?"

"Probably the way is blocked by the ice now. Who can say? That overhang down there—"

"Is not an entrance," I told him.

"There may, however, Bill, be something there. It will take us only a moment to find that out."

He turned forthwith and moved along the edge to that spot where the fissure narrowed and it was filled with snow. I followed. A few moments, and we stood at the bottom.

"Great Heaven!" said I as we moved along between those walls of ice.

"What is it, Bill?" queried Milton, pausing and looking back at me.

"Suppose this ice-mass here above were to slip! We'd be flattened between these walls like pancakes!"

Rhodes smiled a little and said he *guessed* we'd be like pancakes all right if that happened. The next moment we were moving forward again, our steel soles grating harshly, though not loudly, upon the glacier-polished bottom.

"You see," said I as we drew near to the end, "the way to Drome does not lie here. Under that overhang there is nothing but rock. There is not even a crack, to say nothing of an entrance."

"It certainly looks like it, Bill. However, it will do no harm to make an examination. That there *is* an entrance we know. And, if it isn't here—well, then it must be some place else. And, unless we are too late, we'll search these Rocks of Tamahnowis until we find it."

A few steps, and Rhodes halted, his left hand resting against the rock. He stooped to peer under. I exclaimed and involuntarily seized him by the sleeve.

"There it is again!"

He straightened up, and we stood in an attitude of riveted attention. The place, however, was as silent as the grave.

"I know that I heard something," I told him.

"Yes; I heard it that time, too," said Milton Rhodes. "Where did it come from?"

I shook my head.

"Maybe one of the sounds that the glacier makes," he proffered.

"It is possible. But—"

"Well?"

"It seemed to come right out of the rocks; but that isn't possible."

"We'll see about that, Bill."

He pressed a button, and the strong rays of his electric light played upon the dark rock and the blue ice. The light in his left hand, he dropped to his knees and looked under. I heard an exclamation and saw him move forward. At that instant a sound brought me up and whirled me around.

My heart was in my throat. I could have sworn that the sound had issued from some point just behind me. But there was nothing to be seen there—only the walls of blue ice and the blue sky above.

"Must have been some sound made by the glacier slipping or something," I told myself.

I turned—to find that Milton Rhodes had vanished! For a little space I stood staring and wondering, then called in a low voice:

"Milton. Oh, Milton."

No answer.

"Milton."

Silence still.

"Milton," I called once more. "Where are you?"

The answer was a scream, a scream that threatened to arrest the coursing blood in my veins—the sound seeming to issue from the very heart of the rock-mass there before me.

15
THE ANGEL

The scream ceased as suddenly as it had come. I drew my revolver, snapped on the electric light, and, stooping low, looked into that spot where, a few moments before, Milton Rhodes had so suddenly and mysteriously disappeared.

Nothing but the unbroken rock before me. And yet Rhodes had vanished. I turned the light full upon the low roof, and then I exclaimed aloud: the entrance was there!

I dropped to my hands and knees and moved under, the pack not a little impeding my movements. An instant, and I was standing upright peering into a high, narrow tunnel, which some convulsion of nature, in some lost age of the earth, had rent right through the living rock.

Nothing was to be seen, save the broken walls, floor and roof, deep, eerie shadows crawling and gliding as the light moved. The view, however, was a very restricted one, for the gallery, which sloped gently upward, gave a sudden turn at a distance of only thirty feet or so. What awaited me somewhere beyond that turn?

For a few moments I listened intently. Not the faintest sound—nothing but the loud beating of my heart. What had happened to Rhodes?

"Milton!" I called softly. "Oh, Milton!"

No answer came.

I grasped a projection of rock, drew myself up into the tunnel and advanced as rapidly and silently as possible, the light and the alpenstock in my left hand, the revolver in the right. But it was not very silently, what with the creepers. At times they grated harshly; it was as if spirit-things were mocking me with suppressed, demoniacal laughter. Yet I could not pause to remove those grating shoes of toothed steel. Every second even might be precious now.

I drew near the turn, the revolver thrust forward in readiness for instant action.

I reached it, and there just beyond, a dark figure was standing, framed in a blaze of light.

It was Milton Rhodes.

He turned his head, and I saw a smile move athwart his features.

"Well, we've found it, Bill!" said he.

I was drawing near to him.

"That scream?" I said. "Who gave that terrible scream?"

"Terrible? It didn't sound terrible to me," smiled Milton Rhodes. "Fact is, Bill, I'd like to hear it again."

"What on earth are you talking about?"

"'Tis so."

"Who was it? Or what was it?"

"Why, the angel herself!" he told me.

"Where is she now?"

"Gone, Bill; she's gone. When she saw me, she fetched up, gave that scream, then turned and vanished—around that next turn."

"What is she like, Milton?"

"I wish that I could tell you! But how can a man describe Venus? I know one thing, Bill: if all the daughters of Drome are as fair as this one that I saw, I know where all the movie queens of the future are coming from."

I looked at him, and I laughed.

"Wait till you see her, Bill. Complexion like alabaster, white as Rainier's purest snow! And hair! Oh, that hair, Bill! Like ten billion dollars' worth of spun gold!"

"Gosh."

"Wait till you see her," said Milton.

"And the demon?" I queried.

"I didn't see any demon, Bill."

There was silence for a little space.

"Then," I said, "the whole thing is true, after all."

"You mean what grandfather Scranton set down in his journal, and the rest of it?"

I nodded.

"I never doubted that, Bill."

"At times," I told him, "I didn't doubt it. Then, again, it all seemed so wild and unearthly that I didn't know what to think."

"I think," he said with a wan smile, "that you know what to think now—now when you are standing in this very way to Drome, whatever Drome may be."

"Yes. And yet the thing is so strange. Think of it. A world of which men have never dreamed, save in the wildest romance! An underground world. Subterranean ways, subterranean cities, men and women there—"

"Cavernicolous Aphrodites!" said Milton Rhodes.

"And all down there in eternal darkness!" I exclaimed. "Why, the thing is incredible. No wonder that I sometimes find myself wondering if I am not in a dream."

Said Milton Rhodes:

> "*All* that we see or seem
>   Is but a dream within a dream.'

"But come, Bill," he added. "Don't let this *a priori* stuff bowl you over. In the first place, it isn't dark down there—when, that is, you get down far enough."

"In Heaven's name, how do you know that?"

"Why, for one thing, if this subterranean world was one of unbroken darkness, the angel (and the demon) would be blind, like those poor fishes in the Mammoth Cave. But she is no more blind than you or I. Ergo, if for no other reason, we shall find light down there."

"Of course, they have artificial light, or—"

"I don't mean that. If there had not been some other illumination, this strange race (of whose very existence Science has never even dreamed) would have ceased to exist long ago—if, indeed, it ever could have begun."

"But no gleam of sunlight can ever find its way down to that world."

"It never can, of course. But there are other sources of light—nebulas and comets in the heavens, for example, and auroras, phosphorus and fireflies here on earth. The phenomena of phosphorescence are by no means so rare as might be imagined. Why, as Nichol showed, though any man who uses his eyes can see it himself, there is light inherent *even in clouds.*"

I have the professor's book before me as I write—J. P. Nichol, LL.D., Professor of Astronomy in the University of Glasgow—and here are his own words:

"Whatever their origin, they [the auroras] show the existence of causes in virtue of whose energy the upper strata of our atmosphere become self-luminous, sometimes in a high degree; for, in northern regions, our travelers have *read* by their brilliance. But the Aurora is not the only phenomenon which indicates the existence of a power in the matter of our globe to emit light. One fact, that must have been often noticed, forcibly impresses me with the conviction, that here, through what seems common, truths of much import will yet be reached. In the dead of night, when the sky is clear, and one is admiring the brilliancy of the stars, hanging over a perfectly obscured earth, a cloud, well known to observing astronomers, will at times begin to form, and it then spreads with astonishing rapidity over the whole heavens. The light of the stars being thus utterly shut out, one might suppose that surrounding objects would, if possible, become more indistinct: but no! what was formerly invisible can now be clearly seen; not because of lights from the earth being reflected back from the cloud—for very often there are none—but in virtue of *the light of the cloud itself*, which, however faint, is yet a similitude of the dazzling shell of the Sun."

After mentioning the phosphorescence of the dark hemisphere of Venus and the belief that something similar has been seen on the unillumined surface of our satellite, he continues thus:

"But the circumstance most remarkably corroborative of the mysterious truth to which these indications point, is the appearance of our midnight luminary during a total eclipse. By theory, she ought to disappear utterly from the heavens. She should vanish, and the sky seem as if no Moon were in being; but, on the contrary, and even when she passes the very centre of the Earth's shadow, she seems a huge *disc* of bronze, in which the chief spots can easily be described by a telescope."

And that, remember, when the moon is in the utter blackness of the earth's shadow. Of course, another explanation has been advanced; but it does not take the professor long to dispose of that.

"It has been put forth in explanation," he says, "that a portion of the rays of the Sun must be reflected by our atmosphere and bent toward the eclipsed disc, from which again they are reflected to the Earth—thus giving the Moon that bronze color; but, the instant the hypothesis is tested by calculation, we discern its utter inefficiency. Nor is there any tenable conclusion save this:—That the matter both of Sun and planets is capable, in certain circumstances whose exact conditions are not known, of evolving the energy we term light."

All this, and more, Rhodes explained to me, succinctly but clearly.

"Oh, we'll find light, Bill," said he.

All the same this subterranean world for which we were bound presented some unpleasant possibilities, in addition, that is, to those concomitant to its being a habitat of demons—and Heaven only knew what besides.

"And then there is the air," I said. "As we descend, it will become denser and denser, until at last we will be able to use these ice-picks on it."

Rhodes, who was removing his creepers, laughed.

"We will have to make a vertical descent of three and one half miles below the level of the sea—a vertical descent of near five miles from this spot where we stand, Bill—before we reach a pressure of even two atmospheres."

"The density then increases rapidly, doesn't it?"

"Oh, yes. Three and a half miles more, and we are under a pressure of four atmospheres, or about sixty pounds to the square inch. Three and a half miles farther down, or ten and one half miles in all below the level of the sea, and we have a pressure upon us of eight atmospheres. Fourteen miles, and it will be sixteen atmospheres. At thirty-five miles the air will have the density of water, at forty-eight miles it will be as dense as mercury, and at fifty miles we shall have it as dense as gold."

"That will do!" I told him. "You know that we can never get down that far."

"I have no idea how far we can go down, Bill."

"You know that we could never stand such pressures as those."

"I know that. But, as a matter of fact, I don't know what the pressures are at those depths. Nor does any other man know. What I said a moment ago is, of course, according to the law; but there is something wrong with the law, founded upon that of Mariotte—as any physicist will tell you."

"What's wrong with it?"

"At any rate; the law breaks down as one goes upward, and I have no doubt that it will be found to do so as one descends below the level of the sea. If the densities of the atmosphere decrease in a geometrical ratio as the distances from sea-level increase in an arithmetical ratio, then, at a distance of only one hundred miles up, we should have virtually a perfect vacuum. The rarity there would be absolutely inconceivable. For the atmospheric density at that height would be only *one billionth* of what it is at the earth's surface."

"And what is the real density there?"

"No man knows or can know," replied Rhodes, "until he goes up there to see. But meteors, rendered incandescent by the resistance they encounter, show that a state of things exists at that high altitude very different from the one that would be found there if our formulae were correct and our theories were valid. And so, I have no doubt, we shall find it down in Drome.

"Formulae are very well in their place," he went on, "but we should never forget, Bill, that they are often builded on mere assumption and that a theory is only a theory until experiment (or experience) has shown us that it is a fact. And that reminds me: do you know what Percival Lowell says about formulae?"

I said that I didn't.

"'Formulae,' says the great astronomer, 'are the anaesthetics of thought.'

"I commend that very highly," Milton Rhodes added, "to our fiction editors and our writers of short stories."

"But—"

"But me no buts, Bill," said Milton. "And what do your scientists know about the interior of this old earth that we inhabit, anyway? Forsooth, but very little, Billy, me lad. Why they don't even know what a volcano is. One can't make a journey into the interior of the earth on a scratch-pad and a lead-pencil, or, if he does, we may be pardoned if we do not give implicit credence to all that he chooses to tell us when he comes back. For instance, one of these armchair Columbuses (he made the journey in a machine called d^2y by dx^2, and came out in China) says that he found the interior in a state of igneous fluidity. And another? Why, he tells us that the whole earth is as rigid as steel, that it is solid to the very core."

"It seems," said I, "to be a case of

"'Great contest follows, and much learned dust
    Involves the combatants; each claiming truth,
    And truth disclaiming both.'"

"The truth, in this case, is not yet known, of course," replied Milton Rhodes, "though I trust that you and I, Bill, are fated to learn it—some of it, I should say."

He smiled a queer, wan smile.

"Whether we are fated, also, to reveal it to the world, to *our* world—well, as for that, *quien sabe?*" he said.

"Then," I remarked, my fingers busy removing my ice-creepers, "what we read about the state of things in the interior of the earth—the temperature, the pressure, the density—then all that is pure theory?

"Of course. How could it be anything else? All theory, save, that is, the mean density of the earth. And that mean density gives us something to think about, for it is just a little more than twice that of the *surface materials.* With all this enormous pressure that we hear so much about and the resultant increase of density with depth, the weight of the earth certainly ought to be more than only five and one half times that of a globe of equal size composed of nothing but water."*

"Kind of queer, all right," was my comment.

"It is queer, all right—as the old lady said when she kissed the cow. However, as old Dante has it, 'Son! our time asks thrifter using.'"

As the last words left his lips, I straightened up, the toothed shoes in my hand; and, as I did so, I started and cried:

"Hear that?"

Rhodes made no answer. For some moments we stood there in breathless expectation; but that low mysterious sound did not come again.

I said:

"What *was* that?"

"I wish that I knew, Bill. It was faint, it was—well, rather strange."

"It was more than that," I told him. "It seemed to me to be hollow—like the sound of some great door suddenly closing."

---

* "It has been calculated that at the depth of 35 miles, air, subjected to the pressure of a column of matter of the mean density of that at the surface of the earth, would acquire the density of water; that at the depth of 173 miles, water itself, which is eminently incompressible, would acquire the density of marble; and at the centre, marble would have a density 119 times greater than at the surface. *But the comparatively small mean density of the mass [of the earth] proves that none of these effects take place.*"—Brande.

My companion looked at me rather quickly.

"Think so, Bill?" he said. "I thought 'twas like the sound of something *falling*."

There was a pause, one of many moments, during which pause we stood listening and waiting; but the gallery remained as silent as though it had never known the tread of any living thing.

"Well, Bill," said Milton Rhodes suddenly, "we shall never learn what Drome means if we stay in this spot. As for the creepers, I am going to leave mine here."

The place where he put them, a jutting piece of rock, was a conspicuous one; no one passing along the tunnel could possibly fail to notice the objects resting there. Mine I placed beside them, wondering as I did so if I should ever see this spot again.

Milton then wrote a short note, which recorded little more than our names, the date of our great discovery and that we were going farther. This, carefully folded, he placed beside the creepers and put a rock-fragment upon it. I wondered as I watched him whose would be the eyes that would discover it. Some inhabitant of this underground world, of course, and to such a one the record would be so much Greek. 'Twas utterly unlikely that any one from the world which we were leaving would ever see that record.

"And now, Bill," said Milton Rhodes, "down we go!"

And the next moment we were going—had begun our descent into this most mysterious and dreadful place.

16

"ARE WE ENTERING DANTE'S INFERNO ITSELF?"

When Scranton came with his weird story of Old He, I was, I confess, not a little puzzled by his and Milton's reference to the extraordinary scientific possibilities that it presented. At first I could not imagine what on earth they meant. But I saw all those possibilities very clearly now, and a thousand more I imagined. I knew a wild joy, exultation, and yet at the same time the wonder and the mystery of it all made me humble and sober of spirit. I admit, too, that a fear—a fear for which I can find no adequate name—had laid its palsied and cold fingers upon me.

In a few moments we reached that spot where the angel had vanished. There we paused in curiosity, looking about; but nothing was to be seen. The gallery—which from this point swung sharp to the right and went down at a rather steep angle—was as silent as some interstellar void.

"Bill," smiled Milton Rhodes, "he is idle who might be better employed."

And he started on, or, rather, down. A hundred feet, however—we were now under the glacier—and he halted, turned his light full upon the left-hand wall, pointed and said:

"There you are, Bill—the writing on the wall."

I pressed to his side and stood staring. The rock there was as smooth, almost, as a blackboard; and upon it, traced in white chalk, were three inscriptions, with what we took to be names appended to them. That on the right was clearly a very recent one—had been placed there doubtless, at the most but a few days since, by that "cavernicolous Venus" that Milton Rhodes had seen for so fleeting a moment.

It was Milton's opinion that the characters were alphabetical ones, though at first I was at a loss to understand how they could be anything to him but an utter mystery. The letters were formed by straight lines only. The simplest character was exactly like a plain capital T, with, that is, the vertical line somewhat elongated. And it was made to perform the office of another letter by the simple expedient of standing it upon its head. The number of cross-lines increased up to six, three at the top and three at the bottom; and in one or two characters there were two vertical lines, placed close together.

"Evidently," observed Milton Rhodes, "this alphabet was constructed on strictly scientific principles."

For a space we stood there looking, wondering what was recorded in that writing so strange and yet, after all, so very and beautifully simple. Then Milton proceeded to place another record there, and, as he wrote, he hummed:

> "'When I see a person's name
>   Scratched upon a glass,
>   I know he owns a diamond
>   And his father owns an ass.'"

The inscription finished, we resumed our descent. The way soon became steep and very difficult.

"That Aphrodite of yours," I observed as we made our way clown a particularly rugged place, "must have the agility of a mountain-goat."

"Your rhetoric, Bill Barrington Carter, is horrible. Wait till you see her; you'll never be guilty of thinking of a goat when she has your thoughts."

"By the way, what kind of a light did the lady have?"

"Light? Don't know. I was so interested in the angel herself that I never once thought of the light that she carried. I don't know that she needs a light, anyway."

"What on earth are you talking about?"

"Why, I fancy, Bill, that her very presence would make even Pluto's gloomy realm bright and beautiful as the Garden of the Hesperides."

"Oh, gosh!" was my comment.

"Wait till you see her, Bill."

"I'll probably see her demon first."

"Hello!" exclaimed Milton.

"What now?"

"Look at that," said he, pointing. "I think we have the explanation of that mysterious sound, which you thought was like that of a great door suddenly closing: in her descent, she dislodged a rock-fragment, and that sound we heard must have been produced by the mass as it went plunging down."

"'Tis very likely, but—"

"Great Heaven!" he exclaimed.

"What is it now?"

"I wonder, Bill, if she lost her footing here and went plunging down, too."

I had not thought of that. And the possibility that that lovely and mysterious being might be lying somewhere down there crushed and bleeding, perhaps dying or lifeless, made me feel very sad. We sent the rays of our powerful lights down into those silent depths of the tunnel, but nothing was visible there, save the dark rock and those fearful shadows—fearful what with the secrets that might be hidden there.

"The answer won't come to us, Bill," said Milton.

"No, "I returned as we started down; "we must go get it."

The gallery at this place had an average width of, I suppose, ten feet, and the height would average perhaps fifteen. The reader must not picture the walls, the roof and the floor as smooth, however. The rock was much broken, in some spots very jagged. The gallery pitched at an angle of nearly forty-five degrees, which will give some idea of the difficulties encountered in the descent.

At length we reached what may be called the bottom; here the tunnel gave another turn and the pitch became a gentle slope. And there we found it, the rock-fragment, weighing perhaps two hundred pounds, that the angel had dislodged in her descent—which doubtless had been a hurried, a wild one.

"Thank Heaven!" I exclaimed, "she didn't come down with it!"

"Amen," said Milton.

Then a sudden thought struck me, a thought so unworthy that I did not voice it aloud. But to myself I said:

"It is possible that we may find ourselves, before we get out of this, wishing that she had."

If a human being, one of the very best of human beings even, were to voice his uttermost, his inmost thoughts, what a shameful, what a terrible monster they would call him—or her!

And the demon? Where was the angel's demon?

I could give no adequate description of those hours that succeeded. Steadily we continued the descent—now gentle, now steep, rugged and difficult. Sometimes the way became very narrow—indeed, at one point we had to squeeze our way through, so closely did the walls approach each other—then, again, it would open out, and we would find ourselves in a veritable chamber. And, in one of these, a lofty place, the vaulted roof a hundred feet or more above our heads, we made a discovery—a skeleton, quasi-human and *with wings*.

I made an exclamation of amazement.

"In the name of all that's wonderful and terrible," I cried, "are we entering Dante's Inferno itself?"

A faint smile touched the face of Rhodes.

"Don't you," he asked, "know what this is?"

"It must be the bones of a demon."

"Precisely. Grandfather Scranton, you'll remember, wounded that monster, up there by the Tamahnowis Rocks. Undoubtedly the bullet reached a vital spot, and these are that creature's bones."

"But," I objected, "these are *human* bones—a human skeleton with wings. According to Scranton, there was nothing at all human about the appearance of that thing which he called a demon."

"I admit," said Rhodes, "that this skeleton, at the first glance, has an appearance remarkably human—if, that is, one can forget the wings. The skull, I believe, more than anything else, contributes to that effect; and yet, at a second glance, even that loses its human semblance. For look at those terrible jaws and those terrible teeth. Who ever saw a human being with jaws and teeth like those? And look at the large scapulae and the small hips and the dwarfish, though strong, nether limbs. Batlike, Bill, strikingly so. And those feet. No toes; they are talons. And see that medial ridge on the sternum, for the attachment of the great pectoral muscles."

"A bat-man, then?" I queried.

"I should say a bat-ape."

"Or an ape-bat."

"Whichever you prefer," smiled Milton.

"Well," I added, "at any rate, we have a fair idea now of what a demon is like."

Little wonder, forsooth, that old Sklokoyum had declared that the thing was a demon from the white man's Inferno itself. And this creature so dreadful—well, the angel had one like it for a companion. When Rhodes saw her, she was, of course, without that terrible attendant: undoubtedly the next time, though—how long would it be?—she would not be alone.

"Oh, well," I consoled myself, "we have our revolvers."

17
LIKE BALEFUL EYES

According to the aneroid, this great chamber is about four thousand feet above the level of the sea; in other words, we had already made a vertical descent of some four thousand feet. We were now about as high above the sea as the snout of the Nisqually Glacier. But what was our direction from the Tamahnowis Rocks? So sinuous had been this strange subterranean gallery, my orientation had been knocked into a cocked hat. It was Milton's belief, however, that we had been moving in a northerly direction, that we were still under the peak itself, probably under the great Emmons Glacier. I confess that I would not have cared to place a wager on the subject. Goodness only knew where we were, but of one thing there could be no doubt: we were certainly there.

"Why," I asked, "didn't we bring along a compass?"

"I think," returned Milton Rhodes, slipping loose his pack and lowering it to the floor, "that, as it was, we had a case of another straw and the camel's back's busted. Let's take a rest—it's twenty minutes after one—and a snack. And another thing: we wouldn't know whether to trust the compass or not."

"Why so?"

"Local attraction, Bill. Many instances of this could be given. One will suffice. Lieutenant Underwood, of the Wilkes Exploring Expedition, found a deviation of thirteen and a quarter points on the summit of the Cobu Rock, in the Feejees—one hundred and forty-nine degrees. The Island of Nairai was directly north, and yet, according to the compass, it bore southeast-by-south one quarter south, whilst, placed at the foot of the rock, that very same compass said Nairai bore north! So you see that that faithful friend of man, and especially of the mariner, has in its friendships some qualities that are remarkably human.

"Still," Rhodes added, "I wish that we had brought one along. Also, we should have brought a manometer, for the aneroid will be worthless after we have descended below sea-level. Oh, well, the boiling-point of water will give us the atmospheric pressure: under a pressure of two atmospheres, water boils at $249.5°$ Fahrenheit; under a pressure of three atmospheres, at $273.3°$; four atmospheres, $291.2°$; five, $306°$; six, $318.2°$; seven, $329.6°$; eight, $339.5°$; and so on. On the summit of Rainier, it boils at about $185°$."

"I wish that we were headed for the summit," said I. "Eight atmospheres! When we reach that pressure—if we ever do—we'll be ten and a half miles below the level of the sea, won't we?"

Rhodes nodded.

"According to the law. But, as I remarked, there is something wrong with the law. 'Tis my belief that we shall be able to descend much deeper than ten and one half miles—that is, that the atmospheric pressure will permit us to do so."

"That qualification," I told him, "is very apropos, for there is no telling what the inhabitants of this underground world will permit us to do or will do to us—bat-apes or ape-bats, humans, or both."

"That, of course, is very true, Bill."

"And," said I, "we won't need a manometer, or we won't need to ascertain the boiling-point of water, to know that the pressure is increasing. Our eardrums will make us painfully aware of that fact."

"When that comes, swallow, Billy, swallow, and the pain will be no more."

"Swallow?"

"Swallow," Milton nodded.

"Great Barmecide, swallow what?"

"Swallow the pain, Bill. For look you. Deglutition opens the Eustachian tube. Some of the dense air enters the drum and counteracts the pressure on the outside of the membrane. You keep swallowing. The air in the drum becomes as dense as that outside; there is no pressure on the membrane now—or, rather, the pressures are in perfect equilibrium—and, presto and abracadabra, the pain is gone."

"Who would have thunk it?"

"A gink," said Rhodes, "going into compressed air had better think it, or do it without thinking it. He may have his eardrums burst in if he doesn't."

"But why does the Eustachian tube open only when we swallow?"

"To shut from the ear the sounds produced in the throat and mouth. If the tube were always open, our heads would be so many bedlams."

"Wonderful Nature!" I exclaimed.

"Oh, she does fairly well," admitted Milton Rhodes.

"And I suppose," I said, "that the pain in the ears experienced by those who ascend high mountains is to be explained in the same way, only vice versa. They too ought to swallow."

"Of course. At lofty heights, the dense air in the drum presses the membrane outwards. Swallowing permits the dense air to escape. One swallows until the pressure on the inside equals that of the rarefied outside air, and, hocus-pocus and presto, the pain has evaporated."

"I hope," I said, "that all our difficulties will be as easily resolved."

"Hey!" cried Milton.

"What's the matter now?"

"Stop *swallowing* that water! We're got food sufficient for a week, but we haven't got water to last a week or anything like a week. Keep up that guzzling, and your canteen will be empty before sunset."

"Sunset? Sweet Pluto! Sunrise, sunset or high noon, it's all the same here in Erebus."

"You'll say that it's very different," dryly remarked Milton Rhodes, "if you find the fingers of Thirst at your throat."

"Surely there is water in this place—somewhere."

"Most certainly there is. But we don't know how far we are from that somewhere. And, until we get to it, our policy, Bill, must be one of watchful conservation."

A silence ensued. I sank into profound and gloomy meditation. Four thousand feet down. A mile deeper, and where would we be? The prospect certainly was, from any point of view, dark and mysterious enough, dark and mysterious enough, forsooth, to satisfy the wildest dream of a Poe or a Doré. To imagine a Dante's Inferno, however, is one thing, and to find yourself in it is quite another. These are things, by the way, that should not be confounded. 'Tis true, we weren't in it yet; but we were on our way.

I hasten to say, though, that I had no thoughts of turning back. No such thought, even the slightest, was entertained for one single moment. I did not blink, that was all. I believed our enterprise was a very dangerous one; I believed it was very probable that we should never return to the light of the sun. Such thoughts are not pleasant, are, indeed, horrible. And yet, in the very horror of them, I found a strange fascination. Yes, we might leave our bones in this underground world, in this very gallery even. Even so, we should have our own exceeding great reward. For ours would be the guerdon of dying in a stranger, a more wonderful quest than any science or discovery ever had known. A strange reward, you say mayhap, and perhaps you wonder what such a reward can mean to a dying or a dead man. All I have to say is that, if you do, you know naught of that flaming spirit which moves the scientist and the discoverer, that such as you should never—indeed, can ever—seek the dread secrets of Nature or journey to her hidden places.

We rested there for exactly one hour. The temperature, by the way, was 57° Fahrenheit. When we resumed the descent, I was using the phosphorus-lamp instead of the electric one. It was not likely that even our electric lights would fail us; still there was no guessing what might happen, and it might be well, I thought, to adopt a policy of light-conservation also. As for the phosphorus lamps, these would furnish light for *six months*. In this, they were simply wonderful; but there was one serious drawback: the light emitted was a feeble one.

The manufacture of this lamp (at one time used, I believe, in Paris, and probably elsewhere, in magazines containing explosives) is simplicity itself. Into a glass phial is put a small piece of phosphorus. The phial is filled two-thirds full of olive-oil, heated to the boiling point. The thing is hermetically corked, and there you are. When you wish to use your wonderful little pharos, you simply allow air to enter. The space above the oil becomes luminous then. You replace the cork, and the phial remains sealed until there is occasion to restore the waning light, which you do, of course, by allowing more air to enter. As has been said, such a phial will furnish light for a half-year.

These phials of ours were set each in a metal frame and protected by a guard in such fashion that it would take a heavy blow to break the glass. When not in use, they were kept in strong metal cylinders. Of course, the electric light could be turned on at any instant.

There were places where the gallery pitched in a way to make the head swim, many spots in which we had to exercise every caution; a false step might have spelled irrevocable disaster. I wondered how the angel had passed down those difficult places, and many pictures of that mysterious creature, as I wondered, came and went. Well, she had passed down and that without mishap. Where was she now? Indeed, where were we ourselves?

Steadily we toiled our downward way. For a long distance, the gallery ran with but slight deviation either to the right or to the left, though the descent was much broken; I mean now was steep and now gentle, now at some angle intermediate. Rhodes thought that we were now moving in an easterly direction; it might have been north, east, south or west for all I knew. Not a trickle of water had we seen, not even a single drop, which I confess caused some unpleasant thoughts to flicker through my mind.

At five o'clock we were two thousand feet above sea-level; at half past seven, about half a thousand. And we then decided to call it a day. Nor was I at all sorry to do so, even though we might be near some strange, even great discovery, for I was very tired, and sore from the top of my head to the end of my toes. I was in fair trim, and so was Milton Rhodes; but it would take us some time to get used to such work as this.

A very gentle current of air, so slight that it required experiment to detect it, was passing down the gallery. The temperature here was 62° Fahrenheit.

We had stopped before a cavity in the wall, and, in that little chamber, we passed the night, one holding watch whilst the other slept.

My dreams were dreadful, but otherwise the night was as peaceful as any that ever passed over Eden. Neither Rhodes nor I, during that strange, eerie vigil there in the heart of the living rock, heard even the faintest, the most fleeting sound. As the watcher sat there waiting and listening, whilst the minutes slowly passed, he found himself—at any rate, I know that I did—almost wishing that some pulsation would come, so heavy and awful was the stillness of the place.

But a sound we were to hear. We had been journeying for about an hour and a half and had just passed below sea-level. In that place Rhodes had left the aneroid. Of a sudden Milton, who was leading the way, halted with a low, sharp interjection for silence. When my look struck him, he was standing in an attitude of the most riveted attention.

"There!" he exclaimed. "Did you hear that, Bill?"

The air had pulsed to the faintest sound; now all was still again.

"What was it?" I asked, my voice a whisper.

"Don't know, Bill. Haven't an idea. There!"

Again that gentle pulsation touched the ear, and again it was gone. And a strange thing was that, for the life of me, I could not have told whether it came from below or from behind us.

"There it is again!" said Rhodes.

I flashed on my electric light, to the full power.

"A whisper!" I exclaimed. "Angel, demon, human or what? And, great Heaven, Milton!"

"What now, Bill?" he asked quickly.

"It's something *behind us!*"

He started. He turned his light up the tunnel, and for some moments we stood peering intently. Not a moving thing was to be seen there, however—only the moving shadows.

"Again!" said Milton Rhodes. "But it isn't a whisper, Bill. And it didn't come from up there."

"The thing," I told him, "could be hiding in shadow—hiding and watching us."

"It's not up there; it's ahead."

"Wherever it is, what on earth can it be? Whatever it is, what does this mean?"

"That we shall learn."

We resumed our descent, every sense, you may be sure, on the *qui vive*. The tunnel here inclined rather steeply; a little space, however, and the dip was a gentle one. The sounds soon became one steady, unbroken whisper; then a dull melancholy murmur.

Abruptly Milton Rhodes stopped. He turned to me, and he laughed.

"Know now what it is, Bill?"

This was not a moment, I thought, for laughter or anything like it.

"Sounds like the growling of beasts," I said, peering intently down the passage. "I wonder if the angel—there are two kinds of angel, you know—has turned loose a whole pack, or herd, or flock, of those demons."

To my surprise and astonishment, Rhodes burst into outright laughter.

"Well?" said I rather testily. "Why all the cachinnation?"

"Forgive me, Bill. But it isn't a pack of demons—or a flock of those charming creatures."

"How on earth do you know *what* it is?"

"It's water."

"Water?"

"Yes. H_2O."

"Water? I'm from Missouri. You'd better see that your revolver is handy. Who ever heard water make a shivery sound like that?"

"You'll see that I'm right, Bill, though I think that you'll hear first."

Ere long there could be no doubt about it: Milton was right; it was the sound of falling water. I was not in a hurry, however, to admit the fact. I had to let myself down gracefully. At length, though, it was impossible to hold out any longer.

"Must be at quite a distance," I said; "sounds carry a long way in tubes, and that is what this tunnel is."

Steadily we made our way along and down, and, just as steadily, the sound increased in volume. The gallery made several sharp turns, and then of a sudden the sound rose from a loud growl to a roar, and we fetched up and an exclamation burst from us.

It is impossible to convey to the reader the eerie effect of that sudden, strange transition. One moment we were in the gallery; the next we had issued from it and stood in a most tremendous cavern, or, rather, we stood on a ledge or a shelf high up on one of the walls of that cavern.

The opposite side was but dimly visible. The roof swept across a hundred feet or more above our heads. And the bottom? I gazed at the edge of the rock-shelf on which we stood, out and down into that yawning abyss, and I felt a shudder run through me and one through my heart.

The roar of the falling waters came from our right. We turned the rays of our lights in that direction, but nothing was visible there, save the dark limestone rock and Cimmerian blackness.

We then moved to the edge and turned our lights down into those awful depths—to depths perhaps never before touched by ray of light since time began. Far down the beams went plunging and farther still; but we could not see the bottom. Bottom there was, however, for the water was tumbling and growling down there.

I was glad to draw back from the edge, and I leaned against the rock-wall and gazed upon the dark scene in wonder, amazement and in awe.

In a few moments Rhodes joined me.

"Well, what do you think of it, Bill?"

"Milton, this is awful."

"It is. I have never seen a sight more strange and terrible."

"And the angel?" I queried.

"What about her, Bill?"

"How on earth did she make her way through this awful place?"

"Why, along this ledge on which we are standing. There is no other way."

I glanced along that shelf, and I did not like what I saw.

"She's got a better head," I told him, "than I have got. Why didn't we bring along an airplane? I wonder if the way lies down or up, up towards the fall."

We bent over and examined the rock.

"Down," I observed.

"Down," Milton nodded.

Whilst I stood there pondering this and wondering what was down there in the blackness of that frightful chasm, Rhodes moved off to the right and examined the ledge there.

"And *up* too," he announced. "Somebody or some thing, or both, has gone up towards the fall."

"Great Heaven, if we get caught between them!"

"The programme *is* becoming interesting," Milton Rhodes admitted.

For a time we stood in silence, then he said:

"I suggest, Bill, that we go up and take a look-see."

I nodded. So far as I could perceive, one way was just as good— I mean just as bad—as the other.

That shelf was, as a whole, not an easy thing to negotiate, and some spots made my head swim and made me wish mightily that I was somewhere else. Undoubtedly, some thousands of years in the dim and mysterious past, the stream once flowed at this level; at any rate, this is the only theory that, in my opinion, will explain that ledge, and something which we were soon to discover. Not that I ever spent much time in worrying about theories and hypotheses; the facts themselves gave me enough to think about, enough and to spare.

At times the shelf would be twenty or thirty feet in width or even more, and then the going was easy enough; but at other times the space would contract to something like a yard, and then it was quite another story. Indeed, once or twice Milton Rhodes himself, an experienced and fearless mountain-climber, was glad, I believe, that the way was no narrower. As for what those moments meant to me—well, I never posed as a mountaineer or a steeplejack.

For fifteen minutes or so, I believe, we toiled along that terrible place, and then of a sudden came the end. Nothing before us but the bare precipitous rocky wall and the black profundity of the chasm, and up above a ghostly thing crawling, crawling down, ever down, and filling the place with thunder—the fall itself. Where did the water come from? From one of the glaciers? And, a question more interesting, where did it go?

"We must go back," said Milton Rhodes. "The road to Drome does not lie here."

Scarcely had we turned when I started, and then I cried out sharply.

"Look!" I said, pointing with my alpenstock down the cavern. "Look at that!"

Far down the cave a light was gleaming, where a moment before no light had been. And on the instant another shone beside it. A second or two, however, and they had vanished.

"Moving," was Rhodes' explanation. "The bearers of those lights moved behind something."

"No!" I told him. "They didn't move. They just went out. And look! *Again!*"

There the lights were again—gleaming at us for all the world like the dim and baleful eyes of some waiting monster.

18
"THAT'S WHERE THEY ARE WAITING FOR US!"

For some moments those yellow eyes gleamed at us, then vanished. The lids of that waiting monster (so to speak) had closed over them.

I had watched them very intently, and I was sure that there had been no movement of the eyes themselves. Milton, however, was just as sure that they had moved.

"To the right or to the left?" I queried.

"Neither. Down," said Rhodes.

"Then it must have been straight down."

"It was. Down behind a rock-mass or something."

We waited, watching closely, but those yellow eyes did not gleam again through that Stygian gloom.

"Must have been at quite a distance," I remarked at last. "It seems so, Bill; and that means that this cavern is very straight for a mile or more or that it is one of enormous size."

"It may be both."

"It may be, of course," he nodded. "And it may be that those lights were not so far away as they appeared to us to be. One may easily be deceived in such matters."

"We don't know what this means," I said; "but we know this: we're spotted."

"Oh, we're seen, all right, Bill. Our every movement will be watched."

Some minutes passed, during which we stood peering down the cavern and waiting; but no light gleamed forth again.

Then we started back.

"We'd better keep a sharp lookout," I said suddenly. "Remember, a demon doesn't have to come along the ledge to get at us."

"I have not forgotten that, Bill; but we are armed."

As I believe was made sufficiently obvious, the crossing of those places where the ledge narrowed to the width of but a yard or so had been no pleasant matter; but, during this the return, the thing assumed (in my imagination, at any rate) an aspect truly sinister. That we were being watched both of us regarded as certain. That we might at any moment find a demon or a dozen demons driving at us—well, that was a possibility which never left our thoughts for one single second. And, in those narrow places, where the ledge contracted to a mere ribbon of rock, it was all that one wanted to do to hug the wall and make sure of his footing. A frightful place truly in which to meet, even with a revolver, the attack of but one of those winged monsters; and we might find ourselves attacked by a dozen.

It can easily be imagined, then, the relief which I felt when we had passed the last narrow spot, though, forsooth, we might be going towards something far more dangerous than anything that we had left behind us. But the angel had gone down, and where a woman could go, there, I told myself in masculine pride, could we also.

"That is," I subjoined, "supposing that we do not meet ape-bats or something more terrible."

At length we stood once more at the mouth of the gallery. And scarcely had we stopped there when an unpleasant thing flashed into my thoughts—which, as it was, resembled anything but the rainbow.

"Great Heavens!" I cried, peering into the tunnel, which, at the distance of only thirty feet or so, gave a sudden turn to the right.

Something could be in there, very close to us and yet unseen.

"What is it, Bill?"

"Could those lights that we saw have been *here?* Are they waiting in there to dog our steps or to do something worse?"

Rhodes, peering into the gallery with a curious, half-vacuous expression on his face, made no reply.

"Well," I queried, "what do you think of it? We could not tell where those lights were, how far away—anything."

"I don't think that they were here," Milton Rhodes returned. "I think that they were much farther down and *on the other side.*"

"On the other side? How on earth could any one cross that chasm?"

"We don't know what it is like down there. And, of course, I don't *know* that the lights were on the other side. But I believe that they were."

A silence ensued, which at length I broke:

"What is the next thing on the programme?"

"Make our way down the ledge. That is the only way there is for us to go. But first we'll try a little finesse."

He took a position in the mouth of the tunnel, one that permitted him to look down the great cavern. He signed to me to follow suit, and, when I stood at his side, he said:

"Off go the lights."

Off they went, and the blackness was upon us. So terrible was it and so strange and fearful that place in which we stood, I actually found myself wondering if it would not all prove to be a dream.

"Why," I asked at last, "did we do this?"

"To see if those lights that we saw will show again. Those Dromans may think that we have lost heart and started back."

I saw it all now: instead of our advancing to those mysterious being somewhere down the cavern, he would bring them to us.

But they did not come. They did not show even the faintest gleam. We waited there for many minutes, but nothing whatever was seen.

"Hum," said Rhodes at last, snapping on his light. "It didn't work. Wary folk, Bill, these Hypogeans."

"And so," I replied, "we'll have to go to them."

"That's what we shall have to do."

"And," I added, "by doing so, walk maybe right into a trap."

"It is possible, certainly," Rhodes admitted. "But, as the brave Pliny said, *Fortes Fortuna iuvat.*"

"I don't remember much of my Latin, I told him; "but I remember what happened to Pliny. And I remember enough to know that *Fortuna caeca est.*"

"So's Love," returned Rhodes. "And he's pretty clever, too, the little chap is, when it comes to setting traps. But men and women, for all that, still keep going to meet him.

"But in this business now before us," he went on, "it is possible that the trap may not prove so terrible, possible, indeed, that there is no trap at all. Be that as it may, I tell you, old *tillicum*, I certainly would like to see that angel again."

"Then let's go see her."

"That's just what we'll do."

And so we started.

A strange, indefinable dread had its grip upon me, and yet I was anxious to go, to put the thing to an issue. In all probability, we should not have far to travel. Nor, in fact, did we.

The way was much like the one that we had traversed in the opposite direction. One or two spots were even more dangerous than any we had found up there. And, over those narrow, dangerous places, where a false step or a slip of the foot on the smooth rock would have meant a most horrible death—along this airy, dizzy Stygian way, the angel had passed. Well, she was a brave angel, at any rate.

We were descending all the while, sometimes at an angle that I was glad was no steeper. This does not mean, however, that our distance from the bottom of that black chasm, on our right, was decreasing. The sounds that came up from the unknown depths of it told plainly that the descent of the stream was as pronounced as that of the ledge we were following, and perhaps more so.

"And here's something that I don't understand," was my remark as we stopped in a particularly broken spot: "to say nothing of our being below sea-level, here this stream has been pouring down for untold centuries, for how many thousands of years no man can even guess, and yet the place isn't full. Where does all the water go?"

"Think," was Milton's answer, "of all the rivers that, for how many *millions* of years no man can tell, have been running into the sea, and yet the sea is not overflowing."

"I don't see the application of that to this underground world, don't see how all the water—there must be more streams than this one—can possibly return as vapor to the region above."

"I admit," Rhodes said, "that the problem is a formidable one and that, with our present paucity of data, we can not hope to solve it. Still I think that my suggestion is sound."

"But where are the openings to permit the escape of so enormous, for enormous it must be, amount of water-vapor?"

"There may be countless vents, fissures, Bill, ways of egress that man will never know. Whatever the explanation, there can be do doubt that the water is going down and that this subterranean world into which we have found our way is not full."

"But where does it go? Down to some sunless sea perhaps, though, if that hypothesis of yours is a sound one, bathed in light, a light never seen, in that world we have left, on land or sea."

Rhodes was silent for a moment, leaning on his alpenstock. Then:

"It is strange truly, the descent of the waters. And yet it would not, I believe, have been to you so very strange a thing had you known that the sea itself flows into the earth."

"The sea itself?"

Rhodes nodded.

"Surely, Milton—why, the thing sounds like something from Jules Verne or from Lucian's *Icaromenippus*."

"On the contrary," he told me, "it is not a bit out of romance either modern or ancient, but it is a fact that has long been known. At Argostoli in the Island of Cephalonia, the sea flows right into the limestone rock."*

* "The cases are certainly not numerous where marine currents are known to pour continuously into cavities beneath the surface of the earth, but there is at least one well-authenticated instance of this

"Shades of Lemuel Gulliver, but this old ball that men call the earth is certainly, after all, a strange old sphere!"

"How strange," said Milton Rhodes, "no scientist has ever dreamed, though your scientist has thought of things far stranger than any that were ever conceived by your wildest romancer, who, after all, Bill, is a pretty tame homo."

"I have an idea," I answered, glancing down the cavern, "that we are going to find the homos here in this place any thing but tame."

Milton laughed, and then suddenly, without any other answer, he turned and resumed the descent.

For one thing I was profoundly thankful: the wall ran along without any pronounced cavities or projections in it, so that we had little to apprehend from a sudden attack on this our giddy way—except, of course, an attack by a demon. Had the wall been a broken one, any instant might have found us face to face with a band of Hypogeans, as Rhodes called the denizens of this subterranean place.

But how long would the wall remain like that? And, after all, did it really greatly matter? Meeting, sooner or later—and, in all likelihood, very sooner—was inevitable. 'Tis true, I could not conceive of a worse place than this, supposing the meeting to be, in

(cont.) sort—that of the mill streams at Argostoli in the island of Cephalonia. It has been long observed that the sea water flowed into several rifts and cavities in the limestone rocks of the coast, but the phenomenon has excited little attention until very recently. In 1833, three of the entrances were closed, and a regular channel, sixteen feet long and three feet wide, with a fall of three feet, was cut into the mouth of a larger cavity. The sea water flowed into this canal, and could be followed eighteen or twenty feet beyond its inner terminus, when it disappeared in holes and clefts in the rock."—George P. Marsh: *Man and Nature.*

any measure, an unfriendly one. And, from what had happened up there at the Tamahnowis Rocks, I could not suppose that it would be anything else.

This, however, was to prove simply another instance of how inadequate the imagination, when confronted with the reality, is sometimes found to be, for even now we were drawing near a place more terrible even than this—and that the place where we met!

It required but little imagination, though, to make us aware, and painfully so, of the extreme probability (regarded by ourselves as a certitude) that eyes were watching our every movement. But where were those eyes? And what were the watchers? To what fearful thing—or could it be wonderful—were we drawing near at every single moment now?

Some minutes passed, perhaps fifteen, perhaps less, perhaps more; I cannot say how long it was. Of a sudden, however, Rhodes, who was still leading the way, stopped. Of course, I stopped, too. No sound had escaped him, and he stood there like a statue, peering intently straight ahead.

"What is it?" I asked.

"Look there, Bill," he said in a low voice, pointing with his alpenstock, "and tell me what you see."

I was already looking, and already I had seen it.

But what in the world was that thing which I saw?

I remained silent, gazing with straining eyes and wondering if I really saw what I thought that I did.

"What," Rhodes asked, "do you make of it?"

"The thing is so faint. 'Tis impossible, and yet, if it were not impossible it can be that, I would say that it is an arch—part of a bridge."

"Just what I thought myself, Bill. The thing is so strange, though, so very strange, that I didn't know whether to believe my eyes or not."

"And so dim," I observed, "that it may be nothing of the kind. A bridge? Now, who, in the name of wonder, would build a bridge across this frightful chasm? And why? And how?"

"*Quien sabe*, Bill?" said Milton Rhodes.

The next moment we were moving towards it.

"Look!" ejaculated Rhodes suddenly. "Look at that! It goes clear across!"

"Yes," I said, stopping and gazing at that strange dim mass; "it goes clear across.

"And," I added, "that's the place, over there on the other side—that's where they are waiting for us!"

19

THE ANGEL AND HER DEMON

"I shouldn't be a bit surprised," said Milton Rhodes. "And a strange bridge, that, truly. It looks like a ruin, a ruin that has not fallen."

It looked like a ruin indeed. So ruinous did it appear that I wondered how the mass could possibly remain intact. A short advance, however, and the mystery was solved. The hand of man had not builded that great arch across this dreadful chasm; Nature had fashioned it, there in that region of everlasting darkness. It has, Rhodes said, a remarkable semblance to the celebrated Natural Bridge in Virginia.

A short space, and we stood upon it, gazing across. Its width here was about sixty feet. The surface was, comparatively speaking, a smooth one, and it had a rather pronounced slope upwards— a circumstance by no means conducive to security of footing. And a feature that I noticed with some unpleasant misgivings was the diminution of width at the farther end. Just how wide it was there we could not tell, what with the uncertain light that struggled to the spot; but we saw enough to know that that way which we should have to cross was a very narrow one indeed; and on either side was the black chasm yawning to receive us. And just beyond, dim and ghostly as though seen in a dream, stupendous columns rose up and were involved in the darkness of the lofty cavern.

"What on earth are those?" I queried. "It reminds one of a Grecian temple."

"Limestone pillars, no doubt," returned Milton.

"And it's there," I exclaimed, my voice, however, low and guarded, "that they are waiting for us! That, I have no doubt now, is where those lights were."

"I think it very likely, Bill."

"They'll wait," said I, "until we get in that cursed narrow place, and then—"

"And then?"

"And then," I told him, "we had better say our prayers before we start across."

Rhodes laughed. I thought, though, that there was a touch of the sardonic in the laugh. Little wonder, forsooth, if 'twas so, for the thing was fraught with some terrible possibilities.

"What," I asked, "are we going to do now?"

"Cross over—that is, if we are permitted to do so."

If we should be permitted to do so!

I gazed into the black profundity of the chasm, and I tell you that I certainly did not feel happy.

"Why," I asked, "didn't we bring a parachute along? I have an idea that we'll wish before very many minutes that we had done so."

"It is possible," said Rhodes, and his voice and mien were grave, "that we shall. However, Bill, it is cross over—or give the whole thing up and go back."

"Go back? Never!"

"My sentiments to a T, Bill.

"It is possible, though," he added, turning and sending his look along the wall, "that we may find a way out of this infernal place by following the ledge."

"But," was my comment, "not probable."

"'Twill do no harm," he said, "to see."

"But look here: maybe, if we go on a scouting expedition along the ledge, they'll come over here, come across the bridge, and follow us."

"I don't know," Milton answered, "that such a proceeding on their part would make the matter any more serious than we find it right now. The bridge contracts over there to something like a ribbon of rock."

"Holy Gorgons," I said, "haven't we got into a fine pickle, though?"

"I'll tell you what we'll do, Bill: you remain here, like Horatius at the bridge, while I explore down along the ledge."

"I don't like it," I told him. "United we stand—well, you know the rest of it."

He was silent for some moments. Then:

"I think that we can risk it, Bill."

"Very well," I acquiesced, shrugging my shoulders. "But I tell you that I don't like it at all."

The next moment, however, he had turned and was moving away down the ledge. I stepped back to the wall (upon which two inscriptions were traced) and waited the result with such composure as I could summon

At last Rhodes moved behind a projection in the wall. A few moments, and the glow of his light had vanished. He was gone, and I was alone in that terrible place.

The blackness seemed to increase, the shadows to thicken about me and grow denser. But one sound broke the awful silence, which sound seemed to have a quality tangible, crushing—the growl of the water in the abysmal depths of the chasm. And even that sound, as I stood there listening, watching, waiting, seemed to change; it seemed to sink to a murmur, then a whisper, as though evil spirits were hushing it to lull my suspicions and even the very senses of me.

What was that? I started, and something shot through my very heart, chilling and sharp as the needle point of an icicle.

Surely I had seen it. Yes! There it was again, dim but unmistakable, there by one of the great columns—a single point of light, an eye staring at me with a greenish fire.

Yes, there it was. Then of a sudden it was gone.

For a time I stood peering and waiting, the blood throbbing in my ears; but it was not seen again.

I turned and looked down the ledge, and I gave an exclamation that was one of relief and joy, for there was Rhodes just come into view around that projection in the wall.

"What," I asked as he drew near, "did you find down there?"

"We can't go down. The shelf is broken—nothing but sheer wall between. So it's across the bridge for us."

"We may never reach the other side."

And then I told him what I had seen.

"And," I asked, "didn't grandfather Scranton say that the eyes of the demon burned with a greenish fire?"

Rhodes nodded.

"Then what I saw was a demon's eye. But why didn't I see two. Is this a Polyphemus demon?"

"Can't say, Bill. The greenish fire, however, is nothing but re-flected light; in other words, light has to reach them, or the eyes can't shine. In absolute darkness they would not do so."

"It may be different down here in this world. At any rate, that eye shone, though ghostly. And so the angel at least—and Heaven only knows what besides—is waiting there with her demon!"

"I believe so, Bill. There can scarcely be any doubt that the eye which you saw belonged to a demon. The prospect, I admit, is cer-tainly a sinister one."

A silence ensued. Of a sudden Rhodes raised his voice and hallooed:

"Hello there!"

The answer came almost on the instant:

"Hello there—hello there—hello there—hello there—hello—hello!"

"Nobody there but Echo, lovely Echo," smiled Milton Rhodes.

Again he raised his voice, and again the words were thrown back at him.

"Hear that, Bill?" he cried whilst the echoes were still sounding.

"I heard it."

"*That* was no echo."

"No," I said; "that was not an echo."

We waited, listening intently, but that sound which had come with the echoes was not heard again.

Rhodes drew his revolver and examined the weapon most care-fully. He looked at me curiously, and then he said:

"I have no desire, Bill, to disguise the fact that this crossing may prove a most, a most—Bill, it may prove to be the—"

"You needn't tell me," said I. "I know very well what it may mean."

"But we can't turn back, Bill."

"No; we can't turn back."

He reached out his hand and grasped mine. And then, without another word, we started.

I had known some critical, terrible, horrible scenes in my life; but never anything like the suspense and mystery of those moments that now succeeded. What were we to see? What were we to meet? And, horror of horrors, it would be in that place where the bridge narrowed to something like a mere ribbon—the frightful depths yawning on each side, almost at our very feet.

Well, at last we reached it. My head began to swim, so terrible was the place, and I had to stop and get a grip on my nerves. Rhodes too paused, and for some moments we stood there, so near to safety and yet—the mockery of it—closer than ever to mystery and danger and perhaps horror unnamable.

"Now for it, Bill!" said Rhodes. "Keep your revolver ready for instant action!"

And we started the ascent across.

The place immediately before us was so narrow that we could not think of walking side by side. Rhodes was leading. And then it came—when we had taken eight or ten steps, when we had reached the most dangerous spot on that ribbon of rock.

Of a sudden a dark figure, straining at leash, moved out from behind one of the limestone pillars, and two eyes shone as with a greenish fire, and the strong rays of our lights were flashed back in the gleam of teeth. And, behind that demoniac shape, a tall figure appeared, a figure clothed in white, the eyes wide and blazing, the face white as snow and framed in gleaming gold, which fell down in masses behind the shoulders—a figure majestic, one indescribably lovely and dreadful.

It was the angel and her demon!

20

THE ATTACK

That scene, like some terrible vision from the pages of Doré, often rises before me—the tall white figure of the angel, the dark, squatting winged monster before her, and we two men from the sunlit world standing there upon that narrow way, the black profundity of the chasm yawning on either side of us.

The angel had indeed well chosen the moment. If that hideous ape-bat, straining at its leash, were loosed at us, our position, despite our revolvers, would be a truly terrible one. Scarce twenty-five feet lay between that Cerberus and ourselves. In case of attack, we would have to drop the monster in its spring—and only a lucky shot could do that—or the result would be a most disastrous one. For we could not meet an attack there; to step aside or to meet the demon in a struggle would mean a plunge over the edge.

It was indeed a critical, appalling scene, one in which, if I were a believer in the *lex talionis*, I would have no desire to see even my worst enemy placed. Our fate, I thought, was in the hands of that white-clad, white-faced being whom we knew as the angel. The demon, however, as will be seen in a moment, was to take the matter into its own hands, if I may use that expression in speaking of that monster, for hands the thing had none. I can easily see how the demon, in the obscurity of the fog, had seemed to old Scranton a thing that had no shape. But here, the strong rays of our lights turned full upon our demon, the sight was an altogether different one. And a stranger sight surely no man had ever seen up there in that world which we had left, that world so near to us still and yet

367

it seemed so very far away now. It was as though some Circe had changed us into the figures in some dread story of ancient days. And this was what men call the Twentieth Century, the golden age of science and discovery. Well, science doesn't yet know everything—a fact that, I am sorry to say, some scientists themselves are very prone to forget.

"Heavens," said Rhodes, keeping his look fixed on those figures before us, "isn't she a wonderful creature?"

"And it," said I, "an awful thing? And I'd wait a while before saying that she is wonderful. She may prove to be something very different."

The next instant I gave a cry. The demon had made a sudden strain forward. Came a sharp word from the angel, and that Cerberus sank back again. But, though it sank back, that greenish fire in its eyes seemed to burn more fiercely, malevolently than before.

"I think," I suggested, "that it would be a good plan to move back a little, back to a safer, a wider spot."

"Move back? Never!" said Milton Rhodes. "We are here to move forward, not to go back. And, besides, the way widens out a little up there."

I thought this utterly Quixotic; but, of course, if he didn't want to go back, I couldn't make him. And, if he wouldn't step back, neither would I.

"Look," I said. "She is going to speak."

The angel raised her left hand and motioned to us rather vehemently, at the same time uttering some word, or words.

"No mistaking that, Bill," said Milton.

"No; it is as plain as any words could be:

"'Go back!'"

"I am at a loss," said Rhodes, "how to answer."

Again the angel raised her hand; but she did not motion this time, for the demon, with a blood-curdling sound, deep in its throat, strained forward again, and so suddenly and strongly that the angel was drawn forward a step or two. A sharp word, however, from the angel, and the monster settled back, as a dog does after straining at its leash.

Once more the angel fixed her eyes upon us, or, rather, upon Milton Rhodes. Once more she raised her hand to sign to us to go back. But the sign was never given.

At that instant, as the angel stood there with upraised hand, it happened.

That sound came again, only more horrible than before, and the demon sprang at us. Caught thus off her guard, the angel was jerked, whirled forward. There was a wild, piercing cry, which rose to a scream; but the winged monster paid not the slightest heed. It was as though the thing had gone mad.

The woman went down; in an instant, however, she was up again. She screamed at the demon, but it lunged toward us, flapping its great hideous wings and dragging her after it farther out onto the bridge.

Her position now was one of peril scarcely less than our own.

All this had passed, of course, with the quickness of thought. We could not fire, for fear of hitting the angel, right behind the demon; we could not move back; and we could not stand there and let this nightmare-monster come upon us. In a second or two, if nothing were done, it would do so. But what could we do? The thought of saving ourselves by killing the woman—and the chances were a hundred to one that we would kill her if we fired at the demon—was a horrible one. But to stand there and be sent over the edge was horrible, too. And the angel, in all probability, would be killed anyway; that she had not already been jerked from the rock was nothing less than a miracle.

Why didn't she loose her hold on the leash?

These are some of the things that flashed through my mind—yes, even then. I never before knew what a rapid thing thought can be. Oh, those things that shot through my brain in those brief, critical seconds. My whole life, from childhood to that very moment, flashed before me like the film of a cinematograph, though with the speed of light. I wondered what death was like—what it would be like somewhere in the depths of that black gulf. And I wondered why the angel did not loose her hold on that leash. I didn't know that she had wrapped the chain around her hand and that the chain had in some way got caught. The poor angel could not free herself.

Little wonder, forsooth, that she was screaming so wildly at the demon.

"We must risk it!" I cried.

"Hold!"

The next instant Milton Rhodes had stepped aside—yes, had stepped right to the very edge of the rock. The demon whirled at him, and, as it whirled, one of its great wings struck me full across the face. I gave myself up for lost, but somehow I kept my place on that ribbon of rock. Another instant, and the monster would be at Milton's throat. But no! From this dizzy position which he had so suddenly taken, the angel was no longer behind the demon, and on the instant Rhodes fired.

Oh, that scream which the monster gave. It struck the rock, and that Rhodes managed to keep his footing on the edge of that fearful place is one of the most amazing things that I have ever seen. But keep it he did, and he fired again and yet again. The demon flapped backward, jerked the angel to her knees and near the edge and then suddenly flat on her face. The next instant the monster disappeared. Its wings began to beat against the rock with a spasmodic sound.

I gave a cry of relief and joy.

But the next moment one of dismay and horror broke from me.

The monster was dragging the angel over the edge!

21

INTO THE CHASM

Milton Rhodes threw himself prone on the rock and his right arm around the angel's waist.

"Quick, Bill, quick! Her arm—the whole weight of the monster!"

Her screams had ceased, but from her throat broke a moan, long, tremulous, heartrending—a sound to shake and rend my already quivering nerves, to most dreadfully enhance the indescribable horror of the scene and the moment.

I could do nothing where I was, had to step over the prostrate forms, which, in my heated imagination, were being dragged over the edge.

The wings of the demon were still beating against the rock, the blows not so strong but more spasmodic—the sound a leathery, sickening tattoo.

It will probably be remembered that the angel had held the demon with her right hand. I was now on the angel's right; and, stretched out on the rock, I reached down over the edge in an effort to free her from that dragging monster, the black depths over which we hung turning me dizzy and faint.

I now saw how the angel had been caught and that she had been dragged so far over the edge that I could not, long-armed though I am, reach the leash. So I grasped her arm and, with a word of encouragement, began to pull. Slowly we drew the monster up. Another moment, and the chain would be within the reach of my other hand. Yes, there. Steady, so. I had reached down my other hand, my fingers were in the very act of closing on the chain, when,

371

horrors, I felt myself slipping along the smooth rock—slipping over into that appalling gulf.

To save myself, I had to let go the angel's arm, and, as the chain jerked to the monster's weight, an awful cry broke from the angel and from Milton Rhodes, and I saw her body dragged farther over.

"Cut it, Bill, cut it!"

"It's a chain."

Rhodes groaned.

"We must try again. Quick. Great Heaven, we can't let her be dragged over into the chasm."

"This horrible spot makes the head swim."

"Steady, Bill, steady," said Rhodes. "Here, hold her while I get a grip with my other arm. Then I'll get a hold on you with my right."

"We'll all be dragged over."

"Nonsense," said Rhodes. "And, besides, I've got a hold with my feet now, in a crack or something "

A few moments, and I was again reaching down, Rhodes' grip upon me this time. Again I laid hold on the angel's arm, and again she and I drew the monster up. This time, though, I got my other hand too on the chain. And yet, even then, the chain hanging slack above my hand, the angel was some time in freeing her own, from the fingers of which blood was dropping. But at last she had loosened the chain, and then I let go my hold upon it, and down the demon went, still flapping its wings, though feebly now, and disappeared into those black and fearful depths.

I have no recollection of any sound coming up. In all probability a sound came. Little wonder, forsooth, that I did not hear it.

A moment, and I was back from the edge, and Milton and I were drawing the angel to the safety of that narrow way. She sank back in Rhodes' arms, her eyes closed, her head, almost hidden in the gleaming golden hair, on his shoulder.

"She's fainted," said I.

"Little wonder if she has, Bill."

But she had not. Scarcely had he spoken when she opened her eyes. At once she sat up, and I saw a faint color suffuse those snowy features.

"Well," said I to myself, "whatever else she may be, our angel is human."

We remained there for a little while, recovering from the effects of the horrible scene through which we had passed, then arose and started for that place of safety there amongst the wonderful, stupendous limestone pillars. I was now moving in advance, and I confess (and nothing could more plainly show how badly my nerves had been shaken) that I would gladly have covered those few remaining yards on all fours—if my pride would have permitted me to do so.

Yes, there we stood, by that very pillar behind which the angel had waited for us with her demon. There was her lamp, lantern rather, and dark, save for a mere slit.

I looked at it and looked all around.

"We saw *two lights*," I said. "And yet she was waiting for us here *alone*."

"There certainly were two lights, Bill; in other words, there certainly were two persons at least. Her companion went somewhere; that is the only explanation that I can think of."

"I wonder where," said I, "and what for."

"Help, in all likelihood. You know, Bill, I have an idea that, if we had delayed much longer, our reception there," and he waved a hand toward the bridge, "would have been a very different one."

"It was interesting enough to suit me. And, as it is, Heaven only knows what is to follow. This is, perhaps, just the beginning of things."

The angel, standing there straight and still, was watching us intently, so strange a look in her eyes—those eyes were blue—that a chill passed through my heated brain, and I actually began to wonder if I was being hypnotized. Hypnotized? And in this cursed spot.

I turned my look straight into the eyes of the angel, and, as I looked, I flung a secret curse at that strange weakness of mine and called myself a fool for having entertained, even for a fleeting moment, a thought so absurd.

Rhodes had noticed, and he turned his look upon me and upon the woman—this creature so indescribably lovely and yet with so indefinable, mysterious a Sibylline something about her. For some moments there was silence. I thought that I saw fear in those blue eyes of hers, but I could not be sure. That strange look, whether one of fear or of something else, was not all that I saw there; but I strove in vain to find a name or a meaning for what I saw. Science, science! This was the age of science, the age of the jet-plane, the atom-bomb, radium, television and radio; and yet here was a scene to make Science herself rub her eyes in amazement, a scene that might have been taken right out of some wild story or out of some myth of the ancient world. Well, that ancient world too had its science, some of which science, I fear (though this thought would have brought a pooh-pooh from Milton Rhodes) man has lost to his sorrow. And, like that ancient world, so perhaps had this strange underground world which we had entered—or, rather, were trying to enter. And perhaps of that science or some phases of it, this angel before us had fearful command.

One moment I told myself that we should need all the courage we possessed, all the ingenuity and resource of that science of which Milton Rhodes himself was the master; the next, that I was letting my imagination overleap itself and run riot.

My thoughts were suddenly broken by the voice of Milton:

"Goodness, Bill, look at her hand. I forgot."

He stepped toward the angel and gently lifted her blood-dripping hand. The chain had sunk right into the soft flesh. The angel, with a smile and a movement with her left hand, gave us to understand that the hurt was nothing.

The next moment she gave an exclamation and gazed past me and down the pillared cavern.

Instantly I turned, and, as I did so, I too exclaimed.

There, far off amongst the sinter-columns, two yellow, wrathful lights were gleaming. And soon we saw them—dark hurrying figures moving towards us.

22
WHAT DID IT MEAN?

"The help is coming, Bill," said Milton Rhodes. "And that reminds me: I haven't reloaded my revolver."

"I would lose no time in doing so," I told him.

He got out the weapon and proceeded to reload it. It was not, by the way, one of these new-fangled things but one of your old-fashioned revolvers—solid, substantial, one that would stand hard usage, a piece to be depended upon. And that it seemed was just what we needed—weapons to be depended upon.

The angel was watching Rhodes closely. I wondered if she knew what had killed her demon; knew, I mean, that this metal thing, with its glitter so dull and so cold, was a weapon. It was extremely unlikely that she had, in that horrible moment on the bridge, seen what actually had happened. However that might have been, it was soon plain that she recognized the revolver as a weapon, or, at any rate, guessed that it was.

With an interjection, she stepped to Rhodes' side, and, with swift pantomime, she assured us that there was nothing at all to apprehend from those advancing figures.

"After all," Milton said, slipping the revolver into his pocket, "why should we be so infernally suspicious? Maybe this world is very different from our own."

"That's just what I'm afraid of. And it seems to me," I added, my right hand in that pocket which contained my revolver, "that we have good cause to be suspicious. Have you forgotten what grandfather Scranton saw up there at the Tamahnowis Rocks (and

what he didn't see) and the death there, so short a time since, of
Rhoda Dillingham, to say nothing of what happened to us here a
few minutes ago? That we are not at the bottom of that chasm—
well, I am not anxious to have another shave like that."

"I have not, of course, forgotten any of that, Bill. I have an idea,
though, that those tragedies up there were purely accidental. Certainly
we know that the demon's attack upon ourselves was entirely so."

"Accidental? Great Scott, some consolation that."

I looked at Milton Rhodes, and I looked at the angel, who had
taken a few steps forward and was awaiting those hurrying figures—
a white-clad figure, still and tall, one lovely, majestic. And, if I
didn't sigh, I certainly felt like doing so.

"No demon there, Bill," observed Milton, at last, his eyes upon
those advancing forms.

"I see none. Four figures. I see no more than four."

"Four," nodded Rhodes. "Two men and two women."

A few moments, and they stepped out into a sort of aisle
amongst the great limestone pillars. The figure in advance came
to an abrupt halt. An exclamation broke from him and echoed and
re-echoed eerily through the vast and gloomy cavern. It was
answered by the angel, and, as her voice came murmuring back to
us, it was as though fairies were hidden amongst the columns and
were answering her.

But there was nothing fairylike in the aspect of that leader (who
was advancing again) or his male companion. That aspect was grim,
formidable. Each carried a powerful bow and had an arrow fitted
to the string, and at the left side a short heavy sword. That aspect
of theirs underwent a remarkable metamorphosis, however, as they
came on towards us, what with the explanations that our angel gave
them. When they at last halted, but a few yards from the spot where
we stood, every sign of hostility had vanished. It was patent, however, that they were wary, suspicious. That they should be so was,
certainly, not at all strange. But just the same there was something
that made me resolve to be on my guard whatever might betide.

The leader was a tall man, of sinewy and powerful frame.
Though he had, I judged, passed the half-century mark, he had
suffered, it seemed, no loss of youthful vitality or strength. His

companion, tall and almost as powerful as himself, was a much younger man—in his early twenties. Their hair was long. The arms were bare, as were the legs from midway the thigh to halfway below the knee, the nether extremities being incased in cothurni, light but evidently of very excellent material.

As for the companions of the twain, one was a girl of seventeen or eighteen years of age, the other a girl a couple of years older. Each had a bow and a quiver, as did our angel. Strictly speaking, it was not a quiver, for it was a quiver and bow-case combined, but what the ancients called a *corytos*. The older of these young ladies had golden hair, a shade lighter than the angel's, whilst the hair of the younger was as white as snow. At first I thought that it must be powdered, but this was not so. And, as I gazed with interest and wonder upon this lovely creature, I thought—of Christopher Columbus and Sir Isaac Newton. At thirty, they had hair like hers. That thought, however, was a fleeting one. This was no time, forsooth, to be thinking of old Christopher or Sir Isaac. Stranger, more wonderful was this old world of ours than even Columbus or Newton had ever dreamed it.*

The age of our angel, by the way, I placed at about twenty-five years. And I wondered how they could possibly reckon time here in this underground world, a world that could have neither days nor months nor years.

* "Considering that the mean density of the whole earth is only about five and a half times that of water, and that the materials of which the crust of the earth is composed are all compressible in a greater or less degree, so that even at no very great depth the density of the different substances must be greatly increased by the mere pressure of the superincumbent materials, some philosophers have supposed that the effects of pressure must be counterbalanced by the expansive force of a great heat subsisting in the interior of the earth; and others that the earth is not solid, *but merely a hollow shell* of inconsiderable thickness."—Brande

The quartette listened eagerly to the explanations given by our angel. Suddenly the leader addressed some question to Persephone, as Rhodes called her. And then we heard it!

"Drome," was her answer.

There it was, distinct, unmistakable, that mysterious word which had given us so many strange and wild thoughts and visions. Yes, there it was; and it was an answer, I thought, that by no means put the man's mind at ease.

Drome! Drome at last. But—but what did it mean? Drome! There, we distinctly heard the angel pronounce the word again. Drome! If we could only have understood the words being spoken! But there was no mistaking, I thought, the manner of the angel. It was earnest, and yet, strangely enough, that Sibylline quality about her was now more pronounced than ever. But there was no mistaking her manner: she was endeavoring to reassure him, then, to allay, it seemed, some strange uneasiness or fear. I noticed, however, with some vague, sinister misgivings, that in this she was by no means as successful as she herself desired. Why did we see in the eyes of the leader, and in those of the others, so strange, so mysterious a look whenever those eyes were turned toward that spot where Milton Rhodes and I stood?

However, these gloomy thoughts were suddenly broken, but certainly they were not banished. With an acquiescent reply—at any rate, so I thought it—to the angel, the leader abruptly faced us. He placed his bow and arrow upon the ground, slipped over his head the balteus, from which the *corytos* hung at his right side, drew his sword—it was double-edged, I now noted—from its scabbard, and then he deposited these, too, upon the ground, beside his bow and arrow. His companion was following suit, the two girls standing by motionless and silent.

The men advanced a few paces. Each placed his sword-hand over his heart, uttered something in measured and sonorous tones and then bowed low to us—a proceeding, I noted out of the corner of my eye, that not a little pleased our angel.

23
THAT WE ONLY KNEW THE SECRET

"Well," remarked Milton Rhodes, his expression one of the utmost gravity, "when in Drome, Bill, do as the Dromans."

And we returned the bow of the Hypogeans, whereupon the men stepped back to their weapons, which they at once resumed, and the young women, without moving from the spot, inclined the head to us in a most stately fashion. Bow again from Rhodes and myself.

This ceremony over—I hoped that we had done our part handsomely—the angel turned to us and told us (in pantomime, of course) that we were now friends and that her heart was glad.

"Friends!" said I to myself. "You are no gladder, madam, than I am; but all the same I am going to be on my guard."

The girls moved to the angel and, with touching tenderness, examined her bleeding hand, which the younger at once proceeded to bandage carefully. She had made to bathe the hurt, but this the angel had not permitted—from which it was patent, I thought, that there would be no access to water for some time yet.

Our Amalthea and her companions now held an earnest consultation. Again we heard her pronounce that word Drome. And again we saw in the look and mien of the others doubt and uneasiness and something, I thought, besides. But this was for a few moments only. Either they acquiesced wholly in what the angel urged, or they masked their feelings.

I wished that I knew which it was. And yet, had I known, I would have been none the wiser, forsooth, unless I had been cognizant of what it was that the angel was urging so earnestly and with such confidence. That it was something closely concerning ourselves was, of course, obvious. That it (or part of it) was to the effect that we should be taken to some place was, I believed, virtually certain. Not that this made matters a whit clearer or in any measure allayed my uneasiness. For where were we to be taken? And to what? To Drome? But what and where was this Drome? Was Drome a place, was it a thing, was it a human being, or what was it?

Such were some of the thoughts that came to me as I stood there. But what good to wonder, to question when there could be no answer forthcoming? Sooner or later the answer would be ours. And, in the meantime—well, more than sufficient unto the day was the mystery thereof. And, besides, hadn't Rhodes and I come to find mysteries? Assuredly. And assuredly it was not at all likely that we would be disappointed.

This grave matter, whatever it was, decided, the angel plunged into a detailed account of what had happened on the bridge. We thought that we followed her recital pretty closely, so expressive were her gestures. When she told how we had saved her from that frightful chasm, she was interrupted by exclamations, all eyes were turned upon us, and I felt certain in that moment that we were indeed friends. Still Heaven only knew what awaited us. It was well, of course, to be sanguine; but that did not mean that we should blink facts, however vague and mysterious those facts might be.

There was a momentary pause. When she went on, I saw the angel's lower lip begin to tremble and tears come into her eyes. She was describing the death of her demon, her poor, poor demon. Well, as regards appearances, I must own that I would greatly prefer that hideous ape-bat of hers to many a bulldog that I have seen. The others too looked distressed. And, indeed, I have no doubt that we ourselves, had we known all about demons, would have been— well, at least troubled. Little did Milton and I dream that the loss of that winged monster might entail upon our little band the most serious consequences. So, however, it was, as we were soon to learn.

When she had ended her account, the angel turned to us forthwith and went through an earnest and remarkable pantomime. She and the others awaited our answer with the most intense interest. But the only answer that we could give her was that we did not understand. That pantomime had been wholly unintelligible to Milton Rhodes and myself. I say wholly unintelligible; we could see, however, that it had something to do with ourselves and something to do with *something* up above; but everything else in it was an utter mystery.

The angel went through it again, more slowly, more carefully and more fully this time. But still we could not understand.

"Perhaps," I suggested, "she could tell us with paper and pencil."

"Not a bad idea, Bill."

Thereat Rhodes produced pencil and notebook. These he gave to the angel, with a sign that she put it down in the book. She regarded the pencil curiously for some moments, tried it upon the paper, and then—with some difficulty and undoubtedly some pain, what with her hurt hand—she began. Rhodes moved to her right side, I to her left.

Yes, there could be no mistaking that: she had drawn the Tamahnowis Rocks. Then she drew a crevasse and two figures, plainly Rhodes and myself, going down into it. That was clear as the day. Then she put those figures that were Rhodes and I into the tunnel, and, presto, with a wave of the hand, she brought them down to that very spot where we were standing. Clear again, lovely Sibyl. What next? More figures, and more and more; and were they too coming down into the tunnel? Yes, at last it all was plain, at last we wise numskulls understood her.

Were we alone?

Rhodes made it clear to her that we were. But he did not stop there; he proceeded to make it clear to her that we only knew the secret. She was some time in understanding this; but, when she did understand it, what a look was that which passed across her lovely Sibylline features!

"Great Heaven," said I to myself, "he's gone and done it now!"

The look was one of joy, the look of a soul triumphant. In a moment, however, it was gone; her features were only lovely, impassive.

But the thoughts and the feelings which that strange look of hers had aroused were not gone. I felt something like a shudder pass to my heart. Of a truth, this lovely woman was dreadful.

I glanced at Rhodes; I thought that even he looked grave and troubled. Well, so I thought, might he be.

I said nothing, however, until the angel had rejoined her companions. Then:

"There can be not the slightest doubt that they look with great fear upon the coming of people from that world above, a world as mysterious, I suppose, to them as this subterranean world of theirs is to us. And, now they know that they have the great secret also when they have you and me—well, Milton, old *tillicum*, I think it will indeed be strange if either of us ever again casts a shadow in the sun."

"It may be so, Bill," he said soberly. "I did not think of that when I told her. Still—well, who knows? Certainly not I. It is possible, indeed probable, it seems to me, that we may do them, *her*, Bill, a harsh injustice."

"I sincerely hope so."

That grave look left his face, and he smiled at me.

"And, besides, Billy, me lad, maybe we won't ever want to return to that world we have left—that world so full of ignorance, and yet so full of knowledge and science too; that world so cruel, and yet sometimes so strangely kind; that world so full of hate and mad passion, and yet with ideals and aspirations so very noble and lofty. Yes, who knows, Bill? It is possible that we may not want to return."

Was it significant, or was it purely casual? I could not decide. But Rhodes' gaze was now on the angel. And, whilst I stood pondering, she turned and signed to us that they stood in readiness to proceed.

She raised a hand and pointed down the cavern, in some subtle manner making it clear that she was pointing to something far, so very far away.

"Drome!" she said.

"Drome," nodded Milton Rhodes.

"Ready, Bill?"

"Ready," I told him.

And so we started.

24
WHAT NEXT?

For a mile or more, the way led amongst pillars and stalagmites. Oh, the wonders that we saw in that great cavern! The exigencies of space, however, will not permit me to dwell upon them. There is, I may remark, no deposition of sinter going on now; undoubtedly many centuries have rolled over this old globe since the drip ceased, perhaps thousands upon thousands of years. Who can say? How little can scientists ever know, even when their knowledge seems so very great, of those dim and lost ages of the earth!

"One thing that puzzles me," I remarked, "is that each of these Hypogeans has nothing but a canteen. So far as I can see, the whole party hasn't got the makings of a lunch for a ladybug. Can it be that we have not far to go, after all?"

"I think, Bill, that we'll find the way a long one. My explanation is that, on starting for the bridge, they disencumbered themselves of the provision-supply (if they were not in camp) so that, of course, they could make the greater speed. That the angel had a companion back there, we know. We know, too, that that companion—in all likelihood, it was one of the girls—went for help."

"What on earth were they doing there, with the men off some place else?"

"I wish that I could tell you, Bill. And what was the angel doing up in the Tamahnowis Rocks? And all by her lovely lonesome? I wish that you would tell me that."

"I wish that I could. And that isn't the only thing that I wish I could tell you. What in the world are *they* doing *here?* And what at the Tamahnowis Rocks?"

384

"What, Bill, are we?"

"But women!" said I. "Our explorers don't take women along."

"Lewis and Clark took a woman along, Sacajaweah, and took her papoose to boot. And this isn't our world, remember. Things may be very different down here. Maybe, in this subterranean land, the lady is the boss."

"Where," I exclaimed, "isn't she the boss? You don't have to come down here to find a—a what do you call it?—a gynecocracy. Which reminds me of Saxe."

"What does Saxe say, sweet misogynist?"

"This, sweet gyneolater:

"'Men, dying, make their wills,
   But wives escape a work so sad;
   Why should they make, the gentle dames,
   What all their lives they've had?'"

"Bravo!" cried Milton Rhodes.

And I saw the angel, who, with the older man, was leading the way, turn and give us a curious look.

"And that," said Rhodes, "reminds *me*."

"Of what?"

"Who is the leader of this little party? Is it that man, or is it our angel?"

"I'd say the angel if I could only understand why she should be the leader."

At length we passed the last pillar and the last stalagmite. All this time we had been descending at a gentle slope. The way now led into a tunnel, rather wide and lofty at first. The going was easy enough for a mile or so; the descent was still a gentle one, and the floor of the passage was but little broken. The spot was then reached where that tunnel bifurcates; and there were the packs of our Hypogeans, or, rather, their knapsacks. There were five, one for each, the men's being large and heavy.

"You see, Bill?" queried Milton. "Evidently our little hypothesis was correct."

"I see," I nodded. "We have far to go."

"Very far, I fancy."

Also, in this place were the phosphorus-lamps of the Dromans, one for each. These were somewhat similar to the ones that Rhodes and I carried, save that the Droman lamps could be darkened, whereas the only way we could conceal the light of ours was to put them into their cylinders. As was the case with our phials, the light emitted by these vessels was a feeble one. Undoubtedly, though, they would remain luminous for a long period, and hence their real, their very great value. Beside the lanterns, oil-burning, of which the Dromans had three, the phosphorous-lamps were somewhat pale and sorry things; but, when one remembered that they would shed light steadily for months perhaps, while the flames of the lanterns were dependent upon the oil-supply, those pale, ghostly lights became very wonderful things.

"The light," I said as we stood examining one of these objects, "is certainly phosphorescent. But what is that fluid in the glass?"

"I can't tell you, Bill. It may be some vegetable juice. There is, by the way, a Brazilian plant, called *Euphorbia phosphorea*, the juice of which is luminous. This may be something similar. Who knows?"*

Each of the Dromans took up his or her knapsack, and we were under way again. It was the right branch of the tunnel into which

---

* "One dark night, about the beginning of December, while passing along the streets of the Villa de Natividada, I observed some boys amusing themselves with some luminous object, which I at first supposed to be a kind of large fire-fly; but on making inquiry, I found it to be a beautiful phosphorescent Fungus, belonging to the genus Agaricus. . . . The whole plant gives out at night a bright phosphorescent light, of a pale greenish hue, similar to that emitted by the larger fire-flies, or by those curious soft-bodied marine animals, the Pyrosomae. From

the route led us. That fact Rhodes put down in his notebook. I could see no necessity for such a record, for surely we could not forget the fact, even if we tried.

"We'll record it," said Milton, "certitude to the contrary notwithstanding. And we'll keep adding to the record as we go down, too. There's no telling, remember. It may not be so easy to find the way out of this place as it seems."

"You said," I reminded him, "that we may never want to return."

"And I say it again. But I say this too: we may be mighty glad indeed to get out!"

To which I added the quite supererogatory remark that it was clearly within the realm of possibility that we should.

Soon the slope of the passage was no longer gentle. An hour or so, and the descent was so steep and difficult that we had to exercise every caution and care in going down it. "Noon" found us still toiling down that steep and tortuous way. We then halted for luncheon. The Dromans ate and drank very sparingly, though this work gives one a most remarkable appetite. Rhodes and I endeavored to emulate their example. I am afraid, however, that it was not with any remarkable success. As it was, the lunch left me as hungry as a cormorant.

As we sat there resting, the Dromans held a low and earnest colloquy. The two girls, though, had but very little to say. The subject of the dialogue was an utter mystery to us. Only one thing could we tell, and that was that the matter which they were revolving was one of some gravity. Once and only once did we hear the word Drome.

Also, it was then that we first heard—or, at any rate, first made out—the name of our angel. We could not, indeed, at the time be

(cont.) this circumstance, and from growing on a palm, it is called by the inhabitants 'Flor de Coco.' The light given out by a few of these Fungi in a dark room was sufficient to read by."—George Gardner.

certain that it was *her* name; but there was no uncertainty about
the name itself—Drorathusa. Ere the afternoon was far advanced,
however, we saw our belief become a certitude. Drorathusa. I confess that there was in my mind something rather awesome about
that name, and I wondered if that awesome something was exis-
tent only in my mind. Drorathusa. It seemed to possess some of
that Sibylline quality which in the woman herself was so indefinable and mysterious.

Drorathusa. Sibylline certainly, that name, and, like the woman
herself, beautiful too, I thought.

In our world, it would, in all likelihood, be shortened to Drora
or Thusa. But it was never so here. No Droman, indeed, would be
guilty of a barbarism like that. It was always Drorathusa, the
accent on the penultimate and every syllable clear and full.
Drorathusa. Milton Rhodes declared that it was the most beautiful name he had ever heard in all his life!

It was about four o'clock when we issued from that passage,
steep to the last, and found ourselves in a great broken cavern.
The rock was granite, the place jagged and savage-looking as
though seen in some strange and awful dream.

Here we rested for a while, and I, for one, was glad enough to
do so. I was tired, sore and stiff from head to foot—especially to
foot.

Just by the tunnel's mouth, there was some writing on the wall.
Before this, Drorathusa and the older man (his name, we had
learned, was Ondonarkus) stood for some moments. This examination, and the short dialogue which followed it, left them, I
noticed even more grave of aspect and demeanor than we had ever
seen them.

I wondered what it could mean. I felt a vague uneasiness; a
nameless foreboding was creeping over me.

It was futile to think and wonder what it meant, and yet I could
not help doing it. Glad had I been to stop, but, strangely enough,
glad I was to get under way once more. For 'twas only so that we
could hope to get the answer.

Well, we got it—an answer that I wish never to know again.

25

THE LABYRINTH—LOST

We soon saw that we had entered not a cavern but a perfect labyrinth of caverns. I could never have imagined a place like that. It
was bewildering, dreadful, forsooth, in the possibilities that it
limned on the canvas of one's imagination. How in the world could
any one ever have found his way through it? But somebody had,
for there were the inscriptions and signs on the wall. For these the
Dromans kept a keen watch, and the relief evinced whenever one was
sighted showed what a frightful thing it might be to lose the way.

An hour passed, another, and still we were moving in that
awful maze.

"Great Erebus," said I, "but this is confusion worse confounded.
Do you think that we can ever find our way back through this?"

"I've got it all down here, Bill," returned Rhodes, tapping his
notebook. "The angel, *the* leader now, is finding her way through
it: what she can do can't we do also?"

"She isn't through it yet! It is some time, too, since we saw one
of those directions on the wall. The fact is, unless I am greatly
mistaken, our Dromans are becoming uneasy right now."

"Think so, Bill? I confess that I thought something of the kind
myself, but I was not sure that it wasn't only a fancy."

"I wish that I could believe so."

As Rhodes had remarked, Drorathusa was the leader now. And
a striking sight it was—her tall white figure leading the way, the
shadows quivering, swaying, rushing over the broken, savage walls
and deepening to inky blackness in the secret places as we passed.

389

Farther and farther we went, deeper and deeper; but never another inscription was seen. The advance became broken, irresolute. Then suddenly there was a halt.

And at that instant the last vestige of uncertainty vanished: Drorathusa had lost the way.

There was a sudden panicky fear in the eyes of the girls, but it soon was gone. The little party met this most unpleasant truth with exemplary philosophy. There was a short consultation, and then we began to retrace our way. The object was, of course, to return to the last mark on the wall. If we missed it, then Heaven help us!

"Perhaps," I thought, "it will be Heaven help us, anyway!"

And it was.

We reached our objective without misadventure, and then a new start was made. Rhodes and I were greatly puzzled, for it was patent that neither the angel nor any one else knew how we had gone astray. And, not knowing that, how could any one tell which way to go?

"Better get it clear in that notebook," I admonished Rhodes. "Maybe this new start will end up in something more unpleasant than the other did. It's a queer business, and I don't pretend to understand any of it at all."

We went along for a half-mile or so, carefully and with no little apprehension, and then, hurrah, there was a sign on the wall! The route to Drome again! But for how long?

Drorathusa quickened her pace. She was moving along now as though in confidence, certitude even. I have never been able to explain what followed. For a time, an hour or more, that confidence of hers certainly was fully justified. Then came the change. Suddenly we became aware of an unpleasant fact—there was something wrong again. Not that we remained in doubt as to what that something was which was wrong. A few minutes, and we had a fact even more unpleasant presented to our contemplation and incidentally cogitation—again we had gone astray.

Once more there was a consultation, and once more we retraced our steps—I mean we started to retrace them. Neither I nor any one else could tell how it happened. Not that I marveled at our failure to return, even though I could not explain just how we had missed the way. However, it was no longer possible to blink the fact that we were lost, utterly lost in this maze of passages, caverns and chambers.

I raised my canteen and shook it; my heart sank at that feeble wish-wash sound. The canteen was almost empty. Nor was any one of the others, in this respect, much more fortunate than myself.

Our position was a most unpleasant one—appalling even in the grisly possibilities which it presented to the mind.

26
THROUGH THE HEWN PASSAGE

I could set down no adequate record of those hours which followed. It was late now, and yet on and on we went, mile after mile, deeper and deeper but only, it seemed, to involve ourselves the more hopelessly in the dread mysteries of that fearsome place. I wondered if it was my imagination that made it so, but certainly the confusion of those chambers and caverns seemed to become only confusion and the worse confounded.

At last and suddenly came the discovery.

We had entered a long and narrow chamber and were drawing near the end, Rhodes and I wondering if we should find an exit there. Of a sudden there was a sharp exclamation from the lips of Drorathusa, who was some little distance in advance—an exclamation that fetched me up on the instant.

She had stopped and was pointing towards the left-hand wall, her attitude and the look upon her face such that I started and a sudden fear shot through me.

"What in the world can it be?" I said. "I see nothing but rock and shadows and blackness. What has she found?"

Milton Rhodes made no answer. He was moving forward. I followed. A moment, and he was beside the Dromans, his light turned full upon the wall.

"Look at that, Bill!" said he.

I moved to his side, and we stood there gazing, for some moments motionless and silent.

"Well, Bill," he queried at last, "what do you think of that? We are not the first human beings to stand in this spot."

"But probably many centuries have passed since any human being stood here," I said, "and gazed upon that entrance—went into it. I wonder what it leads to. Why should men have cut that passage into the living rock? In such a horrible place. And how do we know that it was made by men? In this underground world, there may be intelligent beings that are not men."

"Well, that is possible, of course," Milton nodded.

The entrance was about four feet in width by eight in height. Above it, there was some striking sculpturing, evidently work of a mystical character. Its meaning was an utter mystery to Rhodes and me, but not, I thought, to our Dromans. Very little dust had accumulated, though, as I have good reason to believe, many, many centuries had passed since that spot was abandoned to unbroken blackness and silence.

Many were the pictures that came and went as we stood there and looked and wondered. Who had cut this passage into the living rock? In what lost age of a people now perhaps lost as well? And for what purpose had they hewn it?

"Well," I said to myself, "possibly the answer to that question awaits us there within."

Rhodes and I moved over to the entrance, and he sent the strong rays of his electric light into the passage.

"About fifty feet long," he observed, "and evidently it enters another chamber."

We started in. We had taken but a few steps, however, when we stopped and turned our look back to the Dromans.

"Not coming," said Rhodes.

Why did they stand hesitant, with that strange look in their eyes and upon their faces? Even the angel was affected. Affected by what? By the mere mystery of the place?

"I wonder what is the matter with them," I said. "Why are they staying out there? I tell you, Milton, I don't like this at all. What's the matter with them?"

"Superstitious dread or something, I suppose," returned Rhodes. "Well, it ill becomes a scientist to let superstition stay his steps, to turn back even if a black cat crosses his path; and so on we go."

And on we went into the passage. When we were nearly through it, I glanced back. The Dromans had not moved.

"Look here!" I said, coming to an abrupt stop.

"What is it now, Bill?"

"Maybe this is a trap."

"A trap? How can it be a trap?"

"How in the world do I know that? But to me the whole business has a queer and suspicious look, I tell you."

"How so?"

"How so? Why, maybe they *brought* us to this hole. We don't know what's in there."

"Neither do they," Milton said.

"Maybe they *do*," I told him. "Maybe they aren't lost at all. Maybe it's all make-believe. Why don't they come in, too? What are they standing out there for, standing and waiting—waiting? What are they waiting for? Probably for their chance to steal away and leave us to our fate!"

"My gosh, Bill," said Milton Rhodes, "your imagination goes like a jumping-jack!"

"Heaven help us if that's what you think when a man would be cautious and watchful!"

"Cautious and watchful. Yes, certainly we want to be cautious and watchful. After all, there may be something in what you say.

"But," he added the next moment, "not much, I think. No, Bill. This is not a trap. There is no faking about it: the Dromans *are* lost."

"I don't like it," I told him, "Why don't they come on in?"

"Goodness knows, Bill. Why won't some people sit down to a table if the party numbers thirteen? And why should *we* stand hesitant? Suppose that they do plan to steal away from us. I don't believe it, but suppose that they do. What then? Are we going to run after them, like lambs after little Bopeep? Not I, old *tillicum*. If they are as treacherous a lot as that, the quicker we part company the better. For, sooner or later, their chance would come."

"There may be something in that," I admitted. "Lead on, Macduff."

A moment or two, and we had stepped from the passage and out into a great and lofty chamber.

"Great Heaven!" I cried, my right hand going to my revolver. "What—what is that thing?"

Rhodes made no answer. He stood peering intently.

"Look out!" I cried, pulling out my weapon and drawing back towards the entrance. "*It's moving!*"

27
THE MONSTER

Rhodes made no response. Still he stood there, peering towards the end of the chamber. Then of a sudden, to my inexpressible surprise, he began moving forward—moving towards that monstrous thing which reared itself up out of the gloom and the shadows, up and up, almost to the very roof itself.

"What are you doing?" I cried. "I tell you, I saw it move!"

Rhodes paused, but he did not look back.

"It didn't move," he said. "How *could* it move? It must have been only the shadows that you saw, Bill."

"Shadows?"

"Just so—shadows."

He moved his light slowly back and forth.

"See that. A certain way you look at it, that thing up there seems to be moving instead of the shadows."

"But what on earth can it be?" I asked, slowly advancing to his side. "And what is that white which, though so faint, yet gleams so horribly? It looks like *teeth*."

"It is teeth," said Milton, whose eyes were better than mine. "But the thing, of course, is not animate. You just thought that you saw it move. The thing is simply a manmade monster, like the great Sphinx of the Pyramids, like the Colossi of Thebes."

We were moving toward it now.

"And look at all those horrors along the walls," I said, "dragons, serpents, horrors never seen on land, in the air or in the sea—at any rate, in that world we have left. And look there. There is a demon—I mean a sculptured demon. And that's what the colossus itself is—a monstrous ape-bat."

"Not so, Bill. See, it is becoming plainer and plainer, and it is unequivocally a dragon."

Yes; it was a dragon. And I wondered if a monster more horrible than this thing before us ever had been fashioned by the wildest imagination of artist or madman.

The dragon (not carven from the rock but made of bronze) crouched upon a high rock, its wings outspread. At the base of this rock, upon which base rested the hind claws of the monster, was a platform some twenty feet square and raised five or six feet above the floor of the cavern. In the front and on either side of this platform, there were steps, and, in the center of it, a stone of curious shape—a stone that sent a shudder through me.

And up above rose the colossal dragon itself, its scaly fore claws gripping the edge of the rock, twenty-five feet or so above the platform. The neck curved forward and down.

The head hung over the platform, thirty feet or more up in the air—the great jaws wide open, the forked tongue protruding hungrily, the huge teeth and the huge eyes sending back the rays from our lights in demonical, indescribably horrible gleams.

"Talk about Gorgons, Chimeras and Hydras dire!" I exclaimed, and it was as though unseen things, phantom beings, so eerie were the echoes, repeated the words in mockery and in gloating. "Why should men create such a Gorgonic nightmare? And worship it—worship the monster of their own creating? Look at that stone there in the center of the platform. Ugh! The things that must have taken place in that spot! The thought makes the flesh creep and the blood itself turn cold in one's veins!"

"What a dark and fearsome cavern, after all, is the skull of man," said Milton Rhodes, "a place where bats flit and blind shapes creep and crawl!"

I turned toward him with a look of surprise.

"That from the man whom I have so often heard sing the Song of the Mind; that from a scientist, one who has so great an admiration for Aristotle, Hipparchus, Archimedes, Galileo, Newton and

Darwin; from one who so often has said that the only wonderful
thing about man is his mind and that that mind, in its possibilities, is simply godlike."

"And so say I again, Bill, and so, I am sure, I shall always say.
In its possibilities, remember. But you shouldn't have had scientists only on your list; you should have added these at least: Homer,
Plato, Saint Augustine, Cicero, Dante and Shakespeare, and, yes,
poor old Job in his Land of Uz. But man is a sort of dual creature,
a creature that achieves the impossible by being in two places at
the same time: his body is in this the Twentieth Century, his mind
is still back there in the Pliocene, with cave-bears, hyenas and
saber-toothed tigers."

I uttered a vehement dissent.

"But 'tis so, Bill," said Milton Rhodes, "or at least back there
beyond the year 1492. The world knows but one Aristotle, one Newton, one Archimedes, one Galileo, one Darwin, one Edison; but
Heaven has sent the world thousands."

"I don't believe it. There are no mute, inglorious—Shakespeares."

"No; there are no mute, inglorious Shakespeares, no mute, inglorious Newtons: the world, this glorious *mind* that we hear so
much about destroyed them."

"Or," said I, "they destroyed themselves."

"You are not making the mind's case any brighter, Bill, by put-
ting it that way. Yes, the mind, the glorious human mind destroyed
them and turned forthwith to grovel in the dust before monsters
like this one before us—before Prejudice, Ignorance, Superstition
and Worse."

"What a horrible piece of work, then, is man!"

"Take the average of the human mind," went on Milton Rhodes,
"not the exceptions and those so brilliant and so wonderful, but
the average of all the human minds in all the world today, from
our Newtons—if we have any now—to your savage groveling in the
dust before some fetish or idol made of mud; do that, and the skull
of man is found to be just what I said—a dark and fearsome cavern, a habitat for bats and ghostly nameless things."

"What a strange, a horrible idea!" I exclaimed.

"The world is proud of its Newtons now," said Rhodes. "But was it proud of them when they came? Whenever I see a man going into ecstasy over the wonders and the beauties and the glories of the human mind—remember, Dante was driven from his country—then I think of these words, written by the Philosopher of Ferney:

"'When we reflect that Newton, Locke, Clarke, and Liebnitz, would have been persecuted in France, imprisoned at Rome, and burned at Lisbon, what are we to think of human reason?'"

"Alas, you poor, poor humans," said I, "you are only a breed of vile Yahoos!"

"Oh, don't misunderstand me, Bill. The mind of man is a fearful thing, but it is wonderful too, as wonderful as it is dreadful; and the more wonderful, perhaps, than it intrinsically is because of the very grossness and the very sordidness that it has to conquer. We are prone, some of us, to think the record of the intellect a shabby one; but, after all, the record is not, all things considered, so bad as it may seem at a first glance to be. It might have been better, much better; but we should rejoice that it is not worse, much worse; that the mind, the hope of the world, has made even the slightest advance that it has. Man, however, is on his way at last. And, with Science on his right hand and Invention on his left, he can not fail to conquer the ape and the tiger, to win to a future brighter even than the most beautiful of our brightest dreams."

"Well," said I, turning and seating myself on one of the steps, up which steps perhaps many victims had been dragged to sacrifice, "this is a fine time truly and a fine place indeed in which to discuss man and the glorious destiny that may await him, in view of the fact that some spot in these cursed caverns may soon be our tomb.

"And," I added, "there come the Dromans."

Never shall I forget that look of awe and horror upon their white faces when at last they stood there in a huddled group before, almost under, the great dragon. Rhodes had seated himself beside me, and it was obvious that this temerity on our part was a source of astonishment to the Dromans. What dread powers they feared the monster might possess, I can only conjecture; but I do know that we could never have induced even Drorathusa herself to thus, on the very steps of his altar, hazard the wrath of an offended deity.

28
I ABANDON HOPE

At last Milton and I arose and proceeded to examine carefully this chamber of carven horrors. By the altar, another passage was discovered. Like the great chamber itself and the passage by which we had entered, this tunnel had been hewn out of the living rock by the hand of man. It was some sixty feet in length and conducted us into a small but most remarkable grotto, or rather a series of grottoes. We advanced, however, but a little way there; a few minutes, and we were again in the hall of the dragon.

We continued, and finished, our examination of the place. Another passage was discovered in the roof and leading, of course, to we knew not where. Then there were those stone horrors ranged along either wall; but I shall not attempt to describe those nightmare-monstrosities, some of which, by the way, had two heads.*

* "The Chevalier d'Angos, a learned astronomer, carefully observed, for several days, a lizard with two heads, and assured himself that this lizard had two wills independent of each other, and possessing nearly equal power over the body, which was in one. When a piece of bread was presented to the animal, in such a manner that it could see it with one head only, that head wished to go towards the bread, while the other head wished the body to remain still."—Voltaire.

The Dromans had drawn back some distance from the altar, and all had sunk down to a seat upon the floor, all save Drorathusa.

Our examination ended, we moved toward the little group. Milton looked at his watch.

"Midnight," he said.

As we drew near, Drorathusa suddenly raised a hand and made a significant motion toward the entrance. Those seated rose from the floor with an alacrity that astonished me. Evidently they were very anxious to quit this chamber of horrors. Well, I confess that I was not sorry to do so myself.

"Shades of the great Ulysses," said I as we moved along in the rear, "are we going to keep up this wandering until we drop?"

"Just what I was wondering myself, Bill. I fancy, though, that our Dromans are beginning to think that a rest would not be inexpedient."

Inexpedient!

Shortly after issuing from the passage, the party came to a halt, and Drorathusa, to my profound thankfulness, announced that the time for rest and sleep had come.

"Sleep?" said I to myself. "Who can sleep in such a place and at such a time?"

From his pack, Ondonarkus took a small silk-like bundle; like the tent that Captain Amundsen left at the South Pole,* one could have put it into a fair-sized pocket. The white-haired girl handed Ondonarkus the sort of alpenstock which she carried, and, lo and presto, there was a tent for the ladies!

Rhodes and I betook ourselves off to a hollow in the wall, where we halted and disposed ourselves for rest. This disposition, however, was a very simple affair: we simply removed our packs and sat down on the floor, the softness of which by no means vied with that of swan's-down.

---

* See *In Amundsen's Tent*, by John Martin Leahy.—
Darwin Frontenac.

I drank a little water, but it seemed to augment rather than to assuage my burning thirst. For a time I sat there, my aching body leaning back against the rock-wall, my fevered, tortured mind revolving the grisly possibilities that confronted us. Meditation, however, only served to make our situation the more appalling. With an exclamation of despair, I lay down, longing for sleep's sweet oblivion. At this moment Ondonarkus and the young man— whose name, by the way was Zenvothunbro—were seen approaching. They laid themselves down nearby, their lanterns extinguished. We had shut off the electric lights, but our phosphorus-lamps, and those of the Dromans, shed their pale and ghostly light around.

Rhodes was sitting up, engaged in bringing his journal forward, as carefully and coolly as though he were in his library at home, instead of in this mysterious and fearful abode of blackness and silence, thousands of feet below the surface of the earth, far— though how far we could only guess—below the level of the sea itself.

When I closed my eyes, pictures came and went in a stream, pictures swaying, flashing, fading. The amazing, the incredible things that had happened, the things that probably were to happen—oh, was it all only a dream?

I opened my eyes and raised myself up on an elbow. I saw Milton Rhodes bent over his book, writing, writing; I saw the recumbent forms of the two Dromans, whose heavy breathing told me that already they slept; over there was the tent, in it the beautiful, the Sibylline Drorathusa and her lovely companions—and I knew, alas, that it was not a dream.

I sank back with an inward groan and closed my eyes again. Oh, those thoughts that came thronging! If I could only go to sleep! A vision of treachery came, but it was not to trouble me now. No; Rhodes was right: our Dromans were lost. If only those other visions could be as easily banished as that one!

Ere long, however, those thronging thoughts and visions became hazy, confused, began to fade; and then suddenly they were blended with the monsters and the horrors of dreams. It was six o'clock when I awoke. Rhodes was sitting up. He had, he told me, just awakened. One of the Dromans was stirring in his sleep and muttering something in cavernous and horrible tones. As I sat there and listened, a chill passed through me, so terrible were the sounds.

"I can't stand that!" I exclaimed. "I'm going to wake him up. It's time that we were moving, anyway."

"Yes," nodded Milton. "Surely, though, we'll find water today."

"Today? Where is your *day* in this place? It's night eternal. And for us, I'm afraid, it is good night with a vengeance."

"Aw, Bill, quit your kidding," was Rhodes' answer.

Now, the thing that I want to know is this: what can you do with a man like that?

Ere long we were again under way. My canteen was now as dry as a bone, and I tell you that I felt mighty sad. However, I endeavored to mask, since I could not banish them, those dark and dire forebodings. When we set forth, it was with the hope that we might find, and be conducted by it to safety, the road by which those old worshippers had journeyed to and from that hall of the dragon. But not a vestige of such a route could we discover.

Hours passed. On and on we went, deeper and deeper. Noon came. No change. No one had a drop of water now. Rhodes and I estimated the distance traveled since quitting the temple of the dragon at ten miles and the descent at something like four thousand feet. This estimate, or rather guess, may, however, have been wide of the truth. We were still involved in the maddening intricacies of the labyrinth.

I confess that our situation began to assume an aspect that made my very soul turn sick and cold. Rhodes, however, divining perhaps what was in my mind, pointed out that we had not been lost very long! and that surely we would find water some place. A man, said he, in the equable temperature of this subterranean world, could live for quite a time without water. I have no doubt that a man could—if he were lying in bed. But we were not doing that; we were in constant motion. The arduous exercise that we were undergoing, our fatigue, the anxieties and fears that preyed upon the mind—each was contributing its quota to the dire and steady work of enervation.

No, I would fight against despair; but certainly I could imbibe no consolation, no strength, either mental or physical, from a deliberate blinking of facts. And one of the facts was that, unless we soon found water, ours would be that fate which has overtaken so many of those who have gone forth to search out the secrets of mysterious places.

During that halt for lunch—and what an awful lunch that was—Milton brought forward his journal, and Drorathusa, by means of pictures drawn in the book, made it clear to us that they would never have missed the route had it not been for the loss of their beloved demon. That, of course, made Rhodes and me very sorry; but, if the demon had not been killed, we certainly should have been even more sorry—and, I'm afraid, in a worse place than this in which we now found ourselves.

This strange intelligence, too, reminded me of grandfather Scranton's wonder as to how *his* angel and her demon had journeyed over rock, snowfield and glacier to the Tamahnowis Rocks through that dense, blinding vapor. I understood that now; they were guided by the wonderful instinct of the ape-bat. How truly wonderful that instinct is, we were yet to learn. Little wonder that Drorathusa mourned the loss of her dear, beloved, her hideous demon!

The bat has in all ages been the personification of repulsiveness, gloom and horror; and yet it is in many ways a very wonderful creature. For instance, it can fly through intricate passages with ease and certitude *when blinded*, avoiding any obstacle in or across its way as though in possession of perfect vision. No marvel, therefore, that some scientists have declared that the bat must possess a sixth sense. The accepted explanation, however, is that the creature discovers the objects, in the words of the great Cuvier, "by the sole diversity of aerial impressions."

However that may be, this wonderful faculty is possessed by the great ape-bats of Drome. Not that it is for this that they are valued by the Dromans. It is because it is impossible for the ape-bat to get lost. It matters not how long, how devious, how broken, savage, mysterious the way; the demon is never uncertain for one single moment. And a singular feature of this most singular fact is that the creature does not have to retrace the route itself, and it does not matter what time has elapsed. It may be a month, years; it is all the same to the demon. He may return to the point of departure by the outward trail, or he may go back in a bee-line or in a line as closely resembling a bee-line as the circumstances will permit.

From this it may easily be inferred how greatly the Dromans value these dreadful, repulsive creatures. When venturing out into the "lands of shadows" or into the caverns of utter darkness, these beasts are simply invaluable. In the "lands of shadows," they never fail to give warning of the approach of the wild ape-bats, those wolves of the air, or of other monsters; whilst, in the dark caverns—into which the wild bats sometimes wander for considerable distances—a man, though he may be utterly lost himself, knows that his demon will guide him safely back to the world of light.

In other ways, however, save as veritable Cerberi, they are of little use, are, indeed, objects of distrust and not a little dread. For they are, as a rule, of a most savage and uncertain temper. Not that the owner fears attack upon himself, though instances are not wanting in which master or mistress has been set upon. To its owner, a demon is truly doglike; but other people had better be careful.

"Since the loss of a demon on such a journey as this may spell disaster, I wonder," I said, "why they didn't bring along more than one."

"Food, Bill, food," returned Rhodes. "I am no authority, of course, on demonian dietetics, but I don't imagine that they fed the monster on canary-bird seed."

On we went, blindly and in desperation, on and on and deeper and deeper into the earth. At length there was a change, whether for good or ill we could not know; but we welcomed it, nevertheless—simply because it was a change. At last we were emerging from the labyrinth. But what lay ahead?

Yes, soon we were no longer in a maze of caverns, grottoes, passages, but in a wide and lofty tunnel. We had made our way down it but a little distance when an inscription was discovered on the right-hand wall. The discovery was made by Rhodes, who happened to be in the rear. A rectangular space, perhaps three feet by six, had been hewn perfectly smooth, and upon this rock-tablet were many chiseled characters, characters utterly unlike any we had seen. Before this spot, we clustered in hope and questioning. It was at once patent, however, that our Dromans could make nothing whatever of the writing.

But we regarded this discovery as a happy augury, and we pressed on with a lighter step.

On to bitter disappointment.

Hours passed. We were still toiling down that awful tunnel.

At last—it was then nine o'clock—the way became very difficult. The rock has been broken, rent, smashed by some terrible convulsion. The scene was indescribably weird and savage. And there we halted, sank down upon the rocky floor. Rhodes and Drorathusa evinced an admirable nonchalance, but in the eyes of the others burned the dull light of despair. And perhaps, too, in my own. I tried to hide it, but I could not disguise it from myself— the numbing, maddening fact that I had abandoned hope.

For a time I lay watching Rhodes, who was writing, writing in his journal. How could he do it? Who could ever find the record? At any rate, even though found, it could never be read, for the finder would be a Droman. It made me angry to see a man doing a thing so absurd. But I bridled speech, curbed that rising and insensate anger of mine, rolled over, closed my eyes and, strange to say, was soon asleep.

But that sleep of mine was an unbroken succession of horrors, horrors at last ended by an awakening as horrible.

Once more I was in that hewn chamber, once more I stood before the great dragon. But we had been wrong: the monster was alive. Down he sprang as I turned to flee, sank his teeth into my shoulder, raised his head high into the air and shook me as a cat shakes a mouse.

Then suddenly I knew that it was not all a dream.

Teeth *had* sunk into my shoulder. I struggled madly, but the jaws only closed the harder. And, horror of horrors, the spot in which I had lain down was now in utter blackness.

Then I was wide awake: the teeth were Rhodes' fingers, and I heard his voice above me in the darkness:

"Not a word, Bill—unless guarded."

"What is it?" I whispered, sitting up. "And where are our phosphorus-lamps?"

"In their cylinders," was Rhodes' low answer. "We want to see without being seen, that is why. I can turn on the electric, of course, at any instant. Wish the Dromans had been nearer, on this side of that rock-mass; I would have darkened theirs too."

"Without being seen?" I queried. "In Heaven's name, Milton, what does it mean?"

"I don't know. Got your revolver handy?"

"Yes."

"Good! Keep it so!"

"But what is it?"

"Did you," said he, "notice that passage in the opposite wall, a few yards back?"

I whispered that I had.

"Well," said Milton Rhodes, "there is something in there. And it's coming this way!"

29
THE GHOST

We waited, listening intently; but the place was as silent as the tomb.

"What," I asked, "did you hear?"

"I have no idea, Bill, what it was."

"What were the sounds like?"

"I don't know."

"Were they loud or faint?"

"Faint—mysterious."

"Great Heaven," said I, "what can it be? How long since you first heard it?"

"Only a few minutes. I can't imagine why the sounds have ceased. It certainly was coming this way. I wonder if it has discovered our presence."

"In that case, we had better look out."

"Well, that is what we are doing."

"Hadn't we better wake the Dromans?"

"I see no necessity for it. When the thing comes—it *was* coming, I know—they may be awakened suddenly enough. The men are farther from the passage of course, than we are, the ladies farther still. It must pass us before it can reach them; and we have our revolvers."

"Yes; we have our revolvers. But we don't know what's coming."

"There!" Rhodes exclaimed, his voice a whisper. "We'll soon know. Did you hear *that?*"

"I heard it. And there it is again!"

"It's coming, Bill!"

It *was* coming. What were we to see issue from that passage? I gripped my revolver and waited in a suspense that was simply agonizing. The sound ceased. It came again. It was a *pad-pad*. Once or twice another sound was heard. I thought that that one was produced by something *brushing along the wall.*

"Look!" I said, crouching forward. "Light!"

The rays grew stronger, casting long shadows—shadows swaying, shaking, crawling.

Then of a sudden the light itself appeared, and a tall figure came gliding out of the passage.

"Drorathusa!" exclaimed Milton Rhodes.

This sudden lurch from agonized suspense and Gorgonic imagination to glad reality left me for some seconds speechless.

"Well, well," laughed Milton Rhodes, pressing the button and flooding the place with light, "isn't imagination a wonderful thing?"

"But," said I, "what on earth does this mean?"

"Look there, Bill, *look!*" cried Rhodes. "Look at that!"

Drorathusa was moving straight towards us, a strange smile on that beautiful Sibylline face of hers.

"What do you mean? Look at what?"

"The canteen! Look at her canteen!" cried Milton pointing excitedly.

Drorathusa stopped and raised the canteen, which was incased in canvas-like stuff. It was wet. Yes, it was wet and dripping.

"Water!" I cried, springing up and rushing toward her.

"*Narranawnzee!*" smiled Drorathusa, reaching out the canteen toward my clutching fingers.

Great Pluvius, how I did drink! I'd be drinking yet if Rhodes hadn't seized the vessel and wrested it from me.

"You must be careful, Bill," he said. "We mustn't drink too much at first."

And he raised the canteen forthwith and proceeded to swallow a couple of quarts.

"For Heaven's sake," I told him, "leave some for the others!"

"Yes," said Rhodes, handing the water to Drorathusa. "We have been kind of ungallant, Bill—hoggish, I'm afraid. But I was as dry as a burnt cork."

Ere he had ceased speaking, Drorathusa was moving toward her companions. How wonderful was that change, that rush from out the black depths of despair! And yet our situation was still truly a terrible one, for we were *lost*. But we did not think of that now. Water, water! We had water now and rejoiced as though we had been caught up and set down in the loveliest of all the lovely glades of Paradise.

A few minutes, and we all (with tent and packs, with everything) were following Drorathusa through the passage, were hurrying toward that spring or stream or pool which she had discovered. What whim, what freak of strange chance had led that mysterious woman forth whilst others slept the sleep of despair, forth into that particular passage? Even now I do not know the answer.

After following its sinuosities for several hundred feet, we suddenly stepped out of the passage and into a great chamber. This, like our sleeping-place was weird and savage in the extreme. Broken rock-masses rose up, in all directions. There were distorted pyramids, fantastic pinnacles, spires, obelisks, even pillars, but they were pillars grotesque and awful as though seen in a dream.

Wider and wider grew the place, more and more broken and savage. Soon even the walls were involved in darkness. The roof, as we advanced, became more and more lofty. Clearly this cavern was one of enormous extent. I began to glance about with some apprehension. How had Drorathusa found her way into such a place—and out again? I marveled that she had not got lost. But she had not, and evidently there was no likelihood that that could happen. She was moving forward, into that place of savage confusion, with never a sign of hesitation, with the certitude of one following a well-beaten path.

Suddenly Drorathusa stopped, and, after making a sign for silence, she said, pointing into the blackness before us:

"*Narranawnzee*."

Narranawnzee. Yes, there it was, the faint murmur and tinkle of water.

We hurried forward, the wall of the cavern emerging from out the darkness. And there it was, a large spring of the purest, coolest water gushing out from the base of the rock, to fall in a gentle cascade and then flow away to a great pool gleaming dark and sullen in the feeble rays that found their way to it.

It was near nine o'clock of the day following when we left that spot. Rhodes and I were smooth-shaven again; yes, he had brought along a razor, one of your old-fashioned, antediluvian scrapers. I actually believe that it was an heirloom from the Man of Piltdown, or perhaps from the more ancient Pithecanthropus erectus himself.

Ondonarkus and Zenvothunbro too had gladly availed themselves of this opportunity to get rid of their beards, which, however, they had kept trimmed close with clippers. Your Droman has a horror of mustache, beard or whiskers.

As for the ladies, they were now radiant and lovely as Dians.

We were following the stream. An hour passed, another. We had advanced five miles or so and had descended probably half a thousand feet. And then we lost our guide; the stream flowed into a cleft in the rock, to burst forth again, perhaps, far, far down, in some black cavern that has never known, and indeed never may know, the tread of any human foot.

For some moments we lingered there, as though reluctant to quit the spot; and then, with a last lingering look at those pellucid waters, flashing dark and sullen, however, as the light moved from them, we pressed grimly on and soon were involved in a cavern so rugged and smashed that we actually began to despair of ever getting through it. But we did get through, to abruptly step out into a place as smooth almost as a floor. The slope was a gentle one, and we pressed forward at a rapid rate.

We had gone perhaps a mile and a half when Rhodes, who was walking in advance with Drorathusa, abruptly halted, cried out and pointed.

Something white was dimly visible off in the darkness. We moved toward it, the Dromans evincing a tense excitement. A cry broke from them, and they made a rush forward.

It was a mark upon the wall, a mark which they themselves had placed there.

We had found the way to Drome.

"And let us hope," said I to Rhodes in the midst of the rejoicing, "that we don't lose it again."

Drorathusa turned her look upon Rhodes and me and pointed down the cavern.

"*Narranawnzee*," she said.

We understood that.

"*Narranawnzee*," said we.

Again Drorathusa pointed.

"Drome," she told us.

That too we understood; that is, we thought that we knew when she meant by Drome.

It was a few minutes past seven (p.m.) when we reached the *narranawnzee*, a fine deep pool without any discoverable inlet or outlet, and there we halted for the "night."

In this spot, the Dromans had left a food-depot, and right glad were we to see this accession to the larder. There was also a supply of oil.

That evening (I find it convenient to use these inaccurate terms) I fished out my journal and carefully brought it forward, up to the hour, to the very minute. I felt blithe as a lark, and so, indeed, did everybody else, everybody save Drorathusa, and even she was somberly happy.

I thought that our troubles were over!

Of a sudden Rhodes slapped down his journal and, to the surprise of the Dromans and, forsooth to my own, made a dive at an oil-container, which Ondonarkus had just emptied.

"At last—our depth, Bill!" he cried.

And he proceeded to ascertain the boiling-point of water, the heat being furnished by Drorathusa's lamp and that of Silvisiris, the older of the young women. Nandradelphis, by the way, was the name of the other, the white-haired girl.

It was a strange, a striking picture truly—Milton Rhodes bending over his improvised hypogemeter, the Dromans looking on with curiosity, perplexity and with strange questionings in their looks.

At last Rhodes was satisfied with the result, that it was as near accuracy as the circumstances would permit.

"We are," said he after computing for some moments in his journal, "at a depth of a little more than twelve thousand feet. The exact figures are twelve thousand two hundred and sixty feet, though we cannot, of course, claim for our determination any high degree of accuracy. I feel confident, however, that it is near the truth. Call it twelve thousand feet."

"Twelve thousand feet!" I echoed. "Below the level of the sea?"

"Yes, Bill; below the level of the sea."

"Great Erebus, I knew that we had descended a long way, but I would never have believed that we had gone down over two miles. Two miles, and more, below sea-level. That is a record-smasher."

"Rather," Milton smiled. "Before us no man (of our sunlit world) had penetrated into the crust of the earth to a greater depth than three thousand seven hundred and fifty-eight feet below the level of the sea. That is the depth of the mine at St. John del Rey, Minas Geraes, Brazil."

"Two miles—over two miles down!" said I.

"And probably, Bill, we are only just getting started."

"But the pressure. We can't go down very far into this steadily increasing pressure, increasing in a geometrical ratio whilst the depth increases only in an arithmetical one."

"But," Milton said, "I showed you that there is something wrong with the law."

"Then how do you know that we have reached a depth of twelve thousand feet and over, if the law breaks down?"

"I don't believe that it has broken down yet. It will hold good for this slight descent which we have made. And, of course, if fact is found to coincide with theory, then our descent will be arrested at no great depth."

"And," I said, "unless the discrepancy between fact and theory is a remarkable one, we will have no means of knowing whether the law has broken down or not. For it is impossible, in this world of utter darkness, to make anything like an accurate estimate of the descent made good."

"We shall have no means of knowing, Bill, unless, as you say, truth and theory are remarkably divergent. Of course, in that case, we should not long remain unaware of the fact. Of the depth, then, we can not be certain; but the boiling-point of water will always give us the atmospheric pressure."

"That isn't what is worrying me," I told him; "it is the pressure itself."

"The pressure *itself*," Milton returned, "would produce no dire effects. It is not the diminuation of pressure that produces the dreaded mountain sickness, as was clearly shown by Dr. Paul Bert. Of educated people, nine hundred and ninety-nine out of every thousand will tell you that the acceleration of the pulse as one ascends to lofty heights, the short, troubled breathing, the disordered vision, extreme weakness, nausea, vertigo, bleeding at nose and lungs in short, all the symptoms of the terrible *mal des montagnes*, are caused by the diminution of the atmospheric pressure. The average human being (such is their explanation) having a surface of about fifteen square feet, sustains an atmospheric pressure of thirty thousand pounds; at an elevation of eighteen thousand feet, the pressure is but one half of that; is it any wonder, then, that a man gets mountain sickness?"

"Shades of ten thousand Gullivers," I exclaimed, "do you mean to say that those nine hundred and ninety-nine are wrong?"

"Certainly they are wrong, so wrong as to cause Dr. Bert to write:

"'It is amazing to find a theory so plainly at variance with elementary physical laws accepted by eminent men.'"

"Well, well," was my sage remark, "I suppose the next thing on the programme will be the statement that it is not the fire that makes the pot boil; it is the heat; and that it is simply amazing to find a man who thinks that he has an iota of brains in his cranium entertaining the belief that it is the pot that boils."

"If it doesn't rain, Bill, tomorrow will be Monday. However, Dr. Bert (Professor in the Paris Faculty of Sciences) proved 'that the lessening of the barometric pressure,' to use his own words, 'is of no account, mechanically, in the production of the phenomena.' Yes, he proved that, to use his own words again, 'it is not the lowering of mechanical pressure that produces the symptoms, but the low tension prevents the oxygen from entering the blood in sufficient quantity.'

"Dr. Bert not only experimented on sparrows but entered the air-chamber himself. As the pressure was reduced, he experienced all the symptoms of mountain sickness.

"'But,' he says, 'all these symptoms disappeared as by enchantment as soon as I respired some of the oxygen in the bag; returning, however, when I again breathed the air of the cylinder.'

"In one of his experiments, the pressure was reduced to 246 millimeters—9.7 inches.

"'This,' he says, 'is exactly the pressure on the highest summit of the Himalayas—the same degree of pressure which was so near proving fatal to Glaisher and Coxwell; I reached this point without the slightest sense of discomfort, or, to speak more accurately, the unpleasant sensations I felt at the beginning had entirely disappeared. A bird in the cylinder with me was leaning on one side, and very sick. It was my wish to continue the experiment till the bird died, but the steam-pump, conspiring, as I suspect, with the people who were watching me through glass peep-holes, would not work, and so I had to return to normal pressure.'

"So you see, Bill, it is the low tension of the oxygen and not the diminished pressure that produces the distress and suffering and even death."

"All this is very interesting, but our problem is not one of rarefied air; the atmosphere *here* is *compressed*."

"And, in compressed air," said Milton Rhodes, "it is the oxygen again that produces the symptoms. Subject a sparrow to a pressure of twenty atmospheres, and the bird is thrown into convulsions, stronger that those produced by tetanus or strychnine, convulsions which soon end in death. If pure oxygen is used, a pressure of only five atmospheres kills the sparrow. But, and mark this, if the air be deficient in oxygen, the pressure of twenty atmospheres does not produce even a tremor.

"So you see, Bill," Milton concluded, "we could descend to a very great depth in an atmosphere poor in oxygen."

"But how do we know that the atmosphere down there is poor in oxygen? It may be nothing of the kind. It may be saturated with it."

"Of course, we don't know. All we know is that we know nothing. And that reminds me of Socrates. That is what he said—that all he knew was that he didn't know anything. And Arcesilaus—Arcesilaus declared that Socrates didn't even know that much! However, hope is as cheap as despair. And, remember, here are our Hypogeans. They can ascend to our world, to a height of eight thousand feet above the level of the sea, and that, so far as we know, without suffering the slightest inconvenience."

"Something queer about that," was my comment.

"It *is* queer, Bill. However, we know that they can live in the (to them) rarefied air of our world: why, then, think that conditions down there, whether five miles down or fifty miles down, will prove fatal to *us?*"

On the following morning, we were under way at an early hour. The route led down a great tunnel; we could not have got lost now if we had tried. Shortly before noon, the welcome sounds of *narranawnzee* were heard, and there was a large stream gushing out of the wall. At times, as we advanced, the stream would move along dreamy and silent; then it would be seen rushing and glancing and again growling and foaming in lovely cascades.

Steadily, save for the noon halt, we toiled our onward and downward way. It was half-past seven when we halted—the eerie silence of the place broken by the soft, musical murmuring of the *narranawnzee*. Again Rhodes ascertained the boiling-point of water. It was 251° Fahrenheit. We were, therefore, under a pressure of two atmospheres; we had reached the depth of eighteen thousand five hundred feet. In other words, we were three miles and a half below the level of the sea!

It seems strange that I awoke, for I was dreaming the loveliest dream, a dream of fairy landscapes, birds and flowers, with lovely Cinderella (she looked very much like Drorathusa) in the midst of them. Nor do I know why I turned over onto my right side, for I was very comfortable as it was. But turn I did. And I was just going to close my eyes, to return to the dreamland of the fairies. But I did not close them. Instead, my heart gave a wild leap, and I opened my eyes wide. The next instant I was sitting up, straining my eyes as I looked into the darkness. Fear had its grip upon me, and I felt my hair begin to stand on end.

For there was something in that blackness, something visible, something *moving!*

Scarcely had my eyes fallen upon this amorphous, ghostly thing when it rose into the air, slowly and without the faintest sound. Up it rose and up, whilst I sat watching, immovable, speechless, as though in the clutch of some uncanny charm.

Up! Up to the very roof of the cavern!

Of a sudden there was a fearful change in its form. Then the ghost, now of monstrous shape, was coming down—*coming down straight towards me!*

30

THE MOVING EYES

I jerked out my revolver; I reached over and gave Rhodes a shake that would have awakened Epimenides himself; then I grabbed the electric light and flashed it upon the descending monster.

I could scarcely believe my eyes. Nothing but the empty air. The monster had vanished.

"What's the matter?" came the sudden voice of Rhodes. "What in Paradise is going on now?"

I rubbed my eyes and stared upward once more.

"Look there!" said I, pointing. "Tell me, do you see nothing there?"

"There isn't anything there, Bill—*now*."

"But there was something there a second or two ago, and it didn't go away."

"Ergo it is still there," said Milton. "But, you see, it isn't. What did you see?"

"I wish I knew. I thought at first that it was a demon, phosphorescent or something. It was up there. I tell you it was up there. And it was coming down, coming down straight towards this very spot."

"Great Caesar's spook!" exclaimed Rhodes.

"I can't understand," I told him, "where the thing went. It was there, and the next instant it wasn't. And yet it didn't go away."

"Turn off your light," Rhodes said quickly. "Turn it off, Bill."

"Great Zeus, what for? You'd better have your revolver ready."

"Revolver fiddlesticks! Off with it, Bill; off with the light!"

The light went off. And look! There it was again, and almost directly over us. It was not descending now but was hovering, hovering, as though watching, waiting. Waiting for what? And it seemed, too, to thrust out arms or tentacula. And look at that! Something started to drop from it—phosphorescence (I shall call it that) dropping to the floor, where it writhed and crawled about like a mass of serpents. Writhed and crawled and grew dimmer and dimmer, faded, faded.

We sat staring at this mysterious, inexplicable phenomenon in amazement, fascination and horror.

"What in the world can it be?" I asked, my voice a whisper.

"Who," returned Rhodes, "would ever have dreamed of such a thing as that?"

"I'm afraid," I told him, a shudder passing through me, "that our revolvers can't hurt a thing like that. It seems to be watching us. Look! Aren't those eyes—eyes staring at us, moving?"

"Eyes? Watching us? Eyes moving? Oh, Lord, Bill!" said Rhodes.

"Then what is it? It's moving."

"Oh, it's moving. But it hasn't any eyes."

There was a momentary silence.

"As for sending a bullet into it," he added, "don't do anything so foolish."

He arose, stepped over and awoke Ondonarkus. The monster was still hovering over the spot. The Droman bestowed upon that ghost but a cursory, careless look, then yawned sleepily.

"Yam-yump!" said Ondonarkus, stretching himself.

Milton Rhodes laid a hand upon the other's shoulder and pointed an interrogative finger up in the direction of the phantom. The Droman gave a careless, airy toss of the hand.

"Drome," said he, then lay down again.

It was obvious from this monosyllabic answer, to say nothing of the manner of Ondonarkus, that there was absolutely nothing to apprehend from this mysterious apparition hovering above us. Certainly, though, there had not been any remarkable clarification. Indeed, in a way, Rhodes and I were more puzzled than ever. Drome, Drome. What could be the meaning of that word? Drome.

"It seems, Bill," said Rhodes, "that we are on our way to a very strange place. As for that ghost up there, it must be a fragment, as it were of the *light* of this subterranean land."

"Suppose it is—a harbinger, so to speak—then what, in the name of wonder, can that light be?"

"That, of course, we can not tell. It may be phosphorescent or auroral, or its origin may be one of which no man of our own world ever has even dreamed. I believe that I forgot to mention, when we were speaking of this the other day, that even human beings sometimes evolve light.* One thing, however, is certain: there is light somewhere in this underground world. And I believe, Bill, that we are drawing near to it now."

"I certainly hope that we are. But look at our ghost. It is moving again—thank Heaven (even if it is only a mass of light) away from us."

"Yes," said Rhodes. "But look down there. There is another one coming."

It came, and another and another. I don't know how many. On they came through the cavern, now lingering, now hovering; on they passed like some unearthly, ghostly procession. And, even

* "A very decided luminosity has been observed to proceed from dissecting-room subjects, the light thus evolved being sufficient to render the forms of the parts (which are peculiarly bright), almost as distinct as in the daylight. . . . Three cases are recorded by Sir H. Marsh, in which an evolution of light took place from the living body. . . . The light in each case is described as playing around the face, but not as directly proceeding from the surface; and in one of these instances, which was recorded by Dr. D. Donovan, not only was the luminous appearance perceptible over the head of the patient's bed, but luminous vapours passed in streams through the apartment."—Dr. Carpenter.

though one knew that these phantoms, so dim and so misty, were perfectly innocuous, were as natural (as though there is anything that can not be natural!) as the light of the firefly, as the glow of the auroral arches and streamers—all the same, I say, the sight of that spectral company, passing, passing, was one indescribably strange and uncanny.

However, a man can get used to anything. I got used to them and ere very long was asleep once more. In the morning, not a single ghost was to be seen. Nor did we see one until near midafternoon. That ghost was all by its lonesome and so dim that it vanished when our lights drew near. But soon they were about us in all directions. One of these phantoms, large, amorphous, writhing (its light so strong that it was bright in the rays of the lamps but not of the electric ones) came crawling along, swaying and shaking, straight toward us. Rhodes and I, as if by instinct, moved over so as to miss it; but Drorathusa and the others walked right into it. As they emerged from the spectral, phosphorescent cloudlet, the light clung to them like wraiths of fog, to be slowly dissipated as they advanced in little streams and eddies behind them.

It was during this afternoon, too, that Rhodes made the first discovery of animal life in this fearsome place—little fish, like those in the Mammoth Cave, totally blind. But, though they could not see, they could *feel* the light. When the rays fell upon the stream, they would drop to the bottom and seek the concealment of the shadow-places. Poor little blind things! What an existence! And yet how like them, after all, are we poor humans! How often have I thought of these sad words of Dr. Whewell's:

"It is not necessary here to inquire why those faculties which appear to be bestowed upon us for the discovery of truth, were permitted by Providence to fail so signally in answering that purpose."

Yes, blind are we, though we have eyes; our souls shrinking from the light to wander, lost and happy and doubting and fearful, in psychic caves and labyrinths more terrible even sometimes than this cavern through which we were making our way—making our way to we knew not what.

We journeyed on until about seven o'clock, when we reached another depot, and there we halted for the night. All were much fatigued, but the Dromans were in high spirits, and ours rose, too. Whether we were drawing towards the end of our strange journey was not clear; but there could be no doubt that a great change was imminent.

To the surprise of Rhodes and myself (nothing in the place seemed to surprise Drorathusa and her companions) not a single light-wraith was anywhere to be seen. The cavern was as black as the deepest pit in Erebus.

And it was still the same when we awoke. How I would have welcomed the appearance of the faintest, loneliest ghost, as we called the small apparitions of light.

We noticed that Ondonarkus and Zenvothunbro, and the ladies also, were at some pains to have their bows in such a position that they could be drawn at an instant's warning. Ondonarkus saw us watching, and, sweeping a hand toward the darkness before us, he said:

"*Loopmuke.*"

That, as we well knew, is the Droman word for ape-bat. Also, he tried to tell us about something else; but the only thing intelligible to us in his pantomimic explanation was that it was about a creature even more formidable than a wild *loopmuke.*

It was with keen anticipation on the part of Rhodes and myself that we set out that morning. For an hour or so, there was no change. Not a single light-wraith had shone in the awful blackness. Then, after passing through a particularly broken and tortuous place, we began to see them. Not many, however, and all were small and faint. Another hour passed, and of a sudden the walls drew together, and the roof came sloping down, down and down until we had to go bended over. Narrower and narrower grew the way, crowding us at last to the water's edge and then into the very stream itself.

Drorathusa and Ondonarkus were leading, Rhodes and I bringing up the rear. Fortunately the current was a gentle one; had it been otherwise, the place would have been simply impassable.

"I certainly," said Milton at last, "admire the man (maybe he was a woman) who first came through this awful place."

The next moment he made a rush forward. Nandradelphis, the white-haired girl, had slipped out into deep water. Rhodes caught her just in time to save her from immersion and drew her back to the shallow water by the wall. Not a cry, not the faintest sound had escaped her, and now she only laughed. Beauty was not the only admirable quality that these Droman ladies possessed.

For ten minutes or so, we toiled our way down that tunnel, now hugging the wall, now following the shallows out into the stream and at times to the other side. Then of a sudden there was an exclamation from Drorathusa, and the next moment we had issued from the tunnel and the stream and found ourselves in a great lofty cavern.

"Great Rameses!" I exclaimed as we stepped forth. "Look at those things."

Rhodes, I found, had already halted and was gazing up at them—two colossi, one on either side of the mouth of the tunnel. These carven monsters (we were, of course, standing between their bases) were seated, and one was a male, the other a female. They had not been fashioned *in situ* but clearly had been brought to the spot in sections. But how had those massive pieces of rock, the smallest of which weighed tons, been raised into their places? Who can tell? It remains, and probably always will remain, one of the mysteries of that lost and mysterious land.

We were getting rather used to strange things now: but, so remarkable were these great statues, for some minutes we lingered there before them.

The Dromans had moved on. We followed, to find ourselves in a few moments before a monstrous carven human head. There was the great pedestal, and there, lying face upward before it, was the great head, that and nothing more.

"Poor fellow," said I as we walked around the caput, "where is the rest of him? And why did they leave the head lying here like this?"

"I have an idea," Milton returned, "that there was no rest of him, that this head was all that was to be placed upon that pedestal."

I suppose that Rhodes was right. One wonders what happened there so long ago, why the great caput was never raised to the place which they had prepared for it. No man can tell that now. All we know is that there the great head lies, that there it has lain for, in all probability, untold thousands of years.

At last Milton Rhodes climbed up and stood upon the chin, in order, as he said, "to get a good view of the poor gink's phiz." And not only that, but he stood upon the poor fellow's nose; yes, he balanced himself on one foot on the very tip of it.

I turned my look to the Dromans with some apprehension, for I did not know what superstitious ideas they might entertain, feared that to them this acrobatic stunt of Rhodes might be sacrilege itself. My misgivings, however, were groundless. The Dromans were delighted. They burst into merry laughter; they applauded vociferously. Even Drorathusa laughed outright.

Little wonder, forsooth, for a pretty figure Milton Rhodes made balanced up there on the poor gink's olfactory protuberance. A fine posture truly for one of the world's (I mean, of course, our world's) great scientists; and I could not help wondering what certain dignified old fellows (Milton called them fossils) would have thought could they, by television or some miracle, have seen him there. And what would the Dromans themselves think? Well, I was glad when he came down and there was an end to that foolishness.

And I put in a prompt remonstrance.

"We," I told him, "have—or, at any rate, we *ought* to have—a certain dignity to uphold. For we are the representatives, as it were, of that great sunlit world above, the world of Archimedes, Kepler, Galileo, Newton, Humboldt, Darwin, Edison—not a world of Judys and Punches."

"Aw, Bill," was the answer that I got, "now quit your kidding."

I ask you this again: what can you do with a man like that?

We soon quitted the spot. The light-cloudlets were all about us now. Some came slowly gliding, some crawling, along the floor;

some along the walls and the roofs. Others floated along overhead or hung motionless in the air. The changes of form were sometimes very rapid and certainly as unaccountable as the masses themselves. Occasionally we would see a mass slowly take form in the darkness and as slowly fade into darkness again. Where did the light come from, where did it go? And the explanation of this uncanny phenomenon? Undoubtedly some electric manifestation, said Rhodes, analogous perhaps to the light of the aurora. That, I objected, really explained nothing, and Rhodes admitted that that was just what it did explain—nothing.

Which reminds me of the beautiful eclaircissement which Professor Archimedes Bukink gave when the little girl to whom he was reading a fairy story asked:

"But what is that flamingo thing?"

"*Phoenicopterus ruber,*" said Bukink!

The spirits of the Dromans rose higher as we toiled our way onward and down. They quickened their pace, and, as we swung along like soldiers marching, they suddenly broke into a song or rather chant, the wonderful contralto voice of Drorathusa leading, the sounds coming back from the dark secret places of the cavern in echoes strange and sweet as voices heard in fairyland.

The light-masses were steadily increasing in number and volume. Especially was this pronounced in the great chambers. Fungoid growths were seen, coleopterous insects and at last a huge scolopendra of an aspect indescribably horrible. From this repulsive creature, the Dromans and myself drew back, but Milton Rhodes bent over it in a true scientific scrutiny and ecstasy.

"Look, Bill, look!" he cried suddenly pointing, "Look at that. The body has thirty-five somites or segments."

"Thirty-five segments?" I queried, scratching my head and wishing that the scolopendra was in Jericho. "What is there so wonderful about that?"

"Why," said he, "in the Scolopendridae of our own world, the segments of the body never exceed twenty-one. And this one has thirty-five. Really, Bill, I must keep so remarkable and splendid a specimen."

"Great Gorgons and Hydras! Keep it? Don't touch the horrible thing. It may be venomous, deadly as a rattlesnake. And, besides, you'll have plenty of time to collect specimens, and probably some of them will make this one look like the last rose of summer. Leave the hideous thing alone. Why, the Dromans will think that you are dippy. Fact is, I believe that they are beginning to think so already."

"Let 'em!" said Rhodes with true philosophic indifference. "People thought that Galileo was crazy, and Newton and Darwin; Columbus was *non compos mentis*,* Fulton was dippy, and Edison was looney. Yes, at one time the great inventor bore the beautiful sobriquet of Looney Edison. Listen to me, Billy, me lad: the greatest compliment that a scientist can ever receive is to be called a sap by sapheads."

All that, I admitted, was very true and truly cogent in its place; but this was not its place, and the Dromans certainly were neither sapheads nor saps. To my relief, and, indeed to my surprise, I dissuaded him from taking the thing as a specimen, and on we went once more.

At length we left the stream, which went plunging into a most fearsome place, into which no man could even dream of following it. Soon after that, the descent became very steep. The going, however, was good, and we went down at a rapid rate. This lasted for two or three hours, and we had descended many hundreds of feet. The slope then suddenly became gentle, and we were making our way through a perfect maze of tortuous galleries and passages, which at times opened out into halls and chambers.

The light was no longer in masses but in streams—streams that crawled and shivered and shook, as though in it spirit-things were immersed and were struggling to break from it. The fungal growths were everywhere now. There were mushrooms with pilei bigger than umbrellas. Shapes as grotesque as if seen through the eyes of madness. There were growths, too, that one could almost think

* "The very children, it is said, pointed to their foreheads as he passed, being taught to regard him as a kind of madman."—Irving.

beautiful, and masses hideous and slimy as so many octopi. A strong and most unpleasant odor filled the place. And here and there, almost everywhere in the strange fungoid growth, were things creeping, crawling—things for which I can find no name, and for some of them I am glad that I cannot.

It was a weird scene, an indescribable scene, one horrible, mysterious and yet strangely wonderful too. A place gloomy and weird as any ever conceived by Dante or Doré. And through it human forms were moving, and its stillness was broken by human voices raised in song; and, moving with those human beings, those inhabitants of a world as alien as that of Venus or of Mars, were Rhodes and I, we two modern men from the great modern world above—the wonderful, the awful world of the sun.

Of a sudden an exclamation rang out—an exclamation that stilled the song on the instant, brought the party to an abrupt halt and the bow of Ondonarkus and that of Zenvothunbro from the cases.

The exclamation had broken from Rhodes; he was pointing into the gloom off to our right, a tense, expectant look on his face.

I peered with straining eyes, but I could see nothing there. A few moments passed, and still nothing was seen. I then turned to Rhodes to ask him what it was; but the words I was about to speak were never uttered. Instead, I gave something like a cry and whirled round. For a sound had come from out the fungoid growth and the darkness behind us, a sound as if of a slimy thing moving, slipping.

Nothing, however, was to be seen there, and silence, utter silence, had fallen upon the spot—silence abruptly broken by another exclamation from Milton Rhodes.

"Great Heaven!" I cried as I whirled back to the direction in which he was pointing. "They are all around us!"

"Look, Bill—*look at that!*"

I saw nothing for a second or two. And then, off in the darkness beyond the reach of our lights, the darkness itself was moving—yes, the very darkness itself.

"See that, Bill?"

I saw it. And the next instant I saw two great eyes, eyes that were watching us. And those eyes were moving.

They were visible for a few seconds only—those great eyes burning with a greenish fire.

"Where did they go?" exclaimed Rhodes.

"And," said I, "what can it be? An ape-bat?"

"That is no ape-bat."

He turned to Ondonarkus.

"*Loopmuke?*" he queried.

No; it was not a *loopmuke*. But what it was neither Ondonarkus's pantomime nor Drorathusa's could tell us.

"I don't think it's as bad as that. But the Dromans are know what it is themselves."

"There!" I cried, whirling round. "Did you hear that, Milton? There's that other thing again—that thing behind us!"

"I heard nothing."

"I heard something, I tell you. That mystery with the eyes is not the only thing that is watching us, watching us and waiting."

Some moments passed, perhaps minutes, in expectant watching, our glances incessantly darting about the cavern, through which the light-mist was moving in troubled, writhing streams, the nebulous, spectral glow of it seeming to enhance the fearsome gloom of that dreadful place.

"I see nothing," Rhodes said at last, "and the cavern is as silent as a tomb."

"But we are *seen*. And, if we don't get out of this, it may be *our* tomb."

"I don't think it's as bad as that. But the Dromans are signing to us to come on—let us hope to a place more pleasant that this one."

I had turned to quit the spot, my look, however, lingering in that direction whence had come those low, mysterious sounds, a direction right opposite to that in which the moving eyes had shone. And scarcely had I taken a step forward when I fetched up, cried out and pointed.

"See that! See it moving?"

A large fungus-tree, its form one indescribably grotesque, was quivering. It began to shake violently. Some heavy body, hidden from our eyes, was moving there, and it was moving toward us.

Of a sudden the tree was thrust far over, there was a squishy, sickening sound, then down it came, the spot where it fell involved in a cloud of phosphorescence, which thinned and faded in the air like dust or mist as it settles.

"Shades of the Gorgons," I cried, "what is in there?"

A sound from Milton Rhodes turned me round on the instant.

"The eyes again!" he cried. "There they are. See them? Have we at last got into Dante's Inferno itself?"

I was beginning to think that we had got into something worse.

Yes, there the eyes were, and they were nearer this time. But that was all we saw, eyes and nothing more. The thing itself was hidden in the fungoid growth and the shadows.

Rhodes raised his revolver, rested it on his left arm, took careful aim and fired.

The report seemed to bellow like thunder through the cavern. There was a scream from the Dromans, none of whom, save Drorathusa, had ever heard a firearm before; and I doubt that even Drorathusa knew what had killed her demon. On the instant, whilst the report of the weapon and the cry of the Dromans were ringing in our ears, came another sound; it was a shriek, high, piercing, unearthly, one that seemed to arrest and curdle the very blood in our hearts.

It sank, ceased. But almost instantaneously it came again; it rose until the air seemed to quiver to the sound.

The effect upon the Dromans was most sudden and pronounced.

A nameless fear, and something worse, seized upon me as I saw it.

They started from the spot as if in a panic, signing to us with frantic gestures to follow.

I started; but Rhodes, for some inexplicable reason, stood there, his look fixed on the spot whence came those demoniacal shrieks. The eyes had disappeared, but in almost that very instant that I turned, they shone again. I gazed at them as though in fascinated horror, forgetting for the moment that there was something behind me.

Up the eyes rose. A black thing was visible there in the darkness, but its shape was amorphous, mysterious. Up the eyes rose, seeming to dilate, and the fire in them grew brighter and brighter, became so unearthly that I began to wonder if I were going insane. The eyes swayed, swayed back and forth for some moments, then gave a sudden lurch into darkness. The shrieks broke, then came again, more horrible, if that were possible, than before.

"Come on!" I cried, starting. "For Heaven's sake, Milton, let's get out of this, or I'll go mad!"

"What in the world," said Rhodes, reluctantly turning to follow, "can that thing be?"

"Let's get out of this hellish place. Let's do it before it's too late. Remember, there is something *behind* us. Maybe monsters in other directions too."

"Well," said Rhodes complacently as he followed along in my wake, "we have our revolvers."

"Revolvers? Just see what your revolver has done. A revolver is only a revolver, while that thing—who knows what that monster is?"

"The Dromans know, or at any rate, they think that they do."

"And look at the Dromans. Fear has them. Did you ever see fear like that before? See how they are signing to us to come on. Even Drorathusa is shaken to the very soul."

"After all, 'tis no wonder, Bill, that she is. Those shrieks! How can it continue to shriek and shriek like that?"

Ere long we had come up with the Dromans, who at once quickened their pace. On we went, casting apprehensive glances into the gloom about us. Those frightful sounds sank as we moved onward. They became faint, fainter still, and at last, to my profound thankfulness, they were no longer to be heard, even when we paused to listen.

"If that," said I during one of those pauses, "is a good sample of what we are to have here in Drome, then I wish that, instead of coming down here, I had stepped into a den of cobras or something."

Drorathusa's eyes were upon me. As I ceased speaking, she raised a hand and pointed in the direction whence we had come.

"*Gogrugron!*" she said.

And I saw fear and horror unutterable well up in her eyes as she said it.

32

"LEPRAYLYA!"

Steadily we made our way along and downward. The light-streams were increasing in volume, the luminosity becoming stronger and stronger, the vegetation more abundant, the weird shapes larger and more unearthly than ever. The silence was broken by the drone of insects—creatures meet inhabitants, forsooth, for a place so indescribably strange and dreadful.

The cavern we were following was very tortuous, our route even more so, what with the twists and turns which we had to make in order to get through that phantasmagoria of fungal things. I do not mean to say that all of those growths were horrible, but most of them were, and some were as repulsive to the touch as they were to the sight.

As we toiled our way through them, my heart was replete with dire apprehension. I could not banish the vision of those great burning eyes, the horror of those shrieks, which perhaps were still ringing out. What if we were suddenly to find ourselves face to face with one of those monsters (or more than one) here in this night-mare-forest?

Gogrugron! Gogrugron! What in the world was that monstrosity known to the Dromans as a *gogrugron?* Well, most certainly, I was not desirous of securing firsthand knowledge, upon that interesting item, for the great science of natural history.

At length the light no longer lay in streams and rifts in the darkness, but the darkness, instead, lay in streams through the light.

The Dromans quickened their already hurried pace, and there were exclamations of "Drome! Drome!"

"Drome!" echoed Milton Rhodes. "I wonder what we are going to find."

"Something wonderful," said I, "or something worse, perhaps, than anything that we have seen."

Rhodes laughed, and I saw Drorathusa (Ondonarkus was leading the way) turn and send a curious glance in our direction.

"Well," I added, "anything to get out of this horrible forest of fungi and things."

Some minutes passed, perhaps a half-hour, perhaps only fifteen. Of a sudden the great tunnel, now as light as a place on a sunless day, gave a sharp turn to the right; a glad cry broke from the Hypogeans.

"Drome! Drome!" they cried.

We all hurried forward.

"Look!" I said as we reached the turn. "The mouth, the mouth! *The tunnel ends!*"

There, but two hundred feet or so away, was the great yawning mouth of it; nothing was visible through that openings, however, but light, pearly, opalescent, mystic, beautiful.

"Drome!" cried Nandradelphis, clapping her hands.

A few moments, and we were standing at the entrance and gazing out over the weird and beautiful scene.

"Drome!"

I turned at the sound and saw Drorathusa, her figure and mien ineffably Sibylline and majestic, pointing out over the strange landscape, her eyes on the face of Milton Rhodes.

"Drome," she said again.

"Drome," echoed Milton.

"I wonder, Bill, what this Drome really is. And I have an idea that this is only the outskirts that we see. Can we at last be near our journey's end, or is that end still far away?"

"Who can tell? This place seems to be a wilderness."

"Yes; a forest primeval."

"What," said I, "are we destined to find down there?"

"Things stranger, Bill, in all likelihood, than any explorer ever found anywhere in that strange world above us."

"No *gogrugrons*, I hope."

Rhodes laughed.

"*Gogrugron!*" said Drorathusa.

And I saw that horror and fear again in her eyes.

The cavern had come out high up on a broken, jagged wall, which went beetling up for hundreds of feet, up to the roof, which arched away over the landscape before us. We were fully half a thousand feet above the floor, which was a mass of luxuriant forest. Glimpses were caught of a stream down to the left, possibly the one which we had followed for so long. I judged the place to be over a mile wide; Rhodes, however, thought that it was perhaps not quite a mile in the widest part. Down this enormous cavern, the eye could range for three or four miles, at which distance the misty light drew its veil over the forest, the dark walls, and the roof arching across.

At times the light quivered and shook and there were strange flickerings, and dartings of opalescent streaks through it—streaks ineffably beautiful and yet, strangely enough, terrible too, terrible as the blades of plunging swords in hands savage and murderous.

Once more Drorathusa raised a hand, and this time she pointed into the misty distance.

"*Le-prayl-ya!*" she said.

Again her eyes were on Milton Rhodes, and, as she spoke that name, I saw in those wondrous orbs of hers one of the strangest looks that I have ever seen. I wondered if Rhodes too saw it. I found his eyes upon Drorathusa, but there was in them so abstracted an expression that I believed his thoughts were far away and that he had not noticed. When I turned to Drorathusa again, it was to find that that strange look was gone.

What a fascinating and mysterious creature this woman was!

"Lepraylya," she said again.

"Lepraylya," Milton nodded.

He looked at me.

"I wonder who or what this Lepraylya can be, Bill."

"King maybe."

"Queen, I hope," said Milton Rhodes.

He drew forth his notebook and pencil and handed them to Drorathusa, pronouncing as she took them that mysterious name:

"Lepraylya?"

A few strokes with the pencil, and Drorathusa had given us the answer.

"You see, Bill?" said Rhodes, smiling. "A woman. In all likelihood, too, the queen."

Drorathusa's Sibylline look was upon him once more—and *she* did not smile.

33
FACE TO FACE

We found the wall even more broken and difficult than it had appeared from the entrance. It was almost destitute of vegetation, a circumstance that contributed not a little to the slowness of the descent. Indeed, making our way down over those pitching naked rocks was a ticklish, an unpleasant business, I want to tell you; at times it was really precarious.

We had halted to rest above one of these difficult spots, and every one was either seated or leaning against the rock, when of a sudden Milton, who was nearest the edge, arose and pointed, pointed down and off to the right.

"Hello!" said he. "What's that?"

All of us arose, moved over and looked.

"Where?" I asked.

"Down there by that strange clump of cycadaceous trees, that clump near those tall trees that look so much like Douglas firs. But 'tis gone now."

"What did you see?"

"I haven't the faintest idea, Bill. But there certainly was something there, and it was moving. And, if I were imaginative, I would probably say that it was watching us, that, at the moment I arose and pointed, it glided back to the concealment of the trees."

"Well, *did* it?"

"It certainly seemed to do so, Bill."

I peered down there again, but I could not see anything moving. There was silence for some moments. The Dromans stood watching, waiting; stood expectant, puzzled.

"Oh, well," Rhodes said, turning a quizzical look in my direction and then to the face of Drorathusa, "we must expect to find live things in that forest."

I saw Drorathusa's eyes fixed upon his face, then, a few moments after he ceased speaking, return to the clump of cycads.

"Live things?" said I. "There may be things in this place of mystery more terrible than any live thing."

"Come, Bill, come. It can't be so bad as you imagine it, or our Dromans wouldn't be here.

"I wish," he added, "I knew what that thing is that I saw."

"Hello!" I cried the next moment, my look raised up to the vaulted roof. "What does *that* mean? Good Heaven, what next?"

The light, which was brightest up along the roof—in fact, it seemed *pressed* up against the rock-canopy like glowing, diaphanous mist—was changing, fading. The wonderful opalescence of it was disappearing before our eyes.

Of a sudden the spot where we stood was involved in a gloom indescribably strange. Up above, the light-mist was quivering and flickering, pale and dreadful.

"What in the world is it?" I cried.

"Queer place, this!" said Milton Rhodes.

"What can it mean?" I asked.

He did not answer. He sent a questioning look toward Drorathusa and her companions. Mine followed. The faces of the Dromans seemed to glimmer ghostlike in the thickening, awful darkness. Upon those pale features, however, was no discoverable sign of alarm, of uneasiness even.

The gloom deepened about us. Pitchy darkness came down with a rush. Far away, and up along the roof, there were pale flickerings and flashes. Then the light burst out, so sudden and so strong that pain shot through the eyes.

Came a cry, and I turned to see Drorathusa pointing, pointing down toward those cycads.

"There it is, Bill!" exclaimed Milton. "There it is again! See it moving?"

I saw it, but it was for a fleeting moment only. And, I thought, I saw something else.

"A little nearer this time," Rhodes told me. "There can be no doubt that it is watching us."

"Evidently," I said, "it is moving over to lie in wait for us. And, unless I'm very much deceived, it isn't alone."

"Hum," said Rhodes. "Queer place, Bill, to go into. Even our Hypogeans, it seems, don't know what to make of that apparition."

They were conversing in low tones, casting searching, apprehensive looks along the ragged margin of the forest.

The gloom was falling again. Denser and denser it grew about us. Fainter, more and more dreadful became those distant flickerings and flashes along the great vaulted roof. Darkness, blackness was involving everything. Dimmer still became the flickerings. The stillness was utter, portentous. There was not the gentlest movement of air. The light gave a last faint, angry gleam and went out altogether.

Abruptly, from out of the darkness, a voice came sounding, and, though I knew that the voice was Drorathusa's, I started and almost gave a cry. I pressed the button, and the rays of the lamp flashed out, lighting up the spot and showing the tall figure of Drorathusa with arms extended upward in some mystic invocation. The others were kneeling, and the words that Drorathusa spoke were echoed, as it were, in their low responsive voices. It was a strange scene, truly the dark, savage masses of rock, the tall Sibylline figure of the woman, the kneeling forms of the others and we two men from the sunlit world looking on in wonder and in awe.

Minutes passed. The wondrous, eerie voice of Drorathusa never ceased, though there were moments when those echoing voices were silent.

Look! Far away, there was a faint, ghostly flicker. Another and another. Brighter they became and brighter still, at last opalescent; soon rocks and forest, soon the whole weird landscape was again bathed in the mystic pearly light.

"What, in the name of wonder," I said, "was it?"

"An eclipse," smiled Rhodes. "Queer place, this."

"Queer place? Can't you hit another tune? You don't have to keep telling me that this is a queer place. I am not at all likely to forget that fact. And I wonder if these 'eclipses' are a frequent phenomenon. Certainly I hope that they are not."

"I wish that I could tell you, Bill, tell you that and a few other things."

"And," I added, "that forest, when the light goes, must be a queer place truly—gosh, I'm catching it from you! But I'll tell you what: I wouldn't like to find myself, in the depths of those woods, face to face with a *loopmuke* or a *gogrugron* or *something* and in that instant have the darkness come down."

"It would be rather unpleasant, I fancy. But unfortunately our likes or our dislikes are not likely to alter in any way the scheme of things,"

The Dromans, all standing now, were singing a low and sweet song of thanksgiving and gladness. Yes, so sweet were the tones that they seemed to linger in the air, for some moments, even after the song had ceased.

We cast our looks along the margin of the forest, but not a single glimpse was caught of that mysterious object, or objects, that we had seen moving down there.

It was patent that the Dromans knew no more what to make of that apparition than we did ourselves and that they looked forward with no little apprehension to our entry into that wood.

The descent was resumed. Were eyes, somewhere below, watching our every movement? I feared that it was indeed so, and, as I well knew, every other member of our little band feared it, too. There was nothing, however, that we could do except descend and face the issue. To turn aside would be futile, for the watcher, or the watchers, would turn aside also to meet us.

Ere long we reached the talus, and our troubles were then over; that is, as regards the descent. But Heaven only knew what troubles were awaiting us somewhere in that forest, to which we were now drawing so very near.

As we made our way down over the rock-fragments, amidst which shrubs and stunted trees were growing, more than once did we pause and send keen, searching looks and glances into the silent recess of that mysterious wood.

Some of those sylvan depths were enshadowed, gloomy; others were pervaded with the strong, transparent light-mist, the objects involved in which *cast no shadows.*

At the foot of the talus, almost beneath the branches of great palm-trees, there was a pause.

"Now for it!" said Milton Rhodes solemnly.

The Dromans were clustered together in earnest but laconic dialogue, their eyes employed the while in a keen scrutiny of the forest aisles and recesses, before us and on either hand.

Insects were in the air about us; one or two shadowy butterflies flitted past; and that was all. Not a leaf stirred; the air was without the slightest movement. No song, no call of a bird broke the silence, which seemed to press down upon us and about us as though it were a tangible thing. It was as if the spot, the forest itself had never known either the voice or the movement of any sentient thing. But, somewhere in that forest, hidden and close at hand, there was something sentient—something, in all likelihood, watching us, watching and waiting. Waiting for what?

Or, came the sudden thought, even now stealing toward the place where we stood.

"This suspense," said I to myself, "is simply awful, is as terrible, even, as that which we knew when we were crossing the bridge, that chasm of unknown depth on either side."

Drorathusa turned to us and pointed in a rather vague direction out into the trees.

"*Narranawnzee,*" she said.

"Evidently, said Milton, "they plan to strike that stream."

"I pray Heaven," I told him, "that we live to see that *narranawnzee.*"

Whereupon Rhodes laughed outright, and the effect of the sudden sound was curious and startling, so great was the tension of our nerves.

"One would think, Gloomy Face," said he, "that you had just issued from the Cave of Trophonius. 'And he never smiled again.'"

"I have an idea, grinning Shaky Knees," I retorted, "that we have got ourselves into a place more awful than any Cave of Trophonius. I don't blink, that's all."

"Nor, Bill, do I," said Milton soberly. "You know, I'd feel more at ease if it wasn't for the presence of the ladies. Why did they come on a journey so hazardous and so terrible?"

How often had we wondered that! We didn't know the ladies of Drome.

We at once got in motion. Ondonarkus and Rhodes were leading, Drorathusa was just behind them, then came Nandradelphis and Silvisiris, whilst Zenvothunbro and myself brought up the rear. This disposition of our little party was as Drorathusa herself had desired it, and she had been at some pains to impress upon Rhodes and me (though there had been no necessity for that) the expediency of keeping our weapons ready for action at any instant.

On we went, deeper and deeper into the wood. Strange forms of vegetation, strange flowers, strange insects were everywhere. How interesting we should have found the place! But there was that *thing*, somewhere hidden, watching us perhaps—following.

Came a sharp exclamation, a dull sound from above; but it was only a bird, a thing of silver and gold, launching itself from off a branch of one of the trees which we were approaching. Away it went sailing, lovely as a vision from fairyland, and disappeared amongst the tree-trunks and foliage.

Five minutes or so passed. Another sound, an exclamation from Drorathusa, and the party came to a sudden halt.

Every one had heard it—a clear, unmistakable but inexplicable sound and from behind. We were being followed!

We stood listening for some moments, waiting; but the sound did not come again. Save for the low melancholy drone of insects, the spot was as silent as a tomb.

We resumed our advance, every sense on the alert. A few moments passed, and then we heard it again. This time it was off to the right, almost abreast of us, it seemed.

Had it thus quickened its movements in order to get in front of us?

We waited, but nothing was seen, nothing was heard.

We had advanced but twenty or thirty feet when a sudden gloom involved the forest. The scene on the instant turned weird, unearthly. This, however, was but a few moments only; then came the light. The advance was at once resumed. But we had gone only a short distance when the gloom came once more, grew so dense that we had to come to a halt.

It lifted, just as I was on the point of switching on my electric light. Then like a bolt came utter darkness. And, even as the darkness fell, there was a velvety sound and a faint rustling from amongst the foliage beside us. With frantic haste I sought and pressed the light-switch. At the same instant Rhodes flashed on his light. A cry of horror broke from me. There, thrust over the top of a great log and but a few yards distant, was a long snaky head with a pair of great blazing eyes fixed upon me.

We were face to face at last!

34
ANOTHER!

I jerked out my revolver, took swift aim, right between those great blazing eyes, and fired.

From the beast came a fearful roar, which seemed to end in a scream, and the long snaky head and neck (no more of the animal had been visible) disappeared.

"Good work, Bill!" applauded Milton Rhodes.

He had hardly spoken when the light came again, strong and beautiful. And the next instant came something else. A dark form, with a gleam of something white, rose into the air and drove straight toward us. I sprang aside and turned to fire, but I did not do so for fear of hitting the Dromans or Rhodes. There came a piercing shriek from Drorathusa, a sound made by cloth-rending talons. The monster had her.

I leaped toward it and emptied the revolver into its side, whilst Ondonarkus and Zenvothunbro sent each an arrow into the body. That of the former was driven with such force that it passed clear through the body and went on for a distance of six or eight feet. And down the beast fell dead, though still quivering, there in our very midst.

I turned and hurried to Drorathusa. Rhodes was already beside her. As I reached her, the darkness came down again upon the place, pitchy and awful. The claws had ripped her dress, from the thigh down, literally into ribbons; strangely enough, the flesh had escaped even a scratch.

Drorathusa was badly shaken, and little wonder, forsooth. It had been a miraculous escape from terrible injury, from a most horrible death. A few moments, however, and she was as composed as though nothing had happened. Truly there was much to admire in this extraordinary woman.

Rhodes and I turned and examined the body, now lying quite still. It was that of a big cat. Strictly speaking, it was not, I suppose, a cat; it was not like anything that we had even seen or heard of. But a cat I shall call it, not knowing what other word to use. The head was long and of an aspect strikingly, repulsively snake-like. So was the neck. This reptilian resemblance was enhanced by the head's being absolutely destitute of hair, save for the vibrissae, which were really enormous. The body was dark, curiously mottled with gray. The breast and the belly were snowy white.

"Hum," said Milton Rhodes. "A strange and terrible creature, Bill. This wilderness must be a real one when we find a carnivore like this subsisting in it. And Goodness only knows of what other beasts it is the habitat."

"Yes. And, with such creatures in the woods, our journey through them is likely to prove an interesting one."

"Most interesting. O well," said Rhodes, "we have our revolvers, and the Dromans have their bows and arrows, to say nothing of their swords. And they know how to use them, too."

"And that reminds me," I told him: "I haven't reloaded my blunderbuss."

"Save those shells, Bill."

"What for?"

"So we can reload them."

"Reload them? Do you think we'll be able to do that in this world called Drome."

"Why not?"

"But how—?"

Rhodes turned like a flash.

"Hear that?" he said. "By the great Nimrod, another one!"

The darkness still lay impenetrable, pitchy. We flashed our lights into the trees, this way and that, all about us; but no eyes were seen gleaming at us, nothing was seen moving save the shadows, and not the faintest sound was heard.

The Dromans were listening intently, but it was patent that they had not heard that sound which had whirled Rhodes about; nor had I heard it myself.

"Are you sure," I queried, "that there was a sound?"

"I most certainly thought that I heard something."

"Look!" I cried, pointing upward.

Through openings in the foliage, were to be seen pale flickerings of light.

"Thank Goodness," Rhodes said, "we'll soon again have light. I hope that this time it will last."

And we soon did—the strong mystic, and yet strangely misty, light pervading the mysterious and dreadful wood, the flickerings and flashes overhead soon opalescent and as beautiful as ever.

We at once (Ondonarkus having picked up his arrow and Zenvothunbro drawn his from the body of the cat) left that spot, to make our way deeper and deeper into that forest, which harbored enemies so terrible and so treacherous.

"Why," I queried, "didn't we camp up there on the rocks, where it would have been impossible (save in one of these periods of darkness) for anything to approach us unseen? We had made a day's good journey; and here we have gone and left a place of safety to camp somewhere in this horrible wood."

"What," returned Milton Rhodes, "would that have been but postponing the inevitable? For into these trees we should have had to go, sooner or later, and the thing would have been watching for us just the same. As you say, we had made a good journey for the day; well, aren't we making it better?"

"It isn't ended yet."

"This place, after all, Bill, may not be so bad as it seems."

"Well, there is one consolation," I remarked: "there is no danger of our starving to death in this lovely Dante's Inferno. Look at all the fruit and nuts and things."

"Yes. From that point of view, the place is a veritable Garden of the Hesperides."

At length we reached the stream, considerably larger than I had expected to find it. At this point where we struck it, the water was deep, the current a gentle one. The rich forest growth hung out over the surface for some distance. There was a soft rustling of leaves, for some of the branches dipped into the water and were swaying to and fro. This and the faint, melancholy whisper of the gliding element were all that broke the heavy, deathlike stillness. It was a placid, a lovely scene.

The attainment of this their objective seemed to give our Dromans much pleasure; but, save for the fact that there was now no danger of our perishing of thirst, I could not see that we were any better off than we had been.

I thought that this would be the end of our march, now a long one indeed. But the Dromans merely paused, then started down the stream; and, of course, along with them went Rhodes and myself.

At times we had literally to force our way through the dense and tangled undergrowth; then we would be moving through lovely aisles—

> "And many a walk traversed
>   Of stateliest covert, cedar, pine, or palm."

We pushed on for perhaps two miles, never moving far from the stream, and then made camp in a beautiful open spot, over which, however, the great branches formed an unbroken canopy of leaves.

A guard was arranged for the night. Rhodes had the first watch.

It was during my vigil that it came—a sudden, fierce, frightful scream, which awoke every member of our little party. It came from somewhere down the river, and it was replete with terror and agony; it was a sound that made the very air quiver and throb. It seemed human, and yet I told myself that it simply could not be. And then it ceased, as suddenly as it had come, and all was still again, save for the gentle, sad whispering of the water.

"What," I exclaimed, my voice, however, low and guarded, "could it have been? It sounded human, but I know that that sound did not come from the throat of a man or a woman."

"I think you are right, Bill," said Milton Rhodes. "What it was—well, that seems to be a mystery to the Dromans themselves."

I turned and saw Drorathusa, who had just issued from the tent, standing beside Ondonarkus and engaged in hurried and whispered dialogue, the troubled looks which she incessantly directed into the forest, in that quarter whence had come that scream, advertising dread and something for which I can not find a name.

"Evidently," Rhodes observed, "they know but little more about this place and the things in it than we do ourselves. "And that is virtually nothing."

"Did you," he asked abruptly, "hear something else?"

"Something else? When?"

"Something besides that scream. And while it was filling the air. And just afterwards."

"I heard nothing else. Did you?"

"I believe that I did."

"What?"

"I can't say," was his answer. "I wish that I could."

"Well," I said, "all we know is that there is something sneaking or prowling about in this wood, that it has just got a victim and that, in all probability, it means to get one of us—maybe all of us."

Rhodes nodded, rather rueful of visage.

"We were fortunate enough," he added "to kill two carnivores—snake-cats; I wonder if we shall be as fortunate the next time. For there is another thing waiting, sneaking, watching, biding its time."

"Another, yes," said I. "But another *what?*"

35
A SCREAM AND—SILENCE

I am afraid that no one slept very well after that. It was about seven
o'clock when we left that place. And I confess that I was more
uneasy, more troubled than I would have cared to acknowledge.
For we were headed toward the spot—at any rate, in the direction—
whence had come that scream. What would we find there? Would
we find anything?

We did.

We had gone about an eighth of a mile. The disposition of our
little party was as it had been the day before; Rhodes and
Ondonarkus, that is, were in the lead, followed by Drorathusa, then
came Nandradelphis and Silvisiris, whilst Zenvothunbro and myself formed the rear-guard. Had my own wishes in the matter been
followed, Rhodes and I would have been together. The formation
assumed was, as I believe I have mentioned, the one that Drorathusa herself desired. The idea, of course, was to have the front
and rear protected each by one of the mysterious weapons of the
mysterious stranger-men, which weapons, undoubtedly, were far
more formidable in the imagination of Drorathusa and her companions than they were in reality.

Certainly our revolvers were in every way excellent weapons,
but I could not help wishing that they had a heavier bullet.

As has been said, we had proceeded about a furlong. The dense
and tangled undergrowth had forced us away from the stream, to a
distance of perhaps three hundred feet.

451

At the moment a sound had fetched me up and my exclamation had brought the party to a sudden halt.

"What is it, Bill?" Rhodes asked.

"We are being *followed!*"

He made no immediate response to that dire intelligence. We all stood listening, waiting; but a silence pervaded the forest as deep as though it had never, since the day of creation, been broken by the faintest pulsation of sound.

Then, after some moments, Rhodes asked:

"Are you sure, Bill, that we are being followed?"

"Yes! I tell you that I know that we are!"

"Well," said he, turning slowly, "I don't see that we can do anything about it, save keep a sharp lookout; and so on we go."

Whereupon he and the others started. I had turned to follow when that sound, low and mysterious as before, stopped me in my tracks. And in that very instant came another—a sharp interjection from Rhodes, instantaneously followed by a scream, the short, piercing scream of a woman.

I should have explained that we were in a dense growth of fern, a growth some ten or twelve feet in height; it was a meet place indeed for an ambuscade. Overhead, too, the branches met and intertangled, affording an excellent place for a snake-cat or some other arboreal monster to lie in wait and drop or spring upon any human or brute passing below.

Now, as I whirled to that exclamation and scream—the danger there behind forgotten in what was so imminent before—it was to find, to my indescribable fear and horror, that my companions, every single one of them, had vanished.

And that which chilled my heart was enhanced by the fact that before me, where Rhodes and the Dromans must be; there was no agitation amongst the ferns, not the slightest movement amongst them. I was alone, alone in that place of dense, concealing vegetation, of silence and mystery. But no; they were there, my companions, right there before me. The ferns hid them, that was all. But why were they so still? Why utterly silent? What had happened?

That exclamation, that scream, the silence that had followed—what did it mean?

It has taken some space to set this down, but it must not be imagined that the space itself during which I stood there was a long one. It was, in fact, very brief; it was no more, I suppose, than fifteen or twenty seconds. Then I was moving forward through the crushed ferns, as swiftly as was consistent with caution, and, of course, with the revolver gripped ready for instant action.

I had covered perhaps three yards, had reached the point where the way crushed through the fern-growth turned sharp to the left to pass between two great tree-trunks; then it was that I heard it— a low, rustling sound and close at hand.

Something was moving there; it was moving toward me.

36
GORGONIC HORROR

Almost that very instant I heard it, that low, rustling sound made by something moving through (as I thought) the fern-growth ceased. My companions! What had happened to them?

I began moving forward, every second that passed enhancing that fear which chilled my heart. For each step took me nearer to, though not directly toward, that spot from which had come that mysterious sound.

Just as I was passing between those great tree-trunks, came a sound that fetched me up in my tracks, came a sudden low voice:

"Oh, Bill!"

I gave a smothered exclamation and dashed forward. Rhodes was safe; at any rate, he was alive. A second or two, and I burst from the fern-growth.

Surprise, amazement brought me up instanter, and the next instant an indescribable horror had me in its grip.

The surprise, the amazement will be explained when I say that there before me stood my companions, every one of them, safe and sound. There they stood, motionless and silent as so many statues, gazing, as though held in a baleful charm, upon that thing before them. Rhodes was the only one that moved as I burst out into the scene.

"I wondered, Bill, why you didn't come. I was just about to call out to you again."

"And I wondered why you all were so silent, after that exclamation and that scream. I understand it now."

Shuddering, I pointed with my alpenstock at that thing before us. "In the name of the Gorgons, what is that?"

"I wish that I knew, Bill. What is your name for such a monstrosity as that?"

A silence of some seconds followed, and then I remembered something, that rustling sound.

I turned, and another shudder went through me. Drorathusa was standing very near that spot from which that rustling sound must have come.

"What is in there?" I asked, pointing.

Milton Rhodes whirled to the direction that I indicated. "In where?"

"In those ferns, behind Drorathusa. I heard something in there, something that was moving."

"When?"

"Some few moments ago, just before you called to me."

A wan smile flitted across the face of Milton Rhodes.

"That was Drorathusa herself moving through that thick tangle of flowers."

"But I tell you, Milton, that it was moving *towards me!*"

"It was Drorathusa," said Rhodes. "You only thought that the sound was moving toward you, away from us. No, Bill; it was Drorathusa. There was no other sound. To that I can swear."

So my imagination had tricked me. And yet how could I be sure that it had? For, in such a moment, with such a sight before him, Rhodes himself might have been the one deceived. In that case, any instant might see Death come leaping into our very midst.

"Who gave that scream?" I asked.

"One of the girls, when we broke out of the ferns and she saw *that*. Nandradelphis, I believe."

This turned me again to that monster and its victim. No wonder that that piercing scream had broken from the girl!

The spot into which we had stepped was, for a distance of perhaps one hundred and fifty feet, almost free from undergrowth. Tall trees, looking very much at a first glance like Douglas firs, rose up all around, but there were other growths; there were twisted trunks and branches that had a gnarled and savage aspect; the light was pearly, misty; all made a fitting setting truly for that which we saw there in the midst of it.

For, sixty feet or so distant, still, white and lifeless, naked save for a skin (spotted something like a leopard's) about the waist, the toes two or three feet from the ground, hung the body of a man.

That itself was shocking enough, but what we saw up above—how I shudder, even at this late date, as that picture rises before me! It was a nightmare-shape, of mottled green and brown, with splotches of something whitish, bluish.

There were splotches, too upon some of the leaves and upon the ground beneath. It was like blood, that whitish, bluish stuff, and, indeed, that is what it was. In the midst of that shape, were two great eyes, but they never moved, were fixed and glassy. One of the higher branches had been broken, though not clean through, and, wound around this branch, the end of which had fallen upon that on which the monster rested, were what I at first took to be enormous serpents. They were, in fact, tentacula. There was a third tentacle; it hung straight down. And it was from this, a coil around the neck and two around the left arm, that the body of the unfortunate man hung, white and lifeless, like a victim of the hangman's noose.

"A tree-octopus!" I cried.

"I suppose most people would call it that. It has but three tentacles, however, and so is a tripus. And that scream we heard last night—well, we know now, Bill, what it was."

I shivered.

"No wonder," I said, "that we thought that the sound was unhuman! In the grip of that thing, the tentacle around his neck! So near, and we never stirred to his help!"

"Because we never dreamed. And, had we known, Bill, we could not have saved him. Life would have been extinct, crushed out of him, before ever we could have got here and cut him down."

"I thought of some dreadful things," I said, "but never of a monster like that."

"A queer place, this forest, a horrible place, Bill," Milton Rhodes said, glancing a little nervously about him. "But come."

He started forward. The Dromans hung back, but I moved along after him, whereupon the others followed, though with great apparent reluctance.

"What I don't quite understand, Bill, is this: what happened?"

"Why, the poor fellow was passing beneath the branches, the octopus thrust down its tentacle, wound it around the victim's neck and started to pull him up."

"All that is very clear. But then just what happened to the octopus?"

"The limb to which the monster had attached itself—see where the limb has been struck, perhaps by a falling tree, and weakened—well, it broke, and down the monster came crashing onto that branch on which we see it."

"That too is quite clear," said Rhodes. "But what killed the thing? The fall, it seems to me, could not have done it."

The next moment we halted, a little distance from the spot where hung the still, white body of the Droman.

"Oh, I see it now," said Rhodes, pointing. "Why didn't I see that before? As the monster came down, it was impaled upon those sword-like stubs of branches, one going through the body, the other out through the face. Face! The thing seems to be all face. And the human aspect of that visage! How like the big face of a fat man!"

That, there could be no doubt, was what had happened. And that Gorgonic horror, in the shock of the fall and its impalement, even in its death-throes, had never loosed the grip on its victim.

"We can't leave the poor devil hanging like that," I said.

"Of course not. And to give him burial will mean the loss of time probably more precious even than we think it. This is a wood horrible as any that Dante ever found himself in."

"We must risk it. We can't leave him like that or the body lying on the ground for the beasts to devour."

Rhodes and I still had our ice-picks, and we at once divested ourselves of the packs and started the grave. And, as we worked,

try as I would I could not shake off from me—the feeling that, concealed somewhere in the trees, something was lurking, was watching us.

Zenvothunbro cut down the victim. Along the tentacle, ran two rows of suckers, like those of a devil-fish. So powerful was the grip, we could not remove the thing; and so we buried the poor Droman, in his shallow grave, with those coils still gripping him.

Forthwith we quitted that cursed spot, though Milton, I believe, wanted to climb up and subject that monster to a scientific scrutiny!

And, as we pushed on through that dreadful wood, it was as though some sixth sense bore to my brain a warning,—vague but persistent, sinister:

"It is following!"

37
AS WE WERE PASSING UNDERNEATH

Something was following us. And we were not dependent solely upon that mysterious sixth sense of mine for knowledge of that sinister fact, either. Sounds were heard. Sometimes it would be a low rustling, as though made by some body gliding through the foliage. Sometimes it would be the snapping of a twig, behind us, off to the right, perhaps, or to the left; never in front of us. Alas, it grieves me to do so, but I am constrained by the love of truth, and by nothing else, to inform the admirers of that great scientist Mark Twain that twigs *do* snap when they are stepped upon. Yes, I wish that we could have had some of those obstreperous applauders of Mark's absurd essay on Fenimore Cooper with us there in that Droman wood! There were other sounds, too, one of them a thing that I could never describe—a faint humming, throbbing sound that seemed to chill the blood in our veins, so weird and frightful a thing that neither Milton Rhodes nor I could even dream of an explanation. And it was in vain that we looked to our Dromans for one. They tried to explain, but their explanation was as mysterious as the fact itself.

Onward we pressed through that terrible place, that abode of snake-cats, tree-octopi and unknown monsters.

At last, and for the first time since we had entered the forest, a current of air touched our cheeks, stirred the foliage and the lovely tresses of the ladies. Soon the breeze, soft and gentle, was whispering and sighing among the treetops. A gloom pervaded the place; the wood became dark and awful, though through it the light-mist was still drifting, drifting in streams that swayed and shook and quivered. Rhodes and I thought that we were going to have another eclipse. But we were wrong. It began to rain, if I may so call that misty drizzle that came drifting down and, indeed, at times seemed to form in the air before our eyes.

I thought that this would stop us, for soon everything was wet and dripping—dripping, dripping. But the Dromans pressed on steadily, grimly. Soon every one of us was wet to the skin.

An hour or so passed, and then the drizzle ceased and the gloom lifted.

Rhodes and I were discussing this strange phenomenon when abruptly he cried out and pointed.

"There!" said he, reaching for his revolver. "At last we have ocular proof that we are being followed!"

Even as he spoke, that faint humming, throbbing sound again filled the air.

"Look there! See it, Bill?"

"I see it."

What I saw was an agitation, slight but unmistakable, in the thicket from which we had emerged but a few moments before.

Something was moving there, something was gliding through the dense undergrowth.

I jerked out my revolver. Rhodes had already drawn his.

"Might as well try a shot," said he, "for it won't show itself, in all likelihood, while we are standing ready to receive it."

We fired almost simultaneously. There was a smothered crash in the thicket, as though some heavy body had given a powerful lurch sideways. The throbbing of that mysterious sound grew faster, louder; the agitated foliage began to shake and quiver violently; and then of a sudden sound and agitation were stilled.

"We got it, Bill!" cried Milton, starting towards the spot.

"For Heaven's sake," I called after him, "don't go over there! Let's get out of this. It may not be dead, and—and we have no idea what in the world the thing is."

"We'll find that out."

I suppose that I should have been going along after him the next moment, but Drorathusa sprang forward with a cry of horror, began tugging at his sleeve and begging him to come back. So earnest was her manner, so great the fear shown by this woman usually so self-contained and emotionless, Rhodes gave in, though with great apparent reluctance.

A few moments, and we were moving away from the spot.

This Rhodes has always regretted; for to this day we do not know for certain what that thing was which followed us for so long. I have regretted it more than once myself; but I confess that I had no regrets at the time.

I say we do not know for certain: we do know what Drorathusa and the others thought that it was; but that is a creature so grisly that it must (at any rate, such is the belief of Rhodes and myself) be placed amongst Chimeras, Hydras and such fabled monsters.

At length, after a long and fatiguing march, we reached the spot where the water goes plunging over a tremendous precipice. The falls are perpendicular, their height at least half a thousand feet. It was necessary to move off to the right for a considerable distance to find a way of descent. The bottom reached, we headed for the stream. There we found the boat which the Dromans had left in their outward journey, and beside it was a second and smaller one.

This strange craft was something of a mystery to our Hypogeans; but Drorathusa found a message, traced on the inner surface of a piece of bark, and that seemed to clarify the matter somewhat. Drorathusa held up three fingers; three men had come in that boat. And one of them, she told us, must have been the man whose body we had found hanging in the tentacle of the octopus. What had become of the victim's companions? Why had the trio come into a place so dreadful? Well, why had we?

Our journey for this day was already a long one, but we did not halt in that spot. We got into the boat and went floating down the stream, to get away from the thunder of the falling waters.

As the current caught the craft, Rhodes turned to me, and, a smile in his eyes, he said, quoting from *The Faerie Queene*:

"'Have care, I pray, to guide the cock-bote well,
Least worse on sea then us on land befell.'"

Drorathusa, who had learned a few words of our language, was watching him, and, after a moment's silence, she waved a hand in the downstream direction and said:

"*Narranawnzee*—fine and dandy."

One thing, by the way, that from the very beginning had intrigued Rhodes and me not a little was the relationship existing amongst our Dromans. It had at first been my belief (though never that of Rhodes) that Drorathusa was the wife of Ondonarkus. Ere long, however, it had become clear to me that wife she was not. But what was she? His daughter, Rhodes had said. And daughter I had at length decided, and still believed, that she was. In short, we put the relationship as follows, and I may as well say at once that the future was to place its O.K. upon this bit of Sherlock-Holmesing of ours: Ondonarkus was the father of all our Dromans except one, Silvisiris, and to her he was father-in-law.

This little mystery cleared up—at any rate, to our satisfaction—we tackled another, which was this: what was Drorathusa. I think it has been made sufficiently obvious that she was no ordinary woman. But what was she? The only answer that Rhodes and I had been able to find was that Drorathusa was indeed a Sibyl, a priestess or something of the kind. And again I may as well say at once that we were right.

But why had they set out on a journey so strange and so hazardous—through the land of the tree-octopi and the snake-cats, through that horrible, unearthly fungoid forest, and up and up, up into the caves of utter blackness, across that frightful chasm, up to the Tamahnowis Rocks, into the blaze of the sunshine, out onto the snow and ice on Mount Rainier?

* * *

It was as though we suddenly had entered a fairyland, so wonderful was this gliding along on the placid bosom of the river when

contrasted with the fatigues, the dangers and the horrors through which we had passed. There was nothing to do but steer the boat, keep her out in the stream; and so hours, the whole day long was passed in the languorous luxury of resting, in watching the strange trees glide past and in making such progress as we were able in acquiring a knowledge of the Droman language. We found the ladies much better teachers than Zenvothunbro and Ondonarkus. In fact, there was simply no comparison. Why they should have proved so immeasurably superior in this respect to the representatives of the brainy sex, I do not presume to try to explain. I merely record a fact; its explanation I leave to those who know more about science than I do.

For three days we glided through that lovely land, whose loveliness was a mask, so to speak, and but made the place the more terrible, for it was a habitat of creatures very strange indeed.

Late in the afternoon of this third day—how strange these words seem! But what others can I use? Late in the afternoon of this third day, we entered a swamp. The current became sluggish, our drift even more so, and right glad were we to put the oars—of which, though, there were only two pairs—in motion and send her along, for that was not a place in which any sane man would want to linger. Besides the oars, however, there were several paddles, and we sent the boat at a good clip through the dark and sullen waters.

Weird masses of moss and weirder filaments hung from the great branches, which at times met over the stream.

We were passing underneath one of these gnarled and bearded arches when there came a piercing shriek from Nandradelphis, accompanied rather than followed by a cry from Drorathusa of

"*Loopmuke!*"

I dropped the oar and reached for my revolver, turned and saw Ondonarkus, standing in the bow, whip out his sword and slash savagely at the winged monster as it came diving down upon him.

38
SOMETHING BESIDES MADNESS

There was a shock, the boat, I thought, was surely going over. Came a heavy plunge, and she righted, though sluggishly, for water had come pouring over the side in gallons. Ondonarkus had vanished. The demon was struggling madly on the surface, one of its great wings almost shorn clean from the body. An instant, and the head of Ondonarkus was seen emerging. Almost at that very second, Milton Rhodes fired at the ape-bat; a convulsive shudder passed through the hideous body, which slowly sank and disappeared.

Ondonarkus showed the most admirable coolness. He did not dash at the side of the boat, as nine men out of ten would have done, but swam quietly to the stern, where he was drawn inboard without shipping a spoonful of water, unhurt but minus his sword.

Two hours afterwards, we reached firm ground, which soon became high and rocky. The vegetation there was sparse and dwarfish, and the place had a look indescribably wild and forbidding. Then at last we came to the end of the cavern itself. Yes, there before us, beetling up for hundreds of feet, up to the very roof, rose the rocky wall—into a cleft in which the river slowly and silently went gliding, like some monstrous serpent.

We passed the night in that spot and in the morning entered the cleft, which, in my troubled imagination, seemed to open wider to receive us.

Oh, what a strange and dreadful place was that in which we now found ourselves! One thought of lost souls and of nameless things. Ere long there was no perceptible current, and so out came the oars again. The place was a perfect labyrinth—a place of gloom and at times of absolute darkness. We were no less than three whole days in that awful maze of rock and water; but, hurrah, it was to emerge into a landscape beautiful beyond all description.

The region was a wilderness, but soon—the day after that in which we issued from the labyrinth, in fact—we sighted our first habitation of man in this world of Drome. The next day we reached a village, where we passed the night. We were much struck by that deep respect with which Drorathusa was received. As for our own reception—well, that really gave us something to think about.

Not that there was any sign of menace. There was nothing like that. It was the looks, the very mien of those Hypogeans that, to say the least, puzzled and worried Rhodes and myself. That Drorathusa endeavored to allay the suspicion or dread (or whatever it was) in the minds of the people was as clear to us as if we had understood every word spoken. The manner, however, in which they received her address but enhanced our uneasiness. No voice was raised in dissent to what she said; but there was no blinking the fact that there was no acquiescence whatever in what she urged so earnestly.

"What in the world, Milton," I asked, "does it mean?"

"Ask me something that I can tell you, Bill," was Rhodes' consoling answer. "You know, when we came in sight of that first Droman habitation, I thought that now our troubles were just about over."

"So did I."

"But we see now that we were wrong, Bill, that we were wrong. It is a queer business, and Goodness only knows what it means."

"It means trouble," I told him.

And the very next day showed that I was right.

We embarked at an early hour the following morning and in another and larger boat. It had a high ornamented prow and was indeed a lovely little craft. This day's voyage brought us to the City of Lellolando. It has a population of about fifteen thousand, and there Rhodes and I had our first sight of the beautiful Droman architecture, as displayed, that is, in the public buildings, for the dwellings are in no wise remarkable. These public buildings are not many, of course, in a place so small, but their beauty was indeed a surprise and a pleasure.

Incomparably the most wonderful is the temple, built upon the summit of a great rounded rock in almost the very center of the city. It was as though we had been transported back to "the glory that was Greece." Yes, it is my belief, and the belief of Milton Rhodes also, that this temple would not have suffered could it by some miracle have been placed beside the celebrated temple of Artemis at Ephesus. Buildings more wonderful than this we were to see, the grandest of all the great temple in Nornawnla Prendella, the Golden City, which is the capital of Drome; but I do not think that anything we saw afterwards struck us with greater wonder and amazement.

"Some Chersiphron," said Rhodes, "must have wandered from Drome and finally made his way up into ancient Greece and taught the secrets of his art there. It is indeed a marvel that the art of the ancient Hellenes and this of Drome are so very similar. And yet they must have been autochthonous.

"But," he added, "I wonder what they worship in that splendid place. Some horrible pantheon, perhaps."

"Let us," said I, "give them the benefit of the doubt. For all that we know to the contrary, these Dromans may be true monotheists."

And this, I rejoice to say, the Dromans are, though, I regret to subjoin, there are some very absurd things in their religion, things dark and even things very terrible.

But I anticipate in this, for it was just after we landed that it happened.

We had started up one of the principal streets, on our way to the house of a high functionary, though, of course, Rhodes and I had no idea whither we were bound. On either side the street, was a solid mass of humanity—many of the young people, by the way, having hair as white as snow, like that of our Nandradelphis. Of a sudden a man, lean of visage and with eyes that glowed like red coals, broke through the guards (a half dozen or so were marching along on either side of our little procession) and slashed savagely at the face of Rhodes with a great curved dagger. My companion sprang aside, almost thrusting me onto my knees, and the next instant he dealt the man a blow with his alpenstock. The blow, however, was a slanting one, ineffectual. With a scream, the fellow sprang again, his terrible knife upraised; but the guards threw themselves upon him, and he was dragged off, struggling and screaming like a maniac.

Of a truth, Rhodes had had a very narrow escape. And what did it mean?

"It might," I said, "have been the act of a madman."

"It might have been," was Milton's answer. "But, unless I am greatly mistaken, there was something besides madness back of it."

39

THE GOLDEN CITY

Our stay in that place was marred by no other untoward incident; but right glad was I when, on the following morning, we were in our boat and going down the stream once more.

"We ought to be safe out here," I remarked at last.

"I don't know about that, Bill," smiled Milton. "The stream is not a wide one certainly, and those bushes and tress that line the bank offer—there, look at that!"

But a hundred feet or so before us, a boat was gliding out from the concealment of a mass of foliage. There were three men in it, and the looks which they fixed upon us were lowering and sinister.

"Look at that fellow!" said Milton Rhodes, drawing his revolver. "If that isn't the chap who broke through with the amicable intention of carving me, all I have to say is that he is his twin brother."

This man was thin almost to emaciation, but his companions were burly fellows, every lineament of them bespeaking the ruffian.

They held their craft stationary or nearly so. In a few moments, therefore, we were drawing near to them. Drorathusa had arisen, and she spoke to the occupants of the strange boat in a rather sharp, imperious manner. Her presence or her words seemed to awe them; and I was thanking our lucky stars that, after all, there was not going to be any trouble, when of a sudden, just as the drift of our boat brought Rhodes and me alongside, their bridled passions burst forth in a storm of snarls, cries and fierce gestures of menace. There was a moment when I thought that they were actually going to attempt to board us. But they then drew off a few yards, though there was no diminution in that storm of abuse, execrations and threats that was hurled upon us. All three were armed, but no motion towards their weapons was made. The reason for that, I suppose was the sight of Ondonarkus and Zenvothunbro standing there each with an arrow to the string. Certainly the fellows did not in any way fear *our* weapons.

Some minutes passed, during which the two boats continued to drift almost side by side and that hideous clamor filled the air. At last, in an attempt to put an end to it, Milton Rhodes raised his revolver and took careful aim. Drorathusa gave a cry and then addressed some rather fierce words to the trio. In all likelihood, she did not know what Rhodes was going to do. He fired. As he was standing and as but a little distance separated the boats, the bullet, which struck just above the waterline, went out through the bottom.

The change was magical. You should have seen those fellows! Whether it was the report of the weapon or whether it was the hole through which the water came spouting in, I do not know; but the taming of those wild men was swift and complete. As soon as they had recovered their wits, round flew the bow of their boat and away they went towards the shore. Our Dromans burst into laughter, even Drorathusa. And that was the last that we saw of those three fanatics.

But why had they done it? Wherefore were Milton Rhodes and I the objects of a hatred so fierce and so insensate?

Nor were we permitted to forget that fact. Intelligence of our arrival had spread almost as quickly as though it had been broadcasted by radio, and along the banks the people were waiting, in twos and threes, in scores and in hundreds, to see the men from the mysterious and fearful World Above—harbingers, in their minds, of calamities and nameless things. Goodness only knows how many fists were shaken at Rhodes and me during the day, how many were the maledictions that they hurled upon us. Happily, however, there was no act of hostility.

"You know, Bill," Milton smiled, "I am beginning to wish that we were back there among those *gogrugrons*, whatever they are, and the tree-octopuses."

This day's voyage brought us to the City of Dranondocrad. There a change was made that certainly did not displease me—from our little craft to none other than one of the queen's own, a long beautiful vessel with oarsmen and guards.

The next day we passed a large tributary flowing in from our left, from out a yawning cavern there. This was by no means, however, the first cave we had seen entering the main one. As one moves through some valley in the mountains, smaller ones are seen coming in on either hand; and so it was in this great cavern of Drome, save that the valleys were caves. In that place, the great cavern itself has a width of two miles or more, and it is four or five thousand feet up to the vaulted roof.

"One wonders," said I, "why the roof doesn't cave in."

"Pooh, Bill!" said Rhodes. "One doesn't marvel that natural bridges don't collapse or that the roof of the Mammoth Cave doesn't come crashing down."

The two days succeeding this brought us into the very heart of Drome, and on the third we reached the Golden City itself.

This, the capital of the Droman nation, is situated at the lower end of a lake, a most picturesque sheet of water some fifteen miles in length. Where the river flows into it and for a distance of about a league down, the lake extends from one wall of the great cavern clean to the other. The walls go straight down into the water to what depth no man knows.

It was about midafternoon when our boat, followed by a fleet of smaller craft, glided out onto this lovely expanse of water. At a point about halfway down the lake, we had our first view of Narnawnla Prendella, the Golden City. I say view, but it was in reality but little more than a glimpse that we obtained. For, almost at that very moment, a dense gloom fell upon water and landscape. Fierce and dreadful were the flickerings along the roof a mile or more above us. So sudden and awful was the change that even the Dromans seemed astonished. There was a blinding flash overhead, and then utter blackness everywhere.

Rhodes and I flashed on our lights. For a time the Dromans waited, as though expecting the light to come at any moment; but it did not come. Along the shore on either side and in the distant city, lights were gleaming out. A sudden voice came, mystic and wonderful; Rhodes and I turned, and there was Drorathusa standing with arms extended upward in invocation, as we had seen her in that first eclipse. Minutes passed. But the light did not come. At last the oars were put in motion again. Dark and agitated, however, were the looks of the Dromans, and more than one pair of eyes fixed themselves on Rhodes and me in a manner that plainly marked us as objects of some superstitious dread—if, indeed, it was not something worse.

Steadily, however, our boat glided forward through the black and awful night.

"What is that?" I at length asked as suddenly there before us some vapor or an obscuring something thinned out or rose from the surface of the water. "It looks like a floating-palace, with a lot of dwarfish buildings floating behind it. That isn't part of the city itself."

"No; but a palace in all probability," Rhodes answered. "Certainly a very large and imposing structure. That must be an island."

And an island it is.

At this moment Drorathusa moved to our side, and, indicating the great building in question, many windows of which were a perfect blaze of light, she said:

"Lathendra Lepraylya."

Her eyes lingered on Rhodes' face, and her look, I saw, was somber and troubled.

So that was the queen's palace.

Soon we would be in the presence of this Lathendra (Queen) Lepraylya.

What manner of woman was this sovereign of the Dromans?

What awaited us there?

I remembered that look of Drorathusa's, and I confess that my thoughts were soon troubled and somber.

BEFORE LEPRAYLYA

One by one, in twos and threes and then in a body, the small craft had dropped behind, and now we were alone on the black waters, across which, from the shores and from many of the boats, came quivering lines of light.

"It must be the eclipse," said Rhodes, "that has affected the Dromans in this manner so remarkable. It is plain, Bill, that there is something about this sudden darkness that is mysterious and awful to these Hypogeans. It must be that it is in some way a most extraordinary eclipse."

It *was* a most extraordinary eclipse, and there *was* something awful about it—something more awful than we thought. And what troubled me the most was this: they seemed to think that we men from the World Above had something to do with this dread dark-ness—already one of far longer duration than any eclipse any living Droman had ever known. Indeed, none such had been recorded for what we would call centuries, and the last had been the har-binger of the most fearful calamities.

We knew full well that some superstition was pointing a fell finger in our direction; but through the mind of neither flickered the thought that this eclipse might so to speak, be metamorphosed into a death-charge against us.

As we were drawing in to the palace, a heavy voice came across the water. On the instant the rowers rested on their oars. Our commander answered the hail, the heavy voice came again, whereupon the oars were dipped and our craft glided in toward the landing-place.

This hailing, by the way, was pure formality, for they on the island knew who we were.

"What a scene!" said Milton Rhodes, his eyes shining. "What a moment, old *tillicum*, is this for you and me! We shall never, in all likelihood, know another such as this is!"

Like a great lovely water-bird, our boat swung in to the landing-place, where she was at once made fast.

And then it was that another strange thing happened.

Rhodes and I stepped from the boat together. Since the light had gone out in that fierce and terrible flash, not the faintest glimmer had shone overhead, anywhere. But hardly had *we* set foot on the island when there came a flash wrathful and awful.

For a few moments, for the flash seemed to travel along the roof for many miles, the palace and the other buildings there, the people, and there were two or three hundreds, the water, the city, the distant walls of rock stood out in bold relief, as though in the glare of leprous fire. Then utter darkness again. It was like, and yet, strangely enough, very unlike too, a lightning-flash; but no thunder roared, not the faintest sound was heard.

Again shot and quivered that leprous light.

And this time cries broke out, cries that fear and horror wrung from the Dromans.

It was, indeed, an awful moment and an awful scene.

"It looks," said Milton, "as though they think that the world is coming to an end."

"Certainly," I nodded, looking about me a little anxiously, "it seems that they think just that. Look at Drorathusa!"

Again she was standing with arms extended upward, as we had seen her at the mouth of the great cave, and once more that strange, eerie voice of hers came sounding. Every one else there, save Rhodes and myself and a little girl who was clinging to Drorathusa's dress, was kneeling. Little wonder that, as I looked upon that scene, with the leprous light flashing and shaking and quivering through the darkness, I thought, for some moments, it must all be a dream.

The flashes became more frequent. The light began to turn opalescent and to shoot and quiver and shake up along the roof.

Then of a sudden the eclipse—what other word is there to use?—had passed and all was bright once more.

For some moments, there was silence, utter, resting on the place like something tangible. Arose a murmur of gladness, and then a song, started by Drorathusa herself, of thanksgiving. Every one, I believe, joined in this anthem, or whatever it should be called, and the voices, rising and falling, produced upon us twain from another world, though we understood but a single word, an effect strange and pronounced.

That single word which we understood was *zur*, which means light. This word is remarkable not only as being a monosyllable—Drome, of course, is another—in this language of polysyllables, but also for a resemblance that will be set forth by the following, which I take from the writings of the great scientist Sir John Herschel:

"In a conversation held some years ago by the author of these pages with his lamented friend, Dr. Hawtrey, Head-Master and late Provost of Eton College, on the subject of Etymology, I happened to remark that the syllable *Ur* or *Or* must have some very remote origin, having found its way into many languages, conveying the sense of something absolute, solemn, definite, fundamental, or of unknown antiquity, as in the German words *Ur-alt* (primeval), *Ur-satz* (a fundamental proposition), *Ur-theil* (a solemn judgment)—in the Latin *Oriri* (to arise), *Origo* (the origin), *Aurora* (the dawn)—in the Greek *Opos* (a boundary, a mountain, the extreme limit of our vision, whence our *horizon*), *Opaw* (to see) *Opoos* (straight, just, right), *Opkos* (an oath or solemn sanction), *Opai* (the seasons, the great natural divisions of time), etc. 'You are right,' was his reply, 'it is the oldest of all words; the first word ever recorded to have been pronounced. It is the Hebrew for LIGHT . . . AOR.'"

And there, down in Drome, is the word *zur*, and it means light. Whence came that word *zur* into the Droman language? Its semblance to *ur* or *or* or *aor* is unequivocal. Is that semblance a mere coincidence? Or did these syllables have a common origin?

Of course, there is no answer forthcoming. In all likelihood, there never will be an answer.

Periods of gloom are by no means a rarity in Drome, so lamps are always kept in readiness, and no Droman would think of beginning a journey into a dense forest without some kind of lamp, lantern or torch. Gloom, then, they accept as a matter of course; but in utter darkness their minds are a prey to fear and to something akin to horror. Superstition is rampant in Drome, and some of the worst species of it have their origin in these very eclipses. Among this strange, and in some ways truly wonderful, people, there is an astonishing mingling of good sense, a genuine love for some branches of science, and a belief in omens, portents, prodigies and other things of that kind, that would make your hair stand up on end.

Probably you will better understand that scene which I have just described—that in the utter darkness—and better understand that one which was so soon to follow when I say that one of their old prophets, as it is recorded in their sacred writings, foretold a time when the light is to go out to shine no more—a time when Drome is to be in a darkness that will last forever and forever.

The song ended, Drorathusa came over and placed herself between Rhodes and me; and then we quitted that landing-place, ascended a short flight of steps, passed through a most beautiful court and then, having ascended more steps, entered the palace itself.

Our little party was conducted straight to the throne-room.

And straight down the great central aisle we went and stood at last before the queen herself.

41

A HUMAN RAPTOR

There is nothing, as we then saw, servile, debasing in Droman court ceremonial. The meanest Droman, indeed, would never dream of kneeling before his queen. A Droman kneels to no man or woman, but to the Deity only.

The sovereign does not owe her queendom to birth, but to merit, or to that which the Dromans deem as such. She is chosen, and she is chosen queen for life, though, if she prove herself unfit for the throne, the Dromans may remove her. I say she, and I mean she. The Salic law excluded a woman from the throne of France; the Salic law of Drome excludes a man; or, as the Dromans are wont to put it. "No man may be queen." A proposition that even the most Socratical Droman philosopher, and Drome has had many a one, has never been known to dispute!

As to the choosing of the Droman sovereign, I should perhaps explain that every one does not have a voice in this. Beggers, prodigals, sociophagites, dunces, nincompoops, fuddle-caps, half-wits, no-wit-at-alls, sharpers, crooks, bunko-men, bandits, thieves, robbers, highwaymen, burglars, crackpots, fools, madmen and murderers, and some others, are all (I know that this is perfectly incredible and awful, but I solemnly assure you that it is a fact) interdicted the ballot.

Alas, it grieves me more than I could ever express to record so sad an instance of benightment in a people in so many ways so truly enlightened and broadminded. But I take pride in saying that, when I had attained to something like a real knowledge of the

Droman tongue, I described to Lathendra Lepraylya herself, at the
first opportunity and in the most glowing and eulogistical language
at my command, though confining myself strictly to the truth, how
beautifully we did those things in the World Above.

I had (yes, I confess it) flattered myself that I would thus be
instrumental in bringing about a great reform, in righting a cruel
injustice. Vain vision, vain alluring dream! As I went on with my
panegyric, I saw wonder and amazement gathering in the beautiful eyes of Lathendra Lepraylya. When I had finished, she sat for
some moments like one dumfounded. And, when at last she spoke,
it was, as old Rabelais has it, as though her tongue was walking on
crutches. What she said was:

"My Lord, Bill Carter!"

And again after a pause:

"My Lord, Bill Carter!"

At this point I noticed that Milton was smiling at me with great
apparent amusement.

"But, then," Lepraylya added, "it must be an allegory. I confess, however, that the meaning, to my poor intellect at any rate,
is involved in the deepest obscurity. Yes, an allegory it must be.
Surely this world that you have described to me exists only in the
imagination; surely it is an imaginary world inhabited by imaginary sane people that are in reality lunatics!"

But this *is* anticipating.

There we stood before Lathendra Lepraylya, the Queen of
Drome.

And what a vision of loveliness was that upon which we stood
gazing! Strange, too, was the beauty of Lathendra Lepraylya, what
with her violet hair. Yes, I wrote violet, and I mean violet. (Her
age I put at about thirty.) The eyes were large and lustrous, were
of the lightest gray, the pallid color of them and the violet of her
tresses enhancing the weird loveliness of her.

With her right hand she held the scepter; one end of it rested
upon the dais, upon the other was a statuette—of Zeeleenoanthelda,
the half-historical, half-mythical first sovereign of Drome. Upon
Lepraylya's brow, in a bejeweled golden diadem, was a large brilliant

of pale green, flashing when she moved her head with prismatic hues and fires.

But this woman before whom we stood was no mere beauty. That one saw at the first glance. Wonderful, splendid, one felt, was the mind of her, the soul of Lathendra Lepraylya.

And not only that, but it was as though there was something uncanny in those pale gray eyes when she turned them to mine. That look of Lepraylya's did not meet look; it seemed to go right into my very brain, to search out its thoughts and its secret places.

At the time it seemed long, but I suppose that no more than a few seconds passed before she turned her eyes to Milton Rhodes, upon whom they seemed to linger.

And what were the thoughts of the queen as she saw before her two men from another world?

We could, of course, only guess.

And here again had superstition and a prophet loaded those dice upon a throw of which the fate of Milton Rhodes and myself depended; for one of the prophets had foretold the coming of men from another world—men who would be the harbingers of fearful calamities for Drome.

The snowy face of the queen was cold, impassive. Even when she slightly raised her right hand and the scepter to us in salutation, not the slightest change was perceptible upon a single lineament.

The next moment, however, there was a change—when she addressed Drorathusa. For each of the others of our little party Lepraylya had a kind word, and then we all moved back a few steps to the seats which had been reserved for us, all, that is, save Drorathusa. She, we at once perceived, was about to give an account of the journey up to the mysterious, the awful World Above.

There was not a vacant seat in all that great room, save one—that for Drorathusa. This was a little to the left of the throne, as one faces it, together with a dozen or so others, all occupied by persons whom I at once, and rightly, set down as priests and priestesses.

Of this small group (small but very powerful) every member save one was dressed in a robe of snowy white. As for the individual in question, his robe was of the deepest purple, and he had round his head a deep-blue fillet, in which was set a large gem, a diamond as we afterwards learned, of a red so strange and somber that one could not help thinking of blood and dreadful things.

We thought that this personage was the high priest, and in this we were not mistaken. He was about sixty years of age, lean to emaciation and with the cold, hard look of the fanatic in his eyes and, indeed, in his every lineament. His face, smooth-shaven, as is the Droman custom, was like that of some cruel bird of prey. Coldly he received, and returned, the salutation of Drorathusa, and dark with malevolence had been the look which he had fixed upon Rhodes and me.

There could not be the slightest doubt that this human raptor purposed to rend us beak and talon.

42
HE STRIKES

Drorathusa began her story.

Lathendra Lepraylya leaned forward, rested her chin on her left hand and listened with the most careful attention. So still were the listeners that, as the saying has it, you could, anywhere in that great hall, have heard a pin drop.

At times, so expressive were her gestures, Rhodes and I had no difficulty whatever in following Drorathusa; but only at times. I have, however, had access to a transcript of the stenographic record of her story (the Dromans, despite the remarkable polysyllabic character of their language, have most excellent tachygraphers) and I wish that space would permit inclusion of it here.

When Drorathusa had finished, the queen, who had several times interrupted with some interrogation, put a number of questions. With two or three exceptions, the answers given by our Sibyl seemed to be satisfactory. But those exceptions gave us something to think about. It was obvious that the queen was troubled not a little by those answers; and she was not, I believed, a woman who would lightly suffer the mask to reveal her thoughts or her feelings.

When the queen had done, came the turn of that high priest, whose name was Brendaldoombro. Up he rose and addressed a few words to Lathendra Lepraylya. Her answer was laconic, accompanied by an assenting motion of her right hand. For a few seconds her look rested upon Milton Rhodes and me, and it was as though across those strange, wondrous pale eyes of hers a shadow had fallen.

As for the high priest, he had instantly, and with a fierceness that he could not bridle, turned to Drorathusa.

How Rhodes and I, as we sat there, wished that we could understand the words being spoken!

"Always, O Drorathusa," said Brendaldoombro, "has your spirit been strange and wayward. Always have you been a seeker after that which is dark and mysterious. And, of a truth, dark and mysterious is the evil which you have brought down upon Drome.

"Never content with what it is given us to know! Always seeking the obscure, the concealed! Sometime, I fear, *even that which is forbidden!*"

At those words the eyes of Drorathusa flashed, but she made no answer.

"Cursed was that hour—cursed, I say, be that peeking and searching and peering that discovered it to your eyes, that record of those who, led on by the powers of the Evil One, ventured up into the caves of darkness and at last up into the World Above itself—a world, as our holy writings tell us, of fearful and nameless things, of demons who, to achieve their fell purpose"—here he fixed his vulture-eye upon Milton and me—"assume the shapes of men.

"But you, O Drorathusa, must needs find that record, that writing which never should have been written. And you must needs turn a deaf ear to our words of counsel and admonition. But you must needs beg and beseech and implore our permission to go yourself up into those fearful places and there see with your own eyes whether that in the writing was true or false. And we, alas, in an evil hour and one of weakness—yes, we did yield to your importunities and your wicked interpretation of our sacred writings, and we did suffer you to go forth."

It seems, however, that just the opposite was the truth—that Brendaldoombro, fearing the growing popularity and power of this extraordinary woman, had been only too glad to see her start for the caverns of darkness, from the black mysteries of which he, of course, had hoped that neither she nor a single one of her companions would ever return.

"Yes, evil was the hour in which you went forth, O Drorathusa the Wayward One. And evil is this in which we see these demons in the shapes of men sitting in our very midst, before the very throne of our queen. Already has God shown His anger, shown it in this darkness which has sent fear to the stoutest heart—this darkness the like of which no living man has ever known in Drome.

"Nor," he went on, his voice rising, "will the Divine wrath be softened so long as we, undutiful children that we are, suffer them to live—these devils that have come amongst us in the forms of men! Death!" his voice rising until the hall rang with the fierce tones. "Death to them, say! Let death be swift and sure! And thus will Drome be spared sorrows, blood and miseries that, else, will wring the heart of the babe newborn and cause it to rise up and fearfully curse father and mother for bringing it into a world of such madness and woe!"

The effect of this impassioned and fiendish outburst was instantaneous and fearful. Something that was like a groan, a growl and a roar filled that great room. One who has never heard it could never believe that so strange and so frightful a sound could come from human throats. The Dromans sprang to their feet—not men and women now, but metamorphosed by the cunning and the diablerie of Brendaldoombro into veritable fiends.

"We're in for it, Bill!" cried Milton, springing to his feet and whipping out his revolver.

I sprang to his side, and we faced them.

Drorathusa, with a fierce cry, threw herself between us and the crowd. We were moving slowly backward, back toward the throne. The voice of our Sibyl rang out clear and full. A moment or two, and it was evident that her words were quieting the mad passions of the mob, for mob, at that moment, it certainly was, though composed of the elite of the Droman world.

Then of a sudden, full, clear, ringing and aquiver with wrath and suppressed passion, came the voice of Lathendra Lepraylya.

Oh, what a vision of fierce loveliness was she as she stood there!

Brendaldoombro had come within a hair's-breadth of achieving his diabolical purpose. And a most ugly vision of thwarted evil was he at that moment. He knew his auditors, though, and he knew his power. Again he raised his impassioned voice. Lepraylya, however, turned upon him fiercely.

"Peace!" she cried. "I bid you, peace—yes, even you, O Brendaldoombro, High Priest of Drome though you are!

"What! You would still make of this room a shambles, stain the very throne of your queen with human blood!"

"They are not human!" he shrieked. "They are demons that have assumed the bodies of men!"

A murmur of superstitious horror arose.

"Ho, guard!" cried the queen. "Guard, ho!"

It is my belief that some cool-headed gentleman had bethought himself of the guard before ever the queen, for it was only a few moments before a score or so of armed men had entered the room and taken a position, in the form of a semicircle, before the throne.

The eyes of Lathendra Lepraylya were blazing like that great jewel on her brow. Those eyes were fixed upon Brendaldoombro, and I actually thought that the old raptor quailed a little under that look of outraged majesty. If this was indeed so, it was for an instant or two only. His look, one of baffled fury, then became fixed and defiant.

"So!" said Lathendra Lepraylya. "What madness is this that I see? What blood-howl is this that I hear? No woman or man in Drome may be deprived of liberty or life without a fair trial; and yet you, yes, even you, O Brendaldoombro, are here striving to make a shambles of the very throne itself."

She raised her hand and pointed toward us.

"If these men are indeed—"

"They are not men!" the old villain shouted. "They are demons who have taken the human shape, to attain here in Drome some fell purpose. Death, I say! Death to these masqueraded devils! Let death be swift and—"

"Peace, I say!" exclaimed Lepraylya, stamping her sandaled foot. "And, if these men from the World Above are indeed but devils counterfeit, could we kill them, O Brendaldoombro? Since when can mere man kill a devil?"

"When they are in the human shape, he can! Death! Death to these fiends who—"

"One can kill their bodies only," interrupted the queen, "and it may be that he can not do even that much."

"Their bodies only? What more," demanded Brendaldoombro, "can one do to any woman or man? Death! Death to these demons!"

"Their spirits would be but loosed from the body, O Brendaldoombro, to move unseen in the air about us, and they could then—if, that is, they really are devils—the more easily achieve their nefarious designs."

"They would be harmless then!" came the ready answer. "They are helpless save when they are in the human form."

"Since when?" queried Lepraylya, her eyes widening in surprise. "Since when did the minions of the Evil One become helpless unless in human shape?"

"You misapprehend, O Lathendra Lepraylya. These belong to a most peculiar order, to a most rare species of bad angel. And," cried Brendaldoombro, "they are the worst devils of all! Death to them before it is too late! Let us—"

"Have justice," said Lepraylya, "as we hope for mercy and justice in that dread day when every human soul—even yours, O Brendaldoombro—must stand and be judged for the sins it has done in the flesh. No human being may be condemned in Drome without trial; and I believe that Lord Milton and Lord Bill are true men, O Brendaldoombro, and no demons. And you would slay them, murder them, these the first men from the World Above, as you would slay a *gogrugron*—if you did not fear it, O Brendaldoombro. Who knows what message they bring to us? Now they stand silent; but, when they will have learned our language, then we shall learn that which is now so dark and so mysterious."

"Dark and mysterious indeed!" cried the high priest. "Signs and portents have been given us, warning us of what is to follow if we harbor these demons amongst us. And I tell you, O Lathendra Lepraylya, you and all Drome shall rue this day if you heed not the dread warnings of the wrath Divine. Darkness I see! Yes, I see, darkness! And earth-shocks! The roof of our world crashing down! Calamities that will overwhelm all Drome and—"

"Silence!" Lepraylya commanded. "Silence, croaker of evil! One would almost think, O Brendaldoombro, that you know more about the angels of the Evil One that you do about God's own. Hear now my word:

"When Lord Bill and Lord Milton can answer the charge that they are demons masquerading in the shapes of men, then, O Brendaldoombro, and not before, shall they be brought to trial— if, indeed, you will prefer that charge against them *then*.

"Such is my word to you, O Brendaldoombro, and to you, ladies and lords all, and on the majesty of the Droman law and of the dread law of God it stands."

43
DRORATHUSA

And so it was that we reached, there in the palace of the Droman queen, our journey's and—certainly a stranger journey than any I ever have heard of and one that ought to prove of even greater interest to scientists than to the world in general.

If, however, what they tell of the region is true, an expedition to the mysterious land that the Dromans call Grawngrograr would make our journey to Drome look like a promenade to fairyland.

But our journey ended there in the palace, and now it is that my story rapidly draws to a close.

Probably you will think that, there under the aegis of Lathendra Lepraylya, we found ourselves in clover. And, in a way, this was undoubtedly so. We were given each a splendid suite of rooms in the palace itself, and our lives were as the lives of princes, save that the close protective guard always kept over us was a reminder that there was such a personage in the world as one Brendaldoombro.

If it had not been for that vulture-shadow, how wonderful those days would have been!

But that shadow was there, and it never lifted. And the worst of it was that everything was involved in the deepest gloom and mystery, what with our ignorance of the Droman language. Forsooth, however, had we been masters of that language, we could not have known the plots that were hatching in the dark skull of Brendaldoombro.

As for the language, we were studying it with diligence, and we really had cause to be astonished at the rapidity of our progress.

As to the high priest, crafty and consummate villain though he was, that worthy found that Lathendra Lepraylya was quite his match and more than his match, as, indeed, was Drorathusa. Against the queen he was, of course, powerless to take any repressive measure; but the case was very different with regard to Drorathusa. He could act in this way, and he did.

She was sent to a distant, lonely, forsaken place on the very outskirts of the kingdom, or, to be precise, queendom. According to all accounts, that spot is really a terrible one. Drorathusa was, in fact, in exile, though Brendaldoombro did not like to hear any one call it that. But almost everybody did or regarded it as such, and there were murmurs, not only amongst the Droman people, but even amongst those priestesses and priests whom the old villain had counted upon to applaud his every word and act.

Nor did time still those murmurs. On the contrary, they grew louder, more persistent. Brendaldoombro was learning that it is one thing to send a person into exile and quite another to banish that person from the popular esteem. Nor did he stop at banishment; he had recourse to the assassin's dagger and the arts of the poisoner. But, in all these attempts upon the life of Drorathusa, he was thwarted by the agents of the queen. Lepraylya knew her opponent, and had at once taken measures to safeguard the life of the exiled priestess, who held as high a place in the esteem of her sovereign as she did in the hearts of the people.

How strange it seems to be writing of things like these in this the Twentieth Century, the Golden Age of Science! But, as I believe I have already remarked, Science hasn't discovered everything yet. This is a stranger, a more wonderful, a more mysterious old globe than even Science herself dreams it to be.

When our acquisition of the language became a real one, we began to learn something of the science of Drome and to impart a knowledge of the wonderful science of our own world. Never shall I forget the amazement of the queen and those learned men of Drome when Rhodes brought his mathematics into play. Problems that only a Droman Archimedes could solve and that only after much labor (what with their awful notation) Rhodes solved, presto—just like that! So unwieldy was the system of notation employed by these Hypogeans that even their greatest mathematicians had been able to do no more than roughly approximate *pi*.

When Rhodes proceeded to the solution of trigonometrical problems, their amazement knew no bounds. And, when he explained to them that all they had to do to become masters of such problems was to discard their cumbersome notation and adopt the simple numerals used by ourselves—well, I do actually believe that that was the straw that broke the back of Brendaldoombro's power! For (strange though it may seem to a world that is more interested in any kind of abracahokum, and especially any kind of political jiggumbob, than it is in science) that brought over to our side virtually every learned man in Drome and a majority of the people themselves. Nor should I forget the priestesses and the priests. Your average Droman is much interested in all things of a scientific nature, and no one more so than the true priestess or priest, though there are, of course, some lamentable exceptions.

Yes, clearly we were men and not demons, else never would we have brought such wonders as these to offer them as gifts to the Dromans.

But old Brendaldoombro had his answer ready.

"Instead," said he, "that proves that they are *not* men; only devils could be such wizards!"

I have often wondered what dark thoughts would have passed through that dark brain of his had he been there the day that Milton Rhodes showed Lathendra Lepraylya, all those learned men and all those grand lords and ladies (ladies and lords, a Droman would say) the marvels of a steam-engine. Yes, there the little thing was, only two feet or so high but perfect in all its parts, puffing away merrily, and puffing and puffing, and all those Dromans looking on in wonder and delight.

Even as we sat there, came word that Brendaldoombro was dead. He had died suddenly and painlessly just after placing his hand in blessing on the head of a little child. Well, they gave him a magnificent funeral.

Peace to his soul.

On the death of the Droman high priest (or priestess) a successor is chosen, in the great temple in the Golden City, by a synod composed of exactly five hundred, the majority of whom are usually priestesses. On the very first ballot, Drorathusa (who was already on her way back from her lonely pace of exile) was chosen.

Priestesses and priests, I should perhaps remark, are free to marry, unless they have taken the vow of celibacy. This (voluntarily, of course) many of them do. Drorathusa, by the way, had not done so.

Came, as last, the day when Milton Rhodes told me that he was going to be married—to Lathendra Lepraylya herself. The news, however, was not wholly unexpected.

Well, every man of us can't marry a queen—though of queans there are plenty.

I take the following from my journal:

"They were married today, about ten o'clock, in the great temple; and a very grand wedding it was, too. Drorathusa herself spoke the words that made them man and wife, for the sovereign of Drome can be married by the high priestess or priest only.

"Now, as she proceeded with the ceremony, which was a very long one, I thought that that pale face of Drorathusa's grew paler still and that a distraught look was coming into her eyes. Then I told myself that it was only a fancy. But it was not fancy. For of a sudden her lip began to tremble, her voice faltered, the look in her eyes suddenly became wild and helpless—and she broke down.

"A moment or two, however, and that extraordinary woman had got control over herself again.

"She motioned the attendant priestesses and priests aside; a wan smile touched her lips as she pressed a hand to her side and said:

"'It was just my heart—but I am better now.'

"She at once proceeded with the ceremony, voice and features under absolute control. Again she was Drorathusa the Sibylline.

"And so they were married. And may they live happy and very happily ever after!"

And then, after the great nuptial banquet in the palace, off went the happy pair in the queen's barge for Leila Nuramanistherom, a lovely royal seat some thirty miles down the river; whilst I betook myself to the solitude of my rooms, there to ponder on the glad-sad lot of man, to hear over and over, and over again, those low tragic words:

"It was just my heart—but I am better now."

"*Amor*," says Saint Jerome, "*ordinem nescit.*"

Beautiful, Sibylline, noble, poor Drorathusa!

44
WE SEE THE STARS

When facing the dangers, mysteries, horrors (and other things) of our descent to this strange and wonderful subterranean land of Drome, how often did I say to myself:

"If ever I get out of this, never anything like it again!"

And I truly believed it at the time, though I should have known better. I should have known—I *did* know that adventure and mystery have inexplicable and most dreadful charms. Indeed, the more fearful the Unknown, the more eager a man (one who has heard the Siren song which adventure and mystery sing) is to penetrate to its secret places—unless, indeed, the charms of some Lepraylya or Drorathusa entwine themselves about the heart. In my case—well, *Amor ordinem nescit.*

Here was I in the Golden City; here was everything, *it would seem to another*, that could conduce to contentment, to that peace of mind which is dearer that all. And yet I was restless and very unhappy.

And the Unknown was calling, calling and calling for me to come. To what? Perhaps to wonders the like of which Science never has dreamed. Perhaps to horrors and mysteries from which the imagination of even a Dante or a Doré would shrink, would flee in mad terror—things nameless, worse than any seen in a horrible dream.

But I wanted to go. Yes, I *would* go. I would go into that fearful land of Grawngrograr—discover its mysteries or perish in the attempt.

And I am going, too. That journey has not been abandoned, only delayed.

It was like this.

I was drawing up, in my mind, tentative plans (my purpose was yet a secret) when one day Milton Rhodes came in, and, after smiling in somewhat enigmatic fashion for some moments, he suddenly asked:

"I say, Bill, how would you like to see the stars, the sun again?"

"The sun? Milton, what do you mean?"

"That I am going back to the surface, out onto the snow and ice of Rainier, back to Seattle. I thought that you would want to go along."

"What in the world," I exclaimed, "are you going back for?"

"There are many things that we ought to have here in Drome; a book of logarithms, the best that I can get, is one of them. We'll get those things, or as many as we can, for it would, of course, be impossible to bring them all. We'll wind up our sublunary affairs, and, hurrah, then back to Drome! What do you say to that, old *tillicum?*"

"What does Lepraylya say?"

"That I may go; otherwise, of course, there would be no going. At first she wouldn't even hear of it. She feared that it might be impossible for us to maintain secrecy—that some of our precious politicians might get down into Drome. I am sure she believes that the kingdom would have more to fear from half a dozen of those sons of Proteus than from an army of sixty thousand men. And, bless her heart, when I think of some of their blunders, asininity, hypocrisy, lying, stupidity, coat-turning and sheer insanity, I am of opinion that there is not much exaggeration, if any, in that idea of hers.

"But I have at last gained her consent. With our large party, there can not be any danger."

I was not sure of that, but I kept those thoughts to myself.

"Of course, I want to go," I told him. "But I want to come back to Drome."

"Most assuredly, Bill, we'll come back to Drome."

"But," said I, "there is something that I don't understand."

"Which is what?"

"We *can't* keep our great discovery a secret. And, as soon as our world has it, adventurers, spoilers, crooks, thieves and worse will come swarming down that passage. We'll loose upon our poor Dromans a horde of Pizarros."

"Did I think for one single moment that what you say, or anything like it, would follow, never one step would I take towards the sun. You say that we cannot keep the discovery of Drome a secret; we can, and we will—until such time as it will not matter. We will come out onto the glacier in the nighttime. Our ways of egress—I suppose we'll have to tunnel our way out through the ice, that there will not be any accommodating crevasse—will be most carefully concealed. No one will see us come out. No one will know of our journeys to and from the Tamahnowis Rocks, for they will be made under cover of darkness. No one will know.

"Fortunately, by the way, as it now turns out," he added, "when we adopted the Droman dress, we did not throw away our pants et cetera, and so, though those clothes are somewhat the worse for wear, our appearance up there on Mount Rainier will cause no remark."

"But our showing up at home," I said, "after so long an absence will cause plenty of remarks and more than remarks. How will we answer all the questions that they will surely ask us?"

"Tut, tut!" smiled Milton. "If all our difficulties could be so easily resolved as that!"

"But how will we do it?"

"We won't answer them, Bill; we'll keep them guessing."

"But suppose we find that Scranton has let out something that will give them a pretty good idea as to what has happened?"

"That might be bad," answered Rhodes. "But I have every confidence in Scranton's discretion. He will, I feel sure, maintain that utter silence which I requested, until the period designated expires. Possibly he may never tell what he knows.

"I believe, however," he went on, "that we ought to leave the world, our world, a record of the discovery. I will set down to the extent that time permits those things which, in my opinion, will interest the scientific world. As for the discovery itself, the journey and our adventures, yours, Bill, is the hand to record that."

"A record?" I exclaimed. "Then why all this secrecy, this moving under cover of darkness and pussy-footing around if you are going to broadcast the discovery of Drome to the whole world?"

"Because we will then have left that world and the way to this will have been blasted up and otherwise closed."

"That," I told him, "will never keep them out."

"I believe that it will. And, if any one ever does find his way down, he'll never return to the surface; he'll spend the rest of his days here in Drome, even if he lives to be as old as Methuselah. Be sure that you put that into the record! The Dromans are human, and so they are not quite saints. But their land is never going to be infested with plunderers or any of our sons of Proteus if I can prevent it, and I feel confident that I can.

"This closing of the way will not mean complete isolation. At any rate, I hope that it will not. For I feel confident that ere very long the two worlds will communicate with each other by radio. There is a possibility, too, though that possibility is indeed a very remote one, that each will even *see*, by means of television, the inhabitants and the marvels of the other."

One or two weird things befell us during our return journey, but time presses and I cannot pause to record them here.

The party was composed of picked men, one of whom was Ondonarkus. We had one ape-bat.

This going up was a more difficult business, I want to tell you, than our going down had been. There was one consolation: we did not get lost.

Onward and upward we toiled, and at last, on the 28th of June, we reached the Tamahnowis Rocks. Thanks to Rhodes' chronometer-watch and the very careful record which he had kept, we knew the very hour.

This was about ten o'clock in the morning. The way out was completely blocked by the ice. Cool air, however, was flowing in through fissures and clefts in the walls and the roof of the tunnel.

We waited until along towards midnight, for fear some one might be about, that some sound might reveal the secret of the rock.

It was about ten o'clock when we began to dig our way out through the ice. The tunnel was not driven out into the glacier but up alongside the rock wall, through the edge of the ice-stream.

Hurrah! At last our passage was through!

And, as old Dante has it,

"Thence issuing we again beheld the stars."

COACHWHIP PUBLICATIONS

COACHWHIPBOOKS.COM

Bestiarium Cryptozoologicum

*Mystery Animals and Unknown Species
in Classic Science Fiction and Fantasy*

Bestiarium Cryptozoologicum
ISBN 1-61646-009-1

Stories of strange creatures . . .

COACHWHIP PUBLICATIONS

COACHWHIPBOOKS.COM

The Sign of the Spider
ISBN 1-930585-28-4

*Lost race and monstrous
arachnid in darkest Africa . . .*

COACHWHIP PUBLICATIONS

COACHWHIPBOOKS.COM

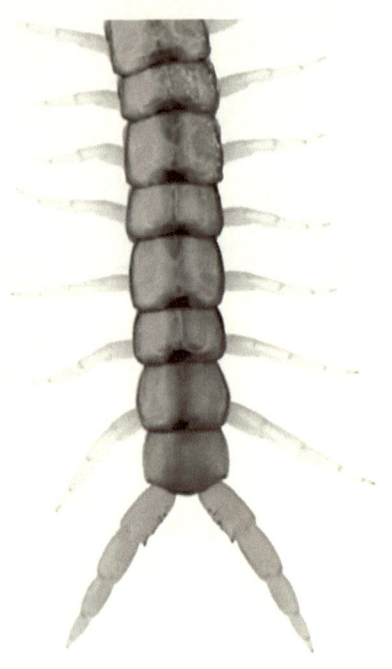

THE GOLDEN CENTIPEDE

LOUISE GERARD

The Golden Centipede
ISBN 1-61646-254-X

African lost race fantasy . . .